Culminating with the international success of *The Polished Hoe* in 2002, Austin Clarke's work since 1964 includes ten novels, six short-story collections, and three memoirs published in the United States, England, Canada, Australia, and Holland.

In 1998 Austin Clarke was invested with the Order of Canada, and since then he has received four honorary doctorates. In 1999, he was the winner of the W.O. Mitchell Prize, awarded to a Canadian writer who has produced an outstanding body of work and served as mentor for other writers. In that year, he also received the Martin Luther King Junior Award for Excellence in Writing. Austin Clarke lives in Toronto.

Books of Merit

MORE

A NOVEL

Austin Clarke

Thomas Allen Publishers
Toronto

Library and Archives Canada Cataloguing in Publication

Clarke, Austin, 1934–
    More : a novel / Austin Clarke. – 1st pbk. ed.

ISBN 978-0-88762-466-7

I. Title.

PS8505.L38M67 2009   C813'.54   C2009-902513-2

Editor: Patrick Crean
Cover design: Sputnik Design Partners Inc.
Cover image: Masterfile

Derek Walcott's poem "On the Cathedral Steps" has been reprinted with
permission from *The New York Review of Books*. Copyright © 2008 NYREV, Inc.

Published by Thomas Allen Publishers,
a division of Thomas Allen & Son Limited,
145 Front Street East, Suite 209,
Toronto, Ontario M5A 1E3 Canada

www.thomas-allen.com

ONTARIO ARTS COUNCIL
CONSEIL DES ARTS DE L'ONTARIO

Canada Council
for the Arts

The publisher gratefully acknowledges the support of
the Ontario Arts Council for its publishing program.

We acknowledge the support of the Canada Council for the Arts, which
last year invested $20.1 million in writing and publishing throughout Canada.

We acknowledge the Government of Ontario through the
Ontario Media Development Corporation's Ontario Book Initiative.

We acknowledge the financial support of the Government of Canada through the
Book Publishing Industry Development Program (BPIDP) for our publishing activities.

13 12 11 10 09   1 2 3 4 5

Printed and bound in Canada

For Emmjaymahdee . . .

On the cathedral steps sprinkled by the bells' benediction
Like water that blissfully stained the scorching street,
You were not among the small crowd in the sun,
So many black against the Sicilian heat.
I never entered the shaded church with its pews
facing the tortured altar, but I hoped to find you:
Oh, I did, halfheartedly, but by now it was no use.
The bells meant nothing or the swallows they lifted;
still I felt you were ahead and I was right behind you,
and that you would stop on your shadow and turn your head,
and there in Sicily turn into salt, into fiction.
I don't know the cathedral's name. It's in Syracuse.
I bought a paper in a language I cannot read.
There was nothing in the paper about this. It wasn't news.

— DEREK WALCOTT, "On the Cathedral Steps"

Why do we expect so little of ourselves? We are worth more, we are owed more . . . we are capable of more . . . why should [we] be no more than Anancy?

— NORMAN MANLEY, Chief Minister of Jamaica

(Anancy is an African folk hero, known to be a trickster; there is an alternative spelling, "Anansi.")

It is because we hate you, you and your Reason, that we uphold juvenile dementia, blazing madness and unflinching cannibalism . . . Come to terms with me, I will not come to terms with you.

— AIMÉ CÉSAIRE, *Return to My Native Land*

THURSDAY

Coming out of the dream, the bells are ringing, and she holds her breath, trying to find out the reason for the ringing of the bells; trying to remember when she had heard the bells ringing like this, "Blang! . . . blang! . . . buh-lang! . . . blang!" coming through the trees in the darkened Park, "Blang! . . . blang! . . . buh-lang! . . . blang! . . . ," and waking to this music, she is entering full consciousness, and can remember how the trees look: straight and black from the ground to the first flaring-out of limbs, dead now on the thin layer of snow that whitens the ground in these cold, teeth-shattering mornings of winter, which she hates, even after thirty years living in Canada; ". . . Blang! . . . blang! . . . buh-lang! . . . blang!" and she remains in the cold bed; and then she turns to lie on her back, and this makes her look up into the dark ceiling, and then all around her, with the eye of a periscope, unable still to pick out the furniture in the room, or see the breaking outline of morning light; or the lights of a passing car, or police cruisers, numerous as ambulances in this neighbourhood, in Moss Park, numerous as black squirrels scampering over the white grass of the sleeping Park; and she imagines that

the ambulances are returning empty-handed, in the dead of
night with silenced siren, without a homeless man with no job,
and with no overdosed sex-working woman strapped down in
the back, with tubes from their nostrils pinned to their chests,
down the front of their clothes pulled roughly aside to accommodate the thin, life-giving, plastic tube; but even so, the ambulance moves with the same speed and emergency over the
thin-coated white street, spewing snow and paper cups like
grass from a lawn mower in summer; just as she is coming out
of it now . . . coming out from the dream she is having, coming out of the warm clutch of "that man"; and it is at this stage
in her awakening, after she turns for the second time, this time
on to her stomach, unable and unwilling to face the darkness
and pick up, from memory, or through invention, the articles
of her life surrounding her: chair and table, linoleum cloth on
the table used as a desk for writing letters to "that man," her
husband, lost or buried somewhere in America, in Brooklyn,
where he went to find permanent employment, the table used
for eating dinner, the one meal in her day when she can sit
with her son, Barrington James, BJ as he is called by everyone,
including his "gangsta" friends, as she calls these friends of his;
and the few neighbours, one on the left, one on the right, and
the man who walks with a four-wheeled walker . . . yes, she is
coming out of the reverie of the clutching embrace "that man"
has her in, and the sounds of the bells of St. James's tolling in the
short distance from her basement apartment, four streets to
the south of the Park, straight as an arrow; and in her mind she
crosses Queen Street, then a small street, Barton, that runs
from Sherbourne to George Street; then a bigger street, Richmond; then Adelaide, and she walks through the small park and
the garden patterned after nineteenth-century ones in London-

England, through the garbage with its smell left by dogs and homeless men; and other things that she does not like to look at, in this short walk from her neighbourhood, and she enters the huge, studded, brown, stained main door of the Cathedral that looks like the door to a castle; and sits down and settles herself in a pew whose seat is padded by a cushion and forgets her life, forgets her son, forgets "that man," forgets the Island where she was born, and had left thirty years ago, as an indentured servant, a "domestic" as she was known to the Governments of her Island and of Canada; for "the loneliness, the loneliness, the loneliness," as she would complain to her friend Josephine; and to her son, BJ—not that she was having a discussion with him; for she had not become so Canadian that she would sit down and reason with him; for he was a child and she told him what to do—simple as that, the way it was done where she came from; and she would discuss it with "that man," the man she was living with, "in common law," the man she had sent for, and had paid for his ticket, and the suit he wore on that cold November night, the man she wanted out of her life—even though he was in America, placing him here in this basement apartment, and making him sit on one of the two red-painted chairs, talking aloud to him even though he was there only in her imagination; and these imaginary conversations did not last long, and then she would remember when they were happy, when they were behaving like man and wife, man and woman, when they spent time in bed, lying like two sardines moistened by the oil and the garlic in a tin of Millionnaires manufactured in Norway; lying in silence, waiting to be sure that their son in his adjoining room was at last asleep (but many times she was sure that BJ pretended he was not asleep); and now she hears the "Blang! . . . blang! . . . buh-lang! . . . blang!" of the Cathedral bells, and tries to decide what time it is, but as she is still lying on her stomach, she cannot tell if the three red digits on her alarm clock, 7.36, refer to nighttime or daytime. *direct attention/make mention/speack about*

She is coming out of her sleep. And she is coming out of her dream, listening to the deep sweet sound of the bells, and she is aware now that today is Thursday, and she thinks she shall not rise from this bed. She has decided she will not go to work today. She pulls the white sheet round her body, tightens the white imitation blanket, then the ribbed white comforter round her body; and as she does this, she realizes that she has transformed herself into a mummy. Wrapped in these three extra skins of her bed linen, she feels sad. The dream is haunting her.

She is unable still to put a name to the tune the bells are playing. The ringing of the bells now connects her back to her dream, cut off before its climax, and she drifts off to the sound of the metal tongue striking the iron skirt of the bell that goes through her body, almost like the man's hand, in the dream, raising her skirt high off her knee, until his fingers reach the soft warmth of her thighs, which makes her jump in surprise and in excitement; and his tongue paints her lips; and she finds the words, awakening from her half-sleep, that what she feels is the same as what she is hearing, the banging of the tongue of the bell against its skirt, moving right and deep into her body, like the sensation of the bells, like the same short sweetness of his impatient kisses, as she lingers on her stomach, as if she is still wandering in her dream, and her dream is a journey; and she is lost, and she is counting the strokes of the bell for direction; "Blang! . . . blang! . . . buh-lang! . . . blang!"; ticking off his kisses, counting them off on her fingers, as she used to do in her class of Mental Arithmetic, years ago back in the

Island, at St. Bartholomew's Elementary School for Girls; and now, counting each smash of iron, listening to the sound that is still going through her body, like a rush that returns and returns, thirteen heavy times in deep disappointment: deep strokes of the iron tongue inside the welcoming skirt of the bell, and she knows now, at this moment, it is time to get out of bed, to let go of her dreaming and escape the power of the bells of St. James's Cathedral. The purpose of the bells is clear: they are summoning her to Communion. But she knows it is time to go to work. She has already decided she will not go today.

The kitchen of Trinity College in the University, where she is the Assistant Manager, Daytime and Supper Meals, will have to survive without her today—and maybe tomorrow too, if she is in the same mood. They owe her vacation days, anyhow, and sick leave. She has worked there five years now. And it is November. And she prays for March and April to come, to bring more warmth into her bones. But she likes the job, especially when she is on the supper shift, seeing all these young men, white and black and coloured, from Canada and England and the West Indies and Puerto Rico, the Bahamas and all over the world, all sitting close and chatting and chattering about their lectures and their classes in Philosophy and Law and Engineering, and gossiping and joking.

But most of all, she liked the way they dressed. They all wore academic gowns to supper. And they looked just like the choir and the clergy when they walked up the aisle on those first Sundays of the month when she took Communion at St. James's Cathedral.

But her joy, because of her position and the prestige of the place she was in, this venerable Trinity College Dining Hall, would sometimes become tainted, as though a dash of vinegar were dropped into it, when she tried to picture her son, BJ, sitting at one of these tables old as the Victorian Age she had read about in library books. "His real, full name even fits this place!" she said many times to herself. "Barrington James, I christened that blasted boy! As if I expected he would turn out to be a success, sitting down in a place like this, *having dinner*. Not *eating food*! Not chomping on hamburger and fries. Stuffing his mouth with potato chips! But taking dinner as a gentleman. How you like that?" And in her mind she would place BJ at one of these heavy brown oak tables, like those used in monasteries and castles in England in the time of Queen Victoria, her favourite English queen. BJ would be dressed in a white shirt, with the College tie smart round his neck, his grey flannel trousers pressed with creases sharp as a Gillette razor blade, his brown shoes shined to reflect his face in them—like dogs' stones, as she would have said if this College was back in the Island—and his College blazer with the crest on the left breast pocket. "Jesus Christ, boy!" she said in her dream. "Jesus Christ, boy! You look like a lawyer! Or a doctor! You look good, boy!" And her imagination would glow in Technicolor, and BJ would replace the student she had chosen in her fantasy as his model. And with these images in her head, her work was made easy— easier; and her eyes would shine, and she would serve the boys larger portions, until the platter was empty and there were only the marks of devoured pork chops left. "If I was in charge of the cooking tonight, I would put a little more black pepper, or even Scotch Bonnet, on these chops, run a little seasoning from back home into them, and with a bone and some fat, for flavour . . . and I wouldn't serve all this damn plain white rice, neither! Oh, no! These boys deserve something special! A little Jamaica red beans and rice. Or Barbadian yellow split peas and rice, and a little piece o' pig tail hide-away in it. These boys deserve more strengthening foods. For their brain!" And she would move through the rows of chairs and oak tables, like a woman light on her feet, skating on ice; smooth; in and out; her face like that of an ice skater she had seen on television, doing Eights. ". . . and Nines, and Tens, and Elevens . . . whatever! . . . if there is such a thing!" But always, in her mind, BJ would be there, installed in a chair, taking his dinner, in this Dining Hall. These were her reveries, these wishes, these possibilities—for to her, nothing was out of her reach. "Let me tell you something, girl!" her Mother told her almost every morning before she left for Queen's College, one of the Island's prestigious high schools for girls. "Don't you ever tell me you can't solve any problem life puts in front of you! You hear me?"

"Yes, Ma."

"Don't call me Ma! Call me Mother. I more-prefer you call me by my Christian name! . . . Ma . . . Baa . . . Baa-baa . . ." And then she laughed.

"Yes, Mother." She can remember it now as if it was yesterday. They were eating roast corn. That commandment became her Twelfth Commandment. Her Eleventh was "Manners Maketh Man."

She remembers one particular cold night on her way home when she accepted the cigarette offered by her friend Missis Proposki, who worked in the College kitchen with her. Missis Proposki was a server, and she helped with the cleaning up. When Missis Proposki gave her the plain-tipped mentholated MacDonald's cigarette, she coughed three times before she could inhale the smoke that rasped her throat like a knife.

"If you wasn't with me," Missis Proposki said, "I never would take this damn road. Not by myself." They were walking along Philosopher's Walk, near the College, towards Bloor Street. "In the *Star* today, I read it on the subway coming to work, another rape . . ."

"I read it too."

"A woman has to be so careful," Missis Proposki said. The cigarette dangled from the left corner of her mouth.

"I forgot to bring my bottle. Must remember to walk with it," Missis Proposki said. She moved her hand round inside her bag, looking for the quart bottle of brandy, bottled by the Liquor Control Board of Ontario, just in case she had brought it with her from the College kitchen. The two of them would take a snap of the brandy when no one was looking; and then would stifle its strength and its smell with squirts of Coca-Cola, through a straw, from the machine; and then toss a Halls cough drop into their mouths, crushing it with their teeth, and laugh at the sound—and she would smile, and tell Missis Proposki how similar the sound of the Halls was to the crushing of roasted Indian corn kernels.

"A beer?" she asked Missis Proposki.

"Why the hell not, girl! Let's turn round. I know a place. College and Spadina. And they plays the type o' music you like. I hear you singing all the time . . ."

"Why the hell not!" she told Missis Proposki.

And so they went back to Hoskin Avenue, and turned left at St. George, taking a right at College, and as they walked they were laughing and telling dirty jokes, as they passed bright blinking lights, and signs advertising rhythm and blues bands and ladies and lap dancing, and blues singers; and she recognized the area, two or three streets north of Baldwin Street, in the Kensington Market where she went to buy plantains, and green bananas, and luscious pig tail, and mackerel floating in brine . . . But she had never gone to this club, El Mocambo, where they were now heading. She remembered her Mother's injunction about walking about in Toronto, "and it so big and wild, by yourself alone at nights! And I reading about these crimes every time you send down a Canadian magazine for me to look at . . . leaving me to wonder what the hell my only daughter doing up there in that damn sinful place!"; and she had read this over and over, in the last letter her Mother had written. They sat down, she and Missis Proposki, in the large room, with the lights so dim she could hardly see Missis Proposki; and just then the band was about to play, and the leader said, "One . . . two . . . one-two-one-two . . . three four!" and she could see the small red dots of cigarettes; and a waitress who wore bright red lipstick, and had beautiful legs, and came and stood beside them, and said, "What will it be, ladies?"; and she took a pencil from her hair and drew small circles on her pad; and Missis Proposki said, "Brandy and Coke! Why not?"; and she said, "Me too!"; and the scantily dressed waitress said, "Two brandy-and-Cokes, coming up!"

"Cigarette?" Missis Proposki said.

"Can we?" she said.

"Others are doing it," Missis Proposki said; and without waiting, she offered the pack of mentholated MacDonald's to her friend. She cleared her throat before she took out a cigarette.

And the waitress came back with the drinks, and served them.

"Where the group from?" she asked.

"American. You want to request something?"

"Just listening," she said. "That's good enough."

"Negro music from Amerrica," Missis Proposki said. "It does something to me . . ."

"'What Love Is,'" she said.

"Eh?" Missis Proposki said.

"'You Don't Know What Love Is,'" she said. "The tune we're listening to. Hear it almost every day on WBLK from Buffalo."

"Oh!" Missis Proposki said. Her face was shining even in the darkened room. Missis Proposki was happy, and her happiness transformed her face and made her look younger, and she held her cigarette the way film stars like Bette Davis hold theirs, in movies.

"If I wasn't so damn tired . . ." Missis Proposki said.

"Me too," she said.

". . . would get up and dance," Missis Proposki said.

"Me too!"

And when she left on the streetcar going east along College, and had waved Missis Proposki good night on the northeast corner of College and Spadina, it was ten o'clock; and the car was empty; and she looked at the five other passengers, sitting at the back of the car, and all of a sudden remembered Missis Proposki's warnings about "the rapists in this city"; and her words about wanting to dance came back to her; and she wondered what really was in Missis Proposki's mind. "Did she want me to dance with her? I wonder." There had been three couples, including two women who clutched each other, their heads on each other's shoulders, dancing to "You Don't Know What Love Is," a soft blues number, thick as syrup, and as sweet, moving to the music as they pressed themselves against their partners' bosoms, eyes closed to the slow saxophone that burned her heart and her body with the fire of memories, and made her wonder when was the last time she had been on a dance floor. "Back home, I would be dancing at the Drill Hall, every bank holiday, every Easter Monday, every club dance, and definitely at every Queen's College Ball. Those were the days!" The streetcar had now stopped at St. George Street, near the Toronto Tuberculosis Centre, across from the building that housed the Public Library. She remembered when she first came here, how the nurse placed her body against the contraption, and she thought she felt the heat, or the electricity coursing through her body; displaying her insides, lungs and heart and liver; and she suddenly became frightened to imagine that the large piece of mica, like a plastic sheet of the X-ray, might actually show the lungs of another patient, and not hers; and that she would be awakened some morning, in the middle of winter, and told by the supervisor to prepare herself, that she was being taken to the sanatorium a long way from Toronto, up upon a mountain in the small town of Hamilton. But then, two years later, they discovered the X-ray of a man who racked his chest each time he coughed, with the name of the university student on it. The student, like her, never had tuberculosis. He was on the bus taking him up the Mountain, a crowded bus full of TB patients, when the error was discovered. She knows this because the student had asked her out to a dance. "Yes! It is as if I am back home. I mean this district. College and Spadina. Apart from the TB place I just passed. I am coming near to the street that Cecil Street runs off! And talking about dances, Cecil Street is the place where, every Thursday night, we domestics danced and ate Trinidadian pellau and curry-chicken, for an admission of seventy-five cents. Three quarters! Dances held by a Mr. Moore. From Barbados.

Look, look! The streetcar just passed the street that Cecil
Street runs off! Beverley! Imagine! Imagine how it is as if I am
revisiting my past. Cecil Street, and the Thursday night dances;
and pellau that didn't have in much chicken, and curry-chicken
that didn't have in much curry . . . and that bastard, pardon my
language! That son of a bitch . . . pardon my French . . .
because he is going to U of T, doing Civil Engineering, thinks
that because I went out with him—once—to one o' these same
Cecil Street brams, which is the name we give to cheap dances
where the music bad . . . he thought he could take me to bed,
on the first date. He thought I wasn't brought up any better
than that! That I didn't have any decency!" And her mind went
back again to the dance floor at the El Mocambo, and whether,
in that short space of time, she had drunk one brandy and Diet
Coke, plus three Jamaica-white-rum-and-Diet-Cokes? "And
what did that woman want, when she said that if she was not
so tired from standing on her feet in the College kitchen she
would have got up and danced? I should have said yes. And see
how she moves her body. And if I-myself wasn't so tired, after a
long day in that blasted kitchen, I would have said yes, and the
two of us could have tripped the light-fantastic! Heh-heh-heh!
My God! Yes . . .

"And the music they played at those Cecil Street brams . . .
by the time the 45s reached us here in Canada, all the music
itself was like it was already rubbed off! The records sticking
and slipping and jerking. But I remember Harry Belafonte.
And 'Day-O.' And 'Stack banana till the morning come! Daylight come and me wan' go home . . .' Those were the days!
Before I became stupid and let 'that man' into my life. Before
I even brought back-up that son o' mine after I got pregnant
with him, that son o' mine, who now giving me such hell . . .

"Those were the days!" she said, as if she was talking to the passengers. All of them were sitting in the three rows of seats at the back of the streetcar; and she figured they were men going home from a long day of temporary, unskilled labour. But how did she know this? she asked herself. She knew because she was once like them. That was what used to be called "Canadian Experience." Yes! She was sure that when they said "You do not have Canadian Experience," they were using the code word for "You black."

Men like these men at the rear of the streetcar are the same men she saw, and got to know by passing acquaintance, who sat in these same seats at the back, thirty years ago. They are the same men who worked ten hours a day, for little pay, six days a week—even on this day—and are now going home. Or are going to their night-shift jobs. Watchmen. Cleaners. "But why do they always sit at the back of the streetcar? When they are so many empty seats up front?"

"Who you take me for?" she was saying, over and over in her mind, as she travelled south on the subway, to Dundas Square. There were many passengers on the subway, and she felt safer in this crowded car. "Who the hell you take me for?" She was re-membering the Civil Engineering U of T student who had first taken her dancing in Toronto. He wore a jacket of blue denim, and on his left shoulder was written in large white letters 6T9. On the back of his jacket was written CIVIL ENGINEER-ING in white capital letters. She had asked him why 6T9? But she can't remember what he told her. The relationship did not last long enough for her to ask the question again.

When she mounted the steps from the subway, she inhaled deeply and walked on, slowly going south to Shuter, passing

young women and men, wondering where they were going at
this late hour; for ten-thirty was late for her; and she a woman
alone, walking in this city late at night, and Missis Proposki
reminding her every night when they parted company to go
their separate ways about "these rapists and molestors . . .";
and purposely not finishing the sentence. She saw her reflection in a shop window obliterated by the bodies of three men,
who seemed to be looking right at her. She became a little
scared and she slowed her pace, waiting for the three reflections to catch up with her. But they did not catch up with her,
and she walked on, and then in another shop window she
saw the same three men. They were on the other side of the
street.

She is becoming really scared now, because there are not
many people on this street. A large vacant lot on her left, and
the Moss Park Armouries and the Park on her right, she feels
like she is walking in the valley of the shadow of death, as her
Mother used to call it.

But she is prepared for any emergency, thanks to Missis
Proposki's warning that lumps all men in this city into the same
bag of "molestors." She takes the cellular phone from the bottom of her leather handbag; flips it open; and starts to talk into
it. Her voice is raised so that the men walking ahead of her look
back. She continues walking and talking; and the men continue
walking with the same distance between them.

"I am outside the door," she says into the cellular phone.

The men look back, and one says to her, "Good night,
ma'am."

"Good night, son," she says to him. "You have a good night."

She flips the cellular phone shut. And puts it into her
handbag.

It was a plastic toy cellular telephone that Missis Proposki had given her as a joke, for her protection.

"These blasted rapists and molestors . . . !"

"You!" she shouted, on that Wednesday night before this Thursday morning, when she closed the door behind her, turning the two keys on heavy locks and then sliding back two bolts. "You!" she said again, and touched the door of his bedroom as if she was giving benediction, as if she was reassuring herself that he was deep in sleep in his bedroom. She moved away from his door, satisfied that he was home. It was going on to midnight.

The lights in the basement apartment, from the bulb in the ceiling at the front door, facing the Park, and the lights along the narrow passageway, and those in the ceiling of the bedroom and sitting room areas, were all turned on. The television was on, with its volume turned down. She kept the television on all day, even when she was not at home. On her bedside table she dropped her house keys, and the small purse that contained her subway tokens; and she ran her hand over the red telephone on the other bedside table to the right side of her double bed, the west side, where she slept.

The telephone started to ring. She looked at her wristwatch. She ignored the ringing. "Who would be calling me at midnight?" BJ came to her mind, but he was supposed to be asleep in his room. And it couldn't be Josephine, her Canadian friend.

She checked to see that the answering machine was on. The telephone rang four times; and the emptiness of her basement apartment seemed to act as a kind of amplifier, making the ringing louder and more frightening; and then it stopped as suddenly as it had begun, and she moved to her bed and started to undress. "I wonder what Missis Proposki really meant by saying she feels like dancing? I wonder. But it was a lovely night." Very carefully, she took the hem of her dress and pulled it up and round her waist, and then covered her face with the silk material. She pulled it over her head and placed it on the bed, and then arranged it onto a hanger, which was covered in silk cloth to prevent the metal of the hanger leaving a stain on her dress. Many nights, less tired than she was on this Wednesday night, she would come home, strip her clothes off, fling them on the bed, take off her panties and leotards in one swipe, and drop them on the bed, flinging on her woollen granny nightgown, and cover her head with the two white sheets, the imitation white blanket and the ribbed comforter. And then she would get out of bed and go down on her knees, after she had put a pillow under her knees, and say her prayers: "Dear Father-God, thank you for taking me through another day . . ."

And then, as if her Mother was talking to her about her laziness and her slovenliness, and her neglect of saying thanks for her life, she would get out of bed, fold her underwear, her brassieres, her slip—when it was winter—and her nylon stockings into a pile, put them on the dresser; and then go back to bed. And immediately get back out of bed, put her silk dress on the ladies' hanger covered in pink cloth; and then jump back into bed. She would fall immediately into a deep, sonorous sleep, breathing through her mouth. And when she awoke the next morning, not knowing what she had done in her sleep, she would for some reason tell Missis Proposki, "Good night, Irene!" And Missis Proposki would laugh and say, "Oh, don't mind you!"

But tonight, on this Wednesday, all of a sudden, sadness descends upon her spirit. She feels lonely. The lights in the apartment, and the rhythm and blues from Buffalo, and the television giving the scores in hockey games, are of no interest to her. She gets out of bed and goes to her son's bedroom door, and says, "You!" But this time it is a whisper, a loving greeting. She walks up to the door, places her ear against the door, tells herself that she can hear him snoring, and goes back into her own bed.

"Rring-rring! . . . rring-rring! . . . rring-rring! . . ."

The sound is louder now, and more insistent, as if the caller can see her through the receiver. "One . . . two . . . three . . . four . . . fifteen . . . sixteen . . ." She counts the number of rings. Nineteen. And suddenly the ringing stops.

There is not a living soul on this street that she could call, at this hour of the night, if she was in an emergency, and ask for help. Her landlord is on one of his long-distance runs to Kirkland Lake. But she knows the 911 number for emergencies. She is two blocks from the Emergency at St. Michael's Hospital; and an ambulance is bound to come before she dies, before the emergency becomes fatal, because she hears them all the time, cutting into the peace of the night, like the wailing of babies.

And the telephone rings again. And it frightens her again. But still she does not answer it. The night closes in; it is late; and she feels alone. She listens to the ringing of the telephone, feeling as though the caller knows she is at home and will not stop until she picks up the telephone. And when she is frightened in times like this, she does nothing. She does not answer the telephone. She does not play back her messages. She does not even turn on the speakerphone to listen to them. She drops into her shell, a carapace, protecting herself from tragedy and misfortune, wiping them from her mind. But the fear remains there, unedited, bare, raw and naked.

And now, for the third time, the phone rings, and she counts the number of rings, and counts along with them— ". . . five . . . six. . . . seven . . ."—and they go on to nineteen. She is convinced that someone is playing tricks with her. She gets out of bed, wraps her housecoat over her nightgown, and goes down the short hall to her son's bedroom. "You!" she says. It is a shout this time. She runs her right hand over the door, and thinks of bursting in upon him, and wonders if this is not a violation; but she ignores all these restrictions and puts a little force on the door. The door swings open. "Thank God!" she says. He sleeps with his door unlocked. "Thank God, you're in here." And she walks into the darkened bedroom, no light coming into it from the hallway, and goes up to his bed, and flings back the blanket and the sheet, even though she can see that there is no body in the bed.

Her body is trembling. She is crying. She holds on to the door, to the wall in the hallway, to the chairs as she reaches them, and then collapses on the bed, burying her head in the pillows, making the pillows wet with her tears. And then she gets up from the bed and stands over the red telephone; and she touches the button to replay her messages. There is only a buzzing sound, like the sound of a telephone off the hook. And then there is a voice coming from the machine: "No new messages . . . remaining time, forty-six seconds."

Earlier in this week, on the Tuesday afternoon, around five o'clock, when she was helping Missis Proposki clear the tables and set up for dinner, she saw an academic hood and gown left on a chair at the high table.

"What's this?" Missis Proposki said. She held them up, away from her face, as if she was holding a dead mouse.

"One of the professors' gowns," she told Missis Proposki. "I'll take it to the Fellows' Lounge."

She took the academic hood and gown from Missis Proposki and went to the lounge; and closed the door.

Missis Proposki was still dusting the top of the high table when she flung the door of the Fellows' Lounge open and said, "Ta-daa!"

"My God!" Missis Proposki exclaimed.

"How I look?" she said.

"Real," Missis Proposki said. "Like one of them."

"You try it on. No professors won't be here yet and . . ."

Before she could finish what she wanted to tell her, Missis Proposki was already fixing her hair, pulling her smock down round her waist, and this took years off her appearance, as she held her arms out, just as she had seen her priest hold his arms out while an assistant threaded his robe and his surplice through them. As though he was ascending the Cross. And Missis Proposki looked younger and more beautiful; and she held her head to one side and smiled, while Idora folded her hands into the shape of a camera and took pictures, saying, "Snap! . . . Good! . . . Another one!" and they were giggling and swirling their bodies this way and the next, and were laughing loudly; and Idora said, "My turn!" and Missis Proposki took the role of the photographer, saying, "Snap, snap . . . snap! Hold your head up. Good!" And like this they walked together back into the Fellows' Lounge, and took the gown off, and folded it, and folded the hood and placed it over the gown.

"You ever thought of night school?" Missis Proposki asked her.

"That's all I think about," Idora said. "After registering at George Brown Community College, since August last year, I managed to make one class. One class! That's all I think about, night school. I am too damn tired on Fridays, when I have to get to my classes, even though I have every other Friday as my off-day. Have I been thinking of night class!"

"Me too!"

Idora wondered whether it was fate, or fatalism, whichever was the correct term; whether there was some deep meaning in their finding the academic hood and gown left on the chair, for them to put on and model; and dream. She had seen her life come clearly before her, in Barbados and even in Canada, that afternoon, when the sun was streaming through the colours in the stained glass windows, transforming the white tablecloth on the high table into a multicoloured one, and touching her apron and transforming it into a "hot dress" that she would wear on a bank holiday, back home; specks of sunlight were climbing the walls of the Dining Hall, all the way up to reach the portrait gallery of former Deans and Provosts and other grey-bearded men whose features were clothed in thick bushes of moustache and beard that made them look more like prophets tumbling out from the pages of the Old Testament than ordinary men who were professors of Latin and Greek, or Philosophy or Logic; or the meaning of miracles.

And then there was another day, a few months back, as she and Missis Proposki and others had finished clearing the tables and cleaning up, and were putting out the cutlery for breakfast the next day, when a stranger came into the Dining Hall. The creak of the heavy oaken door startled her, and she could not move. Idora wondered if the stranger was a thief, intent on snatching a silver sugar bowl, or a cup and saucer, with the College crest on them, as a memento. The stranger had been looking left and right, and was startled when she realized that there was someone in the empty Dining Hall with her, and that Idora had seen her. She could hear the noise of saucepans and knives and forks and soup spoons coming from the kitchen. She walked up to Idora and said, "Do you mind if I have some coffee? I missed dinner. And I am so hungry."

"Haven't I seen you here before?"

"I am in Graduate School," the woman said.

"I know I'd seen you!"

"Thank you. Thank you very much."

"Sit down, child," Idora told the woman.

The woman took her coat off, and her gloves. The lights in the ceiling struck the knives and forks and the glasses on the tables, and made the dining room look vast, and magical.

"Good!" Idora told the woman, who was now sitting. "Let me fix you something."

It is Thursday morning, the bells of the Cathedral have stopped, and she turns over on her back. She is still cold. She moves to her left, and then to her right, and then she tightens the covers round her body and she tells herself that she must look like a dead woman, "a dead," as they say in the Island, a corpse; like the body of that king, or emperor, that she had seen one cold Sunday afternoon, months later, when Josephine had taken her to see the Egyptian Exhibition. And she wondered what it would be like to be dead: to lie right here, in this same bed, left stiff and dead; and after five days or a week, still undiscovered by the neighbour to the left, and the neighbour to the right; and by her landlord, a long-distance truck driver; and then the stench rising from her deterioration to declare that she is at last found; the smell of her stench rising, although it is still winter . . . and she starts thinking if it would be better to be found dead in winter or in the summer . . . and lying in her white bed, with the bedding fitting her like a cocoon, wrapped in a funereal shroud, ready for burial in the frozen grave.

The tiny alarm clock paints her the time, 7.45, in red numerals, like a raw, clearly defined tearing-away of her flesh. The time is 7.46 now. She has lived one minute longer. And she is sad that at this thick velour time of winter, waking in the darkness, getting dressed in the darkness, going to bed in this darkness, even when the ceiling lights and the lamps are left on, along with the television and the radio playing music from Buffalo, even the lights in her basement apartment do not seem able to penetrate the sadness and blackness of her spirit.

This sadness weighs upon her spirit as she tries to call to mind the dream that the ringing of the bells interrupted; and she remembers now how the dream turned terrible. There was a line of men, like soldiers on a march in a green pasture, passing her, in single file, with tall thin-bodied trees surrounding them, and that gave no shade. The horror of her dream, when she got close to the line of soldiers, all black men, and who seemed to be the age of her own son, was that they all had their right hands cut off, clean-clean, at the wrists. And she thought the end of the ringing of the bells—"Blang! . . . blang! . . . buh-lang! . . . blang!"—was like the sudden, final slashes of a cut-lass. All the men were tied to one another, by rope, at the left hand. Just before the dream escaped her body, like air from a balloon, the ringing of the bells had stopped. And she wondered what was the reason for cutting off their right hands. Were they all left-handed?

And now she remembered. The man at the head of the single file of captured soldiers was "that man," her husband, Bertram, only younger. And the man at the rear, a boy, was her son, Barrington James.

It is a cold, dark Thursday morning. The bells are no longer ringing. And her dream has faded. She curses "that man," now in America, in Brooklyn, where he went, he said, to find permanent employment. All the jobs he ever had in Toronto were casual, unskilled, part-time jobs, delivering handbills from restaurants; handbills advertising Tim Hortons coffee, handbills advertising pizza from Pizza Pizza, Chinese food, Wong-Ping Take-Out Chicken Palace, and coupons that offered two chances to win a free Ultramatic adjustable bed. He brought home four of these coupons one afternoon and gave them to her.

"What for?" she had asked him.

"To win!" He said it, she remembered, with the same excitement as if he was placing a bet on a horse at Greenwood racetrack. "Suppose you win!"

"Now, what the hell am I going to do with eight Ultramatics?"

"Take a chance!" he said. "It's life!"

She feels surrounded by her worries, quarried like an animal being hunted down; and disgusted, in her loneliness, with her son, as she would try, on many nights, to locate him in the Park across the street from her apartment, as she looked through her two horizontal front windows, whose sills are below the level of the street. And when she can pick him out from the cluster of his friends, she can see only parts of his body: sometimes his head;

sometimes his legs; sometimes his torso; as if he is cut into pieces, like a side of beef, rendered headless, legless, through the dexterity of a cleaver on the carcass of a slaughtered cow. And as she stands at the windows, she can feel the cold drafts of night breathing down her neck, and along her arms, and see them coming out of her mouth, and her nostrils, like steam; and feel how they enter her cleavage, and sting her breasts like icicles. And the line of young black men walking in single file and tied to one another, by rope the colour of khaki, which runs from one silent body to the next, comes back into her mind, stronger now than when the tableau of frightened black bodies punctuated her dream. They are bent in fear and in fatigue. They are crossing a large green field bordered by thin, tall, leafless trees. And the fear in their eyes flashes across the screen of her disappearing dream.

She has been thinking about her son: hoping he would stop dressing like a rapper, that he would wear a proper uniform to his school at Jarvis Collegiate Institute, less than four blocks away; that he would become like one of the students she cooked for, years ago, and served at the boys' private school; that he would see these students as his role models, these smart boys, black and white, Chinese and Indian, students of this prestigious school for boys, where she peels potatoes and carrots and fries chicken legs and thighs in the kitchen that is large as a hotel's; these boys who wear white shirts and grey flannel short pants, grey stockings pulled up to their knees, blue-black blazers, blue ties with animals on them, and brown leather shoes; and who "walk erect and nice, and talk nice" as they carry their bookbags strapped to their backs that make them, with the humps of weight, look like little camels. She sees these "nice-talking young men"—boys to her—standing at bus stops and on subway platforms—and in chauffeur-driven private cars; and then they would disappear in the flash of the car window when the morning light hit it; and she would see them every day of all the years she worked in the kitchen of the boys' private school. And every day she went to work, tired and cold before she entered the large kitchen, she drew her son's face onto the face of a Chinese boy, in the whim of fantasy, then onto the face of a white boy; and then onto the face of an Indian boy from Pakistan. And finally, onto the face of that one boy who she was told was from the Bahamas. "Close-enough to the Island where I born!" His complexion was two shades lighter than BJ's.

"But BJ prefers to walk, rocking from side to side, as if his testicles are swollen, are enlarged like goadies. Walking like a penguin. The waist of his blue jeans falling almost to his knees. Down below his backside. White do-rag on his head. White baseball cap on top of the do-rag. The peak of the baseball cap pointing backwards. Or sideways. Looking so aggressive in this rap-culture fashion. That he copied from African-Americans. His long white T-shirt. Looking more like a woman's dress than a man's shirt. And thank God. Thank God. He is still wearing round his neck the sterling silver chain, with small links, and a silver cross around his neck that I gave him on his thirteenth birthday. That makes me so happy." And it really did make her proud to see him wearing it. And then his Reeboks, for which she bears the burden of the price, three times a year—"Your foot is growing too damn fast, boy!"

"But sometimes I feel I could kill you!" she says in her mind, to the empty basement apartment, one cold morning as she kneels on the floor covered by a floral linoleum carpet. "Just to look at the way you look!"

Her knees are hurting her. No matter how carefully she sweeps the floor in the living room area that serves also as her bedroom, there are always grains on it, from the basmati rice she buys at the Muslim store on Parliament Street, east along Shuter. The grains of rice escape the tough black hairs of her industrial broom. The broom was "borrowed" from the company where "that man" was the temporary janitor. And besides the rice grains were grits, little white specks that look like small raw diamonds. And this Thursday morning she spends a long time on her knees, while grits and rice grains dig into her knees, and she interrupts her prayers to raise one knee, and then the other, to brush them off and wet her fingers with saliva to clean her knees; and then go back down on her knees.

She wonders if she is being punished for not going to work, and she compares the stabbing pain from the rice grains to that bigger pain suffered by Jesus when the Roman soldiers crowned him with a diadem of thorns; and his side pierced by a spear.

"Hymn three hundred and four!" she says to herself, as if she is talking to Josephine her new friend, or to someone else in the basement with her. She talks to herself, aloud, as if she is conducting a conversation, a dialogue; and she changes her voice to answer the question she poses to herself, and reverts to her original voice, her natural voice, to ask another question, or to give another opinion, in these arguments she is having with herself. "Sunday coming," she says to herself, "I intend to be the first person in a pew, at the Cathedral, to take Communion. And if I happen to change my mind, what do you think of my going up to the Apostolicals? I been thinking of giving the sermon. I been thinking of Jonah in the Belly of the Whale. What do you think of that? I have to call the Pastor and tell him."

She understands her reason for this, this populating of her
basement apartment with invisible, but talkative, people. As a
girl growing up in the Island, she was introspective. But this
habit, the splitting of herself into two or more different person-
alities—in this schizophrenic act is a new, more dangerous psy-
chological matter. In the Island, people, especially women, who
talk to themselves are "tetched in the head"—mad, stark crazy.

"Father-God," she says, now on her knees, with the rice
grains and the grits still digging into the soft flesh of her
knees, "I praying for BJ, my son. Help him." And she recites
the second-last verse of a hymn:

> "Your reign shall know no end,
> And round Your pierced Feet
> Fair flowers of Paradise extend
> Their fragrance ever sweet."

And she is ready to rise from the floor covered with the
cold linoleum decorated in red and yellow and pink flowers,
that she used to walk beside, and sometimes trample with her
"pumps," her word for Reeboks, in gutters back in the Island,
flowers that now are so beautiful on the cold basement floor,
stamped into the linoleum. She thinks again of going to
church, on Sunday, three days away; and she begins an argument with herself. "Should I go to the Apostolicals?" And if
you were not in the same room with her, you wouldn't know
that there is no one kneeling beside her; and that she is referring to the Apostolical Holiness Church of Spiritualism in
Christ. She is an Assistant Deaconess there. For twenty-five
years, off and on, five years after she came to this country, she

has been attending revivals and prayer meetings in the hectic, rhythmic, tambourine-beating small church, whose congregation is entirely West Indian; black; immigrants who worked in hospitals and banks and office buildings as cleaners and sweepers. These women and men dressed each Sunday as if they were going to weddings or five o'clock morning services on Christmas Day or Easter Sunday. And she watched them attending this small church, and saw the pride in their eyes and the joyfulness in their bodies, each Sunday she joined them in the small yard beside the small church. When she took Communion at the Cathedral, she had all the grounds and beds of flowers that grew on all four sides of the building to admire. There was no garden, and not even a wild plant, in the gravel path of her other church.

As much as she tried, she could not get the Pastor to change "Apostolical" to "Apostolic" in the name of his church. He did not see the error when he painted the sign; but he told her, "I like how Apostolical sound. It sound more Biblical."

Before the congregation bought the building and turned it into a church, and gave it this "Biblical" new name at a party one Sunday morning, like a christening back in the Island, with rum and champagne, curry-chicken and baked pork, it was a small-scale slaughterhouse which sold huge pieces of cow, and cow tongue, cow heel, and the testicles of oxen. These testicles were made into "mannish-water," a delicious Jamaican delicacy. And pork, cut with skin and bone and fat, for better cooking and taste; and, with the growing population of West Indians in the neighbourhood surrounding it, goat belly and sheep belly. No, she could never get the Pastor to change the word which offended her knowledge of grammar; so, she and other members in the congregation continued to call their place of worship "the Apostolicals."

"So, Sunday coming, the Apostolicals?" she asked herself aloud. "Or the Cathedral? And I have to speak with the Pastor about Jonah in the Belly of the Whale."

She rises from the floor. She raises her weight on her right foot first. And she finds her balance. And with her left hand on the linoleum, she raises her weight onto the other foot. And she inhales deeply. And sighs. And gradually, slowly, all the while telling herself she hears the creaking of her bones, she stumbles to an almost upright position. She pulls out that part of her white imitation silk nightgown that is sticking into her bottom; passes her hands over the rest of her body, breasts first, stomach second and hips third; and smiles. She is taking today off. And that lifts her spirits slightly, since it means she can, she hopes, put away the frustrations of her life that face her. She has put her husband completely out of her life, and he has become "that man." Her biggest worry is her son. She wishes she had the nerve and the hardness of heart to throw him out of her apartment. Yes.

She had saved for years, every penny left over from her salary after paying the bills. And sometimes, when she wanted the balance of her savings account to reflect her enthusiasm for a larger balance, she added an extra twenty dollars to the deposit slip; and because she was a single parent, she often had to withdraw that same twenty dollars for a deposit on a telephone bill, or for the hydro. But she wasn't complaining. She had her health. "And I have my BJ. But by-God, sometimes I wish he was dead." And immediately she begged God's forgiveness for having these thoughts about her son.

"I wish I had the courage to tell him, to his face, to please leave." And with this feeling of frustration, she made up her mind to take Communion on Sunday at the Cathedral, to help bolster her determination. "But I don't have the courage . . ."

And all of a sudden, the cold November morning sun streams through the two windows at the front of her apartment; and she sees the shafts of light splatter like water from an over-turned glass onto the linoleum floor, and the light becomes like an injection of air into the tire of a car, and it buoys her spirits, and at the same time she can hear the cars passing fast and late, for work, going in both directions; and she tells herself that she can smell the heavy oil and gas fumes and exhausts of these vehicles. And if she could see herself, if she was standing in front of her looking glass that has the shape of a rectangle, and without a frame, secured to the wall by six plastic braces in which she has placed screws, if she could see behind her, she would notice that the light from the windows has drawn the lusciousness and the size of her hips and her thighs through the thin white imitation silk nightgown to look more sexy and magnificent. And with this life in her body, this new lightheartedness, she begins to walk up and down her apartment, at first counting the number of steps, measuring them, right heel touching the toes of her left foot, heel to toes, then toes to heel, walking and measuring like a land surveyor marks off distance, counting the number of "feet" to guess the size of the field. Her linoleum floor, in the bedroom area and throughout the apartment, is like the field in her dream, over which the young men and the boys were walking, tied together, hand by hand, with rope. And she walks over this cold linoleum now, with the sprightliness in her body and especially in her legs, measuring the area, the length and

the breadth of the space in which she lives, touching the tips of
her toes with her heel, right heel to left toes; left heel to right
toes; like a model . . .

She puts her right hand, fingers opened like a fan, onto the
right side of her waist, and she holds herself erect; balances her
body on her bare feet; head held high, haughty and with dignity;
wets her lips, presses them tight together, and releases them, to
give them a more sensual, more seductive appearance and mag-
netism; and moves off, switching her backside from side to side.
She is a large woman, and this action, this movement, takes the
energy from her; but she is determined to transform her narrow
linoleum-lined basement apartment into a catwalk with men
and women, artists and designers, crowded on both sides of
her; and she walks the gauntlet. "But is the right name for it a
walkway? Or a *runway*?" For she is now Naomi Campbell, the
famous model from England. She moves her hips from side to
side, taking short disjointed steps, as if she is determined to put
her hips out of joint, deliberately out of commission. "I am a
model! Look at me! The Canadian Naomi Campbell. On the
catwalk. That's the word for it! *Catwalk*. Amn't I beautiful? Ain't
I beautiful? Am I not beautiful?" And she laughs out louder still,
laughs so loudly that the neighbour on the right pounds on the
wall; or perhaps she imagines it.

She moves from the two front windows, down the middle of
the area used as the sitting room, and says, "Don't touch the
couch, girl!" and then she breaks off her rhythm and walks,
naturally, farther along, until she comes to the king-sized bed,
under which she reaches; and when she rises again, she is even
more regal and black, in a pair of high-heeled shoes, with a
spike for a heel, and in the brightest red leather, "patient-
leather" as she used to call them back in the Island. All the shoes

she wore to the girls' school back in the Island, and to church, at Matins, to Sunday School, to Evensong, and to Saturday after-noon matinees at the Empire Theatre in town, to watch cowboy movies, and to count and cheer on the number of cuffs landed on the cowboy-crook by the cowboy who was the star-boy, were all made by the village shoemaker. In black dull leather.

She is now in front of the full-length looking glass nailed onto the wall; the wall is painted green, verdant and bright and with glossy paint; but it does not make the basement apartment dull and sombre (as "that man" used to protest that it did, when he offered to paint the apartment) because she keeps the lights on always, "burning bright," she says to herself, remembering that one line from a nursery rhyme, or a children's poem; and the television is left on too, day and night, even when she is at work; and the radio is always tuned to WBLK, her favourite station in Buffalo, New York, playing rhythm and blues, and big band jazz, and soul music, by her beloved Supremes and Count Basie and Aretha Franklin, Otis Redding and Ray Charles and James Brown; and she jerks her heavy waist to a stop, tired and breathing hard, and she says to herself, "I have to go on a diet"; as she catches her breath and starts singing "It is a man's world."

In her imagination she is a model, and she goes back to jerk-ing her left hip, hearing the corresponding snap of leather from her high heel; and then she moves her right hip in a sharp jerk, and now she passes the area where her bed stands, white and empty, smooth as marble, like a huge baking pan of icing, like a cake, like a skating rink, empty with only the imprint of her body on it—"This bed. This empty bed. This empty bed."—until she reaches the only bedroom in the apartment, the only room that has a lock and a key. BJ's room. She is not thinking clearly now. Something is bothering her. Did she really hear his breathing? Or was it her imagination? She knows he is not in his room. But she pretends that he is. And sadness of self-deception rattles her body, and touches her gait and posture. So she ends her parading; and the room becomes gloomy even though all the lights, and the television and the radio, are turned on; and she is standing in front of the door that leads to the back of the house, to the garden. Her landlord plants tomatoes and corn and white roses during the summer, in the garden, in which she is not allowed to go. Her landlord is from Trinidad and Tobago. He has secured the wrought iron gate that leads from her back door into the garden with a combination lock. She has promised herself to learn to pick the lock. Or, with luck, sneak the key from the ugly iron lock and have it copied at the hardware store on Dundas Street, where the owner speaks Somali, a second language to English, as if he was born, and had grown up, in Toronto.

But she must turn back now and retrace her steps, walking in the gyrations of the model, Naomi Campbell, who she has convinced herself she is: jerking her waist from side to side, matching the touching of heel to toes in this slow march, parading in the white silk nightgown on her body, showing off her body as if it is now dressed in the latest fashion; with the light coming in through the two windows at the front of her apartment highlighting her hips, and the touch of a chill in the draft that comes with the breaking of dawn in this dark November light; and it touches her body and penetrates beneath the white nightgown, with its thin imitation silk, and she can feel it clutch her breasts and her waist and her legs, but the most decided touch is on her legs. Still, she must complete her surveyor's measurement of the land, the area of the apartment, she had begun, returning to the front of the apartment, through the same spaces, the field over which the line of chained men were walking: "I am coming now to my bedroom, my bedroom space." The bed is still white; and the pillows, all seven of them (three in the space that used to be "that man's" side, three on her side), are white, with the seventh pillow tossed on top of them, and fluffed. It looks like a field, like a section of the Park across the street, on which snow had fallen all night, and the first light of morning shows her, through her windows, the clean, even, pure snow, the same as alabaster, the same as a marble slab of a tombstone, the same as a thick layer of icing on a cake.

She has never seen a tombstone since she has lived in this city; only back home in the Island, where she lived next door to the church and its bordering graveyard, where soldiers and seamen and governors of the Island—when the Island was a slave-colony of England's, where slaves were held and broken and made pliable for Jamaica's cane fields—where white people were buried beneath huge, white, marbled slabs and fitted into tombstones that looked like small buildings. She has never walked so far north along Yonge Street, here in Toronto, from her neighbourhood, to see the graveyards of Mount Pleasant Cemetery—"Who's fooling who? Pleasant?"—to see the statues and the architecture of the dead.

On her white bed, made up as she was taught by her Mother when she was a girl, and afterwards when she was training to be a nurse, back in the Island at the General Hospital, are her toys, her "babies" as she calls them, made by her own two hands: her teddy bears and her panda bears, all made from brown, soft cloth, corduroy and suede, stubby and short as a crewcut, gathered from scraps, from needleworkers' leftovers, and, in addition to this, she has bought scraps from stores along Bloor

Street West, especially at Honest Ed's bargain basement, near the Bathurst subway station. Her babies' eyes are small buttons; and their mouths small dashes of red thread; and there is a necklace of silver-like embroidery around the neck of each baby bear.

There is also a statue of a little boy, a little brown boy, a little brown-skin boy, with black woollen thread for hair; large white buttons for eyes; red silk thread for lips; and small, brown baby booties; and he is dressed in a white shirt with a tie of slashed blue and white, like a college tie; and long grey flannel trousers, and a blue-black blazer. She made this doll when she was still working in the kitchen of the private school for boys. This brown boy is her replica of BJ, her son, made by her own hands, as her image of the role model BJ should follow; and she had created it with artistic fervour, her workmanship like that of a sculptor forming a person from clay. But instead of clay, her choice was cloth: pliable, sensitive to her change of temper and love for him, delicate as her moods. When she looks at it, in spite of the fact that it really does not look like BJ, she nevertheless thinks of him. And she experiences short bursts of joy. But just as easily, this vision of him, which is what she wants it to be known as, makes her more convinced that her life holds more grief and sadness than her dreams for his well-being can accommodate. Her "precious baby," as she calls him when she touches his hair and passes her hands across his cheeks, as she was indulgent and caring, when he was a baby—this temperamental demonstration of closeness does not satisfy her wishes and her dreams for his success in life. And sometimes she cannot see, and does not wish to see, any difference between the doll-baby and her son. She keeps the doll-baby propped up in the centre of the bed, between the three piled pillows on the right side and the three on the left side. She kisses the doll-baby on its mouth every night as she gets into bed, and first thing when she opens her eyes in the morning; always after she has read her Bible, praising God, while most of the time she prays for her son.

She turns the knob of the bedroom door, opens it a crack, looks inside and closes it again. She is convinced that he came home in the night and that he is in his bedroom. Her hope is mixed into conviction. She had heard him snoring. She opens the door a second time and looks in. There is no one there.

Black wallpaper covers the walls. There are drawings of two windows, complete with white curtains, painted onto the wall-paper. BJ has put two small lights, like the bulbs for a Christmas tree, on the windowsills. The windowsills are two straps of wood nailed onto the black wallpaper. And when she switches the lights on, there are only the two blue Christmas bulbs that come on, giving the room a distant, cavelike look, eerie and familiar at the same time, like a cave in which she expects a monster to emerge with a club in his hand, raised to drive the studs into her head. There is a framed photo of his father, Bertram. And a smaller one of her, in a silver frame, beside his bed. The sheets on his bed are black. They are made of cotton. The blanket is black. She starts to shudder. Where has he gone? On the wall opposite the door is a photo-graph of John Coltrane, taken from the cover of his album *A Love Supreme*. She looks at Coltrane hard, trying to see what is the magnetic interest BJ could have in this man who is looking straight ahead, into the distance, looking in the direction of the landlord's garden, at the north end of her basement apart-ment. She likes the serious, sullen, piercing look in Coltrane's eyes. She wishes she knew more about this man. And then she faces another picture, this one of Marcus Garvey. And one of Eldridge Cleaver. And one of three young black men wearing dark glasses and many heavy gold chains round their necks, and their hats are pulled down to cover their eyes. All of them are pointing their fingers at the camera. She has never seen these three young men before. They frighten her. Even in their photographs. All the pictures are trimmed and matted in cheap frames he could have bought from Goodwill stores, or from the Dollarama store on Sherbourne Street, across from the Community Hall with the two lions at its front steps, the lions looking more like house-pet cats reclining on a warm carpet before a fire than beasts from the jungle.

And then the thing that looked like a fishnet nailed to the ceiling of the room, and coming down onto his bed like a veil, like a huge mosquito net; like an amateur artist's rendition of Niagara Falls.

And then the photograph of a man. Strong, firm, hostile eyes, the eyes of someone who is terrified by the very idea that obsesses him, by a thought, an act; lips thin in their anger; eyeballs like bullets. With a finger raised just like her Mother raised her finger in threat, in warning, in caution. On this man's head is a round hat. And on the hat are silver markings of moons and stars in some quarter of the zodiac, and they seem to turn his head into a scene out of the heavens.

Malcolm X!

That is who he is. She has seen his face on the front page of the newspaper that young black men, dressed in black suits, push into her face to buy—wearing these heavy black suits even in the sonorous sweating days of July and August—at the corner of Dundas and Yonge, up and down the sidewalk, pushing the newspaper up to her nose one afternoon, forcing her to be black and conscious of her race, she could see this dare in their eyes, in their short-clipped hair, their tidiness of dress, their clean-cut deportment, confident that she, black like them, and conspicuous along the white sidewalk, could not escape their imprecations of racial allegiance.

"Buy a paper, Sister?" The first words are an appeal. The next, "Buy a paper, Sister! Read 'Muhammad Speaks.' The words of the Honourable Elijah Muhammad." This is now a racial command.

"I can't read," she told the Black Muslim black man once. And to herself she said, "Making me embarrassed before all these white people!"

"Slamm-laikum!" the young man said. She did not know what language this was.

"Embarrassing me in front o' all these white people!"

She turns the knob of his bedroom door, closes it; opens it, as if to get a final look, as she had looked one last time at the roaring waters of Niagara Falls, a memory she took with her on the long trip back to Toronto. And in this final glance, her eyes take in two speakers stained in dark mahogany that blends into the black wallpaper, reaching up to her navel, on which are stacked record albums and CDs; and as her eyesight adjusts to the blackness in his decoration, she sees that the walls are lined with books which almost reach up to the ceiling. Then she closes the door again. "Where could this boy be?"

She looks through the windows, and the windowsills are above her head, even if she tiptoes or stands on a box of empty beer bottles. Now she can see the men and the women and the children passing; but there are only the legs and thighs of women, and the bottoms of winter coats and thick woollen leotards, and the trousers of men, and the briefcases in their right hands. She can see entire carriages and prams in which children are pushed through the thick snow on the sidewalk; and the children do not move, because it is too cold for movement, too cold for laughter, and they seem asleep; or even dead; or perhaps dead asleep, in the cold perambulators; and she can see the women pushing them, see their hands and their jeans and their large handbags; and nothing else; and sometimes she imagines the diapers, soiled and damp; and fresh, in the diaper bags; and she smiles at the flashes of the flowing rich-coloured robes that some of these women wear—she has already labelled them single parents and wives whose husbands have left, for jail, for detention centres, in flight against the breaking of their probation clauses; for love of another woman; and in all this, all this turmoil within families that she reads about in the *Star* newspaper, and listens to on the radio when she is trying to tune in to WBLK from Buffalo, never before, until now, has she been forced to number herself amongst the rising wave of single parents, who float before her front windows, who rise in the cold, dark mornings; push comforters into the children's mouths to keep them quiet; while they throw housecoats over cold, naked bodies, mix Carnation milk with warm water; rub the warm washcloths over the shivering, trembling bodies, across eyes, into creases, underarms, legs, private parts; and put diapers on; and count the number of those sousing in a plastic pail, under the sink, in the space there for baby powder, and then pulling something on, and going down in the elevator already crowded with the smell of bodies and of hope, to enter the eye-clearing, shivering cold morning. And then they walk, too hungry so early in the morning. She remembers the young white woman opposite her in the subway coach, holding the *Star* newspaper high to her eyes, and

the front page is opened out so that she can read the headline
and see the eyes of the black woman in the photograph with a
child in her arms, another one toddling along and the third in
a pram. And then the woman holding the newspaper folds it
together, and she sees the black woman sitting opposite her,
and she looks at her with a crease of worry on her forehead; and
she, the object of the woman's curiosity, wonders if she does in
fact look like a woman going home from work to pick up three
children, between the ages of five and one, from the daycare
centre, or from the babysitter, or from her own sister—"My
mother can't keep them, because she just got a part-time job at
Wal-Mart"—who keeps them for her "since she ain't working,
yet!"; and how many times she had been pointed out, in
glance, in whispered pity, in complete disregard, as a member
of this growing number. The headline that was illustrated by
the photo of a young single black mother screamed in thick
two-inch-tall letters, WHERE ARE THE MEN? She knows
that there is no need to mention the colour of these men. And
there is no need to waste words or reason to argue that she
herself is not one of them. She looks as if she is; as if she could
be; as if she is. These thoughts go with her on the subway and
the streetcar, and the bus, every morning, as she glances at the
headlines when the woman sitting opposite her turns the pages
of the Life section of the *Toronto Star*. The question, in the
newspaper, on radio and on television, is the same: "Where are
the men?"; meaning, as she knows they mean, meaning, as she
knows they know, the black men. Where are they? And she
becomes ashamed to be a black woman, old enough to be a
mother; now, because of her special circumstance (husband lost
in the throng of Brooklyn's unemployed black population, son
who has disappeared), she knows there is no need to state her

exclusion from this category. But more than this presumption that she will join this numbering, this profile, which seems to grow and grow, is her sadness about the things the media says about these missing black men, things she had never heard back in the Island: that they are killers of other black men; that they are gangsters; that they call their own women "hos"; that they are violent; that they sell and use drugs.

"BJ can't be a member of a gang. No! BJ couldn't be a gangster. Oh, God, no! And he won't call a black woman a ho without knowing the next step would be to call his own mother one. Good God, it can't be! Couldn't be! A ho?"

Two Fridays ago, she could hardly climb the fifteen steps up to the second floor of the hairdressing salon; and she had to pause every three stairs and hold on to her knees, and then to her back, and breathe hard as she used to breathe when she was in the sea, and say, "Phewww! Phewww!"; and say to herself, speaking the words as if she was talking to Josephine, "Girl, age catching up with you, girl! And you not watching your diet, and eating all this sticky-rice with pig tails cooked in it, and all this Jamaica-white-rum-and-Diet-Coke . . . a young woman like you . . . and behaving so!"; and eventually she entered the large room and sat beside a woman, one of fifteen others waiting their turn with the hairdresser; and before her turn came, she sat and listened to the women talking.

"The medias? The medias in this blasted country?" one said.

"They're always bad-talking our men."

"That is what the media are for. Downgrade black people . . ."

"You mean black men!"

"Well, of course! Not one without the other . . ."

"And when they had the story, as they did last Saturday, about 'Where the blasted men is,' I had to say to myself. . ."

"But really-and-truly, yuh can't argue with the media for asking this question, though!"

"Cuddear! No, you can't. Fairness is fairness."

"Sometimes I-myself, although I'm a married woman, I does have to ask myself that same question. 'Where the fucking men is?'"

"Fucking white women! That's where! Pardon my French."

And then they all laughed, as if they knew the woman was telling a joke, and that the men were not out running after white women.

"Some of our men married good ones, though!" one woman said. "I mean white women. My sister-in-law is one."

"That is true. But they're in a minority."

"We are accustomed to being in minorities."

"I mean the white women, not—"

"The Gospel-truth!"

"But where are the men?" a woman said; and then laughed out as if she was telling a joke.

She has her own answer to that woman's question. Nobody, no newspaper, no television interviewer, no member of the medias, as they call reporters who enter the ghettos of Toronto and demand answers, not one of those bastards has ever asked her the question. But if they had, her answer to them would have been contained in two words: "Fuck off!" Or, better still, in one word: "Dead!" And she laughs at her cleverness. "Dead," she repeats. "Like the one I said 'I do' to."

Her basement apartment takes up the entire perimeter of the first floor of the house, and it runs from the south of the building, where her front door is and two windows are, backwards to the north, where there is a small garden. The garden is "for my personal usage," the landlord had told her when she signed the lease, when she thought her life was getting the security she had prayed for; when the balance in her savings account was growing with each paycheque. She didn't like the idea of living in a basement; she had never lived in one before; but in this space below the level of the street she didn't have to share bathroom and cooking facilities with strangers, with the other tenants in the house.

There are three steps that lead up to the garden from the back door of her apartment. The wrought iron gate blocks further progress and is always locked. "For safety," her landlord says, "from these goddamn criminals living around me, that live in halfway houses surrounding my property." Her landlord lives alone, in the rest of the two-storey house. He emigrated from Trinidad many years ago; worked for a while as a railroad porter; and then went into truck driving. His soft, smooth skin, the colour of clear honey, fooled her that November afternoon many years ago—seven or eight?—when she answered the advertisement, when he opened the front door to answer the question she asked him, "Is the apartment gone?" At first glance she had taken him for a white man; but when he spoke to her, something told her differently; and to prove it he told her, "Jesus Christ, I hope you don't mistake me for a white man! I is a Wessindian like you. And living in this blasted cold too long. I from Trinidad, man. This country cold, no-ass, eh, girl?"; and when his laughter, infectious and sweet as a hummingbird chirping first thing in the morning, when that sweet sound that reminds her of steel pan and calypso, hit her ears and warmed her body that cold afternoon, she placed him accurately back in

Port of Spain, Trinidad, walking on grass cooled by the dew and
by the wind coming off the sea from the Gulf of Paria, one of
many young men and young women taking their morning exercise round the Savannah.

Her apartment has two windows on the south side, facing
the Park. They look like portholes to her, only that they are rectangular, longer than they are deep; and sometimes, looking
through them to see the people passing, they make her feel she
is on a schooner, watching the waves, and the fish beside the
boat swimming faster, passing her in their silent, surer confi-
dence. So, when she looks through the two rectangular windows, it is as if she is in a submarine; and it is the people, men
and women and children, and toddlers in prams and strollers,
who pass her, in front of her subterranean window-hatches.
They are moving, and she is standing still. She is not tall enough
to see the entire bodies of the people passing, at all hours of the
day and night, in all months of the year, in all temperatures.
She never sees their full stature. She has to stand on her bed to
see three-quarters of a person's body; or stand on one of the
two wooden chairs, which she had painted red; and on which
she and her son, BJ, would sit to eat their meals, especially on
Sundays. Those were good times, happy times, before "that
man" left for America. One Saturday evening, around eight
o'clock, he pushed his key into the front door; and slammed the
door after him; and was singing an old calypso, "Brown skin
girl, stay home and mind baby," all the rage at brams and house
parties during the Second World War; and he walked heavily
down the short hallway, and entered the kitchen and dropped
the plastic bag on the table covered in linoleum cloth; and in all
this time, not a word of acknowledgement, of announcing his
arrival; nothing.

"Brown skin girl, stay home and mind baby,
Brown skin girl, stay home and mind baby,
Going-away, on a sailing ship,
And if I don't come back,
Stay home and mind baby . . ."

And he hummed the next two lines, as he could not remember the words; and his humming turned into a whistling, as he held the large, dark grey plastic bag at the bottom and lifted it just so slightly, and she and BJ's little eyes watched the squirming bodies of the fish oil their way down from the plastic bag, now looking more like a chute, more like a galvanized gutter for rainwater, ooze out of the bag onto the table. BJ saw the eyes move and put his arms round his mother's waist. And she saw the sides, the chests of the fish, the gills expand and contract like the bellows of a concertina; and she closed her eyes.

"Oh Christ, Bertram!"

"When I fry-up these six trout fishes, you going see something, girl! As a matter of fact, the two o' wunnuh going taste something! I frying them in olive oil, with a lil white sugar sprinkle-over them, some lime juice, and Jesus Christ . . ."

"You went to the Kensington Market?" she asked him.

"A hundred! One hundred dollars I win today at the races," he said, touching the fish; and replacing them in a line when they squiggled for their short freedom on the slippery table. "And I say to myself, Bertram, you and the wife and this boy here deserve a little feast. So I cooking a feast for you and the boy. And I even stop at the Liquor Store and buy this bottle o' champagne which a Jamaican fella tell me is a good bottle, for the price. I spending some o' this hundred dollars on my family tonight . . ."

And when the cork from the bottle of champagne popped and struck the ceiling; and BJ looked up and could not find it, and thought it had shot through the ceiling like a rocket, and she followed its sound, and thought too of real rockets; and Bertram poured the drink, badly, and it spilled over on the tablecloth; and they watched Bertram put his face on the linoleum and suck up the champagne, they clapped and cheered his dexterity; and he dipped his finger in his glass and wiped it across BJ's lips. And a short time later, when he had scaled the fish, and had drawn the knife perpendicular over the fish and watched the guts fall out; during the rubbing of the thyme and the garlic and the black pepper into the fish, and when the fire hissed like starlight sparkles dipped in water; and the smell covered them over like the smell of warm sea water; and they listened to each other's chewing as their teeth crunched into the head, eating the bones with the flesh there . . .

"Oh Christ, boy!" she had said that night, referring to other things.

Bertram ate every sliver of flesh from the skeleton of the fish he held in his hand; and he left the head intact, for the last; and she was able to count the number of bones in the fish's spine, and she watched as he sucked out the eyes and then removed the skin from the head, like a surgeon peeling dead skin from a wound; and then when all the "goodness," as he called it, from the fish head was sucked into his mouth, he held the head up to the light, closed both eyes and put the skull into his mouth. They listened to the breaking down of bones, and then they watched him pour the last inch of the cheap champagne into his plastic glass. The stem could be screwed off from the cup of the glass.

"Oh Christ!" she said.

"A hundred dollars I win today!" he said. "One hundred!"

And that Sunday morning, when he climbed the few steps to the landlord's garden, and hung his black suit on the railing for the sun to kiss and breathe on; and he got dressed in time for her to wait for him, after he had bathed BJ and dressed him in his Christmas gift, a new, dark brown jumper, dark brown training shoes made of imitation brown shining leatherette, Bertram announced, "I ready."

And the three of them walked in the clear, bright morning warmth, that Sunday, the first day of summer.

"We going to the Cathedral, boy," he told little BJ, who just giggled. "You learn about cathedrals yet in the daycare, boy?"

Yes, those were good times, happy times, before "that man" forsook her for America. She did not mind supporting him, from her small salary, from various jobs she held down at the same time, some of them temporary, some of them she held for two months, all of them jobs reserved for immigrants; and she had been doing this, supporting him, taking these jobs, for one more year; then for another year, then for two; then for the fifteen-or-so years her husband had lived here, as a man sponsored by his wife; and before that, back in the Island.

The garden at the back of her apartment is overgrown in weeds, tall as sunflower bushes, and rose bushes that look like weeds; but when she stands close to them, on the few occasions in the summer when her landlord invites her for a rum punch, she closes her eyes and inhales the fragrance of the roses, all white, deeply in her body; and the smell changes her entire disposition, and she cries secretly, concealing her tears, as she remembers walking beside the sea, on the Esplanade back in the Island, and smelling flowers and roses like these, but in greater abundance. Here in this city, with its greater wealth and its "things," and its large apartment buildings and condominiums like ocean liners that pass in the night, silent as a dark sea of white clouds, this place with its brand-new-brand cars and SUVs, there is the result that no space is left back, in the city's streets, in which to plant a flower . . . her landlord plants only white roses . . . and she is transported back to Trinidad, where she visited only once, for five days, strolling in the Botanical Gardens and eating coconut-flavoured vanilla ice cream in a café called Green Corner. In this smaller garden, not belonging to her, she can still drink in the colours; and suppress her tears, and smile at the way the clouds become sailing boats going silently in and out of the blue skies; over the dark, scum-covered smelly water of the placid Lake. And she would, in moments of small wickedness in her thoughts, swear that her landlord's protectiveness about his garden conceals the fact that he has planted marijuana seeds amongst the white roses. The smells in this backyard are intoxicating: "too sweet, boy; and damn sweet!" Standing in this garden of smells, on a day like today, she remembers the mosquitoes in July and August, at the cottage she visited once, up in Georgian Bay. This cottage had an outdoor WC, a water closet; and these facilities took her headlong back to the Island; but water closets were common in Barbados. Barbados was colonized, and owned by the English, and water closets originated in England; and here now in Georgian Bay there was hardly any running water, just a bar of blue soap and a galvanized bucket and the large, pure, beautiful lake in which to bathe. And a thick towel that smelled of overripe McIntosh apples. And the largest cake of Palmolive soap she had ever seen: and a pink washcloth. And the water was cold. And snakes the size of twelve-inch rulers took their afternoon baths with her. "Oh shite!" she screamed the first time, at their companionship.

Sometimes, her landlord offers her a drink. On every Dominion Day, he and all of Canada get drunk, and eat hamburgers and steaks slapped on the barbecue, with the blood still dribbling from them, celebrating their new country's coming of age. But usually, and except for these infrequent but joyous warm afternoons in the back garden, when her landlord, who drives a long-distance truck for a company that delivers reconditioned used cars to car dealers in the North, in North Bay, Kirkland Lake, Timmins and Cochrane, when he offers her a glass of his rum punch, she is still not encouraged, nor permitted, even though he always got a little tipsy, to use the garden.

A combination lock, secured from the outside, out of her reach, makes certain of this restriction. But one Dominion Day, when the sun was hot and the "fire" in the rum punch had gone to his head, and he was getting drunk, and drunker, and his words were slurred almost out of recognition, and he peppered his talk with "In your ass!", which is what he said at the beginning of one sentence, and ". . . in your ass, pappee!", drunker and drunker, now in every sentence, she had slipped one of the two keys off the wire ring; got it copied at the hardware store on Dundas Street; replaced it the next time he offered her drinks of rum punch in his garden—this was on Remembrance Day—and she kept the stolen key on the same ring with her own house keys. "Suppose there was ever a fire," she had said to herself, aloud, many times, as she heard the rumble and the high-pitched sirens like frantic voices of the fire engines passing, in such earnestness as if she was talking to the landlord, "and I am seeking escape, and I am running from my basement apartment out into this garden, my only saviour, my only means of escape, and this blasted garden gate is locked . . . and I am here, in this prison, burning alive? Jesus Christ!"

But in all the years that she lived in the basement apartment, she never did use the key to the garden.

If she opens her arms and extends them horizontal from her body, in the first position of exercise and calisthenics, to make her body take the shape of a cross, she still would need another arm's length attached to her fingertips before she would be able to touch the two walls that mark out her bedroom space. Her small bedroom has no door. It is merely a space.

BJ was twelve then; and she was standing inside the wrought iron gate at the back of her basement apartment, looking up into the landlord's garden, and it struck her. Footprints were leading from the fence right up to where she was standing, admiring the snow, and watching and counting the number of times the snow sparkled like crystals, like jewels; and still she could not find the answer to the puzzle in her mind. The footprints in the snow were pointing towards her. The person had headed in her direction; but still, there was no sign that the footprints had entered the basement or turned back. They just pointed in one direction.

One Thursday night when she could not sleep, and her life from those early days came back to her, looking for a job after she had left the domestic service, looking for a room, those days of failure came back to her and made it impossible for her to get back to sleep, and she put on her housecoat and quietly crept along the short hallway to BJ's room. She was sure she had heard a woman's voice. "No! But it couldn't be!" She was imagining things. She stopped moving. She held her breath in case she was making too much noise, breathing. And listened. She thought she heard a voice giggling, a voice expressing pleasure or satisfaction of some kind. She slithered along the hallway right up to his door. It was silent. The hallway was like the track in a subway station. The basement apartment was like a sepulchre. She gathered her resolution. She made certain that in the darkness of the hallway she had the doorknob firmly in her sight. And then she grabbed it and turned it and slammed the door back against the wall.

BJ was sitting on his bed, in his pyjamas and dressing gown, with a book in his hand, reading.

"Mom?" he said, shocked at her presence.

"Did I wake you?" she said.

"Reading," he said, his head again buried in the book.

"I thought," she said, "I thought . . ."

She would measure her son's behaviour against that of many black kids his age, some of whom were killing other black kids; some stealing computers and guns and knives, and watches from passengers on the subway; some breeding women.

"Not women! They are not breeding women!" she had told Josephine. "They're mere children. Girl-thrildren, as we call them! Every time I hear the radio say that a police shoot a kid trying to steal a late-model car, or an SUV, in a chase on Highway 401, I say a prayer in my heart. 'God, not another black kid! Not another one! Not one more black kid, Lord!'" Josephine would listen to her, and shake her head, in equal sadness and confusion. "Once," she went on saying, "I am sure I saw the keys on a ring. A lovely key ring. And I sure, even though I don't know much about motor cars, and automobiles, I swear to you, Josephine . . . as God is my witness . . . BJ had the keys to a Mercedes-Benz on his set o' keys! A Mercedes-Benz? Jesus Christ, Josephine, where that boy get a Mercedes-Benz from?

He worked for it? Well, he would have to steal it, then, wouldn't he?" She began to shake her head from side to side, measuring the sadness in her heart; in her body; moving her head from left to right, her eyes closed; shut tight, her lips pressed and bucked in, living in the future, living her sadness she was sure would visit him. "I don't know how long it will be before a police come banging down my blasted door, asking me if I have a son named BJ. How long the train going take before it stop of this destination?" And then her resistance collapsed. The walls that kept the torrent of water, the powerful wash of flooding, broke, and out poured her grief, and the weakness of her limbs now no longer was able to keep the water within the dyke. "I am still trying to figure-out the meaning of those footprints in the snow in the backyard . . ."

She wanted more from life: not much; just her due. Not even a man; certainly not a husband. That was past tense. But a son who doesn't dress and talk like a rapper; and walk like Stepin Fetchit, the former American Negro comedian; or walk like a penguin; and she wanted a small bungalow house, somewhere in a suburb, Mississauga, or Scarborough, Brampton, or Richmond Hill; even a small town outside of Toronto, far from this downtown ghetto, where sixteen-year-old black boys are shooting one another dead, with guns the Mayor says come from America; committing murder at seventeen, and breeding like pigs at this young age. "Black thrildren fooping black thrildren and breeding black thrildren, adding to the census numbers and the Canadian population. My God, what kind o' image are we reflecting back to the white people? Yes, Lord! Just help me to get my two hands on a little bungalow. I would even go as far out o' town as Barrie, or Orillia, then!"

And sometimes, when she looks out through the glass in her front windows, to the wrought iron fence with its gate that separates her from the human activity on Shuter Street; and at the squirrels, and the pigeons and the white seagulls, large as turkeys for Thanksgiving and for Christmas; and at the raccoons, she is surprised and a little uncomfortable to be so close to these pests, rodents, damn bothers; and then she remembers what she was taught in Sunday School, and in the Girl Guides, about kindness to animals; for Jesus made them all. And she would feel vulnerable to realize how close she is, physically and morally, to the people walking on the sidewalk, in front of her apartment. And her anxiety would become inflamed, to think that a man could spit and it would land on one of her front windows, so close is she to this tired army of humanity. And feel how exposed she is.

And going back in her mind to that morning, she remembers now how she had closed the gate in her wrought iron fence, in case the man with the walker wanted to be social, and talk; or fresh, and wanted to come in. But she knew he couldn't come in because of his walker.

The man moved silently, pushing the walker on its four rubber wheels, coming closer towards her. She stepped back to the sidewalk and stood in front of her gate, deliberately blocking his entrance in case he had ideas in his head.

"I'm John!"

She told herself that she could smell something. She was standing in front of the wrought iron gate, blocking him.

She was cold. She had just come from having Communion at the Cathedral and her high-heeled red leather shoes were cold; and she thinks that it will not be until the month of June that she will feel life and vigour in her body, when she will be able to stand in front of her basement apartment, guarded by the wrought iron fence that reaches her up to her breasts, and that protects her from men such as this one standing so close to her now; and from women too, the sex workers, who talk slow and who shake their limbs as they walk, as if they are suffering from St. Vitus's dance.

"I am John . . . Johnnie!" His four-wheeled walker is slipping away, and he pulls it back and leans on it. "What's yours? You new to this neighbourhood, ain't you!" he says. "Never seen you before . . ."

She feels challenged. This is the first person, man or woman, who has spoken to her.

"I am Johnnie," he says, "your neighbour, at the house just north of Shuter . . . the one where you see the fellas sitting on the veranda, smoking . . . Just kibitzing, you know . . ."

She can see the veins in his fingers and in his face; and smell his perspiration; and she muzzles her mouth with her hand, that is clothed in red leather gloves that are not lined with wool, for this cold weather; and for a moment she cannot open her mouth; and this causes him to have to introduce himself again, all the time she is inhaling a smell that is not cigarette smoke.

"Johnnie's the name?" he says. "I didn't get yours."

"Mistress Morrison."

She shifts her attention from Johnnie to the man walking like a snail on the opposite side of the street. And Johnnie looks too.

"Mike!" he says, as if he was relishing giving her his knowledge about the neighbourhood. "Crazy as a coot! Name's not really Mike, far's I been told. But we call him Mike. The neighbourhood calls him Mike. You ever notice how long it take him to walk to the next block? Lives round the corner there, at the Meighen place. Story is that his sister dropp' him off there and never returned . . ."

Mike is very well dressed for a homeless man, with shoes polished like a policeman's; long black coat, and with a backpack that makes him hunch his shoulders against the weight. She wonders what he carries in his backpack.

"They're druggies!" the man says. "All o' them! The homeless, and the cocaine addicks!" He tells her this as if he is breaking news. His four-wheeled walker suddenly moves away from his grasp for a second; and he grabs hold of it and reins it back, close to his legs, and his arms touch the brakes in the handlebars. "They're all drug-addicks," he tells her, "that's why they walk like that."

And he moved away from her without saying goodbye; and moved slowly down the street, as she watched his back; and just before he turned left at Sherbourne, she read RAPTORS on the back of his mauve windbreaker; and she was glad, relieved that his interference had been short; and that his undesired information had been given to her, that his perspiration was now dissipated in the cold, wet morning.

When she was sure she was rid of him, he came back into view, and pushed his walker right back to her, and said, "You ever seen them in the Park, at night? All these druggies?"

And she went in from the cold.

". . . and one afternoon, it was a Thursday, years ago, I was still working as a domestic, which had me cleaning floors with a mop and detergents that burned my eyes, and caused me to have allergies, from cleaning bathrooms and children's bottoms, and the four floors in that mansion, including the basement

floor, where I first came upon the name Mr. Albert Johnson, a
Jamaican. Lord have His Mercy! I saw the photograph of the
killing. On the front page. And I had to read the full story. I read
the story in a newspaper, the *Star*, I think. The newspaper told
how the police went into that man's home, on a Sunday, and
shoot him dead! My God. My heart burned when I saw the picture in the newspaper. And from then—and according to my
calculations, the shooting had taken place years after I arrived in
Canada—I still can't get that picture out o' my mind. I cut-out
the clipping with a pair of scissors. It was from the newspaper in
a drawer I found it in, and I have it in my bureau, up to today. I
looked at it every night; for nights, at the beginning; and then,
after a while, when the worse wore off, I would look at it just to
remember the past, every November when I have to search
for my Labello Lipsyl, to prevent my lips from chapping and
cracking, I would look at Mr. Johnson in the bureau drawer . . .
just to remember. Even though I was told years later that he
was killed in the month of August, I nevertheless associated his
murder with the month of November, which was one of the
most miserable months of my life in this country, because of the
dreadful weather. And why, you tell me, why still can't I get his
face out o' my mind? And I will tell you why. Every time, every
year, every beginning of winter, every November, my mind
goes back to that face. It was a August when the policeman blew
his head to smithereens! Simple as that, the reason, I mean.
Mr. Johnson's head was covered in blood, in a drawer in the
servant's quarters my employers had assigned for me to sleep
in, fixed up with furniture, books and old magazines, to help
me pass the time during that first winter, when every white person—my employers, the women at the bank, and the woman at
the meat counter in the supermarket—were telling me, 'This is

the worst winter we are having, in twenty years!' You must have heard this strange Canadian saying from other mouths! . . . and to soften the culture shock of coming to Canada. I refused to leave the house where I worked. Yes! But I was telling you about the places we learned to go to, in Toronto, where we could get served, and those places where we were not welcomed. It wasn't like it is now, in them days, boy! Oh, no! Yes, back to those Thursdays. I would go down to Eaton's store, at that time at the corner of Yonge and College, and while-away the time, escape from the work for those few hours, noon until six o'clock, when we had to get back in. I always felt like we were a little like prisoners out on day parole from the Don Jail. Or inmates from the TB sanatorium up on the Mountain in Hamilton, yes! That is how we spent Thursdays. Escaping from the mansions we laboured in, six days a week, to go window-shopping; look-ing at clothes, trying on some o' them, beautiful clothes that we didn't have back in the Islands, and that we couldn't afford to buy in Toronto. And if we had a good clerkesse serving us, who allowed us to touch the clothes—those were the days, boy! And me with thoughts in my head, planning to wear the three dresses that the lady waiting on us told me I could try on . . . and keep them under the dress that I wore in the store, and hope, and in my mind hope against hope, that the commission-aire, the store detective, don't read my thoughts and suspect anything. The three extra dresses got me looking fat . . . fatter than when I became pregnant with BJ, after 'that man' said he would be careful not wearing a French letter. Stupid me! . . . fatter than when I entered the store! And because I am black, and therefore a thief, a shoplifter.

"'Come, let me feel you to see if you have the store's prop-erty under your clothes!' I could hear that bastard telling me . . .

"And we never, never walked too far from the stores where we were sure we would get served, as black people. We got to know which stores served black people and who didn't. This is the first thing you learned as a coloured person in Toronto. I am talking about survival now! Survival, girl! Improvisation, girl. The Toronto General Hospital, it employed a handful o' West Indians. Cleaners and nurses' assistants, and orderlies, pushing the heavy bodies of dead white people on canvas stretchers attached to wheels; and farther up along College Street, and south off College to Cecil Street, where a lot of Canadian Negroes, as they were known back then—coloured people— used to live, and go every Thursday night, to enjoy ourselves at the seventy-five-cent brams held in a three-storey house, on the second floor. Those 'brams' were organized by Mr. Moore, who I told you about, who, before he died, got one of the highest Orders of Honour that this country ever awarded a black man with. Trinidad pellau, my God! I told you about the food already. The curry-chicken-and-rice, my God! . . . with the rice grains hard-hard, like bullets; not much curry and no Scotch Bonnet pepper in the food at all, at all, in this excuse for curry-chicken. But we danced! We danced ourselves sweaty until the middle of the night. Eleven o'clock. Curfew time! Eleven o'clock. Curfew time. For us, the domestic parolees going back into our deten- tion centres. Yes, when, right on the dot, we had to march our- selves right back to our quarters! . . . or so I used to feel. Yes, it was like that . . . and share a taxi, since it was so late . . . and if the taxi driver had a heart, you know what I mean, and would stop for all these young coloured women, out so late at eleven o'clock, on a Thursday night, in Toronto, was . . ."

"Yes! And on another Thursday afternoon we got carried away, and had-ventured farther south on Yonge Street, and came to Simpson's, which was a more expensive store than Eaton's, some of us thought it was a better store too; and instead of minding the directions, we are talking about a place where we could use the bathroom; and we turned left, and walking and walking, looking for a place . . . and found ourselves all the way east on King Street, at Jarvis! Could hardly walk, with the pressure of the need . . . because in those days, you know what I mean! Well, with my two girlfriends, domestics like me, I see this man, who turned out to be a priest, who turned out to be a Dean, who turned out to be my Dean. My Dean! The Dean of the Cathedral. Where I take Communion, on the first Sunday of the month . . . when I do take Communion. Coming towards me, from a restaurant, La Maquette, a name that is French. I was good in French back home. Never came lower than third. But in the Island, I never came across that name of the restaurant, in any French Vocabulary class, or Friday afternoon French Conversation class. But there was the Dean, my Dean, coming out of the French restaurant, on such a cold Thursday afternoon, in November, so many years ago! "Poor fellow!" I say to myself. My Dean, the man I love—in a spiritual, Christian way only, mind you. And I am so proud of him, because, like me, he is from the same Island.

"And I spoke to the Dean in Barbadian. And ask him in French, if I use my French and 'ask if I could use Maquette's facilities, if I ask in French!' By now I had to pass water, bad-bad.

"I worship the ground my Dean walks on, as a member of his large congregation. For the past nineteen-twenty years

now. When I do attend the Cathedral, not as religiously as I
would like, mind you, but on first Sundays, I just love to sit
at the back of the church, in the last row of pews, locked in
safe by the latch on the gate, by the dark-stained gate whose
latch doesn't always work properly, but I am safe sitting there
nevertheless, though the latch is always coming undone. And
very often I am transposed—transported—by the deep, sweet,
mellow voice the Dean uses, in the way he pronounces the
English language in the King James Version of the Bible, if you
please . . . nothing but the best . . . that contains the Old and
the New Testaments, naturally. And he speaks it in a voice and
manner that has a touch of our Barbadian dialect in it, that
always makes me feel so, so . . . good! His voice seduces me,
especially when his accent takes on the feeling of sea water first
thing in the morning, his voice is like the waves covering my
body . . . his intoning of the words in the Bible, mixed perfectly; and in equal measure and meaning. And then, and then
I watch how the Dean mixes the chalice of rich, deep-blooded
red wine with Holy Water, mixed with the crisp voice of
his adopted Canadian accent. Sometimes, holding my hand to
my mouth, like that man that I was foolish-enough to let get
me pregnant, and get married to would do, when he would
come back from the Greenwood racetrack, broke and drunk,
and would hold his hand to his mouth to prevent his vomit
from splashing-over my clean linoleum that I, on my hands
and knees, had just scrubbed . . . barely able to reach the
toilet bowl . . . it is all I can do, sometimes, to control my
emotion for the Dean, when I should be following the words
of the Nicene Creed, or the Collect for that Sunday, and my
thoughts are straying from the cleanliness of the Bible to come
to rest on the carnal knowledge of my thoughts themselves. It

is all I can do to stop from swooning, when the Dean holds forth. I am back there, in my seat at the back of the Cathedral, in the last row of the silent temple of God, vast as a tomb lit-up with pearl candles and lights and marble. It has an effect on me, like I remember when I was a schoolgirl in love, for the first time, when the Dean intone, talking and chanting in the same voice, the prayers and the rituals of the Eucharist."

"The Dean's words soothe and disturb me at the same time, just like how love used to blossom and bloom in my heart, when I was first married, from these very words I am listening to now: '. . . do this, as oft as ye shall drink it . . . in remembrance of me.'

"That first Sunday in the month, when I got up from my seat, my two knees were sore from the kneeling, I could barely walk with a straight back, but I managed to walk up that long aisle to the altar, where I stood surrounded by all the white people in the congregation, polka-dotted amongst the few black faces, and I cast an admiring glance at the flags of all the Canadian armies, victorious in battles fought in countries I do not even know, and in wars, like the First World War, the Second World War, the Korean War, the Vietnam War, and I was even thinking of the Boer War and the one that freed the slaves, I was so carried away, completely lost in the pageantry of flags and memorials. And don't forget the Afghanistan War, and why we are in Kabul . . . one soldier a day, killed by a bomb strapped to somebody's body, his head blown-off just like Mr. Albert Johnson's head, as the *Star* said, looked like a watermelon hit by a bullet . . . My God! . . . and I invented some Wars, to suit the flags; almost, but not exactly . . . my imagination was lively, running away from me; and I surmised as I stood there that I

could see . . . my face shining back at me, in the mirror of the
marble, a reflection, as if I was inspecting my lipstick and eye-
shadow in the looking glass over my bureau, in my apartment,
and farther along the marble aisle, giving back to me the sound
and the fall of my bright red, high-heeled shoes hitting the marble like bullets from a pellet gun that I hear sometimes exploding in the Park; and I was imagining how attractive I must have
looked, sweet and good, standing there at the altar, in the chancel that was like a large slab of marble, shaped like a rectangle,
that told the short history of death of a man whose name I did
not even know. He died in 1876, before anybody even thought
of bringing me into this world. But I wondered if this unknown
man, now a corpse, now skeleton and bones, was buried standing upright, following the construction and the installation of
the memorial, behind this very wall I was passing now, on my
way to take the cup offered by Jesus and by my Dean.

"I am a religious person. Brought up to go to church every
Sunday at eleven o'clock; back in the afternoons, at four, for
Sunday School; and at seven, bright and early, for Evensong and
Service, seven o'clock in the night. Baptised, confirmed, said 'I
do'. . . to that bastard! . . . in Holy Matrimony, washed in the
precious blood of the Lamb, and come white and clear, praise
God . . . Heh-heh-heh! Churches and cathedrals are bound to
be in my blood. This Cathedral of which my Dean is the dean of,
is in my blood, through place of birth, and the nationality of my
Dean. In the Island, we could be related. I am dark. The Dean is
shades less dark than me. Back there, we are members of the
same tribe, of the same family; and one of us would come out
dark, like me; one would come out fair-skinned; one, light-light;
one, light-light-light, almost white, my God! But all related.
With the same blood. And recognizing one another as family.

"I belong, it is true, to another church, though. The Apostolical Holiness Church of Spiritualism in Christ, where meetings are held in an old one-storey building on St. Clair Avenue West, in a rundown section of a neighbourhood the newspapers love to call a ghetto, this building that previously was a slaughterhouse, a place for killing cows and pigs, and more recently, with the increased numbers of immigrants from the West Indians, especially Jamaica, the killing of goat and sheep.

"I like to attend 'the Apostolicals'—sometimes; not too often—as I and the rest of the brethren call the church, as it is our business of bringing Christ to the working-class West Indians, who make up most of the congregation. And the more I think of it, the more I want to deliver a sermon on Jonah in the Belly of the Whale. Services are held one night during the week, for 'revival meetings,' when souls are saved, which I attend on and off; and on Sundays, excepting those that are the first Sundays in the month."

Bright and early one Monday morning, she remembers now, twenty years ago, when she still worked as a live-out domestic servant, she walked into her bank and showed her savings book to the white lady who was the teller, who always smiled with her, and the white lady took her Bank ID Card and swiped it, and smiled "How are you, today?"; and handed her back the book, and her ID Card, and her eyes went fast to the last line printed into the bank book. It said END OF PAGE, in computer print. Above that was a line of asterisks. Followed by seven zeros. Her bank balance was zero. Bertram had cleaned her out.

She never recovered, in all the years that followed, from this robbery, which she called a rape.

"Bertram James. The first two Christian names I had in mind to christen him—meaning BJ—with. Bertram, after his no-good father, Bertram Senior. Or, as the Americans say, Bertram the First! I don't know what 'that man' was ever first in! Certainly not with me . . . But nevertheless, two lovely, nice English names, you don't think so? My son. My only child. We call him BJ. As a nickname. And I am sorry to be running ahead of the story, but this boy now gone and changed his name, the name he was born with, and given at his Baptism, this boy decided to baptize himself with a new name. Rashan Rashanan. Muslim, he say! Now, isn't that just fuckery? Pardon my French. Good God! Born a Christian, like most people in the Island, and most of Canada! And now, with all the turmoil in the world, and with everybody hating Muslims, this boy gone and turned himself into a Muslim? As if he is from India. Or born in Iran. Or Iraq. Or if he come from Afghanistan.

"That is the cross BJ has given me to bear."

Her bedroom is an open section of the small apartment, cordoned off by a blind. From her white-dressed bed, her brown panda bears and other bears, and the little doll, a brown miniature that resembles BJ, her "babies," bears and dolls, guard her seven pillows and her loneliness, and the vast white expanse of her bed; and any time, she can talk with them, and give them her side of the story, and imagine that they give her their own opinions of her argument. Always in agreement with hers.

The clock says 8.50. She thinks she is seeing correctly. She has to focus her eyes and think hard, to see if there are two dots, one above the other, before the 5. And when, in various stages of insomnia, tossing and turning; when she cannot sleep more than three hours, waking in the middle of the night and falling back to sleep, like a limping runner staggering to the tape; she calls the red dot the eye of the giant Polyphemus, the Cyclops. She had laughed and laughed when she first read the Fable of the Cyclops, at the girls' school she attended back in the Island.

These November days now are short and dark. For so many years, when she was a domestic servant, she had left for work in this darkness; travelling by bus, then streetcar, then subway, then having to walk down into the cold Ravine, to the large silent mansion, and remain for eight and sometimes ten hours in the air-conditioned mansion, cold as a refrigerator in an abattoir. When her two-year contract had expired, she became a "live-out" domestic. She became a domestic servant, not because she was educated to be a domestic, but because even though the official Domestic Scheme ended before she came to Canada, she wondered if what she had heard was true, that Canada's immigration policy was a "whites only" policy. Canada did not like coloured people as immigrants. But at the time, as a bright young black woman, she knew it was the easiest—if not the only—means open to her to immigrate to Canada. It seemed adventurous and exciting. And she was young. And she knew she could live with the restrictions of being a domestic—single, and no children—and with the cold; and, at the end of her "tenure," go to university and make a life for herself. "You go! Go!" her Mother had said, clapping her hands in triumph when the official letter arrived bearing the good tidings. "Go! And make a woman of yourself. This Island have nothing for you!"

So she escaped from the Island, through this scheme; and from "that man."

Her Mother hated Bertram. "He's a touch too black!" she told her daughter. "We come from fair-skin people," she explained, "from people who have white blood in them . . . I don't have anything against Bertram. He born so. And that is in the hands o' God. If you understand what I mean . . ." Her Mother told her sternly to go to Canada, and deliver herself from Bertram.

Bertram was an apprentice motor mechanic, in his second year of five he had to spend before he could repair a car without assistance from the supervisor of City Mechanical Motor Engineers. Bertram worked in clothes that were discoloured black; and drenched in transmission oils and brake fluids during the day; but after five o'clock he jumped on his three-speed green Raleigh bicycle and rushed along the Esplanade, with the rollicking sea on his right side, and ticked his way up the Garrison Hill, and rushed into his paling, south of the Garrison racecourse, where he lived with his mother, and dashed bucket after cold bucket of fresh water drawn from the oil drum, with leaves of clammy cherry in it, until he had removed as much of the oil, and the muck lodged beneath his fingernails and in the small cuts and abrasions on his hands and the creases of his palms, that showed the future of his life, if anybody cared to look. And always, afterwards, there was a slight hint of gasoline and oil and car grease that the Barbados Limacol and the Mennen could not hide. She bought the plane ticket to bring him to Canada, for a two-month visit, to soothe her loneliness; and his visa expired; and he showed no interest in leaving; and one thing led to another; and she was pregnant; and BJ was born. A black Canadian baby. An African Canadian! Or, as her Pastor at the Apostolicals called him, "a nice little Barbadian Canadian." And when he was five years old, and she had long satisfied her contractual obligations of being a domestic, she sent him back to Barbados, in the care of a returning domestic, her friend, to his Grandmother. Ten or eleven years later, BJ was back in Canada. His Grandmother, her Mother, had suffered a stroke; and died on the spot. When Bertram was sponsored as a spouse, he had just completed his third year of apprenticeship. He spent his first week in Canada filling out applications for motor mechanic jobs; he walked to all the mechanic garages in the neighbourhood in which they lived; he went through the *Star* newspaper with a comb of fine-toothed diligence and determination; and after two months of single-minded perusal of the pages that advertised hundreds of jobs, skilled and unskilled, that related to repairing cars, he shook his head, took a larger sip of the last of the three forty-ounce bottles of Mount Gay rum he had brought with him, and said, "This fucking Canada!"

Her Mother had told her that because good jobs in the Island were non-existent, and her love life was in shambles, to "go and shake the dust of the Island off your two feet, as the Bible warned you, girl. And shake off the dust of that crook, Bertram, especially. Escape from Bertram. Escape from Bertram. Escape from Bertram." But she was already three months in the family-way for Bertram. BJ was already in her womb. Bertram had got her pregnant as a means of getting control over her, and staying in Canada. She kept it from her Mother as long as she could.

So Barrington Bertram James was born in Toronto, and he was such a beautiful child, of exceptionally good looks and dark brown skin. He took after his Mother.

"Do not return to this blasted island," her Mother had told her in a letter; and with even more vigorous animosity for Barbados than for Bertram in her voice, her Mother added, "This place don't have one damn thing to offer you. Let your good looks and your education rescue you from the inequities of that blasted man you had the misfortune to take up with. But that is not the end of the world! I will bring up my grandchild. Leave him. And you go. Your future does not reside in this Island."

And she left. She had always wanted to go to Canada, to continue her education, go to university, and take a degree in English Literature of the Victorian Era, and become a teacher.

"A teacher! A lowly teacher?" her Mother had screamed. "Why not a doctor? Or a Barrister-at-Law, and come back here, if you can't get Canadian citizenship, and hang out a shingle and practise Law. Aim more higher! Aim more higher! Aim higher! I didn't bring you in this whirl to be a mere teacher!"

She knew that being a domestic servant, on contract, for two years, was just a stepping stone to a bungalow in the suburbs, Scarborough, perhaps; money in her bank account, night school at George Brown Community College, to do her master's, and a nice cheap private, or semi-private, school for BJ, when he came up from living with his grandmother to join her. All these things she saw in her future. And her future was Canada.

In those days, from November almost right into April, she had woken up in this darkness, gotten dressed in this darkness, gone to work by bus, streetcar and subway, in this cold darkness, and when it was all over, at six in the evening (but it was even eleven o'clock after she had cooked and served formal dinner), she retraced her steps on the cold, silent journey home, sitting beside men and women she did not know, who did not speak to her, not even saying "Cold-enough for ya?", no one saying "Good evening" or "Good morning"; leaving her to trudge, alone, over blocks of ice and cold pavement, over thick, heavy falling snow, cold and silent, and she often wondered if it was better for a black woman living in the United States, despite its Civil Rights problems. "Move to America? Or stay in Canada?" She first wondered if all these people were uncomfortable to be so close to a black woman. And then, in time, she was sure that they were. Their silence, with heads bowed in paperback books, was their way of asking her where she came from and why didn't she go back there. It was just like sitting on a bench in primary school, so Cilla, her Jamaican friend, a former domestic servant, had told her in the College kitchen, just before they went out-side to have a smoke. "It is like sitting on a bench in primary school. Child, them racists barn young, eh! Eh? You shouldda hear what a white pickney tell my child. 'You can't sit so close to me!' What the rass is this, eh, Dora? Why we still living in this rass place, tekking this shit? You tell me. You been here, more longer than me." Idora stubbed her cigarette into the thick wall, and Cilla tossed hers into the flower bed, sucking her teeth, in disgust, as she did this, and together, arms locked in sisterly love, or in conspiracy, they went back, silent, into the steamy kitchen. She had not responded to the question. But she knew the answer. Now, she is alone.

She is the only black person in this coach of the subway. "This feeling of being in the minority. . . of inferiority. . . not that I am inferior . . . this feeling of segregation runs through my mind, each time I travel on public transportation. And I should know better, an educated woman like me. But it. . . this thing. . . takes away your better judgment, and makes you be-lieve you're what they paint you and define you to be. Yes. . ."

Back home in the Island, she said "Good morning" and "Good afternoon" to strangers, especially to old people. Her greeting was a show of respect for age. And if it was during a

cricket test match between Barbados and England, she was
brought up to say "Congrats!" to the English team even if they
had defeated her own Barbadian cricketers.

"Lordy-Lord! It hot-hot today, eh!" Even this friendliness
would greet a stranger. Or a Canadian tourist.

"You intend to bring shame upon my head, boy?" She would
hold this conversation with herself. And it would bring back to
her, clear as when it happened on the Wednesday night, the ringing of her telephone nineteen times . . . nineteen times . . .
and she did not know who had called. And deep down she told
herself she really did not want to know who had called. Deep in
her mind, she knew it was about BJ. She feared what she knew
she would be told. And conducting this conversation with herself, now, she knew it was merely a tactic of postponement: the
knock on the door would come. She was sure of it. The knock
will be recognizable. Loud. Aggressive. Frightening. Probably
first thing in the morning. Or the last thing at night.

There was a time, a long time ago, when the circumstance was
different, and he was too young to understand the consequence.
It was a Saturday evening. Time was heavy upon his tender age.
He paced up and down, with thoughts he could not understand
entering his head; and his panic at his isolation in a single cell
made the space of his incarceration much larger, so that he
was buried in the vastness of the small cell; and he could see his
life, his entire short life, in the five hours that had passed. He
was just a child at this time. He did not know why he had been
locked up, not having had a charge laid against him; not having
had a policeman enter the warm cell and interrogate him about
the theft (not alleged, but proven through profiling): the theft

of a kid's bike committed one warm summer afternoon, years ago, when he was eight years old—in August, when he and other boys were horsing around and pretending to be blind. Boys like BJ and Armando and Helmut and Goran did not play with girls in those days, in the West End neighbourhood near the corner grocery store at the head of Grace Street and Bloor West where they lived, where there was a community of Negro people, where these four kids had been trying to raise enough quarters from the other poor members of the community—"Got any money? Even a quarter? A penny would do, then!"—to buy ice cream . . . with a cone? . . . to be shared four ways.

His Mum was working at her second job, cleaning offices, when this hot August day found her in a government office with a mop and a pail of detergent that made her eyes burn, and made her sneeze; this other Italian kid at the same time came wobbly down Grace Street, on his new bicycle, his first, a present bought second-hand at the Society for Crippled Civilians (now the Goodwill store), that his Mama had given him for Christmas; and one of the other three kids took the bike away from the little kid, and the little kid started to cry and straight away ran home with tears in his eyes and told his Mama-mother, and his Pooh-pa just returned from slapping water with detergents in it on the floors of classrooms and offices, and the canteen, in the nearby public school, where he was a janitor; and his sunburnt arms were bristling with black hairs; and his underpants could be seen just above green trousers, the uniform of cleaners, when his son pointed out the "coloured fella, Pooh-pa, the coloured fella is who take my bike"; and all hell broke loose then, with "mama-mias" spewing all over the road; and the cops arrived, screaming down Grace Street going in the wrong direction, to solve this community crime, this ghetto delinquency, because

they were cops, a crime that had begun as a small neighbourhood kid's prank—"I didn't do nothing, occifer, sir!"—and
slam! "Into the cruiser, you little nigger, into the goddamn
cruiser, we'll keep you at the station till your goddamn mother
get home! . . . and come get you."

"Oh, mama-mia! Oh, mama-mia!"

Hail Marys showered the street. And little BJ, not understanding the various languages and accents and dialects being
spewed into his face, no explanation from his three friends who
did not know English and were called home by their Mamas,
no longer within earshot and speaking-distance, so they could
translate the truth; no understanding from the Pooh-pas, ripping the air with their hand gestures, because none of them
worried to attend English-as-a-Second-Language classes at
Grace Street Primary School, or Bloor Collegiate Institute in
the evenings, for their evenings were reserved for their second
jobs. There were demonstrations of gestures made like karate
chops, as they struggled and fought with the movements of
their bodies to find the correct word in English, for the Law.
But BJ's three little friends, who were European, and knew
the translation of these hand gestures, kept their traps shut. BJ
never had the chance, or inclination, never got instruction at
school, in Italian and Greek and German. He did not even
speak English like white Canadians spoke English, they told
him at school. The cops had descended armed with revolvers
drawn and guns; they came with firepower enough; enough to
solve this Serious Crime. "Git, goddammit, git! Into the goddamn cruiser! No! Not in the goddamn front seat, you little
bastard! In the fucking back, you piece of shit, where youse
belong"; and they took him down, and did not book him, just let
him cool out until his washerwoman mother got home . . .

And at long last, the truth about the bicycle was revealed. And translated in its telling. And the kind Staff Sergeant on the desk came with a paper cup of steaming Tim Hortons, "Have a cup, come now, son, have a cup"; and then the Sergeant said it was "a little mistake, if you can understand at your age, I mean, you being such a young little feller, too small to know these serious big things . . . a little goddamn mistake and you happened to be in the goddamn wrong place at the wrong goddamn time . . . to be the goddamn unlucky one that they picked out. So beat it, kid, and don't let me lay my goddamn eyes on you again! Git!"

. . . And now, years later, two policemen had taken him down at another time, to the same Division, and did not book him, but had put him in a nice large warm cell, "goddammit nigger, and more warmer than the piss-pot hole you and your goddamn single-parent mother lives in! You fucking piece o' West Indian shit!" And so they left him there. To stew. And then to confess. And then to give them proof that he was a suspect in a carjacking of a European luxury car.

Time had come and gone . . .

Too young to have known what he had done all those years ago; not knowing what he had done; not knowing what the eight policemen in the four cruisers had done; and now not knowing the exact shape of his fate this time, but wise enough to know he was going to have to face some fate, some history, some sheet, with his rap and his previous arrest on suspicion on it, BJ, now Rashan Rashanan, paced and paced. And then, perhaps, because of the sense of new destiny that his Muslim faith had started to school him in, he suddenly stopped walking up and down. He decided not to worry. Not to be beaten by such a little thing as fate. Or bad luck. Or denial of rights. "Let them come

and get me." He is talking to the four walls. He is talking to
himself. He is confusing defiance for destiny. "Let them come
and get me."

But within his heart he knew what his fate was going to be.
It could be only one thing. His Mother had told him. And he
had listened and had forgotten, until now.

So, he was now calm, confined in the small square space. By
his history. By his fate. By his colour. And by his rap sheet. And
then he worked it out, in detail. His reaction to the violence
he knew they had in mind. With a logic he did not know he was
capable of apprehending, in this circumstance of the steel
that surrounds him, in the four smells of impatience and of
restraint, and of vomit and old, stale urine.

And he lit a cigarette. From his pack of Balkan Sobranie
Turkish cigarettes, filter. And in his mind, for his mind was clear,
he imagined himself taking out the long-playing record, as his
fingers eased it out of its jacket and put it on the phonograph
player. And he remained standing, listening to the words of
John Coltrane's chant, in his imagination:

. . . a love supreme, a love supreme . . .

He began to hear, first, the tenor saxophone like a soft dec-
laration of religious intent, and then the deep voice of the saxophone like a soft imploration to a new god; and then the deep
voice of the saxophone again, curving out the clean pure notes
of the theme, like a scream, like an invocation; and then the
deep voice:

A love supreme, a love supreme, a love supreme . . .

All nineteen times. And in his mind he touched the repeat
button, and "a love supreme" repeated and repeated itself; and
he could see John Coltrane enter the cell with him, and with
this greeting; he was stirred from his reverie by the opening of
the door of the cell, and was led out in handcuffs, to the dark,
cold parking lot. The two police "occifers" walked with him
in the middle. One behind, one in front. He walked in the footprints the leading one had made. They were not in uniform.
The parking lot was empty when they moved off.

"We're going for a little ride . . ."

Now, she lives with a different kind of fear. The fear of waiting.
Of waiting for what she knows will come to pass. Like a mother
in a room outside the Court, waiting for the Jury to return,
waiting for the Judge to return. And she is standing there, in the
crowd of people, witnesses and the accused, the room filled with
the silence of agitation, and fooling herself that she is waiting
for a positive verdict. When she knows what the verdict will say.
When the policeman comes, as he will, tomorrow morning or
tomorrow night, she knows what he will say. ". . . the key from
the Mercedes-Benz . . ."

"Did BJ think I am such a damn fool, or too old, or not hip-
enough not to know a Mercedes-Benz ignition key from one
used to start up a Mustang? Was I born the size I am? . . . I
look so stupid to you, BJ?"

This Thursday morning, her eyes are red from the tears she
has shed, that run down her face all over the white face powder
she uses. As she goes to the bathroom, she sees her face in the
looking glass. And she sees a face, like the face of an actress,
whitened like that of a professional clown, with a line of water

painted onto her cheeks exploding into rivulets of tears and sadness. Tears. Now she stands in front of the mirror, closing one
eye and then the other, to get the correct sightline, to see the
colour of shade she must use. She blinks her eyes three or four
times, fast. She runs her red painted fingers under her eyes, and
then around them. Then she goes to the bureau and returns
with her compact. It is made from a shell that is dark brown, like
tortoise. She sees a smaller version of her face when she unclicks
the cover. She turns the case over, for there is no way she can tell
the cover from the back. It is so symmetrical. She makes this
mistake all the time, even when the lights in her basement apartment are turned up bright. And she touches the white powder
with the brush lightly as a painter testing tone and emphasis.
And when she has painted her face, leaving a mask of whiteness
on her face, like the faces of African women she has seen in books
about Africa, she takes her powder from another container and
subtracts some whiteness from the sharpness of the white face
powder from the colour already applied. She has painted her
face too white. She wants a tint, a colour, a complexion that
would make a white woman look at her two times, on the subway, to make certain if she is really white, almost white, could be
taken for white, could pass. But with Idora it is not a matter of
passing, of fading from one culture into another. She always
wants to look sharp. Yes, sharp! All her friends back in the Island
wanted to look sharp. And were sharp. And they made their
faces whiter than genealogy said they were, and applied more
white powder and white cream, to bring out the sharp sexiness
of their young, vibrating sensuality. Yes! Sharp. And sexy.

   Standing like this, when she does not have to dress for work,
she remembers when she used too much face powder to con-

ceal the true colour of her face, and that had made her look like a ghost wearing an African voodoo mask.

She had been reading her Bible. The Book of Job. And she recited the words of chapter 1, and said, as Job had said centuries before: "Naked came I out of my mother's womb, and naked shall I return thither: the Lord gave, and the Lord taketh away; blessed be the name of the Lord." But she wasn't sure, was not convinced, that she had got anything from the Lord. And if there was some gift, some relief, that she had not been aware of, she knew that she wanted more.

Her bedroom doubles as a living room. In it she has placed a round table and the two red, upright wooden chairs against the wall, at the foot of the bed. Now that "that man" and BJ are out of her life, she eats alone, when she eats at home, when she is not worried about her failure to follow another diet she has signed up for. And she sits on one of the red chairs, facing the bed, beside which is the refrigerator, where the large, thick-armed white couch covered in plastic, and heavy as an overweight woman, sits, in splendid, silent and immaculate white dominion over the rest of the furniture, which is painted in dark brown, and covered in dark brown corduroy cloth, cushions and upholstery.

Now that her husband is gone and her son is missing, she sinks into her loneliness; and sits in her winged-back chair and concentrates on her favourite television shows about cops and robbers and the LAPD; and waits tensely as she sits with blood-curdling fear as she watches murders and guns and men being killed; as she waits for the knock of the police on her front door, banging for admission and evidence.

At her feet there is a coffee table made out of glass, on which she keeps three candles the same colour as the tapered red scented candles that burn on the altar of the Apostolical Holiness Church of Spiritualism in Christ. She makes a promise to go to the Apostolicals on the last Sunday of every other month, and she breaks this promise every month. It is two months now that she has not gone.

She admires the women who sit in the first twenty rows of pews at the Cathedral, and who are in the first two hundred communicants to go up to sip the cup of Communion wine, and are dressed in clothes that tell her they could be—she is sure of this—from Rosedale and Cabbagetown and the intersection of Eglinton and Yonge; and she assumes that the men who sit beside them are all lawyers and doctors and businessmen who sell stocks and shares in the Business District; and are millionaires . . . "At least thousandaires!" she says, chuckling in her heart. "And I am the only one poor as a bird's . . ." And the women of a class above hers are schoolteachers and housewives and lawyers; and men and women who live in the condominiums on the four corners of the land surrounding the Cathedral. "I am the poorest in this congregation!" she says to herself, as she kneels on the soft stool. ". . . who art in heaven, hallowed be Thy name . . ."

But at the Apostolicals, in spite of the bright colours in the women's dresses, reaching down to the middle of their well-formed calves, and the black suits and brown suits worn by the men, she rubs shoulders with all of them, and tastes the disappointment in their lives, and drinks the tears of their disappointments, as she breathes in the odours of aftershave and cologne and the smell of serge and wool and mothballs (to make the serge and the wool last longer). She does not fuss with her makeup or with her face powder or with her face cream when she attends the Apostolicals. Her face and the faces of all the men and women who attend the Apostolicals are the same hue.

She lights candles after six o'clock, every night, in all seasons, when she is home. And she sits alone, and eats her dinner, in the soft fluttering flame of the three red fingers that point to the ceiling, in the light of the naked sixty-watt bulbs that burn throughout the apartment; and the light from the television screen, and the light from the dial of the radio tuned always to WBLK radio station from Buffalo, that brings jazz and soul music and gospel into her gloomy basement apartment. This is the only other light in her apartment. The candles give off a mild wisp of smoke; and she sits and eats with knife and fork; and tapping the sides of her mouth with a folded white cloth napkin.

It was her Mother who had drilled her in good manners and graciousness, and who made her repeat the philosophy "Manners maketh Man"—and "maketh Woman too!"—as if she was teaching her the Commandments. "As a matter of fact," her Mother said, "make this your eleventh Commandment: 'Manners maketh Man.'"

She has lined up three figurines of buxom women on a cigar box on her dressing table. They are wearing scarves round their heads, with breasts and hips in full sensual vigour, skimpy at the waist, dressed in tropical colour and sea-island cotton frocks. Each woman has a cigar in her mouth. The women are Cuban. *Made in Cuba* is written at the bottom of their dresses. *Royal Jamaica* is written on the box. In this box she keeps her earrings and hatpins and a tarnished gold chain, and a pin that has two flags of two countries painted on its enamel, joined as if in a twinned nationalism. One flag has the Maple Leaf, the other the Broken Trident. Canada and Barbados. When she looks at this pin, which she wears every Dominion Day, and on the Independence Day of the Island of Barbados, smaller than Mississauga or Scarborough, her heart is joyful and light, and she is glad to be living in Canada.

And whenever this mood grips her, she would think of going to church at the Apostolical Holiness Church of Spiritualism in Christ, where she could express herself as if she was at a dance, moving her body to the beat of rhythm and blues; and before she even got there, by bus, she would see herself shouting the words of a religious song. Here in her community of West Indians, she was free.

And she expressed this one Friday evening in the summer, when by accident, and for the first time, the Pastor did not attend their Pre-Sunday Friday Night of Preparation, a meeting of the Deacons and Deaconesses, the Church Preservation Board and the Elders, to talk about the sermon, and the range of hymns, the introduction of a guitarist who would play two tunes, and the planning of the annual picnic for the children at a rented cottage in the country. The Pastor sent a message that he had a touch of the flu, but that the meeting should proceed in his absence. He would read the minutes and other notes taken at the meeting, on Sunday. The Pastor's absence was like a release, an excuse to play hooky from school. So, after the group prayed and sang a song, and just before they had arranged the chairs in a semicircle to begin discussing the items on the agenda, something happened. None of them wanted to spend such a beautiful summer evening inside a church (which, as far as Idora was concerned, still held the smell of dead animals) discussing serious religious and community matters. The wind was cool, and the light was bright, and they could hear the music of Bob Marley from the car radio of one of the Deacons. Idora reacted immediately to the beat of the music. The beat was the beat of church music, the beat of the spirituals sung by Aretha Franklin. And she took her tambourine from the cupboard where it was kept, and beat it as if she was tuning it; and with such vigour and feeling that the men and women in the room widened the semicircle of chairs and made space for her, as she moved with the rhythm of the tambourine; and as she caught the beat of the song coming louder now, through the speakers in the Deacon's car, she hit the beat, and the assembly started to dance and sing, mimicking and inventing words, striking hands and palms on the padded bottoms of chairs, made to sound like congo drums; the assembly started to dance and sing, until everybody was standing and dancing and shouting. And some of the women were shouting "Hai-hai-hai!" in tune with the spirit and the spiritual; and Idora was jumping up, and her body was vibrating; and the music grew loud and louder, until some of the neighbours who were not members of the congregation, but who listened through their windows in winter and their doors in summer, came out of their houses and stood at the open doors. It went on for hours, the singing and the nipping from the bottles held secretively with the labels covered. Idora's dress was soaked. She was mopping inside her blouse when a policeman appeared at the door at the bottom of the church and said, "Are you having a revival?"

Nobody bothered to answer.

The men and the women, and then the policeman, laughed.

"Have one?" a Deacon asked him. And offered a bottle, with his hands hiding the label, to the policeman.

"You don't see I on duty?" the policeman said, raising the short brown bottle to his lips.

All the long journey home that summer evening, Idora was mopping inside her blouse, trying to contain the perspiration, and the joy in her heart.

The sides of her legs were sore. But she was breathing joy and religious excitement, in spite of the humidity. And she went back over in her mind and in her body the way she had jumped to the rhythm of Bob Marley's song, and how she had got into the spirit, moving her body, with the tambourine slamming against her thighs, as if she was swirling in a colourful skirt, like the ones the three Cuban statuettes were wearing on her Jamaica cigar box. She had beat her tambourine to make it sound like an instrument playing a bolero. The beating of the instrument had taken her out of a church, out of the Apostolicals' church, outside of any conventional church, and had placed her at a dance, in a trance, moving fast, fast, fast to this enlivening music, this dangerous freedom-giving music, Marley, James Brown; moving to the latest Barry White tune, slow, slow, slow; and sensual; sexy; moving to Ray Charles and Jimmy Witherspoon, slower still; and she smiled and she rocked to the rocking of the subway train, as she had banged her anxiety and her failures in life out of the tight goatskin stretched over the tambourine, like an exorcism . . . as if she was reproducing the body-swaying richness of songs coming through her radio WBLK, over the Niagara Falls, from Buffalo.

At home, she holds her tambourine, with her four fingers tight against the inside of the circle surrounded by small brass cymbals. The cymbals are like ten flaring tongues; like ten flashes of fire. And she smashes it against the heel of her left hand, as if she is angry with her hand, as if her left hand is BJ's bottom she is beating; and then she beats the tambourine in a swinging rhythm of delight and emotional passion. When you watch her doing this, it makes you think she is accompanying the congregation in one of Barry White's popular songs, more sexual than it is religious; and spiritual; but clean enough for a church. The beating is even more physical than any flogging she has ever given BJ. And sometimes she grunts in rhythm with her body swaying, all the while shouting, "Hai, more! Hai, more! I'm-ah running for my life . . . hai! I'm-uh running for my life . . . hai!"

She beats her tambourine in the intricate, pulsing patterns of a jazz-drumming solo, like one by Elvin Jones; and the rhythm section of the Choir of the Apostolicals becomes the sweetness of sound of the John Coltrane Quartet, playing "A Love Supreme."

She is terrified about this story of Jonah, with its savagery and the close connection it seems to have to her own life. Her uncles were fishermen; and one of them lost a leg. It was his right leg. He lost it in the bowels of a shark. And although a shark is not the same as a whale, the point was made in her young mind. And in time she learned to recognize her uncle's approach to her Mother's front door, by the sound of his peg leg, an artificial foot, not measured properly, made from a branch of the mahogany tree, and attached to his right leg by strips of leather and canvas. He walked from then on, and forever, until he died at home, in his bed, with a limp-and-a-shift to his gait. His peg leg thundered over floorboards; on the Saturday afternoon cricket pitch; and in the public road, which was covered by a thick coat of tar, which melted in the sun and left small black specks of tar on the wooden leg.

All the village called him Hoppa-Kickey!, after his Scottish ancestry. She had listened with excitement for his approach, for years and years, when he would come to visit his sister, her Mother, counting before he had even cleared the paling and entered the galvanized gate, anticipating the number of "sweeties" and sugar cakes and golden apples and slices of breadfruit he would bring, as he always did, in a brown paper bag. But now, and as time went on, she blamed herself for being a backslider by her infrequent attendance at church—both the Cathedral and the Apostolicals—and she remembered her uncle and the story about Jonah, and entertained the hope of someday telling it either to a Sunday School class or on a Friday night, when the Assistant Deaconesses were encouraged to testify about their lives, and confess what had happened to them during the previous days of the week.

The three statues of the Cuban women were given to her by "that man," late one Saturday afternoon, when he had returned from the races at Greenwood blind drunk, but spic and span, every crease in order, tie tied firm and correct at the neck, his white handkerchief folded and fitted into his left breast pocket like the three sails of a yacht, and his brown leather shoes still shining from the polishing he had given them the night before. Bertram had a way of tying his laces once in a bow, and then using the two bows to tie them again, so that in snow or in a hurricane, his shoelaces would never come undone. "I hate to see a man with his shoe-lacings untie!" And his wife loved him for these expressions of care and what she called decentness.

At the races, he was a different man. He walked in dressed like a racing steward, or a horse owner, with a folded copy of the *Toronto Star* in the side pocket of his sports jacket, and in

the other pocket a copy of the *Racing Form*, where the horo-
scopes of horses were printed, along with the program for the
day, and a "Tips on Winners," and two ballpoint pencils—a red
one for his hieroglyphics of notes to himself, and the green one
to highlight the complicated tips and cautions and resolutions
he had decided upon. Bertram could not make up his mind on
horses. He changed his favourite as the minutes before a race
dwindled in nervous re-inspection. And he was always bothered
by his Jamaican friend, Paul, "the West Indian expert on horse
racing." Paul's claim to what Toddy, another Barbadian, called
his "precognostications of winners" was, so far as Bertram
was concerned, based upon the two words "Cayn lose!"—pro-
nounced as one word, "can't-lose." And when Paul repeated his
"precognostications," everyone in the group took notice, until
the horses had hit the tape, and the invincible horse had come
second by a length. In the company of these men of great horse
sense, it was beneath their dignity to bet—even two dollars!—
on a horse to come second. "Eh-eh! On the fucking nose,
pardner! On the fucking nose!" And when the winning nose
belonged to a horse on which they had not laid their money,
the expert, keeping his dignity intact, told them, "The fucking
jockey! You see how he hold-back the fucking horse, bredder?
The jockey!"

And they all accepted the expert's opinion. It was a world of
men. Well dressed on a Saturday afternoon, some even with
peacock's feathers in the bands of their English felt hats, blocked
to fit their heads by steam. It was also a gentleman's world. For
it was, after all, the Sport of Kings.

So it had taken place that Saturday afternoon, in hot sun,
with the breeze from the lake strong enough and energizing
enough to put a smile on their faces, to season the small talk,

dirty jokes, gossip about men who "carried on," having women on the outside, and about wives who were having men on the outside, and burying all this gossip at the track before they emerged in the late afternoon, through the turnstiles. Nothing spoken, nothing ridiculed, nothing criticized during the running of the races was ever repeated after the running of the last race. The protocol amongst these men made certain that each member of the group had—was given or was loaned—at least five dollars to bet on the last race. This Saturday afternoon, the man who needed a "trallia" for a bet was Paul, the expert.

"Two dollar to win-place-and-show, on the 10-horse, bredder!"

The last bet. On the last race. On the last day of the racing season, at Greenwood racetrack.

In those days Bertram went to the track the whole day, every Friday, Saturday and Sunday. He "passed-round just to see how things were" on the other days of the week, sneaking off from work to "place one bet on one race."

He had a temporary job, a seven-to-six job, six days a week, delivering advertising brochures. "That man spends all his time, losing every penny . . ." She said this every Friday night and every Saturday night, and repeated it every Sunday night, to herself. His betting and losing sucked the energy she needed to concentrate on her Bible reading, on her textbook on Nursing, and on choosing her dress to wear to church; and sometimes, on a whim, it made her check the bread tin, in which she kept three twenty-dollar bills, for emergencies: money for the cleaners who delivered BJ's diapers; money for Bertram's cigarettes; running out in the middle of the night for medicine; and money for BJ's formula. And taxi fare. In case little BJ swallowed a button, by accident, and had to be taken to the

Emergency Ward of the Toronto General Hospital on College Street.

Bertram's leisure time cut into the hours he was supposed to be delivering pieces of paper that announced sales and bargains for pizza and fried chicken, and the addresses of small neighbourhood businesses. His delivery job included lifting heavy boxes in the warehouse of Swift City-Wide Delivery, situated many miles down in the East End, and a quarter-mile from the Greenwood racetrack itself. And soon he started to complain about a pain in his back; and in her heart she said that he himself was the pain, and that the "pain was in the arse!"; and that the pain should be in his heart, and give him a heart attack; or a stroke; "or a coronary"; and take him from her.

He was screaming now, every day and every night, saying louder and with a condemning anger, "This country? Blasted raciss! Canada? Canada don't welcome black people. So, don't let nobody fool you. All this shite about multiculturalisms! Give me America, any time."

Soon after this, also on a Saturday, he had left for America.

His words made her sad. But on the following Thursday, she helped him pack his cardboard, imitation-leather grip. And on the Saturday, when he took the Greyhound express bus, buying his ticket the previous day from his winnings on the last race, she gave him a kiss, on his mouth, and rejoiced in her heart at his departure. She clapped her hands. In her heart she was beating a song of freedom on the reverberating tambourine, in praise of a new life.

When this joy and deliverance washed over her body, and she was like a child being bathed in a large wooden tub made of cedar, she began again to feel the same excitement that had

entered the dream with her, when the ringing of the Cathedral's bells came over the Park.

"We're going on a date," Josephine had said.
    "A who?" Idora told her. She did not like the way Josephine
said it.
    The "date" was an exhibition of Egypt and of Egyptian kings.
Out of boredom, and sadness that she was now a woman raising a son by herself, living in a basement apartment, she had
walked west from her neighbourhood, then north along Yonge
Street, then west along Bloor, to the Museum; and as she was
walking, in the quiet, cold streets, she wondered what had got
into her head to make her "do such a damn stupid thing, going
on a 'date,' with a woman, and a white woman at that, to a Museum, to look at dead people . . ."
    In her mind, like the striking of a wand, she had turned the
mannequins into real people, and had emptied all these windows
of all the stores along Bloor Street, between Yonge and Avenue
Road. She chose women for the majority of her imagined population. With a few men to match the national statistics of the
population. And she engaged these mannequins in conversation, to make them more like real people; and they were talking with her, and then they walked out of the display windows
of the stores, miraculously without smashing the thick glass,
and walked like models in a parade on a catwalk. And she
walked with them, along the street, and was sure, from talking
with these mannequins, that it was not her imagination that was
making her happy. "I am a free woman!" she confided to the last
woman who stood blonde and naked before breaking out of
her imprisonment, escaping through the glass of the display
window. The woman's eyes did not blink. Her face was not even

turned in Idora's direction. But she knew, mannequin or no mannequin, that this white, naked, blonde model, with perfect skin and breasts and dress size, had heard her words, for she was like her, after all, a woman. "And we women know these things."

The closer she had got to the Royal Ontario Museum, the ROM, the more nervous she had become, and could not understand why she had chosen to walk all this distance from her basement apartment, on this cold Sunday afternoon, to meet Josephine in a place where everyone was dead . . .

It was on a Friday afternoon, on a crowded rush-hour streetcar, that Idora had met this strange white woman—that's how she described her in her mind—a complete stranger, this white woman, who became her friend . . . Josephine! . . . Josephine, who has become her best friend. It was on this streetcar going east along Queen Street that this stranger had squeezed in beside her; and she could feel this woman's body, her warm legs touching hers; and at first she resented this touching; but she soon began to like the familiarity, this welcome sweet sensation, something like a secret acknowledgement of friendship and gratitude; that she was not once again shunned and marooned by herself, on a seat large enough for two.

"Yes, still, when no one sits beside me on a streetcar, I can't help thinking of the sixties and the South, with segregation and ropes coiled into a perfect hangman's knot, and men wearing white robes, as if they are priests, or deans, like the Dean. With the difference that they are too brave to show their faces. Only their eyes through holes, peeping out at you. These men never show their faces. And Josephine tells me that when you go down South, where she went once, the most beautiful thing you come away with is the sweet smell of the magnolia trees, and then the poplar trees. Poplar trees! I know about those poplar trees, from the song that Billie Holiday sings . . . Let me see if I remember the name . . . something about fruits . . . fruits, fruits, fruits . . . Yes! 'Strange Fruits'!" And she clears her throat and hums the tune, which she remembers hearing on WBLK radio, her favourite station from Buffalo.

"'. . . black bodies hanging
From the poplar trees' . . . My God, yes!"

She remembers that afternoon on the crowded streetcar, and Josephine's leg touching hers; and how the sensation of her surprise was like an electric shock; and how, when the touch lasted longer, and had become familiar, how it changed to a welcome, and then to sweet sensation. That she was not singled out this time, segregated as usual, on her seat on public transportation, was astonishing to her; and the longer she and the stranger remained in this unexpected and suspended familiarity, the longer, it seemed, they were each perfectly aware of what was happening. The word "lesbian" came into her head. But no, it could not possibly be this; my God, no. No such thing, so openly and blatantly expressed, in public, on a crowded Friday afternoon streetcar! But then she had asked herself what was public and what was private, in Toronto; and she remembered the joy and the laughter; the gazing and the staring; the music and the speeches; and the presence of councillors and mayors and a Minister of Foreign Affairs, and priests and mothers, at last year's Gay Pride Parade. Nothing in this city, in this regard, was private any more. No! This woman's leg was deliberately touching hers; and she was liking it; and she wondered if she had been having these feelings all this time, and had been concealing them from herself; repressing them; and suddenly she became aware that the streetcar was jerking; and once or twice, before it had travelled the next block, she had been thrown, heavily, against this white woman, this stranger. But it was an accident. And it had happened a third time in that same block; and when the streetcar jerked a fourth time, and their legs had touched again, she ascribed her gratification of touch, and her pleasure at being noticed in this way, to the jerking of the streetcar, and not to her subconscious will.

They began to talk about the weather. They were sitting so close side by side, in the packed streetcar, that neither of them could turn to face the other.

"Cold enough for ya?" Josephine had said.

"I was born here," she had said.

"Oh?"

"Yes."

"Going to work?" Josephine had said. "You're a nurse?"

"I work at the University," Idora told her. And immediately afterwards wondered why she didn't just say she worked in the dining room.

Then, all of a sudden, the streetcar jerked and came to a stop. It had developed electrical problems. And everything went quiet.

"I'm a student. Graduate School. Just went shopping. Wanna see?"

"I don't think so," Idora said.

"Don't mind showing you!" Josephine had said. And when Idora showed no greater enthusiasm, she added, "Which department are you in?"

Idora was beginning to hate this woman. "I'm getting off soon . . ."

"I'll get off with you."

"So you live around here?" she asked her.

"No," Josephine said. "Do you?"

The streetcar blocked all traffic going east; and all the cars honked their horns; and one man on a bicycle tinkled its bell as loud as he could make it ring; and mostly young men, and some women too, screamed profanities at one another—"Foke you, prick! Foke you, too! Prick!"—and it became colder in the crowded streetcar, and she pulled her winter coat tighter over her breasts. The traffic continued honking horns. Voices were screaming, in a pelting of obscenities. She wondered if it was because of the neighbourhood, the place they had found themselves, so close to the Scott Mission, the war surplus store with bayonets; and men lying on the cold corner of Church and Queen Street East. It was past five in the afternoon. "Foke you!" And then someone else shouting, "Fukkoff!"; and some women, who thought they were the targets, screamed, "You fukkoff!"

And it was then, in the cold, crowded streetcar, that this white woman introduced herself. In her hand was a red bag with the name of a store in Yorkville Village. She had seen bags like this one, left in winged-back chairs, or dropped on the soft cushions of Georgian settees and Louis the Fourteenth chairs, "anteeks"; and on the mantelpieces in the mansion down in the Ravine where she used to work. Those bags contained ladies' nightdresses, brassieres or underclothes; and she guessed that the red bag in this stranger's hand held similar articles; and this made her feel vulgar, and confused; and she did not hear this strange woman telling her, ". . . and since this streetcar isn't going anywhere, anyhow, why don't we get off and find a place, and have a coffee? . . . at Tim Hortons? We're at Jarvis. Must be a nice place around here! Do you know this neighbourhood?"

"This neighbourhood?" she said; then, after a long while, "No." She heard the word leave her mouth. It had taken a long time to leave her mouth, like a tricky gob of spittle.

"This snow!" Josephine had said. "What I won't give, right now . . . to be someplace else! . . . like a place where you come from . . ."

They had got off the streetcar, and had to concentrate on the slipperiness of the sidewalk as they walked past the display windows of pawnshops on Queen Street East, just round the corner coming to Jarvis Street, where there were pawnshops of better quality; and as they passed by, she bent her neck to take in and observe the sparkling and the glitter of rich, heavy gold and diamonds in rings and wristwatches; and crystal; and, more than anything, lust for a good lady's wristwatch; and one afternoon in the summer she promised to buy herself one . . .

Ahead of them, on their right hand, was the Moss Park Armouries, now in full military splendour, with the sun glittering from the cannons on the lawn, in silent memory of battles, and from the glass in the windows; and as they passed the corner windows of the war surplus, with its uniforms, worn by Englishmen and Germans in the Second World War, and bayonets, and holsters for small guns and pistols, she remembered how she had thought—and she had immediately laughed at the idea—of buying a gun. "To protect myself, in this neighbourhood!"

In fact, this whole week the *Star* newspaper was carrying feature stories about rapists and gun violence.

"I should buy a gun, though!"

She had never owned a gun. Never seen one close up. Never even touched one. Except the plastic toy repeater she had bought for BJ from Honest Ed's bargain basement store. But that was a long time ago. BJ was still an infant. The repeater gun squirted water, and made BJ giggle. And in the summer, in the Park, he aimed his squirting gun at a cluster of black squirrels cavorting and missed them all.

As she walked beside Josephine that afternoon, she felt the oddness of the situation she found herself in. Josephine was dressed in a custom-tailored black winter coat, expensive black leather gloves and a large woollen shawl, which she uncrossed from her neck, and then crossed again, in a casual motion, across her shoulders. She guessed that Josephine was about her age; roughly her same social class; with a middle-class bearing, unlike hers, which was rural and islander. She and Josephine were about the same size. Heavy in the hips and, from what she could see of the way the winter coat fitted Josephine around the waist, heavy in the thighs, heavy in the legs; heavy in the breasts; and flat in the "botsy"—the bottom. In the design of Josephine's shawl she could see the colours of trees and flowers in the Tropics; and some leaves fallen from the trees, and which matched the tight-fitting dresses of her three Cuban women sculptures.

She has gone back to bed, and it is now Thursday afternoon. She is certainly not going to work. She is not going to move. Wrapped again tightly in the sheets, only her head is exposed. "This is foolishness," she says of her behaviour; this foolishness, this inability, this unwillingness to summon up the energy to get out of bed. She remembers how she had stared at the face of King Tutankhamun the First, in his own robes of death, in the mothballing cloth that had kept him young all these hundreds of years in the stifling, withering heat of Egypt; Egypt, the same country that Marcus Garvey, a man from Jamaica, had wanted to send all black Jamaicans and black Americans back to; the same Egypt, the place where her African ancestry connected her to a group of women who were queens.

She had read this history in library books, at her school and in the Public Library, in the Island, when she was studying for her examination, the Oxford and Cambridge Joint Board Higher School Certificate of Education. And she read about it here, in Canada, in library books, when, once a year, every February of the year, all the public libraries in the city took out their books on black people, buried for the other eleven months of the year, because the library wanted Canada to know how many books about black people they had bought the previous year; and how many books about black people black people were reading, thanks to the Public Library. Books were a dime a dozen, during those twenty-eight days of the year—except in a leap year, when there was a bonus of one day more. Idora borrowed books from the Yorkville Library, during normal months; but when February loomed, she got them for weeks at a time. Idora just loved February, that month called Black History Month. One February, long ago, she had come across that newspaper clipping, in the drawer of a cupboard in her live-in quarters, in the basement of the mansion of her former employers down in the Ravine.

"A black man, Mr. Albert Johnson, formerly from Jamaica in the British West Indies, was yesterday shot dead by a Toronto policeman." The *Star* gave no motive, and not much more information. But in time, and over the years, Idora and other West Indians built their own structure of facts around that single sentence.

She took the clipping, which had served as a book marker, from the mansion.

She has looked at this clipping, off and on, like a woman who remembers anniversaries of marriage and death and divorce, trying to be a better detective than those on the Toronto police force, trying to find the motive for this shooting. The only other thing she knew about Mr. Albert Johnson was that he grew up in Jamaica, and he grew roses. Red roses.

"Yes. And then, sometime much later, there was another Jamaican, who the police shot one afternoon as he was walking down the middle of Bathurst Street, near St. Clair Avenue West, that's in the Jewish neighbourhood, in case you don't know; and this fellow was dressed in a blanket; and nothing else—not a stitch more on his black body, other than the blanket! But he had sandals on his two feet. 'I am Jesus! I am Jesus! I am Jesus!' he was screeling-out to the people, his disciples. His voice reached up to the top floor of the apartment buildings surrounding him, high in the sky, transforming him into a hermit walking in a valley, like in the Bible, a valley in the shadow of death . . . Yes! . . . screaming at the people passing, 'I am your Saviour. I am your Saviour! I am your Saviour, come back from the dead! I am the Second Coming. The Second Resurrection. The Second Messiah.' And this Jamaican man shouting-out, in this loud voice that all of St. Clair–Bathurst neighbourhood could hear . . . his voice was like a clarion, I heard . . . including Cadillacs passing on the way to work, coming through the St. Clair–Bathurst intersection, a common intersection, that the Jamaican-Saviour had now turned into the Red Sea. He had parted the waters. And was now walking on water. He changed the road into water. I think this second tragedy came to pass whilst I was already living in Toronto.

"It was the summer still, when he performed this miracle, holding a broomstick he had sharpened to shape like the staff a Bishop walks with. Or a Dean of a Cathedral Church. Or was it a spear?

"He addressed himself as Burning Spear. Mr. Burning Spear, a Prince of Africa—if you please!

"Then the cops . . . the cops came, and shot him. Shot him, dead, dead . . . dead. Blam! Blam! And a next one . . . blam! For creating a disturbance of the peace. A bullet in his head, between his two eyes. One on the right side . . . that's the one that missed. And the one that hit the target, right in his chest, on the left side . . . his heart. The three o' them just missed forming a cross. A cross of bullet holes. Yes! And for what? For committing the crime of calling himself a Prince of Africa? For disturbing the peace of the neighbourhood? A simple thing, like calling himself a Prince of Africa? You tell me. And that he was Jesus, come back from the dead, to deliver St. Clair–Bathurst neighbourhood from the intersections—I mean the intercessions— of the Egyptians? . . .

"So now, you tell me! What the hell the cops expect from a man, staying up late, night after night, watching American television, and all the violence that they have on it? Especially on CNN?

"But more than that. Could you tell me what do the police of this city have against Jamaicans? Profiling them so?"

"So, I had just left my apartment, the morning in question; heading towards the Eaton's Centre on Yonge Street; and as I remember, I was still in a bad mood from the minute I had stepped on the last step going up from my basement apartment, to bring me level with the sidewalk . . . yesterday morning. Ten o'clock hadn't gone yet, then. It is in bright daylight now, that my two eyes rested on the mess dropped in front my wrought iron gate, and thrown on the sidewalk in front my place. Ripped out of the three green garbage bags. My empty Mount Gay rum bottles. Empty Jamaica white rum bottles. The crusts from the pizza that I had ordered-in, the night; and had put in the garbage bag, with the mouth tied . . . 'cause I had found it too hard to chew . . . with my fillings. The cans that had-in ackee, and green peas, and . . .

"That bastard ripped-open the three green garbage bags, for the whole damn street to see my private business!

"I could only stand up. And look down at the destruction! There, on the sidewalk. Dumbfounded. Men and women passing, for work. A few young whores already out. No more older than fifteen, or eighteen. I don't know what men see in them! Walking their prostitute walk; and having the nerve, with a scornful look on their face, to step-over my private possessions, capsized on the sidewalk, as if they're stepping-over garbage! Did I say garbage? I mean 'shit'!

"And in bright daylight. I see this man. This sammy-coon! Or, sammy-coot! Back in the Island, we would call him that! Five o'clock! In the morning! I happened to been suffering from a touch of insomnia. The whole night, I tossing and turning. The piece o' canvas in the two windows that I would raise, to look out, and see if snow fall during the night; or if there is ice on the sidewalk . . . Three o'clock didn't gone yet! . . . And there. Is this bastard. A man. Bending over my garbage. Pulling things out of my three green garbage bags I bought from the

Dollarama store! That bastard! He is one of the homeless ones that live in shelters, round the corner. Jarvis. Queen. Places east of the pawnshops and Henry's Camera. Places like that. George Street, north of Dundas. And one on Sherbourne near Queen. The Arthur Meighen place, which is where Mike lives.

"All joking aside, now. He has his two hands inside my garbage. Like a man pulling dirty clothes out of a laundry bag. At that point I shout at the bastard! 'Hey, you!' . . . at the top of my voice . . .

"He looked round. And he see me. And he continued to put his two hands inside my garbage.

"'Hey, you! Take your blasted hands out o' my garbage, man!'

"And then, I looked good . . . 'cause it really was kind o' dark, still.

"My God! He was a black man! A black man! The man pulling garbage out o' my three green garbage bags, is one o' we!

"My God-in-heaven! The garbage-thief is a black man! It make my heart bleed . . .

"'You come to that?' I shout at him. 'You don't know you are a black man? You come to this? You lost your dignities? And your decency?'

"My God! Here is this black man. And it hurt my heart to see it. This black man. With a large bag that have GUESS printed on it. In large, big white letters. He had left his bicycle leaning up against my wrought iron fence. A cigarette in his mouth, dangling at the right corner of his mouth. His two hands buried in my garbage! I felt he was assaulting me . . . raping me in broad daylight . . . with his right hand, in a black glove, against my face.

"Digging into my possessions. And that cigarette in the right side of his mouth, dangling, and the smoke going in his eyes, looking like . . . like Edward G. Robinson in a crime movie . . .

"'What the hell are you doing?' I screeled at him, the second time. And do you know what that bastard said to me? On that sad morning, when I was looking out for his dignity as a black man?

"'It is garbage.' He said to me, 'It is garbage, isn't it?'

"That bastard looked me in my two eyes, and said, 'It is garbage.'

"My garbage is garbage! Heh-heh-heh, heiii! All I could do was laugh. 'It is garbage.'"

"So, I am walking north on Yonge; just past the Eaton's Centre; and to tell you the truth, I can't call-to-mind why I am going up Yonge Street, this morning . . . but here I am, with all these problems on my mind, going north towards Dundas Street. Or, the Dundas Park. Or whatever the hell the open space that they build there, to amuse teenagers, is officially called.

"A truck with advertising boards on it is parked near the corner. On the same side as the Square, with the water sprouting like geysers of cold water. And, as in such cases, as you would know if you live in Toronto, a policeman is guarding the installation, in case a piece o' glass fall off, by accident, and kill a pedestrian. And with this danger in mind, as I approach the police-fellow, who is wearing a black windbreaker . . . it could have been a blue-black windbreaker . . . in any case, his windbreaker isn't fitting him properly, because I can see the handle and part of the barrel of his revolver, sticking out. Sticking out with the holster attached. And the snap, or the thing that snaps, to keep the revolver safe inside the holster, to keep it from going off, by accident, and killing an innocent bystander, 'in the wrong place, at the wrong time,' as the same police tell us when they're investigating all these recent 'drive-bys'. . . . all this danger is in my mind, and is visible to me, meaning the gun, although it is snapped into place.

"The feeling comes into my head, sudden. Suppose . . . just suppose I take out that gun . . . and pull the trigger. This feeling comes into my head from nowhere. And I am the daughter of a policeman back home! And this thing come into my mind. Into my body. With so much, so much force and conviction . . . seriousness . . . that my body start to react with fear and with shame for my thoughts. This spasm of madness shake my whole body. And I felt a rush, a hot wet rush and the joy that comes with such a rush, of the act I have in my mind to commit; and my hand start to tremble, my two hands shaking now; and I imagine myself putting my hand on that policeman's holster and pulling out his revolver. My God! And me, a woman! I can see myself holding the revolver in my hand. My mind is remembering the fate of poor Mr. Albert Johnson, whose picture of crucifixion I have on a wall in my apartment. A picture showing how the crime scene looked, cordoned-off with yellow tape, after the cop blew Mr. Johnson's head to smithereens, like a overripe watermelon, as I said before.

"My God! Yes!

"I see my hand take out the revolver from the policeman's holster, in my imagination. And point the revolver right at his head, also in my mind. And put my right-hand index finger . . . and although I am left-handed, I can still use both my right hand and my left hand, as the case may be, with the same ease . . . and pulling the trigger. Blam! Blam! Blam! Yes!

"Three times. To make sure that if the first bullet did not hit him, the second one would! And the third one would kill-him-off! Dead! Yes!

"One for Mr. Albert Johnson. One for the other Jamaican, the Prince of Africa. And one for the future—for my son, as worthless as he is. Just in case. Yes, one for BJ, now calling himself Brother Rashan Rashanan—if you please. Yes!

"I am like a Mafia-woman! Peter paying for Paul. Paul paying for all. Me, a woman with these thoughts of murder, thinking so; and acting so; and wondering, where are the men? Where are the men? Where are the blasted men gone? Where the blasted black men? My God! Where the men is?

"Me, a woman crying in the wilderness! Rachel, weeping for her thrildren, and shall not be comforted, because her thrildren . . . her children . . . are naught. Are not. Her children are nought. Cannot be found. I reeking havoc and murder . . . revenge for all the things . . . the beatings and the killings and the singling out in profiles, and the picking out in lineups to identify suspects and guilt, in police stations . . . that the police, and this policeman's brothers—which is what Josephine tell me is the term they use for one another to strengthen their brotherhood with, one with the other . . . and that they have been perpetrating, Josephine told me. Or perpetuating . . . What is the blasted word? The Jamaican man planting his red roses. The other Jamaican dressed in a blanket to cover his African nakedness, and keep the cold and the winter from out his chest, to cause him to get consumption in his two lungs . . . TB. This poor man, walking through Forest Hills, then down in the middle of Bathurst Street, thinking he is a Zulu, and imagining he is some nomad crossing the Sahara Desert, convinced he is really Jesus, as he called himself three times; and that he is the new Christ parting the waters of the Red Sea. A simple, harmless, disturbed man, armed with a piece o' stick, walking along the Bathurst–St. Clair area, with that piece o' stick he sharpened to look like a spear, holding it in his hand, saluting Haile Selassie, behaving as if he is still in Africa, believing he is not in the Jewish District of Forest Hills, and that he is a Prince of Africa. And blam! The police exterminate him! With one bullet. To the head. Blam!

"And scrape him up off the street, like you would scrape shit that you stepped in, from off your two shoes . . .

"And then they throw a tarpaulin to mark the spot, and yellow ribbon, like a garland, to rope-off the grave.

"And so, my hand touches the revolver. It is cold. And heavy. My hand is quivering so . . . Look! I take the revolver out with my right hand, and transfer it to my left hand. I am both right-handed and left-handed, at the same time, as I tell you before. But it is so heavy that I have to hold it with both my two hands, to get a good grip on it. And to get a grip of myself. And for that moment, when my two hands touch that cold revolver, all sense, all common sense, all reason, all the teaching of respect for the laws of the land, that my Mother brought me up to believe in, all Commandments went clean out of my head. My God!

"I am a madwoman, now. Like one of those inmates in the Mad House on Queen Street West. Number 999. And for that moment, corresponding with the sudden loss of reason and common sense, I feel this surge of power, mixed with this hot, wet rush of joy. I am holding all this power in my hand. The power to shoot a policeman. Yes! They are profiling too many of all of us. All of us. Especially Jamaicans.

"But then, what people call reality surge-through my body, as strong as the power of madness, and the substitution of reason; and I see, in less time than it take me to extract the revolver from the policeman's holster, two carloads of police appear. Surrounding me. The Tactical Squad. With bulletproof jackets. And machine guns! Not simple revolvers now, boy!

"Sireens wailing. Ambulance and fire engines and police cruisers surrounding me, surrounding the whole block, blocking traffics. They have me flat on the cold pavement of the Dundas Square. My bubbies cold against the concrete. A boot in the crux of my neck. Another boot in the pit of my back. Somebody has my right hand twisted-back behind my back.

"The pain travelling through my entire body. My blood turns into fire. Liquid. Hot molten solder. My God! And then into ice.

"And two new hands, two more hands up my two legs, inside my thighs, searching and asking me and at the same time wanting me to answer-back the owner of the two hands, namely, if I have more guns, hidden under my clothes . . . up my crutch. Yes . . .

"And girl, as I am telling this to you, I close my two eyes and I press down on my teeth, the second I feel that policeman's hand touch my pussy. The sudden feel of his hand, cold as a piece of ice, much more colder than the barrel of the revolver I had held in my hand, in my imagination, in my mind; as I am there on the cold pavement, with that policeman's hand up my crutch . . . My God! Yes! . . . in case I have more guns hidden up in there . . ."

She was glad she was wrapped in her white skin of sheets and blanket and comforter when the light struck the glass, shining through her windows.

It broke into her apartment, covering the entire area, including the corners, of her bedroom, searching, jerking, retracing spots already covered, like a high-powered battery searchlight in wartime.

She stopped breathing. And stopped moving. She played dead. Just like the grey squirrel she had seen in the Park, trying to escape an attacking dog; had played the possum.

The beam traced out the perimeter of her two front windows. And then it painted the outline of her body, moving softly and slowly as it rode the curves of her breasts and her belly. She could see the light travel over her body, and she thought of the statue of the Egyptian queen, now lifeless as any mannequin in the window of the Holt Renfrew store on Bloor Street; dead, and naked on a slab of smoothened marble.

She wanted to appear dead. She was indeed a statue, something left over from an age of marble and stone and eucalyptus and embalming oils. A body on a slab of marble tombstone.

Pap-pap-pap, pap! Puh-pap-pap! Puh-pap-pap! Pap-pap-pap-pap-pap!

Guns are fired in this neighbourhood more often than fireworks displays organized by City Hall. And these guns are in the hands of teenagers. Hardly do these kids live to be twenty. "And it scares me like hell, when I hear that they carry guns to school. Teenagers having guns! . . . My God, back in the Island, we carried to school a compass set for Geometry, a set-square for Arithmetic, an ink bottle with ink in it, for writing; and for Penmanship; and a metal ruler, with twelve inches on it. We weren't into centimetres, then. The heaviest thing in our bookbags was a Ferrol bottle, filled with lemonade. And I sure as hell didn't use that Ferrol bottle to open somebody's head! And all these guns! Children taking guns to school. And missing

their targets, my God, that is the worst thing. They can't shoot
straight. And kill the right person, another gangster, instead o'
killing innocent bystanders. I walk these streets, especially the
street I live on, and I quake in my boots, as I walk in the darkness. As the poem says,

> 'I stand in my boots and I wonder, I wonder;
> I stand in my boots, and I wonder.'

"I wonder when a stray bullet is going to come in my direction. Yes, Lord, save me! And another thing. You could tell me
why a boy, carrying a gun in his bookbag, or backpack, like a
gangster or a cowboy in a cowboy-movie, firing that gun, and
missing his intended target? And instead of facing the music, he
run-off like a blasted coward? You can explain this cowardice
of gun-toting teenagers, to me? You think that a boy carrying
a gun in his backpack, instead of a bottle of ink; or milk, or
lemonade, to drink for his lunch, could . . . I can't go on. I can't
take more of this violence. I am scared to walk the streets, even
in broad daylight. And when night does come, I am walking in
the middle of the sidewalk, away from the bushes and the
houses, and my two ears are pricked, listening to every noise, a
murmur from a mouse, every footstep from a man, his breathing . . . if there is a change in the rhythm of his footsteps
behind me. Even though the street lights are on. The way I
see it, I am a woman walking in darkness. In the valley of the
shadow of violence and guns and death.

"One night I am walking home. It is only eight o'clock. But I
am talking on my plastic cellular phone, pretending I am talking
to somebody. Talking loud. The street black. In front of me,
not a soul. Behind me, not a soul. But my heart is in my mouth.

Because I am a woman. And this is Toronto, which Missis Proposki insists is the murder capital of Canada. I am trying to appear brave, in case somebody in the darkness watching me. In
case a murderer, or a rapist, or a crook, or a man, is hiding in the
darkness. And to protect myself, I imagine that every man on the
street is one o' them. And all of a sudden this thing comes out of
the shadows. I froze. My skin turned suddenly cold. My heart
stopped beating. Cold sweats now, girl. I push my hand in my
handbag to see what I have to save my life. Anything that is
heavy, in the way of a weapon. Or sharp. Just in case. I am searching, hoping to find something. Hoping for something, anything,
to find for protection. Not a nail file. Not a scissors. Not even
a razor blade. Nor one o' them Afro combs to pick the knots
out o' my hair with. I talking 'bout the times when women wore
Afros. Nothing. And then the person comes up to me, and just
as I could smell his breath, he was so close, my God, I wet my
pants . . . I not ashamed to tell you . . . and that was it. I surren-
dered. In my body and in my heart, I gave in. He got me now,
girl. He got me now. And I even said to myself the answers to
the questions I read in the *Star* that a man like him would ask a
woman he is about to assault and molest. And then, murder.
And when he spoke, he had such a nice accent. This nice voice.
'Would you happen, miss, to have a cigarette? Or some spare
change, for a coffee?' I not really listening to him. My mind is on
the condition I am in . . . you know what I mean. But I opened
my handbag, took out my change purse. And gave him every
cent, to my name, that I had. A five-dollar bill, two loonies, and
the quarters. And five pennies. I will never forget that night . . ."

"In this neighbourhood, as I see it, and as I can bear witness
to it, a man who walks with the help of a four-wheeled walker

reminds me of the code of ethics of this community, namely, the wisdom of the three monkeys: 'See no evil; hear no evil; speak no evil.' I see men in the Park exchanging small packets for small tubes of dollar bills, rolled-up tighter than a cigar, and I look off. I hear some of them shouting at women, and I feel sorry for the women, but I do not lift a finger. I see and I don't see. I hear a man tell a woman, 'Wait till I get you home, bitch!'; and already I can hear the screams and the heavy hand of the man's injustice landing on the woman's face. And the screels of her children . . . his children? Perhaps not his children. I remember the men in large expensive cars, talking, although I couldn't hear what they're saying; and nodding their heads, and helping the sex-working women up onto the high running-boards of their fancy cars; and all the time, I am listening to the ringing of the bells in the Cathedral's tower, keeping me company . . . the bells and the sex-workers . . ."

". . . now, 'bout that fella I was telling you about!" Johnnie, her neighbour who walks with a four-wheeled walker, with brakes, was telling her. He was leaning on her wrought iron fence. She kept her hand on the gate. Her hand covered the latch. "Didn't ya?" Johnnie said. "Didn't ya heard about him, didn't ya? Was in the papers. The papers was filled with it, the one who likes boys, the peddafillia-fellow. Didn't ya hear? He's your neighbour. Didn't ya know he's a neighbour of yours? That house up the street west of you, there on Shuter, and slightly north . . . just before you get to Dundas Square, in the back, by Ryerson . . . George Street. Up in there, isn't it?"

Johnnie walks away from her, his walker moving slowly over the snow, before she can answer him.

"The pedophilia-man won't come after me, though," she said to herself. "Not a woman my age."

One day she saw a man on television, by the name of Mr. Godfrey Cambridge, from Harlem, an "Afro-American," as he called himself, on *The Ed Sullivan Show*, a repeat, explaining why it was "racially un-cool"—his words!—for Afro-Americans to eat even a slice of watermelon in public. "Not in public, brother! Eat it under cover! Not in public, sister! If you have to eat it, for cultural reasons, eat it in the privacy of your kitchen, with the blinds pulled down! Preferably, when there's no whites around to see!"

She had almost choked on the seeds in the piece of watermelon in her mouth. But she was able to clear them from her windpipe. Four polished black seeds, with pieces of red, thick flesh stuck to them, came out. They looked like small clots of blood.

She stopped eating watermelon after this, in public. She loved watermelon.

"I wish I could share this new knowledge about eating watermelons with every black man and black woman in Canada! And if 'that man' didn't run out on me, I would share it even with him!"

But no more than one minute after Mr. Godfrey Cambridge had started in with his jokes she started to remember her personal history of Canada. Her invisible visibility made her seethe with anger and rage for the police and for white people, but it also made her feel guilty, inferior, sorry to be so visible and to have her situation so often smeared in big headlines and colour photographs on the front pages of the *Star*. Everybody who sat in the same subway, who saw her walking the streets, especially a street with rooms for rent, knew—from reading the same *Star* newspaper—that there . . . there across the street, knocking for five minutes now on a door . . . there was one of those black women . . . call her that! Yes! That's right, call her by her name! . . . There is one black woman, one coloured woman, and—shhhh, now!—call her by the real name you know her by . . . a nigger, who ain't gonna be on this street after sundown . . . Yess! . . . the whole street, the whole area, knows that she is a victim. Victims, her Mother always said, deserved to be killed. Molested. Victimized.

But was she a victim? Was she too hard on herself?

"And another thing. White barbers refusing to cut black men's hair. The fellow I went out with, for two weeks, the Engineering student, when he was a student, he and four other students from the University drove in a car from Toronto to Windsor, Ontario, to join a sit-in against the racism of white Canadian barbers refusing to cut black, curly, curled, nappy-knotty black hair, in Windsor. And one in Chatham, too. Don't talk about Toronto! And another thing: applying for jobs and being told the job is taken. And going to an interview and being told, 'We will call you!' And waiting for the call, because they were well-brought-up, Christian-minded Commonwealth students, members of the same family—Lester Pearson told them so!—waiting for that call, like when the roll is called up yonder, they would be there; and meanwhile, I know six out of ten West Indians who were waiting for the roll to be called up yonder; and waiting; and waiting; and in the meantime, decided to register in Graduate School, in Sociology and in Economics; and after three years, got their MAs, and their LLBs, and their Teacher's

Certificates from OISE, and got married, and had thrildren, and the blasted telephone ain't ring yet, man! And why do I still tell myself that I like this country? Why? Why? Why?

"I look into my looking glass over my bureau, and I look at my face to see how my tears have dissolved my face, that I just painted to make me look different. As if the applying of all this white powder will make me more invisible. And more accept-able. I pass the face cream all over my face first, to soften-up my skin, to moisten it. I don't really like the word *moisten*, because it has other connotations, you know what I mean? As a woman yourself, you would know what I mean. Soften-up is my choice. And then I wipe all that off. And then I take my brush, dip it in the round face powder bowl, inhale the sweet smell, close my two eyes and inhale deeper, and then, with my two eyes still closed, I touch my face, round my two eyes; then down my left cheek, then the right, under my ears, to make sure that I do not have two colours, one white and one black, to my face, then under my neck a little more. And when I am done, I am like a bloody ghost. Sometimes. For a second, or two. Until I soften the glare left by too much white powder. Soften the glare. I like that word. And when all is said and done, and I put the brush back into the pow-der bowl, and I take my left index finger and wet it in my mouth, and rub it in the corners of my two eyes, lifting up the false eye-lashes, and do the same under my two eyes, and then round my mouth . . . but what a lovely mouth! What a lovely mouth, my Mother gave me in her genes. All the Morrisons in Barbados have the same lovely mouth. I wonder if this is not the attraction I have for my Dean. My God, we could be family!

"I am surprised, sometimes, to look at my face in my looking glass.

"And look at me!"

"But look at you!" she says, peering into her full-length looking glass. "Look at you!" And she looks at herself, staring into her face. "Big eyes. Big lovely black eyes. Nice ears. Not a bad mouth. Firm and confident. A nice sweet mouth. Full o' perfect lily-white teeth! My God, how time has cured my skin! And my bubbies. Pressing them. Feeling-them-up every night, and every morning—when I remember—for cancer. And my back-side. A proper, big, sweet Barbadian bottom, looking just a little too much African. A bit too African for my taste. A Watusi. Look at me!"

One day last winter, she had given BJ ten minutes to clear the corner at Jarvis and then she put her winter coat on, and covered her head with a large woollen hat, pulled down over her eyes, to hide her identity; and then she put on a pair of Bertram's winter boots. The boots swallowed her feet, and made it diffi-cult for her to walk and keep him in sight; and she held her head down, each time he looked around, although she was far behind him, out of sight. He continued walking on Jarvis Street, passed the hotel on the corner, going straight north. For a few moments she lost him. The snow was falling thick, like a curtain, people and cars and the buildings were all white, curtained in the cold slippery sidewalk. She had fallen three times already. "This blasted snow!" she said, but made a greater effort not to slip again, and fall. Falling was the worst part, "a big black woman like me falling on this white sidewalk, looking like a fool . . . don't even know how to walk on the damn sidewalk in winter!"; and she was living here so long. And then, it must have been the thickening snow that was now a curtain cutting him off from her, or it might have been her preoccupation about falling . . . he had disappeared. She walked on, in the thick snow, sliding occasionally, and came to his school, Jarvis Collegiate Institute, hidden almost in the snow; and stopped. She could not decide whether to turn round and go back home or enter the double door, and walk up the two flights of stairs and go into his classroom . . . ask where he was . . . and satisfy herself.

The idea to follow him, and check on him, had come suddenly, impulsively to her. But when she brushed the snow from her eyes and her coat; and when she inspected her appearance, she felt ashamed to be seen like this, at her son's school.

She had lost him. She walked cautiously back down the steps and walked more slowly going back along Jarvis Street, back to her basement apartment.

She was determined to catch him offside.

Her mind went back in time to the footprints she had seen coming from the back gate of the house, right up to the gate the landlord had kept locked. She had studied the footprints for days, until the temperature rose and obliterated the prints, which looked like the footprints of a giant.

At this time she had a second job, working as a cashier at a discount supermarket in the neighbourhood. She likes this job; and after the first two weeks she discovers how she can take home as many groceries as she likes, without paying full price; and when the idea hits her, she is startled by its efficiency; and she convinces herself that she is not shoplifting; but is, as Josephine explained it to her, "ripping off the exploiting international corporations. And it is your duty as a person from the Developing Third World to rip them off."

"I don't see it so," Idora told her. "I would call it stealing."

"How can a poor woman, living alone, steal from a million-aire? And a few groceries, at that?"

Idora does not like Josephine's argument; and she thinks that what Josephine has put into her mind is stealing. But she plans to do it anyhow. She has to bring BJ into the plot; and she smiles at her clever way of keeping an eye on him at the same time.

"You come to the grocery store, punctually at four-forty-five, on Wednesday. Wednesdays are the days when the men and the women in the Parliament Street neighbourhood do their shopping, and the store is crowded on Wednesdays. You are not too young to understand that the neighbourhood is a neighbourhood of working-class poor people. Manual labour-ers and taxi drivers and janitors and maids . . . and whores . . . you're not too young to know this! . . . and pimps, too. I am sure you know what pimps are. But remember that there're also community college students and Ryerson University stu-dents living in this neighbourhood. I just love to see them with their backpacks, going to classes. Men and women going after degrees in Engineering and Computer Sciences, from overseas universities in countries that do not speak English, even as a fourth language!" She laughs at her wit. "In this city of Toronto, we employ these highly educated men and women as taxi driv-ers. Or put them to clean offices. A lot o' them are parking lot attendants. I am telling you all this for a reason. You understand why I am doing this?"

He nods his head.

"You understand why I am doing this?" she asks him a sec-ond time.

And he nods his head a second time.

"You understand why I am telling you this, boy?"

"Yes, I understand."

She is nervous. But she does not want to lose her calm. She laughs.

"Prepare yourself," she tells him. "You are a very intelligent young man. Now, there is a science to filling a grocery cart with groceries. And we're lucky that the grocery carts at this store are some of the best in Toronto. They are made of strong wire . . . I just love these grocery carts. They are made of wire, as I tell you. They look so nice. Their wheels are made of rubber, and they don't make noise when you push them." She laughs again. And BJ does not. He is nervous even listening to his Mother. "Quiet as a mouse. These grocery carts move just like English perambulators back home."

So, BJ arrives at the appointed hour, nervous, looking round to see which man in the crowded store looks like the store detective. The store is crowded. She has given him a list. "Read this and learn it by heart. You have a good head for memory," she tells him. And she places her hand on his shoulder; and she feels the warmth of his affection.

BJ begins to fill the grocery cart with every item on the list, following his Mother's directions as well as his own impulses: candy and bubble gum; and soda pop; and every kind of meat— steak, lamb chops, cuts of pork loin that she had planned to eat on Saturday coming. And she even has a few items she knows he loves: Bounty candy bars with a seam of coconut inside the brown chocolate coating; and Diet Sprite.

The noiseless perambulator of a grocery cart is packed. The groceries reach above rim. BJ comes to her checkout register. He is the only customer in the line. She takes all the items he has selected, one by one, and in a calm, calculated manner she rings each item into the cash register. She smiles each time she looks at him, each time the bell in the cash register rings. She empties the large grocery cart of each item. The total is a fraction of the actual price. BJ is trembling. He is chomping on his chewing gum, as if he is eating chips. She hands him the receipt. The total says fifteen dollars and ten cents.

And BJ pays her. He hands her the same twenty-dollar bill that she had left on the kitchen counter. It was left beside the bread tin, painted with faces of white Canadian children with bonnets on their blond hair, in the same tin that she kept sliced white bread in.

"Smile, boy! Smile!" she tells him. "Smile! Why you so nervous? . . . As if you are a thief . . . Smile! Show your teeth. So smile!" And she smiles with him. And he tries to smile, and . . .

He is so nervous that he has trouble steering the packed grocery cart in a straight line to the closest exit in the store; and then he sees a security guard, a man he takes to be the store detective, coming towards him; and the man is approaching him as if he is walking in slow motion, and the two of them are in a movie; and BJ abandons the grocery cart in the crowded store and disappears through the nearest door that has a red EXIT over it . . .

"I know I've set a bad example for my son. I am no role model at all. I regret I've misled the boy, so. And I know full-well I misguided my son. It is so difficult teaching this boy manners and good behaviour and discipline. I don't know how he is with his teachers . . . That morning when I followed him, he disappeared in the snow. He has good grades at Jarvis Collegiate. Nothing below B-plus. But I don't know if he says 'Good morning' to people older than himself.

"I know that, soon, he will be questioning everything I say to him. This country is like that. Children can talk-up into their parents' face. The Law gives them that right. The more time he spends in the Park, the more he disobeys me.

"I see him, evening after evening, when I am home before him, fading into the matching darkness of the night, hidden in the shade of the maple trees; sitting in a group of men . . . I can see him . . . at least I can see his outline from my front windows . . . and I can even see the way he sits on the Park bench. The bench is made out of cement and tough wood and iron rails for arms.

"And one of these days he will say to me, 'You're not my fucking father! You can't tell me nothing, ho!' Ho? Ho, eh? I'll break your arse first, boy! Call your Mother a ho? That will break my heart . . ."

And that Wednesday in the grocery store, when the rubber wheels did not move smoothly from her cash-out register to the exit door, and she had lost him in the crowd, she stood with her cash drawer open and watched the security guard, and the store detectives, walk up to another cashier and stop beside her; and guide the woman to the back of the store; and she does not remember to close her drawer with all the money in it; and the security guard dressed like a policeman, but without a gun, takes the woman into the little room that has no window, just off the storeroom, where the employees leave their winter boots and their coats; and she could hear, from where she is standing, the heavy bolts slamming when the security guard locks the door; and she imagines how his hands move swiftly over the woman's body, beginning with her chest, then her waist, and down the front of the woman's slacks, which she wore under her dress . . . and Idora walked away, down the aisle, her cash register still open.

She has watched them pass her wrought iron fence, with deep disregard, these immigrants, these foreigners, proud in their dress and in their haughtiness. She felt that they hated her. She has heard that they called people like her "those Negroes."

One of them spoke in an African language. It was only then that Idora knew that the woman was African. Idora has never spoken, never exchanged two words, "Good morning" or "Good night," with an African woman, let alone an African man, although she sees them every day passing, in their robes, in their bright colours, as if they are all going to the Caribana Parade. They pass by, and she looks at them, and comes to no conclusion. It is as if they are figures painted on the street, like a background scene in a play. And she does not understand any of the languages they speak. Her Jamaican friends call themselves Afro-Canadians, or African-Canadians. "You could talk so," she tells them. "You had Marcus Garvey! And he wanted all o' you to go back and populate Africa. Me, now? I am pure Barbadian. I leave it to you, and to the African-Canadians who celebrate Black History Month, to call yourselves Afro-this and Afro-that. Me? As I say, I am pure Barbadian. And that is good-enough for me, darling."

She watched them all the time in this neighbourhood, from behind drawn blinds, walking on the streets; and standing side by side with them, on the Sherbourne bus, and then in the sub-way, going to work. And in the late cold afternoons, like this November, she watched them with young children held by hand, or packed into baby strollers. Some were dressed all in black, from head to toe, with a black shawl wrapped round their face, hiding their identity. Some wore shawls with a slit, a thin line, like a slash of mascara, across their eyes. She wanted to tell Josephine that they looked "like foreigners," but she thought that would sound racist. But to her they looked strange. Like omens. "They look like black spirits."

She said this to herself. No one, except God, would know of her racist sentiments, and accuse her of being prejudiced towards immigrants; towards people from Muslim countries; and towards Africans.

"Leave me a Barbadian," she told Josephine, "and let them be African and Muslim, which they are."

Idora and Josephine had worked together, sorting letters, in the graveyard shift, for one month, during the Christmas rush, at the post office. When they had got their paycheque, Josephine said, "Let's go to the States! Why the hell not?"

"The States?" Idora had replied, surprised. "America? I really don't like America." And then she added, "It's too racist."

"We'll go by Greyhound," Josephine said. "Won't cost much."

"And why the hell not?" she then said, imitating Josephine.

She then became confused: making frantic arrangements in her mind about where to leave BJ. "He could stay with Missis Proposki. He could stay with Pastor James. He could stay by himself in the basement apartment, he is man-enough!

My God, if-only he had a Grandmother living in Toronto!
Only-if Bertram . . ."

She is going to America. By Greyhound bus. For a long weekend.

Idora had a sweet memory of her last visit to Josephine's condominium, when, because there was no game, they could not
watch hockey, and spent the night instead eating potato chips
and drinking Heineken beer, and watching repeats of *As the
World Turns*; and recalling previous weeks' episodes; and mem-
orizing certain portions of the dialogue. She wanted to knit
their friendship with a stronger wool, with a more delightful
and colourful pattern.

    When Josephine told her that night that *As the World Turns*
was also her favourite soap opera, Idora got up from the red
leather loveseat, walked over to Josephine on the matching
leather couch, and put her arms round her, and squeezed her a
little.

    "You too?" Josephine said. "Is that what that's for?"

    That evening, their relationship became a stronger friend-
ship, which had been, until then, a respectful acquaintance. A
happy, relaxed friendship was born. Idora would help Josephine
cook dinner, or lunch, and she would throw her red leather
high-heeled shoes into a corner, as she would do in her own
basement apartment; and they very often sat in the same red
leather loveseat.

    "Why do Canadians call this a loveseat?" she asked Josephine
one evening. The snow came thick past the large picture window that was half the space of one wall, looking south into the
lake. Josephine was opening a bottle of white wine.

"You mean that?" She rested the corkscrew on the counter, took the cork out, got two long-stemmed glasses, flicked her finger against the cup of one of them, listened to the "plinggg," and held them up to the light; and said, "I think it's because we as Canadians believe in love. How does that sound?"

"It sounds like BS," Idora said, "if you'd pardon my French."

"I never thought of it," Josephine said, pouring the wine. "Incidentally," she added, holding her wineglass to the light and twirling it, as if she was looking at an X-ray, or at the negative of a photograph, "do you remember that night?"

"Which night?"

"Try to think of it."

"What do you mean?"

"When we first met."

"When we first met? It was an afternoon . . . on a streetcar."

"No, it wasn't!"

"Wasn't it?"

"It was at night . . . in a dining room . . . Dining Hall . . . and it was cold; dinner had finished. And I was hungry, and . . . are you remembering?"

"Wait! Wait, now!" Idora said, clapping her hands. "You are that girl? I remember now. Hair wet and covered in snow, and shivering . . ."

"Yes! Yes!" Josephine smiled. She got up and sat at the dining table, and tried to imitate herself that night, as she opened the heavy creaking oak door of the College's Dining Hall. And they both laughed out loud, Josephine imitating herself, and then imitating Idora bringing her the tray with food from the kitchen.

They had such noisy, rollicking, laughing times watching television; and Idora sometimes helped Josephine replace her books on the bookshelves, after Josephine had rubbed her eyes red from concentration and study, and placed her spectacles back on her face, her eyes remaining bloodshot; and watching Josephine do this, Idora would have time to admire, and envy, with no animosity, Josephine's tremendous intelligence. Josephine had begun to read poetry to Idora. She wrote a poem to Idora one night, when the snow was like water in the Lake, not far from Josephine's condominium, when the snow was . . .

"Deep as my love for thee,
Deeper than the sweet taste
Of water from Lakes
Going. Stale through loss
Of this my love . . ."

"What are you telling me, girl?" Idora shouted. Shock, shame, anger . . . and love, which she could not define in precise terms, but enough to clear up the misunderstanding, as she thought it was; or the daring demonstration of an emotion that had not been declared . . .

She went to Josephine. There were tears in Josephine's eyes. And in her own eyes too. And they clasped their arms, for comfort, for explanation, for the greater bond, the greater love, the purer love that two women sometimes share, round each other. And, like this, they remained in each other's arms.

Idora was standing in front of the bookcase, running her hands over the titles of the books; from left to right; and when she had absorbed as much as she wanted to, she reached up and started from the topmost shelf, and worked her way down to the floor.

Josephine's condominium was like a library. Most of her books were about what she called Women's Studies, but with the emphasis on Victorian Literature and Modern Literature. Idora remembered her short-lived days as a student at the Erdiston College of Education, back in the Island; and now that she was more comfortable in Josephine's company, she began to behave as if she was in her own library. This love for books, and her admiring Josephine's library, suddenly struck her as being strange; and ironical. The only other reading material in her basement apartment, apart from the Holy Bible, *Hymns Ancient and Modern*, Standard Edition, the Book of Common Prayer, and her textbook on Biology, was *Canadian Woman*, *Dell Horoscope*, *Cosmopolitan*, an old copy of *The Negro Digest*—and an old copy of *Muhammad Speaks*, which the well-dressed black man, with the shaven head, had given her on the sidewalk across from Dundas Square.

"Imagine! Not a damn serious thing to read, other than *Dell Horoscope*. At least I can find what my birth sign tells me about my weight! And *Woman's World* magazine that somebody left on the subway! And I calling myself a woman with schooling? What have I done with my life? Back home, I used to live in the Public Library."

Josephine came and stood beside her. She was drinking her second glass of white wine.

"My books," she said, as a woman would say "My baby." Idora smiled and started to read aloud the titles of books, twelve of them, placed neatly on the top of a radio.

"*Women and Madness. Women and Madness?*"

"That's what it says!"

"Written by a man, I guess!"

"A woman."

"She must be a madwoman, who—"

". . . by Phyllis Chesler . . ."

"*Backlash: The Undeclared War Against American Women*," Idora read, "by Susan Faludi . . . *Literary Women: The Great Writers*, by Ellen Moers . . . George Sand . . . Shelley . . . Dickinson . . ."

"That's a good one," Josephine said.

"*Feminist Theorists* . . . edited by Dale Spender. Dale is a man? Or a woman?"

"Dale . . . Dale . . . Dale . . . Sounds like a man to me. I never checked . . ."

"*Feminist Criticism: Essays on Literary Theory*," Idora read, "edited by Elaine Showalter. Now, that's a woman!"

"That's a woman for ya!" Josephine said, in mock exuberance.

"*Mismatch: The Growing Gulf Between Women and Men* by Andrew Hacker," Idora read, as if she had suddenly become impatient by the titles, and wanted to get it over with, as quickly, as dismissively, as possible. "*Father–Daughter Incest. Father–Daughter Incest?* What? . . . By Judith Lewis Herman. Did you read this?"

"Yes," Josephine said.

"Liked it?"

"No."

"Should I?"

Josephine moved into the bathroom. And when she came back out, she was smoking a cigarette.

"I never seen you smoking before . . ."

"Sometimes I just have to . . ."

"*Women Who Run with the Wolves* by Clarissa Pinkola Estés, Ph.D. . . . *The Ministers Manual* edited by James W. Cox, 1997

Edition . . . *Auto-da-Fé*—is that how you pronounce it?—
Auto-da-Fé, by Elias Canetti, Winner of the 1981 Nobel Prize
for Literature . . . Virginia Woolf, *A Room of One's Own* . . .
and *Virginia Woolf: The Impact of Childhood Sexual Abuse on Her
Life and Work* by Louise DeSalvo . . ."

"Yes," Josephine said. "Yes."

"Yes what?"

"Just yes," Josephine said, with the same lack of emotion.
"Would you mind putting them back in the same order . . .
please?"

And Idora did that.

One Friday night, they watched hockey. Toronto playing
Montreal.

They had just eaten a dinner that Josephine made. She was
not fond of Josephine's cooking. Not enough salt; too little pepper. The carrots were hard; and a little raw—meant for women
concerned with health, on health kicks; on vegetarian diets,
who crunch them in their mouths, and demonstrate how good
they are for you. And there was no Island Windmill Hot Pepper
Sauce to give the food flavour. But the hamburgers, from "free-
range" cows "were grain-fed," Josephine said.

She watched Josephine cut into her hamburger. She watched
the blood run out of it. The hamburger was smothered in fried
onions, with tomato ketchup, which slithered, and looked more
like clotted blood than Heinz. And expensive Green Pepper-
corn Mustard from Clovis, France. When Josephine placed the
hamburger in front of Idora, on the plate that had two pheas-
ants and roses engraved on it, she thought she was looking at a
large wound, a life-sore, a piece of somebody's limb, swimming
in blood.

They drank imported beer; and the two of them shouted and laughed and hooted and screamed, while they encouraged Montreal "to beat the shit outta Toranno!"; and they shared their happy favouritism. They ate potato chips, stuffing handfulls of Pringles into their mouths, already full; and some of the chewed-up chips were flying from their mouths as they screamed, and wolfed the chips down.

"Kil-lim! Kil-lim!" they went back to screaming. "Kill the bastards! Kil-lim!"

The score was now three–love . . .

"Kil-lim-kil-lim!" Josephine shrieked. "Fuck! He missed . . ."

It is her first visit to the United States of America. She does not like America. It is too racist. But she is with Josephine, a white woman, her friend, and anything that is racial and racist, "racialistical" to use Josephine's word for it, anything that smacks of "racialisticalism," she is confident that Josephine will handle.

They sit in the middle of the bus, side by side.

"Window seat?" she asks Josephine.

"Yes. But you have it."

Through the window she sees the building behind the bus terminal, and the people on Bay Street, going to work, the late travellers, and taxi drivers, and they all seem as if she is observing them from a distance, through curtains of voile.

She struggles with her bags.

Josephine unbuckles her navy blue backpack, drops it on the floor, takes a large paperback book from it, and then a plastic bag, and adjusts her seat.

"Where are your things?" Idora says.

"In my bag."

"Where're your clothes?"

"I have a sweater, a pair o' jeans, and what I am wearing."

"You are wearing only those in New York?"

"Water?" She takes two large plastic bottles from her back-pack and hands one to Idora. "Want some?"

She unzips the plastic bag and offers Idora the open plastic bag. It contains pieces of raw carrot that look like the heads of spears; and three McIntosh apples, and celery sticks, and a smaller plastic bag that contains two large brown buns. And then, as if she has just remembered something important, Josephine says, "Coffee! I brought two Tim Hortons, extra large, double-double." She takes the two plastic cups from her handbag, and steam is still rising lazily from them, and she puts them in the slot for cups, one on her side, one on Idora's. When she lifts her coffee from the slot, the plastic cup is still hot.

"No, thank you," she says. Josephine is offering her a McIntosh apple. "I'll have one later on," she lies, "when we are on the road."

Josephine adjusts her seat some more. The bus driver makes an announcement, the engine roars, and they are on the road.

Josephine is soon sound asleep. And snoring.

And Idora is left alone to press her face against the cold window, to admire the Gardiner Expressway, which turns into the 401 West, and she sees the roof of a building and then more of the building, and recognizes where she is now. It is the place she went for an appointment once about a rent-controlled government apartment. It all comes back to her: she is dressed in a black dress; her hair is tidy; she had visited the hairdresser the day before; and she has cleaned her fingernails, and has polished them in a mild colour of red; and she sits upright before the supervisor, her back straight; with her hands hidden beneath the supervisor's desk, because she is scared; and the supervisor asks her if she is married—"Yes."—if she has children—"Yes." —and how many children would there be?—"One."—and would this be one or two children?—"One."—a boy or a girl?— "Boy." And the supervisor smiles and tells her that she will have to put her on the city's List of Unfortunate Indigent Single Women; and then the supervisor tells her, "Look, you are a member of a visible minority, and in this office we know that you are exposed to rape and sexual abuse . . . our statistics verify that profile of women like you . . . there're cases on file of physical abuse that you suffer, and this happens when the surrogate father, or the boyfriend, turns up, if you know what I mean . . ." And Idora sits there in front of the huge polished desk, in which she sees her face, before this woman who tries to hide the fact that she is chewing gum during the interview; and she starts to cry, and tries to hide it, as the woman in a brown dress with long sleeves says, ". . . and all these things are recorded in official documents, in City Hall, in police statements . . ."; and Idora imagines that they are marked on police blotters, too . . .

Ninety-five percent of the women having interviews or waiting for interviews are black. She looks around her, and concludes that they are all single parents. There are no men.

"Carrot?"

It is Josephine. She shifts her position in her seat and searches in the plastic bag for a spear of raw carrot. Idora takes the blanket from the overhead rack and spreads it over Josephine's legs, and raises it up to her neck.

"Thank you very much, but no."

She lifts her brown paper bag from the pocket in the seat

before her, and opens it, and takes out a plastic bottle large as Josephine's bottle of spring water; and unscrews the cover. Josephine puts her hand on her nostril.

"You can't drink that on the bus!"

The smell of the rum is strong.

"Have a drink, girl, do!"

"Suppose the bus driver . . . or the other passengers . . ."

"He would have to come close-enough to me to kiss me, to know what . . ."

And she pours a drink into a plastic cup and hands it to Josephine. Josephine takes a deep sip, smacks her lips, and smiles. She sits upright in her seat.

The scenes pass by . . . she can hear Josephine snoring . . . and she sees the land crippled in white and winter, and she reads the signs and remembers some of them from the weather reports on television . . . the Escarpment . . . the airport . . . and she tells herself not to remember that night, many years ago, when Bertram arrived at the airport, "pissing-drunk," but she remembers from the weather report Guelph Line; and then the bus turns and she is travelling towards Niagara Falls . . . but it comes to Hamilton, and a sign says HAMILTON MOUN-TAIN . . . and so many years ago, when she had two dates with the West Indian Engineering student, whose X-ray for tuberculosis was mixed up with hers; and that brute comes back in her mind; and she sees his large Afro, and his university blazer, and his fingernails which he bites down to the quick; and how they would bleed! But here is the Mountain, the Hamilton Mountain; and this takes her back to the Ontario Tuberculosis Centre on College Street. She wonders what her life would have been, had the mistake with the X-rays involved

her . . . St. Catharines . . . "Wonder what happened to that
bastard? I hope he graduated! . . . Beamsville! Beamsville?
I know a West Indian who is a teacher who used to live in
Beamsville . . . I think he became a principal . . . Ethan
Mings! Talk about barbecue spareribs in the summer! Not a living soul in Beamsville can touch Ethan's spareribs!" And she
opens her brown paper bag. The odour that rises is stronger
than the smell of her rum punch. Josephine opens her eyes.

Idora hands her a large breaded and baked chicken leg, and
a small plastic container of macaroni and cheese pie; and of
course the plastic cup of rum punch; and so they travel on
towards the vast land of freedom and liberty, with the winter
light blinding their eyes through the large windows; and Idora
repeats the name of every town and cut-off that they come to:
"Niagara Falls on the Canadian side . . . and Buffalo, where
we stopped to pick up people, and WBLK, my God! . . . Glen
Falls . . . Albany coming into sight a few miles more . . .
Highland, Hempstead" . . . wondering if sometimes a bus
driver ever loses his way; hoping the line marking the embank-
ment is part of the road; that the driver knows about driving at
such high speed, on ice; and she, one hand gripping the arm-
rest, praying for the bus driver to reach their destination safely,
with all aboard! . . . and Josephine, with her eyes closed, enjoying the macaroni and cheese pie, and the fried chicken . . .
"Rochester, I've heard about many times" . . . "Schenectady,
New Paltz . . . did he go off course, and is now lost?" "Nanuet,
now!" . . . and Josephine eats three more chicken legs, and
opens her book, and reads for a little while; and then her snoring, light, almost like a mild regret, rises; and Idora continues
to call out the names of towns, and feels small, smaller, travelling along the vast highways, as she drinks one more rum punch.

She pulls the blanket farther up on Josephine, and she closes her eyes, and thinks of New York.

This trip was to be an adventure. The opening up of a new world. And the fact that they were making it three weeks before Christmas, in New York, with all the glitter and the tinsel and the sound of music oozing out of shops and stores and bars, added to their excitement; and as soon as they arrived, they wandered and wondered in joy, as they rambled through the crowded streets. They even found themselves humming Christmas carols played by groups of men and women dressed like Santa Claus and some in Salvation Army uniforms.

All of a sudden, Idora started to think about Bertram. She began to wonder whether she might find him somehow, down here in this crowded city where he went to look for work. But how would she get away from Josephine; and go up from Park Slope to Brooklyn; and when she got there, what would she do; who would she ask to tell her where he lived; and who would know him, or remember having seen him in Brooklyn, from the words in her description of him? And suppose in all the years he had been living here he had changed beyond recognition? Was he even still here?

"But 'that man' just got on a bus one Saturday night," she told Josephine. "And that's the last time I saw Bertram. Five to seven years now. I don't remember exactly when!"

"So long, eh?" Josephine said.

"So long," she told Josephine. "He probably won't recognize me. With all this weight I put on!"

In an exchange of confidences, Josephine was telling her about a man she used to date; and then married, on the spur of a moment, after a night of drinking beer. A policeman. And she told Josephine that she was a married woman.

"Was," Idora said. "He left . . ."

"His name was Brandon," Josephine said. "My Ex."

"Is he dead?" Idora asked.

"He was a cop when I knew him," Josephine said. "That's what I mean."

"And when he stopped being a cop?" Idora said.

"He may still be a cop. For all I know, he may be in Toronto! I think he is. Who knows? Things happen."

Idora could hear the raw animosity in Josephine's voice. And she said, in sympathy, "Yes, things happen."

"Yeah!" Josephine said, with more edge to her voice. "Shit happens!"

"So, you went with a cop," Idora said. "A cop named Brandon."

"He's a cop, all right," Josephine said, "and his name was Brandon."

"Well, tell me about it!"

"I'm going to give you Brandon's story one of these days . . ."

"My father was a cop," Idora said. "Not my real father. The man my Mother married. And then threw him out after eighteen months. But he was like a father to me . . ."

Josephine was the one, she remembered now, who had introduced the idea (and had coached her in it) of how to steal from supermarkets and grocery stores, and international corporations which robbed the poor of all races and countries; the weak and the homeless and the uneducated, especially in the Third World. "Daily and senseless. Ripping them off," Josephine said.

"Ripping off is a revolutionary act," she explained. She ripped off bookstores, clothes, food in cafeterias, everything she could put her hands on. Idora remembered how Josephine bragged about her revolutionary acts, which is what she called them, and she remembered too how Josephine had held the cigarette, a non-filter French Gauloises, that she used to go to Montreal by bus, on weekends, to buy; and how the Gauloises dangled from the left side of her mouth; and how she had closed her left eye against the sting of the smoke; and how, after each pull on the cigarette, she exploded into a coughing that seemed to tear out her guts; and how she had said, "Politically, I am a revolutionary intellectual. It is my moral right, my religious duty, to rip off these fucking American corporations, that exploit the poor of the world. Especially the international corporations. It is the duty of international socialists, and the Women's Liberation Movement, to do so."

"I hope you are not trying to turn me into one o' them, girl!" she told Josephine; and then laughed.

She had remained unconcerned about the international corporations, and was less than fervent about the Women's Liberation Movement, and as for stealing food from grocery stores . . . ! "What would my Mother, Miss Iris Morrison, hundreds of miles from Canada, say? And what would she do, if she heard?" Radio and television and newspapers, and word of mouth, letters and long-distance telephone calls, and the gossip of her community, her community of West Indians, were themselves international corporations in the way they used communications. "It would cause my Mother to commit suicide." But it was true that Idora hated the uniforms of security guards because they made them look like real cops, with guns; guards who stood, holding their nightsticks, as if they were holding automatic guns, aimed to shoot black people, automatically assuming they were thieves and criminals. In her imagination she saw their nightsticks turn into huge penises, to screw the women and girls of visible minorities. She hated even to look at security guards. They made her think of more newspaper clippings and photographs of the sixties, and the Civil Rights Movement in Birmingham and Atlanta, Newark and New York. And Detroit, just across the river. Pictures of that bastard Governor George Wallace, and a Mr. Faubus, who was either a governor himself or a sheriff. And this made her think of that clipping she has on her fridge, showing the handsome head of Mr. Albert Johnson, from Jamaica, which was blown to smithereens, with his brains exploding. Blam! One shot. And that made her think of the roar of the cold water bursting from fire hydrants, pouring out in torrents.

"One of these days," Idora said, "you must explain this relationship. Brandon talks to you about these things, doesn't he? You must know a lot about policemen. You must have a lot of stories. I am sure that policemen talk to one another. And to their wives."

"We weren't together that long!"

"But long enough, though, eh?" Idora said. And she caught herself, and realized she was being unreasonable. "I can understand how you would feel, not wanting to talk about it."

"I can talk about it!" Josephine said. "I can talk about it!" She was angry. "I can talk about it! I can fucking-talk-about-it! You want to hear me talk about it? You want to hear? How they beat up people? Especially coloured men? You want to hear the details?"

"I understand it is hard for you to talk to me about these things."

"Because you are black? And I am white?"

"Because you are white."

"Oh, I see! After we've come all this distance on a goddamn bus to New York, you are now—"

"I don't mean it that way," Idora said.

"So, how do you mean it?"

She and Josephine had stayed in the same hotel room, to save money. She was overcome by the tallness of the hotel, and by the surrounding landscape of highways and cars; and the colour of the skies, and clouds, overcast and dolorous; and the number of planes, which seemed to come so close to the picture window at which she stood, beside Josephine.

And on the last night in Brooklyn, after they had returned from their walk, and had eaten two hamburgers each, and chips, for dinner; and drunk an entire large bottle of California white wine; she began to think of Bertram again.

"I have a headache," Josephine said, all of a sudden. "Think I'll lie down for a while . . ."

Idora did not answer.

"Why don't you have another drink?" Josephine said. "Or a coffee . . . I'll get up in a while . . ."

"Okay," Idora said. And at that moment her plan to find Bertram took hold of her.

She walks to the escalator and goes down to the front lobby. She stands outside the hotel, in the cool night, under the hotel canopy, watching the traffic come and go, with men and women in them, laughing and playing their music loud; and the night is getting cooler, and she is hearing all this laughter and loud music, and she wants to move her body to it, and dance as she waits for a taxi. And she takes her woollen tartan scarf from her neck, and wraps it round her head, as she has seen Muslim women on her street back in Toronto do, hiding their faces; and she clutches the front of her dress. She tells the taxi driver, "Fulton Street, please," and when he asks for a street number, she tells him, "I will know it when we get there"; and he tells her, "Lady, Fulton's a big street"; and she ignores him; and after a while she notices the name on a sign, and she tells him, "Stop here." She gives him a tip of two dollars. She pulls the scarf tighter round her face, exposing only her eyes through the slit in the cloth, and she hugs her waist, tightening the coat round her body. It is colder now. It is crowded and noisy. The street is filled with men and women and children. She walks, as if she has a purpose, businesslike, through the crowd, along the busy sidewalk; and inspects the face of each man coming towards her; and she becomes a little frightened, a little anxious, because not having seen "that man's" face for so many years—ten years? fifteen years?—"Suppose he has changed?" in all that time. "Five to ten years is a prison sentence, a long time!" . . . and she also inspects the backs of men walking ahead of her. And all this time, a car is driving slowly behind her, following her, with its lights turned off. She notices this and walks faster. She catches up to a group of men, and touches the shoulder of one of them. Something in this particular man's walk reminds her of her husband. "Bertram?" The man turns, and moves his eyes up and down her body. He seems to like her body. "Bitch, you selling something? Or you giving it away?" Just then, a voice from the car following her shouts, "Over here!" The car stops, the door opens, and a voice says, "You not safe up here, lady." It is the taxi driver.

On the long way back to the hotel, she sits silent in the back seat, with her eyes closed and her hands placed over them, while her tears seep through her fingers . . .

Idora returned to their room at the hotel, took a shower, and prepared for bed. She brushed her feet. She rubbed the right foot under the sole of her left foot; and then her left foot under the sole of her right foot. When she was a child, back in the Island, she did this every night, to clean the sand and the dust from her soles, accumulated during the day. And she has been doing it every night, in Canada, even though she does not walk barefooted, even in her apartment. She then tucked her woollen pink granny nightgown between her legs, and pulled down the nightgown as far as it would go, covering her bottom, her thighs, down almost to her calves. She was a little self-conscious lying beside Josephine, in this nightgown. It was the first time in her life she had slept in the same bed with a woman.

She began to count sheep. "One . . . two . . . three . . . fourteen . . . fifteen . . ."; and she saw the cow jump over the moon; and ". . . fifty-five . . ."; and then, with no warning, she was deep in sleep; and the next minute, she was wide awake.

Disappointed, and unsatisfied, she got out of bed, using the light coming through the sheer blinds at the windows to guide her. The picture window showed her much of the New Jersey land-scape (Josephine had told her that it was New Jersey), and some of Manhattan, and other parts of Brooklyn. All this lay before her now, a picture of haze, of cold temperature, and of distance.

She opened a door. It was off their room. She wanted to use the bathroom. She stood outside the door. For a moment. Then she closed the door behind her. Before her, in the long distance of the hallway, lay the broadloom, rich in a floral pattern. It stretched yards down the hallway, and stopped at a sign that said EXIT, in four red letters. And was illuminated, like a name on a store. The letters were bright. But they were not flickering. She turned, to the left. And then to the right. She then knew that something was wrong. She wanted badly, now, to pass water. The lights above the numbers on the rooms were dull—were they dimmed because it was past midnight? or because of her eyesight?—and showed her that she was not where she thought she was. She was not in her basement apartment, going to her bathroom to pass water. She stopped. She noted the numbers on the four doors she had walked past. She had forgotten the number of her room. She was in terror. Was the door locked by itself, when she closed it? Automatically? The red EXIT sign glowered in the distance, down the broadloom carpet. It was the brightest of the EXITs. The only sign she could read. She tested the doorknob of Room 3030. Then she tested Room 3032. Both were locked. She turned around. And she walked back on the other side of the hallway. She tested Room 3029. Her heart leapt into her mouth. The room was locked. How many rooms had she passed to reach this door? She was standing under the EXIT sign. And then she placed her hand on the doorknob of Room 3027. At that moment the elevator gave off a ring, telling her somebody was arriving. She stood in fear, wondering . . . She waited. She heard the elevator door open. She waited. She was naked. She realized it for the first time. No one came out. The elevator gave off another ring, and continued its rise. She touched the door of Room 3027 again. The door opened to the soft, lowered light inside the room; and to the peaceful, regular, subdued noise of Josephine's snoring; and the skies through the picture windows were awake; and she could see Manhattan in the distance; and she imagined she could see Toronto and Canada; and the tall buildings surrounding her; and this gave her comfort. Everything was like a miracle.

She picked her woollen grandmother nightgown up from the cold tiled bathroom floor, where she had dropped it to take a shower, minutes earlier . . . in the dream? Or had she actually undressed? She put the nightgown back on. And got into bed. She lay beside Josephine. In the narrow single bed. Now it had become suddenly too small for their two bodies. Her stomach was touching Josephine's bottom. "But suppose somebody had come out of the elevator? . . . My God! . . . And suppose it was a man . . . or even a woman . . . ?"; and she got up, and made her bed on the couch; and soon sleep overwhelmed her . . .

FRIDAY

"Blang! . . . blang! . . . buh-lang! . . . blang! Blang! . . . blang! . . . buh-lang! . . . blang! Blang! . . . blang! . . . buh-lang! . . . blang! Blang! . . ."

The bells are now serenading her, lulling her, in thirteen lighthearted strokes, as if laying down the foundation of their sounds, and then taking up the theme and carrying it in another direction; and she does not mind the repetition of the thirteen strokes. The music of the bells is drawn out into another phrasing; and the music becomes as if it is a warning that she is climbing towards some expectation. And then the tolling becomes more sonorous and deep; and changes to "Bang! . . . Bang! . . . Bang! . . . Bang!" striking off the time. She convinces herself she is able to recognize the tune the bells are playing. It is now a lullaby. Yesterday, she had heard the bells striking like a metronome keeping time.

These are strong strokes. Like blows delivered to a fragile body; or a solid lash from a bamboo whip; that lands with a snapping sound upon a man's back that is covered in sweat, just like the single file of men tied at the wrists who walked through her dream, two nights ago.

"Blang! . . . blang! . . . buh-lang! . . . blang! Blang! . . .
blang! . . . buh-lang! blang! Blang! . . . blang! . . . buh-
lang . . . blang! Blang! . . . blang! . . . buh-lang! . . .
blang! . . ."

"So, you are afraid," she says, as if she is talking to the pad of
writing paper. "So, you are afraid," she says, not moving the
fountain pen to make the first word, "afraid that I cannot face
your absence in regards of my yearning for affection, in my
loneliness . . . in your absence." She stops, tries to remember what she has written in her mind, and realizes that she is
repeating herself. She mentally erases the last three words.
"In Brooklyn that time, with Josephine, if I was to be asked
why I took the taxi that cold night in December, to be truthful,
I can't give you a reason. I wanted to see you, and I didn't want
to see you. If I was a woman who walks with a gun, I would have
shot you when I saw you. If I saw you. And then, in a next mind,
I would not have harmed you. For, as I say, 'God don't like
ugly! God don't like ugly, boy!'

"Your absence gives me a more powerful sensation than
your presence.

"As I said before, I was working two jobs, sometimes three,
just to see how fast that bank account would . . . as if it was like
a woman with child . . . would climb and climb like a pregnant
woman's belly. Climbing for me and for you. And little BJ . . .

"But I am dreaming. Was. I am still dreaming. I am living in
a land of foolish dreams."

Her rage devours her. It makes her think of how she imagined stripping the policeman's gun from his holster. The reliving of this fantasy makes her body react, and she shakes
in anger.

She makes a promise that when next she is with Josephine, she will tell her about the night she sneaked out in the taxi; she will tell her about her son; and about "that man," that she too had had a husband who turned out sour, bad; and she will tell her that she is glad for their friendship. And she will have to tell her that her son, BJ, does not like white people; and she will tell Josephine that she did not bring him up to hate white people; and she will have to tell Josephine that he turned out this way after he joined that gang of boys who stand in the Park all hours of the night, in all seasons, wearing black baggy clothes and head-protecting hoodies to keep out the cold, to keep out the wind, to keep out prying eyes, hiding in the darkness of the Park.

Her anger surges again, and she wonders why she must confess all this to Josephine. And she purges her mind of these considerations, as if she is ripping up the pages of the letter she had mentally composed, and wipes away all trace.

Instead, she decides that she will depend more upon her Bible; reading it first thing in the morning, and last thing at night. It will keep her mind off carnal thoughts. She knows she must accept Josephine's friendship and enjoy it, as she enjoys watching hockey with her; drinking Heineken beer and eating Pringles potato chips; and not say another word about her son; and "that man." She feels sad. She pours herself a strong Jamaica-white-rum-and-Diet-Coke; and takes a sip. "I should start watching my weight! All this white-rum-and-Diet-Coke, with all this carbon in it! . . . must be the cause of my sadness."

Idora knew the embarrassment she would face if she met her son on the street.

She feels she will have to dodge him to save herself the embarrassment of meeting him on Yonge Street, or in Dundas

Square, or somewhere in the Eaton Centre, with his white "do-rag" tied tight round his head, and underneath the do-rag a white baseball cap with *Blue Jays* written on it; and his trousers falling off his backside, making his backside look flat, and exposing the white elastic in the waist of his white Jockeys . . . in full view of the street . . .

She would run and pretend she didn't know him . . .

". . . and wearing his cap with the peak backwards, as if he is a gangster, for the whole street to see."

Josephine was her best friend in the world, she would swear to that, never mind Josephine was always talking about dead things and dead people, about the Victorians in Victorian Literature, which Idora always confused with the Moderns in English Literature. Victoria was her "favourite Monarch" who ruled over England and over the Colonies, Dominions, Territories and India, beyond the seas, and who made certain that the sun, the same sun which set every evening at six in the Island, never set on the British Empire. And she regarded every British writer, including Virginia Woolf, Shakespeare and Dickens and John Milton, to be Victorians. She had endowed the Victorians with everything that was good, and of good report, since she had read this somewhere in one of Josephine's books.

But there was, as she had come to confess just a few days before, a certain sadness that tinged her relationship with Josephine. The fact she had gone out with a cop; and BJ was beginning to say things about Canadian people that sounded racist to her. She kept his sentiments to herself, and this burden added to the hurtfulness of his words.

"My English teacher," BJ told her, "is the main one."

And she took that to mean he disliked all Canadian people.

"White people? To be exact?"

He did not answer her.

His racial attitude saddened her. And he told her, "It's in the Bible. The thing about the same tribe living together. And different tribes living together. Like all Mormons living together with all Mormons. Jews with Jews. I read it in the Bible," he told her, "in your Bible. And in Africa, like the Kikuyus living in their own tribes, and other tribes and so forth . . ."

"These blasted views are written in the Bible? In my Bible, you say?" she shouted. "In my Bible?" She became very angry, and ashamed, wondering how Josephine would feel, wondering when the time would come when he would voice these sentiments to her. "How would my friend feel?"

She had had this short conversation with him before he had converted to Islam.

"But I still don't know which Bible you are talking about? Or whose Bible?"

On this Friday morning, she turns her body over, with some effort, and is lying on her stomach, with her arms outstretched, as if she is on the Cross. Her breasts are flat against the white comforter. She imagines that she can see her blood coursing through her veins and other parts of her body, through muscles and ventricles and whatever is the proper name for tubes through which her blood flows; and she knows through feeling and through instinct that her right breast is more tender and sensitive than her left breast.

She wants to find the proper words in which to clothe her prayers: words to convey her sincerity and show a better understanding and control over her prayers; she wants the words to cleanse the bad taste from her thoughts that were left by the

dream of the one-armed men. She is seeking words that will
change the gnawing, nagging anxieties that persist. She wants
to find words that can raise her, in body and soul, from these
black days, from this basement apartment, Thursday, when it
started; and now today, Friday. She plans to continue her vigil
for the next two days as well. Four simple days. Four simple
days which she has come to feel are her days of atonement. She
is a woman walking in a desert of narrow lanes, over bramble
and broken glass, with jagged stones cutting red, thick marks
into her feet.

In her bedroom, her eyes pick out a colour photograph. It is
standing amongst bottles and vials and cosmetic jars; incongru-
ously close to her Bible, beside which is the Book of Common
Prayer, which she has forgotten to return. It is therefore "still
borrowed" from the shelf in the back of the seat where she sat,
two Sundays ago in the Cathedral.

The photograph stands out from the others. It sits, in its rectangular, shining, fake gold frame, like a statue. In the photograph,
a man is standing beside a small boy, in front of a snowbank.
The snowbank is in front of a store which has KENTUCKY
FRIED CHICKEN written in lights along the entire front of
the building. Both the figures in the photograph are dressed
in very dark brown clothes. It is early December. White and
deep in snow; and cold. The man wears a short, dark brown
leather jacket. The boy is wearing a snowsuit of the same dark
brown colour as the man's leather jacket. In this outfit, the two
of them look like Eskimos, zippered up to their ears, covered
with dark brown mufflers, wearing brown oversized gloves and
large, dark brown woollen caps strapped under their necks;
and brown woollen scarves. Their complexions are identical.

When this photograph was taken, on that cold December morning, Santa Claus, in his annual parade along the main streets in Toronto, Bloor Street and Yonge Street, joined in by T. Eaton Co., the largest department store in the whole of Canada, had just crawled past them.

The man and the boy had been standing in front of the KFC store for one hour now: shivering, stomping one foot and then the other on the pounded white snow, as if they are both small boys wanting to "go pee-pee." The photograph catches the boy waving at Santa Claus. He is looking in the wrong direction, however. Santa Claus has already passed by. The man beside him is not waving. He is not smiling.

As she lies on her back, her body still in the shape of a cross, looking at this photograph, this tableau, she remembers every one of the years following the morning it had been snapped; and she remembers that Santa Claus did not wave back to the little boy; and that it was at that moment, after she had pressed the red button that closed the shutter of the Kodak box camera, with a click, that the little boy started to cry. And that the man in the picture beside him had said, "Shut your blasted mouth, boy, and stop embarrassing me in front these white people."

The man is her husband. Bertram. The small boy is her son. BJ.

They did not, ever again, watch the Santa Claus Parade.

She gets down now, on her knees, beside the bed. There is a smell on the white cotton sheets. She places her nostrils to the sheets and inhales, and immediately gives up. There is a smell. She does not know the smell. She tries to concentrate on her praying. And it takes a long time for the first words of communion with God to come to her.

"I can't succeed with you, this morning," she finally admits. "I can't reach you this morning, at all, Father-God."

She gets up, rubs her knees to bring back the circulation into them, adjusts her pink woollen nightgown from sticking to her body, passes her hands over her hips; smiles to herself, at the shape of them; and still makes a mental note to eat less heavy, greasy food, so late at night, and then go to bed almost immediately afterwards; and finally she touches her breasts, lovely and heavy, and resting on her chest in majestic lure and shape; and immediately thinks of cancer.

"Cancer?" she says defiantly, daring it. "What you telling me?"

Her index finger and her thumb touch her right breast, for lumps; and as her index finger and thumb touch her left breast, squeezing that too, for lumps, not knowing if she was really safe, she makes a promise, for the third time that week, to take up the appointment Josephine had made for her to get a breast examination.

"Father-God, another day. Another cold day. Another dollar, as Canadians say. And just as cold."

She walks through the cold hallway of her apartment, the twelve paces that it takes from her bed to the bathroom, and sits on the porcelain pink toilet seat, and immediately she can feel the cold draft, colder than the air coming through the ill-fitting two front windows, clutch at her legs.

"Pardon," she says. She has just passed gas. She says "Pardon" whenever she passes gas, whether in private or in public . . .

She looks up at the colour print of a man with a red beard, hanging from a nail over the wash basin. The beard has two points at its end. Strong, piercing eyes, a thin face and a sallow complexion, with the strong expression of a hypnotist in his brown eyes, which, after all these years, still makes her uncomfortable to look directly into this man's face, when she is sitting on the toilet. The man's heart is painted onto the white robe he is wearing. The man's heart is bare. And it is painted in sharp outline. Red as blood. Something like a diadem, or a crown, but made from two branches of a tree that are thick and plaited, with thorns or needles that stick into the man's head and bring forth large drops of blood from the man's skull.

She wonders if these branches have come from a sycamore tree . . . like the ones she grew up seeing in the Island . . .

Whenever she looks at this picture of Jesus Christ, she remembers the pain from the needles of a poisonous black cobbler, cousin to the edible, delicious sea egg, that pierced the heel of her foot that she accidentally walked on once on the beach in the Island. The pain from the cobbler in the soft, thick skin of her heel reminded her of the early pains of childbirth.

It is to this man's face that Idora now raises her head, with her eyes closed, as she passes water. The water hits the bowl in loud squirts, which turn deep blue from Sanibol Automatic Toilet Bowl Cleanser, high as a tenor voice, gurgling and laughing. As a little girl climbing Bishop's Court Hill in the humid afternoons, a pair of mules walked ahead of her, hauling a huge cart packed with brown hemp bags filled with brown sugar, white bags of flour, and other groceries, salt fish and lard oil, climbing the hill with her in the still-hot sun, and she remembered that the sound of the urine from the brace of mules was similar. And she and her girlfriends would laugh, as the urine hissed as it touched the hot tar road. It created a rising mist, and the aroma of strong, fresh urine rose to sting her nostrils, and she and her group of schoolgirl friends would cover their faces with white handkerchiefs, that were embroidered with red roses in two corners; and turn their faces away from the stinging, fumigating smells. And then they would break out in giggles.

It seems as if Jesus's body is coming alive; his raised hand seems to be moving, conferring some benediction upon her, as she is slouched on the small throne of the toilet bowl; and it looks also as if he is saluting her, personally, with two fingers, shaped in the salute of a Boy Scout. It is her unseeing understanding of this gesture of comfort that causes her to say, "Thank you."

"Going to work, the other day, I am holding on to the metal bar in the subway coach, standing over a woman who had just asked a teenager, a girl wearing a school uniform, sitting beside her, 'to please take your boots off the seat, if you don't mind. I am sorry to have to ask you to . . .'

"The snow on her boots was melting. The student put her other foot on the seat . . . and then this student tells the woman, 'And fuck you, bitch! You're not my fucking muvver!' And the other passengers hear the girl. And they hold their heads down. Some were looking into their newspapers. Some were reading their paperback books. Some placed their hands with knitted fingers in their laps. And the girl in the school uniform says, 'You're not my fucking muvver.' For the second time. And the woman turned redder in her face. She looked as if she had put too much strawberry powder on her face; and meanwhile, still the passengers remained silent, for the next two stations, until the girl pulled her feet from the seat and dropped them on the floor, and dropped her winter boots on the floor

too. The snow on them flew off. And the passengers remained
silent. And the girl's footprints formed by the sludge and the
snow on them remained on the leather seat. The schoolgirl
stood up. She came to her stop. Bay. She adjusted her backpack.
And she walked to the door. Just before she stepped onto the
platform, she turned around. She then raised the middle finger
of her left hand. She made it look like a small prick. She thrust
it, with so much violence, into the air, like a symbol, right into
the woman's face, as if she wanted the woman to feel it, to physically feel it, as if it was being pushed up the woman's arse; or her
other private parts . . . that I shed tears, for her . . .

"The subway door closed behind the little girl. She was
still thrusting her finger in the air. She was talking and walking
backwards. At the same time. On the platform. Thrusting the
middle finger on her left hand in the air.

"And then the passengers in the coach immediately began to
talk, amongst themselves, saying what they should have done,
if . . . and what they would have done, if . . .

"And the lady who had spoken to the girl broke down in
tears . . ."

"The subway train I transferred to was less crowded; and it
was warmer inside the station; and my two feet were tingling,
as they were beginning to thaw out; and I could feel my blood
coursing through my feet and my entire body, rising through
my legs and thighs and waist and breasts, leaving me warm,
and tense as I sat there all by myself; and I started looking at
the other passengers; and I smiled, pretending, as my son, BJ,
would say, 'to be cool'; but not one person smiled back at
me; and this made me feel that I wasn't so cool, and caused me

to think, 'Did I pass the Accent under my two armpits, this morning?'

"I tried to hold my nose down to sniffle under my two arms. But couldn't.

"Some of the women with whom I had smiled now smiled-back; and this caused me to be even more self-conscious. This made me wonder, 'Why don't I learn to like this place, more?' And then I said to myself, 'How could I leave Toronto? And go where? Follow that blasted man, to America?'"

She took the letter from Bertram out of her handbag, an old one, where she had placed it. She had pinned a common pin as a marker at the end of a sentence. She began now to read the same sentence aloud, to herself: "Me and you was never the kind of husband and wife to talk about sex in the open as I hear men here in Amerrica do, in barber shops, in the liquor store, and at the races which I go now and then but not too often. Everything here in Amerrica is sex. Out in the open and as a consequence I find myself thinking about nothing else, wondering if in my former life with you I was man-enough to sat-isfize you. A fellow tell me about a book I should read called *The Joys of Having Sex*, if I remember the name right. I know you never read this book and if you ever did you must have hide it from me. That is a joke I making, but I have not read *The Joys of Having Sex* myself, in case it have in things and pictures showing me those things namely masterbaiting and so on and so forth. I can only mention these things since I am doing it from afar. I am here and you there and I do not have to face my shame, or embarrass you. Sometimes and in particular at night in the room that I am renting I gets some funny thoughts entering my head and I only telling you these things now to tell you that I is a man who spends his time looking for a permanant job and when not on that mission I spends my time watching horse racing on television as I do not have the money to go to the track itself as often as I would like since cash is a . . ."

A woman who had just boarded the subway stood for a moment, deciding whether to sit beside Idora; and when the woman did, shuffling her petite body wrapped in a large black winter coat that had no arms, that looked like a soldier's great cape, and sat down beside her, Idora became embarrassed. She was sure that the woman had already read part of the letter, as she was deciding whether to sit beside her or stand. "And to imagine that this complete stranger had read his words, so personal, so new, and so unsettling . . ."

So Idora folded the page in half, and concealed the secrets of "that bastard's" sexual confusion; and tightened her hand into a fist; and waited for the train to move. She gripped the folded pages with such passion and force that her hand started to hurt.

"Cold-enough-for-ya?"

It took her a while to realize that the woman was speaking to her.

"Cold-enough-for-ya?" the woman said, again.

"Oh, no!" she told the woman.

"Where're you from?"

"This cold doesn't bother me at all!" Idora told her. "I am from here."

"You don't talk like a Negro-Canadian!" the woman said, in a pleasant voice. "But where're you from before that?"

"I like the cold!" Idora told her. "I was born here."

"I know," the woman said, in a pleasant voice. "But where're you really from, before that?"

"I was born here."

The woman smiled. After a while the smile disappeared. The woman then took a thick paperback book out of her handbag, cracked the pages down the spine, found her spot, and instantly was absorbed in it.

Idora's feet were warm now. And she stretched her legs out to their full extent. The subway train was rounding a corner, and Idora's shoulder touched the woman's.

"Sorry," she told the woman.

"You're welcome," said the woman.

". . . that would result in a orgassim as a consequence to make me come . . ."

She paused. She could sense the woman's eyes on her letter.

The subway coach became warm, and it invigorated her, and made her feel like she was lying in the sun, back in the Island; and her skin was being touched by the rays of the five o'clock morning sun; and she was in the sea water, in some kind of a trance; and she could taste the salt in the mouthful of sea water she had swallowed by accident . . . When she looked up, the woman who had been sitting beside her, reading *The Stand*, by Stephen King, was no longer sitting beside her.

"The train is travelling fast now. It is crossing a bridge; and I can see glimpses of sky, and it looks blue as sea water; but the trees are white, branch and trunk and a few leaves, at this time of the year in Toronto; but back in the Island, the trees are tall, some of them; and majestic; and are royal coconut palms and sea-grape trees, and they surround the beach where I am bathing, in my imagination; bathing and rollicking in the waves, and shouting and screaming with complete abandon and enjoyment. And without warning, the trees turn white again, and the skies are dark grey; and I am back in Toronto."

"The train crosses a bridge. I glance up at the route map to check the station I have to get off at. Yonge Street. One stop west from Sherbourne, where I must get off. The next time the subway train stops, I read BROADVIEW, printed on the cement wall of the station. YONGE, my stop, has not yet come up; and I am getting a little anxious, and start to feel lost, and feel I am alone in the entire subway train; alone in Toronto on this cold morning, like how I would sometimes find myself alone in the wide sea; so I look again at the route map.

"My anxiety is growing. I am now heading East. I feel I am in the suburbs. I have no idea how many stations I already missed; don't always see their names on the walls of the stations, as I am going headlong on the speeding train, sitting backwards, going into the suburbs, in the wrong direction."

She pushes the four yellow pages of the letter deep into her handbag, and feels the hard spine of her textbook. And this touch increases her anxiety, agitates her, lost as she is now, on this subway train; lost and without roots, without anchor; too embarrassed to admit that she is lost; too ashamed to ask for assistance.

How can she confess that she is lost? A big woman like her? Conspicuous amongst so many white people? To one of these strangers? Ask for directions? And expose herself as an immigrant, a visible minority, a Jamaican, even though she is not from Jamaica?

"Such a long time . . . Twenty years now? Twenty-five or twenty years," she figured. "Twenty!" she says to herself, shortening the thirty years, this time spent here. This time she is careful to keep her voice low. "Eighteen, or nineteen? Could be twenty-five . . . Thirty." Why is she having such difficulty remembering the number of years she has been living in Toronto? Any one of these men and women holding on to the metal poles in this subway coach with her, if they had to answer the question "How long you're here?" would, in the snap of a second, know the answer . . . and would blurt it out, "From birth, eighteen years ago. I am born here!" And now, on this cold morning, travelling without direction, the train suddenly slows down to enter the next station . . . GREENWOOD.

"Greenwood?" The word comes out a little too loud. People look at her. "Is this the same Greenwood? A name that I know? And hate? As much as I hate 'that bastard'! My God, this is the very place where they race racehorses!

"The anger at 'that man' from the last twenty-five years . . . fifteen, or so in Canada, five in America . . . comes back into my body. It washes over me, completely, and drains all life from me, just as the salt sea water of the waves back in the Island washes my body, but with cleansing effect, and puts me into a state of retirement, and calmness, incapable of acting or of resisting—like a purgative.

"The sight of GREENWOOD brings back his words as though from the grave: for I had buried him now, and have stomped on his grave."

"And I did-know," she recalls "that man" telling her, that Saturday night, around seven o'clock, "I did-know it was the last fifty dollars I had in my pocket and I did-know it was the last penny to my name that I had in my hand, the last fifty dollars. But I say to myself . . ."

She could picture him standing in front of the man selling him the ticket; and she could also picture the postman knocking on her front door, with the letter in his hand. She hated postmen; as much as she hated police who pull guns on young black men; and her hatred mixed with her anxiety that the letter in the postman's hand was bearing the bad tidings of a summons, a notice from the Small Claims Court. For the unpaid electricity bill. She opened the door, and the postman placed the letter in her right hand, just like a quarterback slams the ball into the hands of his running back. "Good morning!" he said; turned; and went back up the steps. It was a letter from City-Wide Collection Agency Incorporated, informing her that they will be suing her for the late payment on her furniture. The payment was six months late. And it was from that day on that she picked up the letters left through the letterbox, and placed them in a neat heap, and put a weight on them, and looked at them, every evening after work, and every morning after she had said her prayers; and had made the sandwich for BJ's lunch and placed a five-dollar bill between the folded brown paper bag, that previously contained her bottle of Jamaica white rum from the LCBO, and a paper napkin, in a plastic bag with a zip lock on it; and left it on the dining table; and including in her morning devotions a word for help (praying, when she remembered, "for help, Lord! Help to help me pay these blasted bills!"); and left them unread; and unpaid. The hydro. Furniture. Bell Telephone. Rogers Cable. The Bay, for the colour television bought on account two years ago. And her two credit cards, Visa and Master-Card. These unopened letters from her creditors gathered and became taller than the pile of letters she had written, over time, to her husband in America, and did not post because he had forgotten, in all that time, to write a return address on his letters.

"We owe the Hydro. We owe fifty dollars for the Lectricity," he had said. "We owe a payment on the couch that you buy. Plus a hundred-and-something dollars in back-rent. I did-know all these things and I faced those realities 'cause I am not so careless or thoughtless not to know the realities of my financial obligations but suppose, as I say to myself, suppose I get lucky 'cause I had to look at the other side, too! Suppose. Just suppose. Just suppose I did-catch the horse that went off at five-to-one odds! That bet could have saved we . . . if-only the horse had-win. Only-if-the-kiss-me-arse horse had-win.

"Fifty dollars on the nose! Multiply that, by twelve! You know how much money that would be?"

"That man" back then had chosen Sundays, not out of disrespect for the Church or jealousy of the Pastor, but out of his unquenchable thirst for racehorses. He would be restless from the Thursday night preceding the Friday, which was his favourite day at the races, checking the favourites in the *Racing Form*, scribbling in the margins his notes to himself; and he would get up early on the Friday, and take a leisurely shower; singing at the top of his voice, discordant over the lyrics of a calypso, or a blues number, and also finishing with a few scatting choruses of John Coltrane's "A Love Supreme," now that he was introduced to jazz by his Jamaican friend, who took him, sometimes after the races, to the Montreal Bistro on Sherbourne Street. He would shave, and brush his brown leather shoes for the third time; and check the seams in his trousers, tie and untie his tie with the paisley pattern until he got the correct length, and lastly, use a clothes brush on his blue blazer, which was single-breasted, with the coat of arms of the motor mechanic's shop at which he was apprenticed. He wore this proudly. His Jamaican friend would ask him, almost each time they met at Greenwood, "Hey, bwoy! Is Oxford you went?" And they would laugh. And fall into their routine, careful and unchanging, more like the rites of superstition: go to the men's bathroom; wash his face and his hands; refold his white handkerchief; buy a beer, and drink it standing up, as he went over, with his friend beside him, his selections of horses for the day. He never bet on the first race. He would take the first of three hamburgers after the third race. And he always carried a twenty-dollar bill, hidden in a pocket of his wallet, in case he lost all his betting money. And he had strict "rules," as he called them: never announce the size of your win; never announce how much money you have put on a horse; and never change your bet because somebody says, "Can't lose! Can't lose!"; and a few more which developed along the way. Bertram did not talk during the running of a race, but bit his lips, the top one and then the bottom one; nervously; and would assist the horse he had picked, saying, "Come on! Come on! . . . Come on!" until the horse passed the finish line.

He took streetcar, subway and bus to get to the track; would slip out to Greenwood to bet, not just two dollars on a horse "to win, place and show," on each race, like a "common racetrack tout," but would place his money, to those standing close to him, as if they were in a circle of brotherhood, to demonstrate his equine expertise. He prayed, silently, that the day would end with a win. "Lemme win a ten-dollar Exactor! Lemme win one! Straight. Or a two-dollar Tri'! Lemme catch a horse going off at twenty-to-one, and bet him on the nose . . ."

"On the fucking nose! . . . On the nose, to-rass! . . . That horse can't lose! Can't lose, mahn!" the Jamaican said, all day, from twelve-thirty, when they arrived, until five o'clock.

Or, that he will win; and he will have enough money for the rent and for the arrears owing Bell Telephone and the Hydro; and Sears; and to Marty Millionaire second-hand furniture store, on Queen Street East and Parliament, for the two upright chairs which she had painted red; and for . . .

"The train is now moving beneath the top of the land. My mood, and the fact that I am now travelling under the earth, makes the fluorescent lights above the advertisements in the car grow dim. I am alone. And the subway car is crowded; passengers are jammed against passengers, men against women. I am sitting on a seat large enough for two more passengers; and I am certain people are damn hesitant to sit down beside me, as if they're scared they will touch me. 'This same situation, two times in one morning.' I say this to myself. 'Nevertheless, I am not really worried about this segregation. It happens all the time. So regular. That I am starting not to notice it.' I cannot see the seat across the aisle from me. There are too many passengers in-between. Most of them seem to know one another. But perhaps this friendliness exists only in my imagination.

"Some are talking. I can't follow their conversations. They are speaking English, but in a dialect that is different from the way I talk, different from mine, and that comes from their own communities, up in the suburbs that I have never been; nor don't know about. Some are laughing. To me, all of them seem so rich, so comfortable and so confident. Privileged. They are dressed in this same privilege. They all seem to know where they are. And where they are going.

"'This train, this train,' I start to hum under my breath, 'this train is bound for Glory, this train!' And then I start thinking of

my Mother. And I say, 'I remember my Mother. My Mother just
came into my mind.' And then I find myself making the Sign of
the Cross; and I say, 'God rest your soul.' The three schoolgirls
look at me, as if they are reading my mind.

"I hardly have any close friends. The number of close friends
I could count on one hand, if I had two fingers cut off—well, it is
not exactly as bad as that! I have Cilla, my Jamaican friend. And
Missis Proposki. And Josephine, of course! But I can walk the
streets of Toronto, Jarvis to Yonge, Yonge to Wellesley, Church
to Front, going to the No Frills, or to Dominion's, to the TD
Bank, to shop at the Dollarama in College Park to buy toilet
paper and Kleenex, or the Eaton's Centre, even walk from my
basement apartment, and go through the back, to the Cathedral
Church, and never-ever meet anyone I know, not one soul, not
one recognized face to say 'Hi' to; or enter a short conversation,
like 'It damn hot, eh?', with; or, a more normal greeting, 'This
damn cold! Brrrrrrr-uh!'—in all the time I living in Toronto!

"No one I know have I ever seen on television. A simple
thing like that. Not last night, not last week, not last year; never.

"The only people like myself, black people like me, who I
see on television are young men, boys BJ's age, whose views,
and character and attitudes the newspapers write about, are in
terms of violence. And from amongst their numbers, they never
write a story about a black boy talking about his success at Jarvis
Collegiate, or his plans for the future . . . becoming a doctor,
or even a teacher! Nothing on television or in the newspapers
ever shows me young black men achieving more. More than
the plight they are in. Or, achieving more than the image that
the same television and the same newspapers type-set these
young black men in. But I see these armies of 'visible violent
minorities,' as the media calls them, and as the Prime Minister

makes new laws and new prisons to confine them in; and I was privileged to overhear private conversations by the pool, and over the pool table; and at dinners down in the Ravines of Toronto, when I was in domestic service. I say it all the time, 'Never do you see a young man BJ's age and complexion—have you ever seen one?—on television, with a book in his hand! My God! Perhaps, with a basketball! But certainly, not with a book!' I say it all the time. And nobody isn't listening to me. Who is me? Yes! But I have seen many of them with a ball in their hands, bouncing it on the sidewalk, making sounds that in a strange way sound like muffled gunshots: pap! pap! pap-pap-pap! pap! pap! Bullets. 'Don't get caught in the crossfire, boy, by mistake! Don't be one of the unlucky ones to be in the wrong place at the wrong time!' As if you have control over that!

"Balls they play basketball with—basketball balls!—banging them against the boards, and on the cold pavement. Football balls, too; but thrown in the Park. Baseball balls, in the summer, thinking about the Blue Jays. Balls and more balls! But I have never had a conversation with any of these young men, on the street, bouncing balls . . ."

"Even those three black young men, shackled by the policemen of the Special Tactical Squad in the Park, last summer. The policemen were dressed as if they were going to Afghanistan to fight, in bulletproof vests, helmets that reminded me of astronauts, or racing-car drivers, or Nazzie soldiers in the Second World War; yes, all the faces on television are of men and women who do not have my black complexion; and when I do catch a glimpse of their black skin, they are in paddy wagons, looking through the chicken wire and the grilles like monkeys in coconut trees . . . travelling backwards from me . . . or shading their features, shielding their identities and their faces, from beneath 'hoodies' or a policeman's jacket that the policeman, outta pity, lend them to hide their faces with . . . the same police who just arrested them . . . thrown over their heads to hide their identity from me, a woman, a woman who could be their mother. And I ask myself, 'Where are the blasted men to protect us: mother and child? Where any o' those men is?'"

"But they look like my son, BJ. Now, alias Rashan Rashanan—if you please!"

"The pounding of my heart, in its irregular beat, slammed me into thinking about Rashan Rashanan.

"Where are you, boy? Where could you be? You are breaking your Mother's heart. But I will never, nevertheless, go to the Division in this neighbourhood, to report you missing. Not if I have any pride!

"That telephone ringing nineteen times—nineteen times!—could have been from the Division, calling me to report something about BJ. But won't you, as a mother—even as a distant-cousin—hesitate to contact the police?

"Back home, the police like the schoolteacher, we were brought up to co-operate with. They were like our parents. We knew them. They lived with us in the same village. One could be our first-cousin. The next, our second-cousin. At any rate, we were related. And we worshipped at the same church! Back home. But here, in Canada, which I love—the money is good when you get it—but it still isn't home. And the police sure-don't make me feel it is home.

"So, I can't see myself voluntarily going down Shuter to the Division, and pour out my heart to a police, strange as it seems, strange as it is for someone not black to understand. Even if it involve my own flesh and blood. You think you can understand what I mean? You think you have the understanding to see what I'm saying? I won't blame you if you don't . . ."

The train jerks slightly, and she loses her balance; and when it settles down, travelling as if on rubber rails, she looks across the aisle at three young men. She knows, from instinct, that she has passed her stop. When the train stops at the next station, it says BATHURST. She is lost; but not really lost. The three young men are no older than her son, BJ. They are holding on to the pole, talking. She is holding on to the vertical pole, not far from them, but within earshot, more or less . . .

She tries to listen to their conversation. They lower their voices. And she pretends she is not listening. And they start again, joking with one another: giving high-five slaps of the hand; touching the knuckles of folded right fists; bending over; and jiving. She knows this kind of skylarking: she has watched BJ in the Park, many times from her basement windows. But there is something serious, almost sinister, about these boys, as she calls them, that alarms her and makes her uncomfortable.

She feels frightened by them. Their character and their behaviour are already presented to her as truth, in the images the newspapers paint them in; and although she knows in her guts that she cannot trust the newspapers, still something about the way these three boys reflect the assumptions made by the media about young black men makes her pose the question: "But suppose, just suppose, the newspapers are right?" And she feels more sad than fearful, that a big woman like her, old enough to be their mother, or grandmother, is, in broad daylight, on a crowded subway train in this city, scared of three damn inner-city black kids! "What is Toronto coming to? What are we coming to?

"There's something about these three, though! . . . Something . . ." These three young men look so young. One looks like a child. Thirteen or fifteen. If that.

The subway train stops before it actually reaches the next station. She wonders if someone has jumped on the tracks, and taken his own life; if someone has been shot . . . if the power has gone out of the train. And she feels anxious, stuck in the stalled train, so close to these three young black kids, whose conversation she is still trying to listen to, even though they are whispering, and talking in their neighbourhood vernacular.

". . . and the mafucker come up to me, man. In my face? . . . Mafucker fucking with me, man."

"Yeah! Nigger playing he baaaad. He ain' bad."

"Mafucker messing with me, man . . . if you know what I am saying. Dissing me, man!"

"Nigger don't know you carry your piece with you, wherever you go? . . . Come closer. Dig it, brother . . . the sister behind you's digging our rap . . . she be listening . . . check it out . . ."

They glance over at Idora; and then they ignore her; and then they go back to their conversation, glancing occasionally at her. They give one another high-fives, and continue talking.

"Weekend's here, bro! Friday," one says, giving the other two a folded fist, in ritualistic exaggeration. "Yeah." And he laughs a giggle that has no giggle in it. "We don't have to do shit in class, today. That's why I like Central Tech. The Tech be the coolest high school in the city to hang out in . . . chill like a mafucker . . . see what I'm saying . . . ?"

"And to deal." And they all laugh at this. "Don't have to do a fuck in school, today, if you see where I am coming from."

"Yeah . . . I see where you're coming from, bro-therrr."

"You should've deal with that nigger, a week ago, when we had him, you say you was gonna—"

"Chill, lil brother."

The third teenager laughs. There is a dangerous sneer on his lips. "Nigger in your face, and shit like that . . . playing he baad . . . and you ain't off the mafucker! I wouldda off the fucker, there and then! But, ain't that a bitch! We ease-up on the clown, and miss the opportunity to fuck-him up, once and for all! . . . see what I'm saying."

"He diss me, man."

"Yeah. He diss you, bro-therr."

"Mafucker in my face, telling me shit, like he's—"

"Shee-it."

"And when we tell him to bring in the BMW 'cause we had a deal . . . gave our mafucking honour on the deal . . . mafucker cop-out. Ain't that a bitch!"

"SUV went through our hands."

"He diss you, man."

Idora watches the youngest, trying to get into his heart, into his mind; and place him in a rec room or a den, amongst the men in his family, brothers and father; and uncles; and she grows more angry at him, because he is so young; is still young enough to be saved, before it is too late; and she says a prayer in her heart for him, that God would save him . . . and she imagines herself leading him, with her left hand . . . the hand nearest the heart . . . up the short aisle of the Apostolicals, just as she had walked behind Pastor Brown and her own son, BJ. He

is just a child . . . a little child . . . and . . . and she knows he
has to measure up, in height and in behaviour, in bragging and
boasts, to these other two who tower over him . . . for he is just
a child . . .

The other people in the coach are not interested in their talk,
they can't understand it, anyhow; and the performance of these
three black boys is of no political or financial benefit to them;
they could be dead, they could disappear, and their absence
would not be missed; let alone observed; and she wonders if this
disregard is caused by their ignorance of the English language,
spoken with a different accent, and that they consequently cannot, and do not want to, understand the language being spoken
in front of them. Is this version of English, that these three
black kids speak, so foreign to them? Is it really English-as-a-
Second-Language that they are speaking?

"Was always a crazy motherfucker. Mafucker's been crazy
from then, if you see what I'm saying . . ."

"Yeah," the second one says.

"Yeah," the third one says; and adds, "When them cops tried
to ride him off the highway, the 401 coming east, mafucker
panic like a woman, and crash the fucking BMW! Ever heard
such shit? The fucker fucked up! BMW went up in flames. And
the son of a bitch ran!"

"Where he running?"

"Was he ever in track and field, at Jarvis?"

"Down the mafucking 401, if you see what I'm saying . . ."

"Mafucker ran like a mafucker, that first time."

"At his second initiation to earn his colour, and deal with the
Merceedee-Benz, mafucker crash the mafucking wheels! Ever
heard such shit? Drove the Benz in somebody's garden . . . and

he banged into a wrought iron fence trying to scale it . . . and fucked up the deal, bro-therr! Fucked up the fence, fucked up the Benz, fucked up! And nearly killed himself."

"And ended up hiding behind a flowerpot."

"Was something else!"

"Was somebody's garden, too."

"A fucking flowerpot, fucked up the deal, bro-therr . . . if you see what I'm saying."

"Yeah," the first one said.

"Yeah," the second one said.

"Yeah," the third one, the leader, said.

"Yeah. We gotta take him down."

"Yeah," the youngest one said. "Gotta close him down, if you see what I'm saying?"

He puts his right hand inside the right pocket of his jeans jacket. And she gets scared; and wonders what he will pull out. And instinctively she moves aside, out of his range, in case . . . She is aware that her breath has come back to her, as he puts the chewing gum into his mouth; and then passes the package to the other two. BJ comes into her thoughts. He eats his chewing gum like this: noisy and slapping in his mouth, like bubble gum.

"We take the mafucker down, this weekend. Deal?"

"Chill, bros. You know what-I'm-saying? We going let him stew a little more longer . . . We have him any time we want the mafucker. See what I'm saying?"

"We know where he hangs."

"We know his crib."

"I scope the mafucker. For two weeks now . . . if you see what-I'm-saying."

"Where the mafucker hangs . . ."

". . . west of the Park . . ."

"Regent?"

"Moss. South o' Dundas."

Idora drops her handbag.

The lights in the train go out. One minute later, but really it seems like an hour, so terrified is she, the coach is suddenly flooded in fluorescent light.

"Saturday!" the boy who is the leader exclaims. "Party-time!"

"I got me a gig," the second one says.

"Not me," the third one says. "My Mum's off this weekend. Rent's due today. It's Friday, isn't it? Have some bills to slip to her, like I been doing since my Mum got sick, and gets only part-time work, these days, and sometimes not even that. And my Dad passed last month. Had a case in College Park, some serious shit, a week after he had the stroke. Some serious lucky shit be going down! Saved by the bell!"

"Damn, little-brother, that is some heavy shit!"

"That was heavy, brother."

"Chill! Later," the first one says.

"Respect," the second one said, and offers a fist full of knuckles.

"Peace," the third one said.

And they hug one another, with a clenched fist placed against the other's heart, slapping one another on the back with the other hand. And they give high-fives; and slaps with the palm and the back of the palm.

"We got the mafucker," the leader says. And he walks slowly, rocking from side to side, in his jeans which are falling off his backside, to the door. The train has now reached the Bay station, coming east. "Mafucker's gone Muslim! Can you dig it? Changed his name. Can you deal with this shit? Change his name to a' Islamic name . . ."

And just before the rubber-tipped doors come at him, he says, almost in a whisper, "To a Muslim name. But Muslim or no Muslim, mafucker's mine . . ."

And the rubber-tipped doors slam shut . . .

She is in total darkness. The lights have gone off, again; and she is the only person in this coach on this subway; and it is going fast, faster, the fastest she has ever been driven into this blackness. And in the temporary darkness, she imagines that her son is in the Park; and that he is playing on the swings with the younger children, boys and girls, and he is helping a little girl out of her pram, and with the help of the child's mother he is settling the child onto the wooden seat of the swing, and makes sure she is clutching the rope carefully. And before the swing reaches its zenith of delight and screaming, the child's giggling voice says, "Haiii! . . . Higher! . . . Higher!" in rhythm with the arc marked out by the swing, which is now like an instrument measuring beat and movement, in music, in contrapuntal precision. And she wants the child in the swing to be BJ, so that she might protect him; and not push him too high into the unknown space above her head.

The doors of the subway coach open again, and she hears a soft, reassuring puff-like sound, like a kiss placed on the side of her face.

"But. But . . . I am ashamed to confess it, but I started following him, started tracking him down, like a detective . . . to see for myself what he was up to. Spying on him. To find out the women that he is hanging around with? In these days of AIDS and other diseases going round, you never know. Nowadays! And what my two eyes observed, that boy is not going round women! No! Not mature women! They're girls! Children. Kids, then! The boy is going after these chicks. That's what he calls them. And I see them wearing these dresses down to their ankles.

"And all these chicks changing the nice Christian names that their Godmothers baptize them with, at birth when they were born, at their Baptism and their Confirmation, into all this Black-to-Africa stuff . . . I mean Back-to-Africa. A whole new generation of black kids, chicks as he calls them, is renaming themselves, with different names.

"No more Cynthia—which is such a lovely name. No more Stella—another lovely name. No more Eileen. No more Mary-Jo—a nice saintly name. No more Linda! No more Mayann—a nice First-Nations-sounding name.

"All the rage, now, is Effefume. Reffefume. Peffefume. African names. All the rage now, girl.

"And every February, everybody is practising Black History Month, and renaming themselves into Africans!

"Aissatou. Sidime. And Toure.

"What is wrong with Pearlene? Or plain Pearl, or Pearlie? Nice Christian names!"

"In the table beside the head of the nun's cot of a bed, in the bedroom in which 'that boy' sleeps, there is a drawer. The drawer has a knob that looks like silver. And I opened that, searching for clues. 'But what clues could you be searching for, woman? And if you do come across some clues, how the hell would you know they are clues?' I was pretending to be a detective. 'What clues? Clues to prove that he is such an arse as to sell drugs? Or is a little pimp? Clues to connect him to that gang of three I met on the subway? Clues to justify my thoughts about throwing him out of the house? How will I find them? What clues could I be looking for?'

"So, I had opened the drawer. The contents were neatly arranged. A copy of the Holy Koran. I had not seen this book before. My two hands were trembling, to touch it, and leaf through the one thousand eight hundred and sixty-two pages in the edition I held in my hand; and I decided that, as I had the book in my hand, I might as well turn the pages; so I flipped the soft, silk pages, and they came to rest at page one thousand five hundred and thirty-six. I selected section number twelve. It said:

"'Prophet!
When believing women come
To thee to take the oath
Of fealty to thee, that they
Will not associate in worship
Any other thing whatever
With God, that they
Will not steal, that they
Will not commit adultery
(Or fornication), that they
Will not kill their children,
That they will not utter
Slander, intentionally forging
Falsehood . . .'

"It was too much for me to bear, to read, and listen to; too close to the truth and the hurt in my own life. I closed the book. And I put it back, in its place.

"A string of black beads, with a crucifix attached to it, was the next thing I passed my hands over, inspecting it. The beads looked like black pearls. A box of Sheik prophylactic condoms was next. 'Thank God, at least he is protecting . . . the chicks!' And then. A brown envelope. With TD written in green on it. An envelope about two and a half inches by six and three-sixteenth.

"In the envelope, there was a bank book. A savings account bank book. The balance was twenty-eight hundred dollars, in crisp Canadian fifties. I was happy and I was scared, at the same time. That he was banking money, and where the hell he got this money from? Drugs passed through my mind. My monthly rent, which the landlord hasn't increased in three years, is two hundred and fifty dollars, every fortnight. That being every two weeks. I owe him back-rent, for three months now.

"'I could have put this money towards the rent, BJ! And what am I going to do with all this money now, BJ?'

"In the pages of the savings bank book were fifty-six fifty-dollar bills, dry and as crispy as the biscuits I buy in Chinatown.

"'Where the hell all this money from, BJ?' I asked him this question, even though I knew he wasn't in the room to answer.

"I slammed the door shut. And walked out. Then I went back into the bedroom and opened the drawer. And recounted the money, thinking of the many times, countless times, I didn't have food to put on the table, I was so broke I couldn't buy a carton o' milk . . . and I went through that period of shoplifting a few groceries from the No Frills, before I got fired for something else. And all this time, in all this time of my misery, and

my worries with money—the electricity, the threats to cancel
my credit cards, the First Division Court, and back-rent . . .
and this criminal—he would have to be one to have all this
money!—and BJ has all this money in a drawer. And knowing
that his mother is a single-parent, almost on welfare, on the
rocks, almost on welfare. The edge of disaster. Wrecked into
poverty and hunger. Well, I don't understand this life.

"I searched the drawer a second time. And recounted the
twenty-eight hundred Canadian dollars.

"My hand touched another envelope. Smaller, this time.
Much smaller than the one from the TD Bank. And when I was
shaking out the contents, and the contents fell out into my
hand, I was looking at a silver chain with a large shining silver
cross. My birthday gift on his thirteenth birthday.

"I unclipped the clasp, and decorated my own neck with
the silver chain. I been wearing it ever since. I walked out of
the room, left the door open, humming to myself, 'A Love
Supreme' . . ."

"At least, when 'that man' left for America, he bequeathed to
me the pleasure of listening to that Mr. John Coltrane. And I am
getting to like him so much, I don't understand what is happening to me. 'A Love Supreme.' It is my favourite, nowadays. You
won't think that, for years, the three o' them, he, BJ and Mr. John
Coltrane, drove me crazy with all this tuk-music that they call
jazz. And this Mr. John Coltrane playing so many notes so fast!

"And the next thing is this new Bible of his, the Holy Koran.
My God!

"I humming 'A love supreme, a love supreme,' almost all
day long these last few days. And how many times, before I say
my prayers, have I heard this tune? How many more times dur-

ing the weekend, blasting-down my two ears, am I listening to
'A Love Supreme'?

"And being curious . . . you won't believe this! . . . don't
laugh . . . one morning soon after 'that bastard' left for America, I made it my business to turn on the CD player and listen to
what this Mr. John Coltrane is saying in the song, for myself.
I had a little trouble getting the damn thing to work, at first.
Yes! But I sat down on my bed, and listened to this Mr. John
Coltrane chanting 'a love supreme, a love supreme, a love
supreme,' over and over and over . . .

"And guess what I discovered? The damn boy was right! It
took me a while, as I tell you . . . but four times I played 'A
Love Supreme,' over and over and over and over again; and I
counted every last one of those 'a love supremes'!

"Then . . . don't laugh . . . I found myself chanting-along
with Mr. John Coltrane! 'A love supreme, a love supreme, a
love supreme' . . . nineteen times! Lord have His mercy!"

"Remember those schoolgirls? The three I saw on the subway
the other day? Let us consider those schoolgirls I saw on the
subway. Let us look at those schoolgirls I saw on the subway,
the other day! And let's look at me. Always tense on the subway,
holding my head down, as if I am afraid to look anybody in his
eye, or her eye. And in the streets in summer, when everything
looks so nice and fresh and green, and you can smell the flowers,
but I am always with a frown on my face. Vexed with the whole
damn world. Why?

"Is this the difference between me and them? Between black
and white? Is it?

"Is it this that makes us different? They are always smiling,
because they have something to smile about. And me, always

cold, always tense as I said, always frightened and scared, and frightening. Because I am a visible minority?

"Looking dangerous. Looking threatening. As if I am about to hold up the nearest convenience store. Or buy gas and speed-off without paying. Or steal an SUV. Rob a bank. Not the TD, I like them. Or start shooting in a crowded street. Like that Boxing Day, when a girl was in the wrong place. When it happened. Poor girl . . .

"Sometimes, I myself cannot tell you the reason why I feel the way I feel. Carrying all this anger in my heart. All this grief. All this rage. Tension. And very often all I can think to do, and do, is sing myself to sleep . . . and hate like hell to be able to get up.

"Poverty is hell!" she says aloud to the ghosts of her basement apartment, with whom, and to whom, she has been talking for years now. And then she sings the words she remembers from the popular calypso that was the winner of the Road March in 1994, in Trinidad. It was one of the songs she and the group of Deaconesses and Churchwardens had sung and danced to in the yard of the Apostolicals, that afternoon in the summer, years ago. She remembers now how she beat her tambourine as if she was at a dance, and how the Churchwardens started slow, to remember the words of the calypso, and the moves of the dance popular as the calypso; and how she moved her body, and for moments lost her control, and moved her "bodyline" as if she was at a Saturday night one-shilling dance at the Drill Hall, back in the Island.

"Poverty is hell!" she says now, announcing the title of the calypso.

And like magic, a portion of the words of one verse comes back into her memory.

"Cockroach gone in the condensed milk,
Who left the condensed milk open?
Come here, you picky-head good-for-nothing!
Mommy get vex and she blood get hot,
She throw some lashes in their you-know-what . . ."

And Idora dances and dances, swirling and shaking her head from side to side, and is imagining all the time she swirls, and her head is getting giddy, and the room is a blur, and the bottles of her cosmetics, and her Bible, and the photograph of little BJ and his father, and the Book of Common Prayer and the hymn book she had "borrowed" from the Cathedral, and the animals made from brown corduroy and other remnants, including the figure of BJ dressed to look like a university student—all these were joined in one fuzzy landscape, and still she moves, beating the heel of her right hand into the palm of her left hand, as if it is her tambourine; and when the whirling scene is too much, she takes aim and plops down, in the middle of her unmade bed. "Poverty is hell!"

Sometimes, when she is in the subway waiting for a train, she sings the opening two lines of a Pentecostal song, "I Am Running for My Life." She has sung this song, many times, standing on the subway platform, oblivious to the press of strangers encircling her. "I am running from myself," she sang these words once, not realizing she had changed them.

SATURDAY

The basement apartment is in almost total darkness. As she awakens, her spirit is light, and the darkness only laps at her exuberance this morning. But she slips from joy to sadness; and back again, too easily. She hums the Pentecostal song "I Am Running for My Life." This song has become her second favourite, to "A Love Supreme."

It is a sad song. A woman, leading the singing at the Apostolical Holiness Church of Spiritualism in Christ, one Sunday, sang this song the first time she heard it. Humming it now helps to take her mind off the fears she has for her son.

"Pap, pap! Pap-pap-pap, pap-pap-pap! Pap! Pap! Pap-pap-pap-pap-pap!"

The short, sharp, shattering noise pierces the morning light air, like fingers being broken.

"Pap, pap! Pap-pap-pap, pap-pap-pap! Pap! Pap-pap-pap-pap-pap!"

Idora struggles with the stiffness in her joints caused by inactivity, making it difficult to jump from her bed. She is too weary. But she is able to turn off all the lights, and the television.

The radio is playing softly: gospel music from WBLK in Buffalo. She rolls, more than jumps, over on her side, and slides her
body under the bed, where it is darker; and safer . . .

The shooting continues.

She is tasting the violence. If she could put a sound to taste,
and a colour to sound, she would have to say that it is like tasting
her own blood; and that the colour is the sensation of a knife
being driven into her chest, all the way down into her belly.
Stuck in the small space under the bed, she is shaking; shivering.
She waits for ambulances, as she imagines seeing them speeding
down Shuter Street. The sirens will announce police, ambulance, fire engine, and the lights from all three will start playing
on her front windows. Just like that night, many weeks ago,
when the beam from the torchlight had played havoc on her
front windows, and on her nerves. But now, there are no sirens.
There are no shouts. There are no cars passing. Just the noise of
guns. "Pap-pap! Pap-pap-pap! Pap! Pap-pap-pap-pap!"

And then, all of a sudden, there is the sound of running feet.
Frantic. Seeking escape. Then of a second pair of feet running.
She moves farther into the darkness that has now turned into
blackness, deeper under her bed. There is the sound of glass. Of
breaking glass, smashed on the hard, cold concrete of the sidewalk. The running feet are coming in her direction. She is now
pressed against the wall, under her bed, at the farthest end, away
from the running feet that seem headed for her basement apartment. Idora sees them in her mind. She sees them scaling the
wrought iron fence. She stops breathing. And listens.

"Fuck!" a voice shouts.

She does not recognize the voice. And she blames her position under the bed for her faulty hearing. The footsteps of the
man running away change pace and rhythm. There is a short

silence. Then the sound of wind, of breath, being forced out from a body. A blow. Like the sound of a suddenly punctured car tire, losing air. Then a bang. Someone has crashed into the wrought iron gate. And there is the sound of glass being smashed again. And the crushing of the pursuer's feet on glass. The first set of feet stop. The second pair has caught up with him.

"Mafucker!"

She knows now that there are two men: one running, the other running away.

"Fuck!"

"Scoped you, mafucker! Told you we was scoping you, mafucker."

"Don't! Don't!" The voice is weak, and pleading. She is too far away, too far under the bed, to recognize the voice. But she knows it is a man's voice; a voice that is blurred by the pleading and the surrender it expresses. The weeping and pleading are pitiful and painful to hear.

"Don't! . . . Don't! . . . Please . . ."

"Pap-pap!" And then a short pause. And she imagines that the early morning outside her basement apartment is in deeper darkness. And then, a final "pap!"

Something heavy drops beside the wrought iron fence. And the fence shakes, vibrating like a loose string on a guitar. Idora is silent, dumb, and frightened. She stays in the darkness under the bed for a long time, among the spiders' webs and balls of dust.

She imagines that it is quiet and peaceful outside in the Park.

"Suppose one pair of those feet is of a dead man; and he is lying in front of my wrought iron fence, propped up now, against my gate! Suppose those cruel words of abuse I heard are the same voices I heard on that afternoon on the subway train! Suppose this is no dream, like my other dream: the one that laid this curse upon my life. Suppose I am hearing once more, exact as true memory, or the playing of a documentary film, the words that the ringleader used to pep up his gang with the violence of paying back, which he and his gang thought was their duty to carry out: the retribution of the gang."

In bright daylight, this Saturday morning, the men and women already passing could be her witnesses, should she require their evidence, should she take it upon herself, as a good citizen, and walk the short distance to the Police Division, she thought; and she knew it was her lack of courage, her lack of closeness with the police, that had made her hesitate to be brave enough to come outside, to see for herself . . .

She delayed opening the front door of her apartment, for she did not want to see (she could imagine it); she did not want to see the evidence; did not want it too close to her front gate; she did not want to see the evidence of brutality, and the destruction done by the fleeing feet so early this morning.

She wants to put it out of her mind. And imagine it had never happened. She could even see in her mind the amount of broken glass she would have to sweep up.

She climbs the five steps to reach the level of the sidewalk. They are narrow steps. She has to walk sideways to climb them safely. Plastic bags, pieces of paper in which hamburgers and pizza were wrapped, are blowing across the street from the dying grass in the Park, and they end up on the sidewalk, on her side of Shuter Street. There is no body. And as she climbs, a few pieces of paper, some used condoms, and plastic Tim Hortons and unnamed coffee cups, crushed into various shapes of flatness, greet her.

And still there is no body.

She sees three beautiful flowers, one yellow, two red, in the garden bed. She has some difficulty remembering the name of these flowers. But then it comes back to her. "Hibiscus!" She uses a large white plastic bowl, normally for kneading bread for making dumplings, to water them. Whenever her landlord came back from his long-distance trip to Timmins, he would give her a hug and say, "Thanks for increasing the blasted property value of the house, girl!" She would draw the water from the tap and mix it with stale tea. Josephine had told her about this. "Stale tea mixed in lukewarm water is no different from Miracle-Gro. But, without the chemicals. And it's cheaper!"

Mike had come early this morning, and he was drawing parallel to her, on the other side of the street.

At the same time, the man with the walker, dressed all in dark blue—windbreaker, work shirt that lumberjacks wear, trousers and sneakers—walks towards her from Jarvis Street, on the west. He is using the walker like a child taking its first steps. The hair on his face gives him a grisly look that makes her feel a touch of terror whenever she stands beside him; and it makes him look old; and his eyes are deep blue and like steel, and he has a large brown mole that turns red in the summer, in the middle of his chin, and another one at the end of his top lip. She can't believe the size of his ears, which are the largest of any man's in the neighbourhood. They make her feel he is always listening to things. They stick out from his head. "Bat-ears!"

she says to herself, remembering the ears of one boy she knew back in the Island.

"And how're you, today?" he says, walking almost as slowly as Mike.

"Not bad, yuh know!" she says, smiling.

"Heard the shooting, early this morning?" he says.

"Woke me up," she says, "all this shooting . . ."

"Just across there!" He takes his right hand off the handle of the walker, to point out the Community Centre.

She is distracted; far from here on this street, in another world of wishes and fairy tale, and dreams, when this man first wheeled his walker down the street to greet her; but now, tugged from her dreams, she begins to listen more attentively to him, and she holds out her hands to greet him. He had gone on talk-ing as if she had been listening. ". . . and I saw it all from my front window. There was three of them, at first. Then four, as another one joined them. The fourth one was on his bicycle, one o' those mini-bikes. The first one of the three, the leader, went up to the fellow on the bike and pushed him off. Off the mini-bike. That started the whole thing, and then the pushing, and the pushing turned into the fighting. And I think that is when the shooting started . . . I hope I never get catched in a crossfire, and can't cash my pension cheque! You don't feel scared to live in this neighbourhood, these days? I sure as hell do. The first three is who had the guns. The fourth fellow, far's I could see, didn't have no gun. It was him who was doing all the shouting and the begging and the pleading, 'Don't! Don't!', which caused the other three fellas to beat him up some more . . ." She was now picturing things, seeing them at first fuzzily in her mind; refusing to accept the realism of the images drawn by her imagination; and then, in the harshest of acts, brutally executed. The man with the walker went on talking; and when he thought he had given her the full story of his evidence as a witness, began to push the walker slowly towards his rooming house.

He stops pushing his walker and, without turning to face her, says, "The fourth fellow, the tallest of the four, somehow looked familiar, even in the darkness and the morning haziness . . . somehow I thought he was similar in looks . . . the same size . . . to your boy . . . Good for him, he got away from them. Just run off. And far's I could figure, from the angle my place is to right here, I would swear he jumped over your fence there, your front gate, and get away."

His words are like an accusation, and she feels the guilt of abandonment, of parental neglect, of her sin.

The neighbour's walker has stopped. It has struck a brown Tim Hortons paper cup. Coffee flows through the mouthpiece in the cover. Mike, on the other side of the street, has stopped walking; and is standing looking at no one, and nothing, in particular. There is a white plastic bag at his feet, like a buoy in a placid sea.

The fence reached her, when she opened the gate, to the bottom of her breasts; and under her armpits, when she stood inside the gate.

There was no body. There was no death. No murder. Only rumours and reports that make her weary and sad.

But most of all, she felt she had sinned . . .

. . . she was surprised, a woman like her, a member of the congregation of St. James's Cathedral Church, taking Communion almost every first Sunday of the month, and in addition to this,

deliberately to broaden and acknowledge her religious her-
itage, a member of the Apostolical Holiness Church of Spiritualism in Christ, an Assistant Deaconess there, to discover that
the Book of Jonah contained only four chapters, and was less
than two pages long. She had thought of choosing a passage
from the Old Testament to read, for her preparation of the sermon she wanted to deliver on Sunday. She liked its language,
old and formal; like molasses moving over stones in the sun, like
that richness, the richness of the wisdom of old people . . .
Wanting to put her finger on a passage of Scripture which would
admonish her against coveting her neighbour's horse, and his
ass, and her neighbour's goods, she wanted to be able to pick it
out from the Bible with her eyes closed. So, she had begun to flip
through Hosea, and Joel, and Amos—names she grew up hearing in the Island, names of boys she played with, who turned
into men—and then, Obadiah. Obadiah! Oh, Obadiah! What
a romantic name! That was the name of her first boyfriend. The
boy from her village. The boy who "got her maiden-kiss."

Jonah would do. Out of the 813 pages of text in the Old Testament, in her Bible, "set forth in 1611, and commonly known
as the King James Version," with 248 pages of text in the New
Testament, making a total of 1,061; plus four pages of maps of
Canaan; the dominions of David and Solomon; showing the
kingdoms of Judah and Israel; Babylon, Assyria; Media and
Susiana, countries of the Jewish captivities; and Palestine—
the Book of Jonah was four pages long. Jonah would do. So,
she chose Jonah:

> Now the word of the Lord came unto Jonah the son of Amit-
> tai, saying, "Arise, and go to Nineveh, that great city, and
> cry against it; for their wickedness is come up before me."

It was late that Saturday afternoon when the thought had struck her. She would wear her silk dress to church on Sunday; not to the Cathedral—although she had not completely made up her mind about this—but to the Apostolical Holiness Church of Spiritualism in Christ; although again, she had not quite made her decision. She felt the strong urge to do something, some act of redemption, of confession, something created by herself, to give reason to this withdrawal from life, from the Thursday, through Friday, and now Saturday; knowing she would rise on Sunday.

She made three telephone calls: her most exhaustive act for the day. The first was to her Pastor. There was no answer. She did not leave a message. One hour later, she made her second call to him. His voice on the message machine said, "Jesus saves. Let Him save you too. Call again, and we will talk to Jesus together." She became tense; and when she thought of it, she became more than angry, as she heard his voice, so distant and without emotion. She wanted to inform him that she would like to give the sermon on Sunday. She called him the third time, and left a message.

She had been neglecting the Apostolicals. But what joy, and sisterly love, and brotherly closeness, and brotherhood, and spiritual satisfaction would fill her body and her soul, to appear, after her long absence, dressed in such angelical white silken splendour!

She thought of making a statement, a testimony, a few words of praise and Christian satisfaction; thankfulness, after the end of Communion at the Cathedral; but she knew, as she fantasized on the possibility, that she was braying to the moon. It would never happen. It could happen only at her Apostolicals. And in the congregation of her Apostolicals.

She would bathe early on Sunday morning, make all the preparations, cooking, cleaning, household chores, before she left home; and that would free her to enjoy her return to "the community of sisters"; have time to chat with the other women who were not members of the Social Services Committee, and other members of the Board of Deaconesses—twelve of them, selected by the Pastor, one for each month of the year.

"For every woman that he want to feel-up, you mean!" one Brother in the church had said; and then laughed; and the small circle of chatting friends laughed too; and closed their eyes; and laughed louder; and something like tears, water in the eye, tears of laughter, came to their eyes, and they used their large white handkerchiefs to wipe away their playful "mischievious-ness," in the Brother's words . . .

And she would help serve the Church Brunch of peas-and-rice and curried chicken; help the Pastor count the money stuffed into five collection bags made of purple velour cloth, rich and red, and thick as sugar cane sling. Each has a golden cross worked into it, by the Decoration Sub-Committee of the Board of Deaconesses, the President of which body was a seamstress.

She, Idora, would help the Pastor decide which portion of the collection to take home, for his own "religious sussinance."

"Because," he always told her, "spreading the Gospull of Christ our Father-God, teaching the word o' God, and taking care of the souls of my flocks, is a costly business, an investment to assure their place in Heaven, praise God, Sister. A' expensive, exacting business! A religious sussinance we're providing, Sister Morrison."

The three days and three nights, beginning on the Thursday, that she has lived through, her recollecting and reliving these memories and experiences, had represented, symbolized, the thirtieth day and the thirtieth night—each day in her bed, on her back, symbolizing ten days in the Bible's "forty days and forty nights." She knew she was bound to suffer through all this time, in sackcloth and ashes demanded by her religion, and her sense of Christian retribution.

In the past three days, she had got to know the patterns and architecture of cobwebs, and the habits of spiders, and little things like slugs, that come out in winter, and moths from the makeshift clothes closet.

But she thought she was looking into the heavens, to God, where she knew the release and absolution from her ennui on this burning bed would come from.

She got to know by heart, and would close her eyes and reconstruct them, every cobweb formation, and every spot on the ceiling where the weak winter sun touched, at the exact time, each day; and she remembered the reflection on the ceiling of her basement apartment that a truck lumbering past, in the thick snow, had left for one moment only. She got to know and learned to live with all these shadows and reflections. She accepted them as ghosts and spirits; and sometimes, in better mood, as living persons she would talk to; and hear them answer her. She got to know the movement of the people next door; she began to imagine the slow pacing of Mike, the homeless man; and her friendly, nosy neighbour, the man with the walker who told her about the bullets fired in the Park; she learned the habits of her neighbours on both sides, living in the ground floor apartments, and above her head: could hear their toilets flushing; and hear the thunder of slamming toilet seat covers; and got to know whether it was a man or a woman using the toilet.

She heard them, as they shouted at each other, as they prepared their meals, as they went about their business. And she
heard them "having sex," fooping and blowing and screaming
and moaning, "Hunhnnh, hunhnnh, hunhnnh," and "O Jesus-
son-of-Mary!"; and did not know what that meant—were they
Catholics?—even though it happened two nights in the week,
after she had stopped hearing the voices of children. And then
the silence afterwards—but then the volume of televisions would
blare. Sometimes she was in a quandary about whose television, and whose "Hunhnnh, hunhnnh," she was listening to:
the neighbours on the left, above her head; or the neighbours
on the right, above her head?

These items of knowledge about her neighbours became
large and important. They were like pieces of a puzzle she had
not earlier bothered to study, and put together.

She got to learn what hour the postman came; and how many
people in a day knocked on her front door, and went away without worrying to wait for her response: the ladies from *The Watch-
tower*; the delivery of notices for pizza of three denominations;
and fried chicken, KFC and Mary Brown's chicken legs; and one
old man with a broom and a shovel, who wanted to shovel her
snow. And she got to know how long they stood, for decency's
sake, at her door, wondering if "Anybody home? Hello?"; and
then their patience would give out, and their manner turn to
disgust. And they would leave only after pushing paper through
the letter slot, or giving the door a kick, with their winter boots.
And she listened to each fumbling hand push these pieces of
paper, brochures and other materials which she never read,
through the letter slot in her front door.

Idora read her Bible, day and night. It brought a certain arrogance, an air of long-suffering, into her ordeal. She even thought of her bed as a cross on which she had been hanging for three days and three nights. She decided once again to lie low, to remain "dead," for the intended four days and four nights. Cover herself in sackcloth and ashes. And repent. She read the narrative about the parting of the waters. She read about the Flight of the Israelites, which she accepted as her own plight from the malefactions of Canada; and Toronto; from the hurt this city throws upon black people, especially women. And she identified with the plight of the Jews, for even back in the Island, people in Clapham Village and St. Bartholomew Village, and villages surrounding, made the same comparison, and measured all adversity with the Flight of the Israelites from the Land of Pharaoh. She read about King David's craving after the flesh of Bathsheba, the wife of his favourite General of the Army, wanting her body in sex. She viewed this story of lust and carnal knowledge clearly; without symbolism or interpretation; and she thought of her own thoughts of sexual covetousness and un-Christian desire.

But the one story in the Bible which touched her admiration best . . . if not worst . . . was the story of Jonah in the Belly of the Whale.

She had read it over and over, until she knew it by heart, practically; punctuation and all.

She was born in an Island. All round her, in her village, and in others throughout the Island, were boys who were christened Jonah. She knew many little Jonahs. She played children's games with many little Jonahs. There was even a calypso called "Jonah," about a little boy named Jonah!

"Jonah, you take a bake here?"
"No, Pa. No, Pa."
"Jonah, I say, you take a bake here?"
"No, Pa. No, Pa."
"One gone, one gone, one gone."
Well the power fly-up in the old man' head,
And he nearly kill poor Jonah dead.
With a wap! Wap-wap! Wap! Wap-wap!

There were always sharks lurking around groups of children bathing in the sea, who would be hollering with joy, "Haiii! Haiii! Haiii! Haiii . . . !; and "skinning cuffings," diving off the shoulders of bigger boys, into the placid warm waves. But she had never really seen a whale. There were no whales in that part of the Caribbean Sea round her Island, joined to the Atlantic Ocean which washed her Island. She was confusing what she read in school books in Standard Seven, at St. Bartholomew's Elementary School for Girls, with her memory of the words used in the Bible, to describe Jonah's whale.

But Jonah rose up to flee unto Tarshish from the presence of the Lord, and went down to Joppa; and he found a ship going to Tarshish: so he paid the fare thereof, and went down into it, to go with them unto Tarshish from the presence of the Lord.

And she would lie on her bed, and do nothing, just lie there, and allow the life to remain in her body, or have it leave her body, if that was God's wish and judgment. She was waiting for something to happen. Even death.

And she would wait for night to come, as she had waited

for Thursday night, Friday night and Saturday night; and then listen to the different sounds of each night, its stillness, and its encroaching misery, when pain is deeper, loneliness blacker and problems thicker. She would lie and wait for the darkness outside to come into her bedroom, which remained in its own darkness— the lights in the apartment turned off, and the television left on, with the radio station in Buffalo, now that she was nearing the end of her days and nights of sorrow, of flight and escape from what was her fortune and her fate—escape from her own Nineveh.

She became, in this abstention, stark as a rainy Ash Wednesday, a woman more dead than alive. And in her transfiguration, in her flight from Tarshish, her flight from her first job in Canada, in a mansion down in the Ravine, her flight from the Island, and her flight from Bertram, and her flight from Mr. Rashan Rashanan, she was turning into the woman she had been pretending she was not. A woman from an Island. A visible minority. An immigrant. A black woman.

"You are a member of Canada's Black Diaspora," Josephine had said. Idora was shocked that Josephine knew anything about blacks and diasporas. The first February of their friendship had come and gone, without a murmur from Idora about Black History Month.

"A who?" Idora said now, with some pique in her voice.

"Diaspora!" Josephine had repeated. "You are defined as a visible minority. And whether you like it or not, you are a member of Toronto's Black Diaspora."

"I would tell you a bad word, if I wasn't a Christian-minded woman, and if . . . !"

Josephine's comment caused Idora to think about friends and friendship; and this thing called "diaspora." The only diaspora she had heard of was the Jewish Diaspora. "Does Josephine think I am Jewish?" she asked herself, seriously; and wondered if she looked Jewish. Idora knew she had one friend. So, which other friends, forming a group, a diaspora of black women, was Josephine talking about? Idora knew that when she did not answer her telephone, ringing now more than nineteen times some mornings, during these first three days of withdrawal from life—it must have seemed to those calling—she wondered if the callers thought she had taken her own life; that she had drawn a line, with the razor she shaved her legs and her armpits with, across the thick veins of her left hand; and killed herself; ended her four days of torment; and caused them, her "friends," to think that she was already dead.

"Me? I am too young to belong to a diaspora," she then told Josephine.

"It is a Saturday afternoon, a few months ago. The first time Josephine is visiting my basement apartment. Earlier, I was ashamed to invite her to visit me, after I saw where she lived, and had such lovely times at her condominium. I have made peace about that, though."

"I have to go shopping," Idora told Josephine that Saturday afternoon. She was thinking of shopping at the Kensington Market, which some of her West Indian friends were still calling by its original name, the Jewish Market, because most of the owners of shops and stalls that sold living chickens, and vegetables and braising beef and cheese, were Jewish merchants. She had bought chickens still living; and sometimes, after she had put them into her basket, she heard a fluttering of feathers and claws.

"I'll go with you." Josephine was excited. "I know a lovely store for dresses. You're looking at dresses, aren't you?"

"Food, girl! Food!" Idora said. "I'm tired of all this Canadian food. I need some real food. Pig tails and salt fish!"

Josephine showed her distaste by the grimace on her face. "Yuk!" she said, imagining the taste of pig tails and salt fish. "I thought you were going shopping . . . for dresses."

"You don't like my name," Idora said, teasing her, "and you don't like my food. Have I ever told you I don't like your cooking?" And she laughed, and Josephine laughed too. And then she got dressed in warmer clothes.

Idora and Josephine walked to the corner of Sherbourne and Shuter; and stood at the bus stop; and the wind from the Park was blowing cold; and it made them turn their backs, and face the inside of the bus shelter. The wind, trapped inside the shed, was colder.

"Jesus!" Idora said. "Christ!"

"Why would you stay in this goddamn country?"

"I'm crazy! Mad!" Idora said. "I ask myself the same question, every November. Sometimes in September. And recently, with all this 'global-warming shit' I see on television, I am beginning to think that the winter begins in April!"

"Won't you go back to Barbados, and live there?"

"Yes and no!"

"With me, it would be yes!"

And they got off at Carlton Street, and transferred to a streetcar, going west; and when they reached Yonge, then Carlton Street became College Street; and Josephine said, "Streetcars! The last time we were on a streetcar together . . ."; and Idora completed the sentiment, and said, ". . . the damn thing broke down. I hope this one don't!"; and Josephine laughed when they reached Yonge Street, and they both looked out the windows, on the left and on the right, admiring the view and the people walking with their collars and scarves pulled up to hide their faces.

"My stamping grounds," Idora said. "All around here!" She pointed out the street leading to Cecil Street, and the building which housed the large Lillian H. Smith Library; and the Ontario Tuberculosis Society; and she told her about the mix-up with the X-rays; and Josephine was cheerful and excited, and behaved as if she was a kid going on a school outing. And Idora was just as cheerful, and changed her personality, and behaved like a West Indian, pronouncing words with an Island lilt and cadence, and adding, as if in increments, more West Indian words and inflections than before. And she didn't even worry to see if Josephine was following her.

"Whenever I go to the Jewish Market—which is what we called it years ago—I become more West Indian than when I left my apartment. You know what I mean? And I stop behaving like a Canadian . . ."

"Like going home, you mean? Like going back to your culture?" Josephine said.

"Nothing so serious, girl. Is just the smells and the things. And the taste of things that I intend buying," Idora said. "I know these ingreasements in this Kensington Market . . ."

Idora then added, "Greasing your insides!" And she jumped up, taking Josephine's hand in hers, and steered her out of her seat, with a little difficulty, as Josephine was sitting in the window seat. It was the same position Idora had taken when they travelled to America by bus. Josephine allowed Idora to guide her, down the aisle, brushing women and bouncing men as she followed Idora's lead. The streetcar conductor had been pleading with the passengers from the time they transferred at Sherbourne and Carlton, and at each subsequent stop, "Move down the aisle, please! Move down the aisle, please!" And after they disobeyed his pleadings, he said, "I am not moving this street-car, ladies and gentlemen, until you move. Please, move. Please. Move down the aisle!" They moved one inch farther down the aisle.

Idora, with Josephine holding on to her handbag, forced herself through the crowded streetcar, touching and brushing people in order to reach the door. And they got down, and stood beside the shelter, up at the corner of Spadina Avenue and College Street. A crowd of men and women, but mostly women, and children, are crossing the wide street, some against the lights, and re-forming themselves in a current of people, four deep, side by side, and touching one another, and seeming to enjoy the closeness. And in all this time Josephine remained silent, looking left and right, at people and at cars passing and at the stores, and looking back at the moving lights of the Silver Dollar club, even though it was only two o'clock in the afternoon.

"Sorry," she was saying often. A woman from South Asia had just brushed her arm.

"Oh!" she said at another time, when a woman, looking Jamaican to Idora, came right up behind Josephine, touched her on her hips and said, "Sarry, ma'am . . ." And passed Josephine, whose eyes were bulging, who did not know what to do, with this closeness and familiarity.

"Oh, sorry! Sorry!"

"No problem, child!" the woman said, increasing her speed, holding her empty straw basket through her right arm. There was a large red, blue and yellow flower worked into the plaits of the straw basket.

"You have to learn how to walk on Spadina, girl!"

Josephine continued window-shopping, and saying "Oh!"
and "Sorry!" every few steps along Spadina Avenue.

"There's an art to walking in these crowds. Move with the
flow! Move with the flow," Idora told her. "We're heading to
Baldwin. And turn right."

Straw baskets made from a firmed straw and varnished in
blond and dark brown tints; and racks of T-shirts, and plastic
flowers, and valises and women's dresses, moved slightly in the
cool wind, as if they were carousels that were not working properly. Josephine could smell the various scents of incense from
China. The tins of Chinese and Indian herbal teas were like
Christmas decorations, and she paused once or twice, with
Idora walking ahead, to admire the drawing of a pastoral
scene, presumably of a tea plantation, of Premium Ceylon
Orange Pekoe. The tin is square and bright green. She turned
it around and looked at all four sides, and saw that it was pack-
aged in Sri Lanka by Lee Valley Tools Ltd. One side gave the
history of the tea.

She picked up a second tin. She struggled with the pronun-
ciation of Shui Hsien, China Oolong Tea. She turned the tin
over and it showed rivers and lakes and steep hills and a farm-
house and trees.

Idora was now holding dresses up to the light, to check their
fit; and then placing them on her chest, to check their quality,
and their fit, and whether they were the right colour for her.
At her feet were baskets of cleaning pads, green and yellow;
some of wire that looked like gobs of gold; and she looked
around and did not see Josephine on the sidewalk. She looked
around again, scanning the crowds of people on the sidewalk.
She could not pick out Josephine. And then, suddenly, out of
the crowd of people from many different countries, she picked

out Josephine's white skin. She had been completely swallowed up in the races of people. Idora thought of this. It was the first time she had noticed, so deliberately, the cultures of people in this market. All these faces. All these languages. All this noise. All these colours. Josephine came up to her, holding her hand up in the air in triumph.

"Look!" she said loudly. The faces on the sidewalk looked round, wondering what had happened. Josephine held a large cylinder of Chinese incense in her hand.

"Your first purchase, girl."

"So, this is the Kensington Market!" Josephine said. "The former Jewish Market? How come I go to classes less than three blocks from here and I never knew this place existed? . . . And so many visible minorities, and—"

"Don't say that! Don't call them visible minorities. Don't call us visible minorities. I am not any damn minority. Visible or invisible!"

"People of all colours, then. Various colours. And cultures. Do you shop here every day? The same as I would go to the supermarket?"

"Special occasions," Idora said. "But when I show you where I shop, you'll understand."

"My God! . . . as you always say!" Josephine said. "My God! This is a different world!"

"Isn't it, eh!"

The shop had a display of plantains in baskets at the front, on the sidewalk. Some were ripe to a colour of yellow; others were speckled yellow and black, and were softer; and Idora fried these in oil, and floured them in white flour and in cornmeal. And green bananas, for boiling; and for giving men stamina, so Idora told Josephine.

"Truly?"

"Trust me, girl! Or ask any of these Jamaican men in this store!"

"My God!"

Scotch Bonnet peppers, in colours of yellow and green and red, were displayed in large paper bags; and there were sweet golden apples from Barbados, and fresh ginger, and pieces of sugar cane, one or two feet long, bottles of hot sauce, from Barbados and Jamaica, and looking like bottles of cosmetics from fairy-tale islands in the Pacific Ocean; and when she placed her hand on Josephine's waist, to usher her into the shop itself, the smells of this food struck them in the face, and the level of conversation, and the sound of voices, each person talking at the same time, and giving advice to the owner of the store, and getting back advice, "Not tummuch water, now, when you boiling the breadfruits, sister! Not too much!"; and Josephine got into the mood, and was touching women as she moved past them, asking them pardon, and saying, "Oh! Sorry!" And one woman, thin and beautiful and with a fierce face, if you watched her eyes too long, said, "What you sorry for, girl!"

"Sorry!" Josephine said.

And the entire store burst out in gut-wrenching laughter. And Josephine joined them.

"What you say this cost?"

"Have any ripe avocados?"

"This breadfruit come from Trinidad? Or Barbados?"

The entire store burst out in laughter.

"What happened?" Josephine asked.

"Tell you later," Idora said.

"Tell her now! Don't shame!"

"It's a joke!" Idora said. "It means that you joking if you ask for a Barbadian breadfruit, when every Jamaican claims that the best comes from Jamaica! Understand?"

"Trying to . . ."

"Any mackerel, this week?"

"These okras not fresh!"

Josephine walked behind Idora, and beside her when the space in the shop allowed; and when no one was looking at her, and when she thought no one was noticing her, she touched the green bananas and the plantains, both the yellow ones and the speckled ones, and the tins of ackees and tins of green pigeon peas, the bottles of Barbados Limacol and of Kola Tonic drunk back home.

And then the assistant opened two white plastic pails, and a whiff of pickled pork and of mackerel came through the small shop like a breeze of beautiful fragrances. Pig tails. Salt beef. And mackerel.

Idora took off her winter coat. And she rolled the sleeves of her dress up to her elbows. And she put her hand into the bucket with the pig tails. The liquid tightened her pores and her veins. She felt the tightening caused by the warm, beautiful brine. She used a pair of tongs, and moved the pig tails round and round in the same direction and motion, and said, ignoring Josephine behind her, "Yes! Yes! Yes!", counting the number and the selection of her pieces. Josephine moved farther away from her. The mackerel was more difficult to select and take out of its pail. It was more fragile. Three fair-sized plastic pails contained the pink of the pig tails, the dark brown of the mackerel, and the reddish, thick flesh of the corned beef, like pieces of limbs cut off in war.

"What are you going to do with those?"

Idora could feel the scorn in her friend's voice. No one in the store heard what was said.

They were still calling Josephine "sister," and asking her if she is enjoying herself.

"You know how to cook this food?"

"She know how to eat it, though!"

"You get accustom to it. Is real food . . ."

"Bring she back, again. Bring she back again . . ."

"Buy she a sugar cake, whilst she here!"

"Buy her a brown sugar cake."

"Why?"

"Buy she a sugar cake to suit her colour."

"A white sugar cake?"

"Give her the choice. Give her her-own choice."

"What colour you want, Josephine?" Idora asked her.

"White," she said.

The entire store applauded.

"Yes!" they all said. "Yes! Yes, girl!"

Idora had bought her "ingreasements" in the West Indian store in the old Jewish Market, now the Kensington Market: pig tails, juicy and with enough skin and fat to add taste to the green peas and basmati rice she was going to cook . . . and Josephine had been admiring the Vietnamese and the Chinese and the Japanese and the black people who, to her, were all Jamaican . . . ; with fresh thyme, and coconut cream; green bananas; over-ripe plantains for frying in flour mixed with bread crumbs; fresh okras, cornmeal for making cou-cou; large brown eggs; salt fish, and two cans of Jamaican ackee . . . and Josephine stared at the South Asians and the Koreans and could not really tell the dif-

ference between them . . . for the appetizer of ackee-and-salt-
fish; and steamed green bananas, with the hard-boiled eggs in
it; and some of the fried plantain added. With the main course
of peas and rice . . . "Basmati rice, if you please!" Idora told
Josephine, who had called three times to check her address, and
the directions to get there; and Josephine realized, with some
shock, that she was the only white woman in the shop . . . Idora
had already given her the address, three times at least . . . And
oxtail stew made from a special recipe one of the cooks at the
College had given her. It was going to be a feast. It was going to
be like Christmas! As they walked out of the West Indian shop,
laden down with the "ingreasements," Josephine admired the
cheese shops—two, side by side—and the shop that sold bread:
French sticks, muffins, buns and Jamaica hard dough bread, and
croissants; and when she passed the vegetable shops, she made a
note to herself to come back here, on her own. In the meantime,
the two of them were going to eat all this food, and drink, and
laugh and tell dirty jokes, and stories of the men in their lives;
and if Josephine had eaten too much—as she told Idora she
intended to do—Idora herself was going to place Josephine on
the floor, rub her belly with coconut oil, and "roll" her over and
over and over—over the cold linoleum—until she sobered up,
and came back to life, and her belly had gone back down, as if
they were, all of a sudden, back in the Island; and . . . and . . .
and Idora was going to let Josephine do it to her—grease her
belly with the remaining coconut oil; and roll her, and roll her,
and roll her . . . on the ground, and . . . and . . . and . . .
Josephine kept the pictures in her mind of the shops that sold
nuts, cashews, peanuts, pistachios, and nuts from Latin America
that she had not seen before; and then the Portuguese fish
stores where the fishes lay on the vast table lined with white

oilskin cloth, and seemed to move, squiggling for breath: king-fish, shark, red snapper, and other colours of snapper which Idora did not know existed, and eel and dolphin, "which," according to Idora, "Canadians call by a different name, since dolphins are played with by children wading into pools and looking at the glass walls of aquariums, and Canadians do not eat pets." And at the end of their shopping expedition, Idora took Josephine to the Silver Dollar for a beer.

"We should come back here," she told Josephine, "some-time. A Saturday night when the weather is warmer. And dance."

"I don't know the last time I danced!"

Idora had cleaned her apartment with a diligence she had not known since "that man" left. She had bought Chinese incense in Chinatown; and Khong Guan Extra-Light Chinese Cream Crackers, a one-pound tin in the shape, roughly, of a coffin. It reminded her of her own lunch tin, back in the Island, a tin that originally contained Rankin biscuits, which her Mother, Miss Iris Morrison, had soaked the label, to get it off, in warm water, with blue soap, and turned it into a lunch tin, looking like a silver-like coffin for a baby; and every morning her Mother filled it with egg sandwiches, whose edges were trimmed; and wrapped in greaseproof paper. "Your strength goes through your mouth," her Mother told her every morning, placing the lunch tin in Idora's bookbag with her own hands. In the Market, she had bought also peanuts in the shell; and West Indian sugar cakes, black ones, pink ones and white ones. It was going to be a feast of food she used to eat on bank holidays, back in the Island. And red candles would be on the table. And Heineken beer and Mount Gay rum, and three large plastic bottles of Diet Coke;

and a forty-ounce bottle of Ontario red wine. And Jamaica white rum.

Josephine eventually found the address, after having checked a fifth time, to be sure; and in less than five minutes after her arrival, was completely at ease; taking her shoes off, and tossing them into a corner, with her winter coat and gloves, now sprawled on the bed, after she had sat in them for some time to get warm, in the drafty basement; and smiling as she did this; and feeling at home in the small space, gloomy already at four in the afternoon, even with all the lights on. It was an overcast day in the first week of December.

Idora remembered another day when she had invited Josephine to dinner, and she had arrived with two bottles of white wine—French Chablis.

She had stomped her expensive leather boots on the mat, inhaled the smells that came at her, and for the hours of her visit made no comment on the cold drafts, or on the neighbourhood, some of whose homeless men Josephine could see passing before the windows, and cursing. And these men walked with their shoulders hunched into their necks like turkeys, stiffened and cramped, because it was so cold.

They began to talk about the men in their lives. Idora about Mr. Rashan Rashanan—if you please!; and "that man." And Josephine, after two glasses of white wine, about the men, usually graduate students, whom she used to date, out of boredom. The wine was loosening her tongue. Idora could see that.

And Josephine broadened her conversation, and talked about the time she dated a policeman named Brandon.

"Don't you remember I told you in New York that I had dated a cop?" Josephine told her. "I think he's still in the police force! He may be. He may not be. I don't know."

"A cop?" Idora said. Her voice held more disappointment than disgust.

"For Chrissakes! Yes! He's a cop! Or was. What's so wrong with that?" Josephine said. "For Chrissakes . . ."

"Nothing. He was your boyfriend."

"Yes! And he told me things. Things I don't feel like telling you."

"I won't want to hear them!"

"You might learn something."

"I wonder," Idora said. "I wonder if Brandon is in the Division that serves this neighbourhood . . ."

"Could be. Who knows?"

". . . and if he was . . . if he knows anything 'bout me! . . . and about BJ!"

"You mean if he knows you personally? Why would he?"

"Oh, nothing. I was just thinking . . ."

She remembered the telephone ringing nineteen times that night, and then a second time . . .

As Josephine talked, Idora prepared the meal: washing the ox tails and the pig tails in warm water with lime juice in it; putting the salt fish in cold water; peeling the onions, and snapping off the ends of the okras, a test that they were still fresh; and mixing some cornmeal in a deep bowl, with water, until the cornmeal absorbed all the water . . . she knew this was cheating on the ordinary and traditional way of stirring meal-corn cou-cou, but it prevented lumps, little balls with raw cornmeal inside them, from forming; but Josephine did not know anything about this; "What the hell!" Idora thought; and then said, "What you don't know, don't hurt!" . . . and peeling potatoes; and drinking Mount Gay rum . . . along with Jamaica white rum . . . both with a drop of Diet Coke. "Girl, lemme taste the goodness in these rums, do! . . . The best in the world!"

". . . not that I am being snobbish about dating a cop," Josephine was saying, with a slight slur in her speech. "'Cause Brandon was not the kind o' cop you see in *L.A. Law*. I went to school with him. Out West. He lived on the farm next to ours. In a little town. Not far from Regina. We walked to school; going and coming . . . no school bus . . . in those days. In the spring and fall, not bad. But in winter . . . fuck! And we just loved it! Sometimes my Mum would ask my Dad to hitch the horse and buggy, and we'd ride to school. Brandon always held my left hand as he held the reins, like a brother, and as brother and sister we sang songs as we went. Songs we learned in school and Sunday School. No such things as HMV nor CD stores in our town. Brandon . . . he was a typical Western kid. A football-playing type who wanted to play for the Saskatchewan Roughriders. But he wanted most to be a cop. In the RCMP. He practised being a detective, even in high school. Solve little problems in class. Someone stole someone's lunch and ate it. Who ripped off whose bike? Or broke into whose locker? Things like that. He tried out for the Riders, but was cut after the first trial. The only thing outstanding about Brandon was that he was born in the town of Brandon, in Manitoba. West of Winnipeg . . . It is really a nice little town . . . the kind o' town you see on Christmas cards."

"So, Brandon from Brandon."

"You got it, kid! . . . Brandon killed squirrels. Could kill a squirrel with a snowball, packed hard as a baseball. Plop!—is that the sound of a snowball hitting a squirrel? And then the guts and the blood explodes! And Brandon killing himself, laughing . . ."

"Brandon the Killer from Brandon!" Idora said.

". . . was handsome. And a real killer. With the girls, I mean."

"That's what I mean!"

The smells of the cooking were thick. The basement was getting warmer. It must have been the drink. Josephine took her woollen cardigan off. Drops of perspiration began to run down Idora's temples and fall into her cleavage. She mopped her breasts with a Kleenex tissue, a balled-up yellow one. She removed the blankets from the front windows and opened them a crack, to let in fresh cold air.

A squirrel was crawling on its belly in the middle of the street, ducking in and out of traffic, which made Idora think of the two squirrels in the maple tree, which she thought were screwing. When she looked more carefully now, she realized that this squirrel was, in fact, walking on the electric wire leading into the Park. Its movement was projected and enlarged, by the sun, onto the street.

"Come! Come-come," she called out, "come quick!"

". . . so, Brandon all of a sudden announces he wants to be a criminologist. But he flunks the exam, so he settles to be a cop. The Brandon police force, since with the RCMP he couldn't—"

"After killing all those black squirrels?"

"Who said they were black?" Josephine said. "Me? I said so?"

"Because most of them are."

"I never thought of it that way! You putting any meaning on 'black squirrels'? Like, is it a code word?"

"Oh, shit!" Idora screamed.

Some of the thick, brown, oily sauce had spilled from the spoon she was tasting it in, and had fallen on the back of her right hand.

"Butter!" Josephine said.

"Waste my butter?"

". . . so, he settled to be a cop."

"A cop who grew up killing squirrels."

"Yeah, a cop with a rap sheet of killing squirrels."

"I hate squirrels too. Can't stand the bastards!"

"Is that so?"

"What became of him?"

"Of who? Oh, Brandon!" Josephine said. "That is another story." She poured herself a full glass of Chablis. "Last time I saw him was in Regina, one summer after I graduated . . ."

"You hungry?"

". . . and I heard Brandon leaves Regina and comes to Toronto, to go to community college . . . from a girlfriend. Seneca College, it seems. He changed to George Brown, which was nearer where he had an apartment. Then I hear he drops out of George Brown after one month. It had something to do with visible minorities, I don't know . . . or multiculturalism. 'Too many of them here,' he used to say, 'not like back in Saskatchewan.'"

"'Them'?" Idora said.

"Who?" Josephine said.

"Black people?" Idora said.

"He didn't like the invisibles no more than the visibles," Josephine said. "Brandon used to say, 'All these Chinese and Filipinos and Latin Americans and Indians and black people . . . black Americans and Somalians and Pakistanis . . . back in Brandon, we didn't have too many of these people,' Brandon used to tell me. 'A man could move around better, in them days! Canada was ours!'"

"And you believed Brandon?"

"Brandon starts telling me a story. About the Ontario Police College, and about how pissed he is, that he can't get in a community college to study Criminology. Too many of these people from Pakistan and black America, and other coloured places, blocking up the system. Too many multiculturals. And he, a Canadian-born. Not a goddamn Canadian immigrant, he used to say, can't get admission; and how he started hating the fellows who got in, especially three coloured fellas, goddamn blacks, who weren't even born here. 'The Afro-cops,' he calls them.

"'Anyways, here I am,' Brandon tells me, 'still pissed off at three universities, and four community colleges, for not admitting me! And here is this little coloured shit coming on strong. You know what really pissed me off? You really want to know?' Brandon tells me. 'He came at the top of the fucking class!'"

"Let me turn down the heat, under this food," Idora said. "I want to listen to you. We could eat later. Let me hear your story."

". . . and the coloured fellow got the Baton of Honour, so Brandon told me he decided to fuck him up. 'I made up my mind to fuck him up, in every way possible,' Brandon said, laughing."

"Well, if I didn't know you, I would never hear it from the horse's mouth," Idora said. "But I could imagine."

"Brandon says more. 'I just didn't like the little coloured shit!'

"Brandon told me he broke into the coloured fellow's locker, and wrote N-I-G-G-E-R, in capital letters and with a black Magic Marker. And left the locker door open . . ."

Josephine poured herself another glass of wine, almost to the brim; and went on telling Brandon's story. And Idora threw the half-inch of rum, now weakened by the melting ice that remained in her glass, into the kitchen sink. She poured a fresh shot of the Mount Gay rum halfway up the glass, over fresh ice. It was a stubby glass, painted with figures in bright colours: cocks with blooming combs and feathers and goggles and beaks, in red, yellow, green and white. The white spots were the eyes of the fowl cocks. She dropped two more ice cubes into her glass. And filled the festive, ugly glass with Diet Coke.

For a long time there was silence in the basement apartment. The red candles flickered. Idora could hear the footsteps of people passing. A man cried out, "Fuck!" Idora thought she had heard that voice before. And when Josephine moved, to refill her glass, Idora jumped a little, so complete was her speechlessness in the face of the story she had just heard. "My God!" she said. And then she said nothing else, for a long time. "These things still go on in Toronto?"

"You haven't heard all," Josephine said.

"I lost my appetite," Idora said.

". . . so, this is Brandon telling me this story," Josephine said, pouring another glass of Chablis. "'We're cruising around, after two in the morning, and we've just reach the Eaton Centre going north, passing Dundas Square, towards Gerrard Street, when my partner says, "Look!", and when I look I see this coloured fellow. My partner says, "Let's go after him. Put a scare in his black ass. What the fuck! It's a quiet night." I tell my partner, put on the lights and the siren, and as if I didn't know how the little shit was gonna react, the little black bastard dash across Yonge, against the lights; ducking in and out between cars, fucker almost got himself killed, then he rush from the laneway leading to the back of the Delta Chelsea Hotel, down Gerrard to the back of Ryerson, up that street in front of the Administration Building, as if he is heading back to Gerrard Street and Church, where those fucking gays and queers and dykes hang out, at the place they dance, the Paddock, at the bottom of McGill and Church. You get to know this fucking city, crawling with immigrants, backwards when you are in Toronto. Mixing with them. I made my partner turn the lights off, and the siren. And I get out. And with my night uniform melting in with the blackness of the night, and my black uniform, I creep up on the piece o' shit. And true to custom, precisely as how I had predicted he would behave, he behave. The shit fit the profile of suspects' behaviour. We're trained to understand how they will behave, and anticipate their reaction. "To Foretell and to Anticipate" is my personal motto for the fucking Force. Not that shit about "Serve and Protect." Serve who? Criminals? Protect who? More fucking immigrants coming into my Canada as criminals? And more criminals really coming in as immigrants, every day! Well, drop around Dundas at University. You'll see 'em! I mean, for fuck-sake, with all the violence in the black communities surrounding Toronto, who the fuck is safe? . . . Incidentally, I love being on the Force in Toronto!

"'Anticipate! We're trained to anticipate how the shits will react to law enforcement. We didn't shout at him. We didn't stop him. He was too far from the car, so I couldn't stop him. We didn't try to arrest him. He is in the public road, obeying the law, by walking. But the moment he seen the cruiser, he start acting guilty as hell. And I believe, from my training, that he *is* goddamn guilty. Goddamn guilty. Guilty of something. A guilty man, regardless to colour, race, religion, ethnic—what is this thing they call it by?—ethnisissum? Ethnicity . . . or multiculturalism? Whatever the fuck it is . . . no man, regardless to colour, race, religion, ethnic or multicultural, will run when he see a cruiser unless he is fucking guilty of some fucking crime. No matter how small! And that goddamn coloured piece o' shit was, according to my training, guilty for-god-damn sure. "What you up to, sir?" I ask him, when I caught him. Making sure to call him *sir*. "Fuck you!" he tell me. I lost it, right there. Immediately. My partner had to pull me off the fucker. I beat the shit outta him, that night!'"

"'I'll tell you something, Josey' . . . he called me Josey . . . 'You look at a kid like that, and you know he's a nanimal; and you feel that if you don't do something to him, the next time you see him again, he will either be robbing a convenience store or shooting innocent teenage girls out shopping. Or, raping your daughter. You don't know if he's carrying a gun. To shoot you with. But the odds're goddamn pretty-high he's carrying a weapon on his person.'"

"Bathroom," Idora said, getting up. She went into the bathroom and slammed the door shut.

Josephine was living inside Brandon's words now, as if his words were her words; and as though it was her story too. And although she was annoyed by the interruption of Idora going to the bathroom, she did not show it. She took the occasion to pour herself another glass of wine. She looked at the bottle. The bottle was practically empty. Both bottles that she had brought were. She did not normally drink so much. She glanced at the stout bottle of Mount Gay rum, and at the bottle of Canadian red wine, and dismissed it; and then, admiring the outline map of the Island of Barbados on the label, showing where the rum in her hand came from, wondered how it would taste; but instead, she twisted the cover from the top of the Ontario red wine Idora had provided.

"Leave the door open, please," Josephine said, "so you can hear the story."

Idora did not respond. Josephine waited a moment. Idora still did not respond.

"Just a peep, then," Josephine said, eventually.

Idora remained silent in the bathroom.

"The Victorians were famous for farting, as you should know," Josephine said to the empty room. "Especially at formal dinner parties . . . like this one we're having." Her words were coming out slow and unwieldy. "Look carefully at a picture of Victorian dinner parties, and you'll see. There's always velour drapes ringing the dining room? They're there for a purpose. The diners, men and women . . . ladies and gentlemen of society . . . the Victorians believed in democracy. But democracy of the aristocracy . . . Their custom was to leave the dinner table and go behind the velour drapes, drop their pants, and to fart, and to shit. You won't see it in the photos, but there was always a line of very expensive chamber pots with beautiful designs of the English countryside on them, shellacked, and manufactured by the best potters during the Second Industrial Revolution . . . you get the pun? Josiah Wedgwood was one o' them, one of the best amongst them . . . And these were lined up, the chamber pots, behind those velour drapes, for their relief . . . I mean for the release of the gentlemen's and ladies' bowels. And the servants had to change these potties . . . heh-heh-heh! . . . as the demand demanded . . . after washing them and polishing them, you understand . . . I'm repeating my words, heh-heh-heh! . . ."

Josephine had continued talking all the while Idora was in the bathroom, with the door closed. The wine was having its effect upon her clarity; but she returned nevertheless to Brandon's story.

"'What's your name?' Brandon asks the coloured kid.

"'I ain't telling you shit, Pig!' Brandon tells me the kid says. 'I know the law. The law says—'

"'And before he could finish, I slammed the little shit against the door of the cruiser, banged his fucking head, a little, on the hood, to soften-him-up. And I had my nightstick up his ass. "What did you say your name was?" He give me some fucking Muslim name. "You's one o' them terriss from Afghanistan that I read about in the *Star*? Eh? Eh? You's a fucking terriss? You planning to blow up the CN Tower? Eh? Eh? We could send you to Grantannomo for that, you know, boy! Eh? Eh?" And with each *Eh*, I push my nightstick a little more higher up his . . .'"

At this moment, Josephine heard the toilet seat slam. She now heard the toilet flushing. And then water running, full blast from the tap. And after a few seconds she heard the jarring noise of the door latch. Idora comes back into the room, wiping her hands with a towel.

"You didn't hear when Brandon beat up the kid . . ."

"Pardon me, child," Idora said. "But I didn't hear one damn word of what you said Brandon did!"

In the distance, in the black night, came the tolling of bells, ringing mournfully, in what the Sexton of the Cathedral had told her was "a change-ringing mode." She did not, even though she was a member of the Cathedral Church, know enough about bells to know if the bells she was hearing could be called a tolling of bells, a pealing of bells; or were simply a change-ringing of bells, meaning that the peals were repeated.

"Blang! . . . blang! . . . buh-lang! . . . blang! Blang! . . . buh-lang!"

"Are they the Catholics, then?" Josephine said. "I could have passed their church coming from the Eaton's Centre, to your place?"

"Blang! . . . blang! . . . buh-lang! . . ."

And in this beautiful sound, soothing in the night, like a song sung by Sarah Vaughan, that rips the heart out, that embraces the body and makes it tingle in spasms of joy, the deep, passionate caresses of the voice in the bells . . .

"Blang! . . . blang! . . . buh-lang!"

. . . took them into a sound sleep, that fell upon them quickly, helped on by the rum and the white wine they had been drinking . . .

Just before Idora fell off into the warm waves of the sea, asleep, with tender hands massaging her body, and was washed and rocked in the salt water, blessed like a labourer in the fields is blessed by the deep sleep his tired body falls into, and just after she had checked to see that the oven and the stove were turned off, and the food was saved, she heard Josephine snoring . . .

By the Saturday morning, the third day of her withdrawal, the silk polka-dotted dress of blue and white, that had been creased, was now like tissue paper; and it stuck to her body. Four of the buttons down the front had come off; the thin white threads were broken off, as she had turned in her sleep, and changed position. Her brassieres had remained fastened at the back. But her breasts were partially in and partially out of their cups; and sometimes, both had managed to squeeze out, a little.

She had started, by the Friday morning, to feel herself getting weaker and weaker, even though she spent all day lying on her bed. And she was beginning to feel she was getting smaller. Losing weight. She wondered about holding a measuring tape round her hips, or round her breasts, or round her waist. She was just getting smaller. And she was sure of one thing: she was getting older, a woman advancing in age, for no reason she could put her finger on. But there was, remarkably, a touch of exultation in her manner. She had just struggled from lying on her bed, and had found the tape measure in the Jamaican cigar box. Her strength was weak, as when she had suffered for a weekend with the flu. Her hands were shaking as she tried to hold the tape measure round her hips, round her breasts, round her waist. She was thinner. This had happened only once in recent years. And it was caused by a diet she had followed. The diet was on television. It had coincided with the time she realized that BJ was missing.

"Is he missing? Is that boy playing tricks with me? Pretending he is missing? More like missing in action, if you ask me, if that is what MIA means! As if he is doing it on purpose, to send his mother to an early grave! That blasted boy! But God, you know how I love him . . . is only that I lost the ability, the tact . . . what is a more better word for a mother to show her heartbreak over a stubborn, wilful, handsome . . . a boy with brains . . . I pray to you, Lord, to bring him through his life, safe. Safe-safe . . .

"I am losing weight," she said, confidently. "My Mother always said that when a woman loses the weight she has put-on from eating too much food, and drinking rum-and-Cokes, she will usually live longer, because her heart won't have so much work to do . . . whatever that means!"

But in the morning, on the Saturday, after the early morning shooting, a sour taste came into her mouth. A dryness. It couldn't be that she had not used her toothbrush in three days. It couldn't be caused by not using toothpaste. This sour, dry taste was so similar to that vile fragrance that sealed her mouth on the Sunday morning of the weekend her Mother told her she had fever. And she had been given a half-pint tumbler with a parrot painted onto the cheap, thick glass, and she could see the pools of lime juice, drifting round the glass like lazy spills of scum on the surface of the glass; and she could smell, even though her nostrils were a little plugged, the raw, thick, brutally crude shark oil, and the weaker smell of the snap glass of Mount Gay rum, which floated lazily in the glass with the parrot on it. She wished the parrot would let go a curse; or come alive; or be injected with life, and break the glass. But her Mother held the glass to her lips, and said, "Drink!"

She wished she had that power over BJ. She wished she could tell him, when she came home from the College kitchen, "Bed!" Or, "Sleep!" Or, "Nine o'clock! You have homework!" Or, "I am going to cut your arse with this tamarind rod, until you learn obedience! You hear me?" . . . and have him comply. "Compliance," she said; and immediately forgot what else she was going to say about it. "Compliance . . ."

The measuring tape was still in her hand; held lazily; like a twig, or a branch, or a long stem with a flower on it; or like the elongated peel of a sweet potato which she had tried to complete in one long unbroken snake of a skin. "Compliance to me?

Or, compliance with me?" . . . Whenever she thought of BJ, she wondered if there were other mothers, in her position, and mothers better off, who had the same problem of having no compliance from their children, especially the boys.

"The boys, the black boys, are always the targets of the blasted system. The blasted target of the system. They are always killing-off our black sons. And when that isn't the case, our black sons are killing-off one another. As if there is a holy war of envy and self-hating self-importance to the act.

"This dryness in my mouth . . . !"

It was like the sensation of a very unripe, she would call it "young," fruit, a golden apple, or a green pawpaw, when the milk of the fruit, the unripe juice, touches the tongue like glue, like fine sand, like sandpaper rubbed on the tongue.

The measuring tape is still in her hand. She is calmer now. "I have been punishing myself, my mind and my body, too much. I don't have the strength to carry on this expiation too much longer. I had hoped, I was wishing, that my four-day retreat would cleanse me, the easing of my mind, the purging of my body, like that Sunday morning when I had the fever and my Mother gave me the awful rum toddy to drink."

She pulled the measuring tape through her fingers, reading off the inches; and then she held the metal tips; and folded the tape into half; and then she wrapped one end round the metal tip, and did this until it formed a tight ball; and then she got up from the bed, and stood beside it, and tried to measure herself. She stood beside the bed, and applied her measurements with the tape onto the white sheets, and saw then the length and width of her body, as if it was no longer containing life . . . "The Lord giveth; and the Lord taketh away."

From dust we come, back to dust we go . . .

"Suppose," she had begun thinking, "just suppose. Suppose my body can't take any more of this punishment. And I suddenly stopped breathing. Suppose my mind cannot withstand this torment, any longer? And my mind snapped. And I become mad . . . insane . . . off my rocker . . . gone . . . gone-off . . . gone in the head? Tetched! If any of these things should happen to me, who is there, in Toronto? Who is there, in this street, Shuter Street, in the whole of Toronto, who would find me . . . ?"

And if it happened, she thought, when BJ was not in the apartment . . .

"But BJ, Mr. Rashan Rashanan—if you please . . . You do not know that I know that you stripped your neck . . . took off! . . . of that lovely silver crucifix, with a silver chain, that I bought from McTamney's pawnshop jewellery store on Church near Henry's Camera, for your thirteenth birthday, for you! You know that I know? Matching an anniversary of your arrival in Canada . . .

"That little brute. He doesn't know that I notice he has something else round his neck . . . a gold chain, and a different pendant. Something with a star attached in the middle, to the moon in first quarter . . . looking like a slice of watermelon. My God! . . ."

"And since Barrington James may not be here when it happens, when I do drop dead, who would call 911? And inform the authorities? Or, if I was still breathing, who would come and give me mouth-to-mouth resuscitation? A man from off the street? Placing his mouth to my mouth? Or a little prostitute?

Off the street, as the only person available in the emergency, to blow her late night alcohol-stained breath into my mouth? And she would be responsible, therefore, for calling on her cellphone the noisy, whirring sirens on the police cruiser, on the EMS ambulance, on the fire engine that would screel down Shuter Street . . . and stop, making a greater commotion than a shooting, in front of my wrought iron gate . . . ? And so saying: so done; and the sex-worker did call 911, and I am transformed into a 'red alert,' and if I should die, and if there is no one to notify nobody . . . anybody . . . my God! No Mother now. She dead long ago. No son now. I don't know where to find him. Nobody to carry a message. No husband, now. 'He is lost!' as James Brown says, in his song 'It's a Man's Man's Man's World.' He's lost, James Brown! He's lost! Lost in America.

"And Josephine. Poor Josephine. Josephine lives so far from me, down into the suburbs!

"These thoughts of death, these thoughts about dying, are getting darker, or getting more black; and they break in on my simple attempt to concentrate on Jonah in the Belly of the Whale. I have considered eating a little food, putting something in my belly, to help break the fasting, to help break the gas in my stomach; to curtail my flying from ordinary life to an escape flight of repentance. I have been calling on Josephine. She doesn't know how much. And all the time I spend trying to find Barrington James! Walking in the wilderness to do so, with the dust and the storms that visit deserts; in the wild wind that bends me in half, bends me against the force of a hurricane in the wind, searching for Barrington James in the wilderness of Toronto. I am Idora. Idora, crying in the wilderness for my son, BJ; and he cannot be found, because my son, Barrington James, is naught.

"Who do I choose, who can I choose, to be the harbinger? Who can I tell that I am dying? Josephine? Or Barrington James?"

"And you want to know something-else that I remember, that I had put out o' my mind? I don't really know why I did it. I don't know if I could give you a real reason; or not. When I think of it, though, I can only say that I wanted to look for the boy, but I didn't want anybody to know it was me looking for my own son. What kind of mother I would look like? You want to know something that I never confessed to, before? I am a woman that is scared. Frightened. Afraid of facing the truth, in case the truth is too painful. But the truth is the truth.

"It was a Friday evening, after I had come from work at the College. I decided, on the spur of the moment, to get dressed in a camouflage. I had not rested my two eyes on that boy for days. When I get home from work, he's always out. And when I am at work, I don't know where the hell he is . . . if he went to school at Jarvis Collegiate, or if he is hanging out in the Park, with his girlfriends . . . where? I gave up a long time ago looking for him. And then I changed my mind, and looked for him. Blood more thicker than water. However. I decided to look for him this Friday evening in question because, as I should have told you, I wanted to see the truth.

"So, I got dressed. To look for my son, BJ, who, as I told you, is now living under a new name—answering to Rashan Rashanan—if you please!

"And guess what kind of clothes I got dressed in? Let me go through it with you.

"I opened my trunk. The trunk I arrived in Canada with. A steamer's trunk that was all the rage, in those days. From under my bed, with the leather straps and the ribs of wood running up and down, and with two locks . . . I still have the keys . . . and the smell! The strong smell of leather and fine cured wood and paper-lining, the minute I turned the key to unlock the trunk! My God!

"The steamer's trunk which I brought from Barbados, as I said, was now filled with sheets and pillowcases and dresses too small for me to wear . . . all this weight I put on . . . some old love letters . . . my birth certificate, BJ's birth certificate, Bertram's birth certificate . . . junk, if you ask me . . . and the fine white dust, like sand off the beach, but really the crumbled dust from the Recochem mothballs . . . All I want to say is that I got dressed to go looking for Rashan Rashanan—if you please! In my steamer's trunk I found most of the things.

"First I tied a red silky-like scarf tight round my head; hiding my hair, fitting like a skullcap. Next, I pull down my slacks, a pair of cotton ones I wear in the summer, down almost to cover my instep. Next, I chose a pair of Mr. Rashan Rashanan's school shoes which he hardly wears. Black. Then a shirt, a blue shirt. Then another shirt with long sleeves and a tunic collar. I just love to watch these Muslim ladies, Africans and South Asians from Pakistan and Bangladesh, when they pass wearing their robes! Bertram left a pair of khaki pants when he left. I put on that, too. Next, the first shawl. Round my neck. A second shawl of a different colour round my two shoulders. And pulled the long black T-shirt over my brassieres. Then, I took off my skirt and my slip; and put on a pair of men's silk pyjamas; red; and pulled them up over my panties. I then put on a black jacket, 'that man's,' that was too large for me. But this was the fit I wanted. And I pulled the red tablecloth off the table. This was to be my outer shawl; and one of my black silk shawls—a Christmas gift from an employer, which I never wore—wrapped round my features, covering my two eyes. But with a space, a slit, left large enough for my two eyes to see through. My eyes were unseen, hardly visible, just like the eyes of the ladies passing on the sidewalk, in my neighbourhood, are invisible to see, are difficult, if not impossible, to see, or look into. When you see these Muslim women, particularly on Fridays, in their silk dresses and shawls and their long dresses over their slacks, all you could do, as I do, is shake your head in jealousy and in wonder at their presence. It is like magic, like queens and princesses sliding over the landscape of Moss Park neighbourhood! Like white swans gliding over water that is like a sheet of ice . . . only thing, they hardly ever wear only white. Just the men. In white caps, and long-sleeved white tunics and white trousers.

"You can't see my two eyes. Just as I can't see the eyes of Muslim women when they wear their head scarf.

"I am wearing this Eastern raiment. I am in disguise. I went through my front door. Climbed carefully up the steps, from my basement, to reach the sidewalk. I have to be careful because I have on so much clothes. So many layers! That I began to feel like a Muslim. And a funny thing happened to me as I reached the sidewalk. I remember walking along Yonge Street, and waiting at the corner by Dundas Square, for the lights to change, and with all the people congregated there, this hand pushed this book, a small book, more like a pamphlet, in my face. 'It is free,' the hand said. And I looked in my hand, and I see a yellowish little book. *Islam Is . . . Introduction to Islam and Its Principles.* I put it in my handbag so nobody won't see.

"I felt protected, dressed as I was, in all this Eastern raiment. And I stood up for a while, watching people pass, and some smiled with me; and from behind my protection, with my eyes hidden, I looked straight into the faces of men walking towards me. Some of the men said, 'Slamm,' in a soft voice I could hardly hear. Some said, 'Slamm-A-lake-um,' soft-soft that I could hardly hear their voices. But that is what I heard. I heard those words. For on the odd-chance, I would hear BJ practising these greetings and salutations. 'Wah-lake-um Slamm'; and many-is-the-time, I swore, that he was learning to be multilingual, practising another language. And I mimicked the same thing, too . . .

"I crossed the road, to enter the Park. Men are gathered on the benches. Women wearing Western clothes, sweaters and blue jeans and running shoes, are rocking babies in their prams. Others on the swings. Though it is getting chilly . . .

"'. . . Wah-lake-um! . . .'

"Sometimes two hands are open, fingers of the left touching the fingers of the right hand, and they are placed at the lips, as if to whisper a blessing, and the bow of the head, and 'Wah-lake-um' again . . .

"And I can't dare to open my mouth to try to give the correct reply to this greeting. But manners and common-sense come in all cultures; and I bow. And some of the men smile, and bow, and say, 'Slamm A-lake-um!'

"'. . . I am turning right now, into the track marked out by the traffic of shoes, and I am near the tennis hard courts, and I can see the Moss Park Armouries, and I turn east again, and come face to face with the high fence of the tennis court; and for a moment, made smaller by the height of the wire, I imagine myself behind this wire, in the exercise yard of a prison . . . and I think of my son . . . I am crossing the outfield of the baseball diamond. I am unnoticed. I am just a Muslim woman, walking across the Park, in the wrong direction, too close to the baseball players, too near to the fence of the tennis court, too close to men playing, to be noticed, and taken seriously in the midst of their games. But I cross the outfield of the baseball diamond, beside the soccer field, beside the basketball courts; and back again, closer this time, to the swings, completing the cautious rectangle of my journey in search for my son.

"And suddenly . . . suddenly, like a rush of energy throughout my body, I had this feeling of fear. Deep. And deeper than that fear, a loneliness such as I never experienced before . . . not even the three days of my confinement to bed—as voluntary and self-inflicted as it is. I felt so sad for my son. I pictured him alone in a large room, painted white, in a building with spires, a mosque. And I saw him there, somewhere in this city, there, lonely without friends, not knowing the language of his new religion too good and too articulate. My God! This was a more brutal purge, a more painful self-flagellation, than my three days and three nights lying down on a bed with unchanged linens!

"And I wondered if he didn't miss his friends? Even his friends in the gang! I wonder what he would do, kneeling in a mosque, kissing a carpet, no matter how beautiful it is . . . how he would live?

"Learning a new language is one thing. You can fool people that you're fluent.

"Learning a new culture, and a new religion, is something-else-altogether-different!

"The first person, who no longer had interest in shooting baskets, a young black boy, like Rashan Rashanan in size and dress; with his friend, a young white boy, said to me, 'Hey, lady! You's one of them terriss?'

"And then he laughed. And his white friend laughed.

"'Mafucker!' the white kid said; and slapped his friend a 'high-fives.'"

Before she had said her prayers that Saturday morning, and read her Bible, she became very confused. She had Bertram's grey construction socks, with a red rim, on her feet. Her feet were cold. And the association of the socks with their owner brought thoughts of writing him a letter into her head. She postponed her prayers.

She got up from the floor covered in linoleum, and brushed the rice grains from her knees; and sat at the table. Her writing pad was on the table. She put the pad into the top drawer of her bureau, imagined ripping up the letter, even though she had not written one. She has been living through times like these, absurd, self-constructed puzzles, the answers to which she knows even before she has given herself the puzzle.

She is expert at destroying imaginary letters written to him.

She was still suffering the sadness she imagined was now BJ's fate: learning a new language, choosing a new culture, learning a new religion. The sadness was so deep that, although it was not yet Lent, she chose to sing Hymn 92. She sang the first two verses, without opening her hymn book, aloud, just as she used to sing it in the choir of the Glee Club of her school, in morning Assembly during Lent; and more recently at the Cathedral, in Toronto.

"Forty days and forty nights
Thou wast fasting in the wild;
Forty days and forty nights
Tempted, and yet undefiled.

"Sunbeams scorching all the day;
Chilly dew-drops nightly shed;
Prowling beasts about Thy way;
Stones Thy pillow, earth Thy bed."

It had been such a beautiful day when Josephine made the suggestion, extending the invitation to her to go with her, back home; out West; on the Prairies, to Regina, Saskatchewan, to spend a long weekend on the farm where she grew up.

"Regina!" Idora said excitedly. And that night, late, she dreamed about an invitation to that same city, with the unbelievable cold weather, read by a very sexy, beautiful woman on the Weather Channel, who always dressed in a red skirt just above the middle of her generous thighs, pointing, indicating and demonstrating her knowledge of rainfall, snowdrifts, avalanches, isotherms, hurricanes, and just plain cold weather. Idora, aghast at this woman's knowledge, and shape, not believing that temperatures could drop so low anywhere on God's earth, followed the pointer in the weather-woman's hand— "There's another name for it. A Canadian name . . ."—as the miniskirted woman told Idora about something called "wind chill factor."

"Regina?" Idora said. Her disbelief was registered in the high pitch of her voice, and in the shock contained in it.

"Regina," Josephine had said.

"Regina!" Idora said again, playfully.

The two of them were playful in voice and manner.

"You will see where I come from."

Idora had been ecstatic. Here now was this woman, this friend indeed; and a friend by her act of kindness; inviting her to her home way out on the Prairies, a place she had seen only in a geography textbook written by a man named Dudley Stamp.

"A-S-M," her geography teacher, also an Englishman, had said, giving the clue for easy memory of the names of the Prairie Provinces, from West to East.

"Alberta! Saskatchewan! And . . . Manitoba, sir!" she would shout, after waving her hand to attract the teacher's attention, and to demonstrate she had a high Intelligence Quotient.

She was going to Saskatchewan! Lord! Saskatchewan! Where all that wheat grows! "But, in all the years I lived in Canada, I never rested my eyes on a blade o' wheat, growing!"

And to celebrate further, she had thought immediately of going on a diet. She would go on a diet. She should go on a diet. She should forget about a diet. She had already spent three days not eating. She didn't need to go on a diet. It was fourteen days ago, this Saturday, that she was to prepare for her departure, by plane with Josephine. But she knew, quite simply, that before that she would have to stop eating so much food. She was confused. But in her confusion and anxiety, she knew she had to be able to fit into the three dresses she had already chosen to wear to Regina: one to wear on the plane; and the other two to parties, and the museum, and the art gallery, and to friends' homes Josephine planned to take her to, on neighbouring farms.

Idora had never been on a farm. She wondered if Josephine's parents grew wheat on their farm. She was behaving like a new bride, choosing her trousseau for a trip to Niagara Falls.

When the fourteenth day had come and gone, she did not lose enough weight to fit into any of the three silk dresses, including the blue and white polka-dotted dress she had got from a former employer, which she planned to wear on the plane. But she packed the three dresses, nevertheless; and looked at them admiringly, with a little anger, but still was able to run her hand over their rich, soft material, caressing them; and as she moved her palms over the dresses, her mind travelled back, over years, when she would caress her son's baby bottom, and his entire body, oiled in coconut oil, and rubbed down with Barbados Limacol, an astringent lotion, refreshingly soothing, like "a breeze in a bottle," the advertisement boasted! She had been ready to suffer the cold of Regina, which "was a dry cold," Josephine had assured her; and walk deep in the snow in leather boots high up to her knees, like those worn by soldiers and jockeys, and cowboys; and have the fresh, clean, bitter Prairie "dry, cold" wind bite into her face, and make her cry, bringing tears of joy to her eyes; and, if they were tipsy enough, and had drunk a little too much white wine and dark rum, they would frolic in this "dry" different "cold" of Regina, fall into snowbanks, and scream till their lungs filled with content, because no one would be near enough to hear their rebellious cries of joy, the land was so interminably vast.

She was like a girl going on her first date. She was like a woman going to a graduation dance. She was like a woman who had achieved more happiness than she had been accustomed to having. She was like a new woman.

She was going West, to Saskatchewan, on a seven-day holiday with her friend, Josephine. "It's not so cold," Josephine had said, again. "The cold is a dry cold."

Idora went back in her mind to *A General Geography of the World*, the book written by Dudley Stamp. As Josephine talked,

Idora realized that she had heard all these things about the Wild West, as she called it, back in the Island; from her teacher from England. The Wild West had always intrigued her: she loved reading detective magazines, and the few newspapers from Canada which trickled into the Island, about the number of women that men killed; of the shootings on the Prairies; of the "red Indians"—nobody in his decent, correct mind would dare to call them "red Indians" today!—and about one man, a miner, who put a knife to the baked turkey on the Sunday table, and then put the same splattered carving knife, with the remnants of skin and grease on it, to the neck of his wife; and then to the neck of his wife's mother; and then to the neck of his first daughter, aged nineteen; and followed this up by putting the same knife to the neck of his daughter's sister; and then plunked the knife back into the skeleton of the baked turkey, and walked out into the everlasting cold night, with its "dry cold," taking a road between his wheat fields that were bearing no wheat at this time of year, it was in December, then allowing his legs to take him to the highway, walking in the direction of the city and civilization, painted on the distant horizon by the lights of buildings.

He reached the police station, stomped his feet four times, each foot twice, on the wire-meshed mat. Said hello to Bill, the Staff Sergeant. Said hello to Jim, the Corporal. Sat down. Lit a cigarette he took from a green box from the left breast pocket of his black and red lumberjack shirt, marked MacDonald's Plain; and, as the article in the *Canadian Murders* magazine had said, he told the RCMP, "I just killed them, Bill. My whole family. You know where to find the bodies."

The magazine said that the RCMP testified that the farmer's name was changed "to protect the innocent."

It was the week before Christmas.

The huge balsam Christmas tree, that the farmer had cut down, and had erected in his living room, still had the lights on when Bill, the Staff Sergeant, and Jim, the other RCMP officer, arrived; and the family's presents were under the sparkling white lights which winked and went out, and came back on again, like eyes, in some kind of gruesome rhythm, identical to a beating heart. Idora liked this story in the *Canadian Murders* magazine, and she circulated it among her girlfriends, at the private school, like a library book.

"You ever heard of the farmer who killed his family, one December night?" Idora asked Josephine. "And gave himself up?"

"He was from Regina," Josephine said. "The biggest mass murderer in the West, until Olson . . ."

She remembers that her valise was packed, and how she looked at it each time she passed from the bathroom to the dining room; and how she placed it into a corner, took it out and removed it again. In her valise were the three silk dresses. She then placed the valise on her bed. The bed was made up. She had placed a red bedspread on top of the white, ribbed comforter. The pillows were fluffed. The linoleum on the dining table was covered with a red tablecloth. Her red candles, which she bought from the Dollarama store along with the bouquet of artificial flowers, are already lit. The glow of the candles, and the incense, and the rich red of the tablecloth, give the room an elegance that she herself did not know was possible. Not since that Christmas, many-many years ago, when she cooked for three days, and Bertram had carved the turkey and the joint of roast pork, and the ham flown up from the Island, did she feel so festive.

Her favourite radio station, down in Buffalo, past the Falls which she remembered seeing that Sunday when Bertram almost ditched the hired car, WBLK, and more recently on her trip to New York with Josephine, is playing rhythm and blues, and torch tunes. She is listening now to Dinah Washington. "What a Diff'rence a Day Makes"? Indeed! What a difference a day makes! Sometimes, as on this very day, the difference occurs in the same day, before twelve o'clock.

She had unlocked the valise, and looked at the three special dresses she will wear in Regina, and the jeans outfit she will wear on the plane—she has changed her mind about the polka-dotted silk dress—and she examines her panties too, and her pair of red silk pyjamas, and the two pairs of men's construction socks, and the two long-sleeved imitation woollen nightgowns. The nightgowns have elastic at the wrists, and a pink ribbon at the neck, giving it a kind of ruff-like touch; and on it are Canadian flowers. She knows the names of these flowers. Four-leaf clovers. "Why can't they give you simple names?" she says to the flowers. "Why can't they name you by colour? Or why not just call you 'flowers'? A flower is a flower, is a flower," she said; and laughed at her cleverness. "Back home, we call a flower a flower. A flower is a flower!" She moved to her clothes cupboard, which she calls a bureau, four feet tall with double doors which do not shut tight, but have to be helped with a wedge of wood "that man" had cut and planed with tools at work; and she opened it, and took out a pair of white denim slacks, "to knock-about in, in Regina!" But to welcome Josephine, that afternoon, she chose a grey sweatsuit, the size to match her weight, but which, however, exaggerated her breasts. Her breasts are like two lovely, ripe shaddocks—the child of an orange and a grapefruit, after grafting.

Idora looked at herself, as she passed before the looking glass nailed to the wall between the bedroom and the bathroom, and she laughed. "Looking good!" she said to herself in the looking glass. "Looking good-good-good, girl!"

It is only eight o'clock on the Saturday evening. It is a cold day. In the Park, the benches that have iron seats are hard as rock; and a man who has no home, and must spend the night in the Park, could be frozen onto the thick, intractable wooden seat. She can picture the City workers, the following morning, Sunday, attempting to peel him off the wooden seat now turned partially into ice. The last neighbour she has seen has just walked his dog. And the dog has done its business on the frozen grass. The snow covers the grass. The owner of the dog puts his hand into a plastic bag, which he then turns inside out. He takes up what the dog has dropped; and as he does this, he cheers the dog, saying, "Doggey, doggey! Good doggey!" The dog wags its tail.

The lights are burning high on the electric poles. From her apartment, she can see almost the full length of the blackened poles. A light snow is powdering the lights and the trees. The lights are not strong enough to cut through the falling snow. And she has to peer through the window, straining her eyes, to see the haze that the coldness of the night causes. The haze stands still, like a faded picture. From where she stands, at the front window, Idora can hardly make out the features of the person sitting in the Park. She cannot make out if it is a man or a woman. In this neighbourhood, she does not even try to know. She does not try to catch a man's eye. She passes men, and women pass by each other. They pretend they are invisible to one another. Like enemy ships that turn their lights off, the closer they get to each other.

There is a figure of a man in the Park. She can barely make out that he is sitting on a bench by the swings. He is a mere outline. A cut-out. His face is buried in the blackness of the night. He is hidden in the blackness of his clothes. Idora thinks she recognizes the style of his clothes. She can make out that he is wearing a hood, like the ones that monks wear on their robes, covering their heads from the cruelty of winter. This hood worn by the figure in the Park, which Idora knows as a "hoodie," and its colour, which matches the man's complexion, is worn, she also knows, to hide the man's face, and protect his identity. Not from winter. But from the police. In this entire neighbourhood, the kind of "hoodie" a man wears reveals its wearer's character. A rush of blood comes to her chest as she imagines the "hoodie" on BJ's head. And not even she, his mother, who has looked on his face since birth, can recognize who is concealed by a simple piece of cloth. She thinks this "hoodie" projects like a sneer on the mouth, or the winking of an eye, or the tight pressing of the lips.

"What do you think this 'hoodie' really means?" she had asked Josephine.

"It means a hood," Josephine had said, "something that hides something, from somebody. Nothing new about that."

"Something to hide something, then?"

"The first President of the United States," Josephine had then begun to tell her, ". . . was he the first, or the second? . . . whatever! . . . the point is, that this President thought that Negroes—his word for it!—Negroes were untrustworthy. And he based this conclusion on the fact that the blackness of the Negroes' face prevented the casual observer from recognizing any change of emotional expression, on the part of the Negroes, from a particular stimulus. The Negroes' face was one solid blob of blackness. Incapable of registering emotion. A face like the face of Othello."

And Idora, who knew something about George Washington, added that "He Slept Here," meaning in Barbados, as a wooden sign said on a house in Barbados, for three whole weeks, the length of the bout of influenza that nearly killed him anyhow, after he left for America by ship; he also left "an offspring of three pretty little coloured darkie 'pickininnies'"— Barbadian-American mixed-race Negroes. He did not leave them his surname, though. He took that back to America, intact.

"That is what I know about George Washington," Idora had told Josephine. "That is how come George Washington happens to know so much about the absence of change in the emotional expressions of Negroes! . . . Is that what you called it?"

"Did he really sleep in Barbados?" Josephine had said.

The colour and the size of the "hoodie" on the head of the man sitting on the frozen park bench makes him almost invisible. And it does not distinguish him, as a Canadian Negro, from an American Negro. "But look at the shirt he's wearing. Look at its bulkiness. And the T-shirt, the sweater, and the windbreaker. Don't you see, by the way they are worn, even in his dramatic, sun-setting silhouette, that there is something pitiful . . . comedic? . . . about the picture painted of this man?

"Don't he remind you of Charlie Chaplin? Of course he does!

"But better still, and to me, his clothes paint him in the image, with the same 'fizziogomy,' as Stepin Fetchit.

"Of course, you know who Stepin Fetchit is!"

"I certainly do not! Why should I?"

"Let me tell you, then," Idora had told her. "This is the story of Stepin Fetchit. Listen. Stepin Fetchit lived in Harlem. He was a famous movie star. He became a millionaire. He was paid the most money of any 'coloured' Hollywood actor in the history of Hollywood. He was a comedian, like Charlie Chaplin. Remember that. It is important. He was a Hollywood superstar. He had a white woman. A Duesenberg motor car. With a rumble seat. And a dog. After partying with his friends and parting with his money—you remember the blues number—about spending your money on your friends?—the one Jimmy Witherspoon, and Billie Holiday, made famous!—'Ain't Nobody's Business'?—well, Stepin Fetchit started singing the blues; and found himself in that position: flat broke.

"White woman gone! Duesenberg gone! Doggone!"

Two men sit in the same darkness as the figure wearing the "hoodie," in a warm, ordinary brown car, parked on the south side of the street, with its engine running, in soft silence, just in case . . . These two men extinguish their cigarettes. They sit like spies. They wait like two cats wait, preparing to pounce on a rat. It is their job to wait in darkness, to catch rats and people. In the blackest blackness of the night. And to recognize the blackness as criminals. They call these criminals "dangerous shits."

The figure gets up. She can see this. The iron park bench makes a small sound. She imagines this. The figure walks directly towards the parked car. Idora is watching. The two men inside the car shift in their seats. They pull out their revolvers. They hold their fingers over the triggers. The figure is a few feet from the car. She cannot see this part in the darkness of the Park. But she sees the man walk close to the car. And she sees that he can touch the dark brown paint of the car, if he wants to. They can blow his brains out, at this short range, if they want to.

She sees the man as he moves to go behind the car, and cross the street from there. Straight for the wrought iron fence. Their right index fingers are still on their triggers.

She sees him looking as if he is about to open the gate in the wrought iron fence. Her gate. She hears it creak. The man's face is covered, by the "hoodie." The hinges of the gate creak. This gate could do with a squeezed drop, or two, of 3-In-One oil. She knows this. She had promised to go to Canadian Tire. The man closes the gate. He does not climb down the steps. She wishes he would do that. And then she hopes he will not. He closes back the gate. And turns to walk back into the Park . . . And she wonders if he had, at last, recognized the ghost of his enemy.

"Now?" one of the men says.

"Not yet."

"What we gonna write this up as, in our report?" one says.

"Home-invasion."

"Breaking-and-entering . . . and attempted sexual assault," one says.

"Do we know that a woman lives there?"

"What the fuck does it matter, in this community?" the same one says.

"Let's just put down common assault, with intent . . ."

The figure has reached the sidewalk, near the purring engine. Just at that moment, an ambulance coming west from Regent Park breaks the silence of the night with its screams of an emergency, heading towards St. Michael's Hospital. Suddenly the headlights of the police car go on high beam. The figure is blinded in the brightness. And then the figure bolts behind the car and disappears in the blackness of the night.

One had just said, to his partner, in a low voice, barely audible, "Let's blow his fucking brains out, Brandon!"

And the other policeman said, "We got the shit now! Let's . . ."

SUNDAY

Idora is in the belly of a fish. And her basement is the fish, and she is engulfed and enveloped in its darkness and its hollowness. Not one familiar object, not her "babies" nor the three sensual Cuban "ladies" who have lived with her, all these four days and four nights, is now of any help or succour; none gives her a sense of place and time. None of her "family"; the objects she created and gave birth to, and loves; not her stuffed teddy bears, twins; or her animals made from brown cloth and corduroy; and "Little BJ," which she had come to call the statue of her son, made with such love and care from a piece of brown velveteen cloth, in the uniform of the boys' private school where she worked in the kitchen; not her skin lotions, her photograph of her son, little at the time, in his brown snowsuit zippered up to his neck, that turned him into a brown sweet pet; or a little brown Santa Claus; not one of these objects—"babies," as she called them—now holds any attraction or power of distraction, for her; nor is able to move her away from the feeling that she is lost, that it is she who is in the Belly of the Whale. So, she renounces all these objects, as she lies under the three sheets and the thick white blanket which now become a different kind of gaping belly, and swallows her up. She is in a different kind of hell. And she throws them on the cold linoleum floor—the teddy bears, the animals, the figure of BJ and the three clay sculptures of the Cuban women, sparsely dressed in clothes that stick to their bodies, as if they have just come out of the sea. She stomps on them. On all of them, these figures which she used to call "my family." The head of one Cuban woman is crushed. The legs of another Cuban woman, dancing the bolero, are flattened by Idora's foot. She sweeps them off the pillows on her bed, and from the top of her bureau. "Happy riddance!" she cries out now. She walks over the broken arms and legs, necks and knees, of her "family." And as they cry out to her, for pity, she is frightened by their human-like wailing. She has committed matricide. For they are, and have been, for many years, her "children." And then to be murdering them, her children, her babies? She wonders if she has done the same thing to BJ. In a way of speaking, perhaps. In a way of speaking, certainly. She trembles at her cruelty, and at the same time is urged on by it—in a satisfying frenzy. She takes up her "babies" from the floor, and rearranges them back in their proper places, back on the top of the shining mahogany bureau, back on the six pillows on her bed, three on each side.

Collapsing from her rage, under the white comforter that brings no comfort.

Three of the teddy bears had been gifts from Josephine. She had brought them back from a conference on Modern English Literature, held at the Royal Victorian Society of Saskatoon, Saskatchewan, Canada.

These were the first of her "babies" that she had sought to destroy.

She remains under the darkness of the blankets, covered from head to foot, sometimes with the Bible between her legs; sometimes under her feet; sometimes under her body, under her breasts. Sometimes, in this darkness, she feels she is carrying a child in her womb, if only for the pain of her depression; and sometimes she convinces herself that it is really the other way around, that she is the child inside her own belly, inside the Belly of the Whale; inside her own womb.

But she has never seen a whale—not in the flesh. Only on the label of a rectangular tin that holds sardines, where there is a picture of a man. He is a fisherman. He is wearing an oilskin mackintosh. The mackintosh matches his oilskin hat. There is a spear in his hand. But when she moves the can opener to get at the fish, the fish are "Millionnaires," the size of smelts. The spear is not a spear, like the one the Prince of Africa brandished down Bathurst Street. It is a harpoon.

The only whales she knows are buried in stories, in waves, in books, in fiction. Ahab and the Whale! And in a bottle of cod-liver oil.

The Commandment of her Mother's sacred belief in "the regular working of your bowels, girl," vouchsafed that on the first-Sunday-in-the-month, of the twelve months in the year, of her entire adolescence, "as long as you living under my roof, girl! You hear me?", castor oil—or cod-liver oil, or shark oil, all of which tastes to her, she imagines, like the oil from whales—is poured down her throat—as religiously as Saturday becomes Sunday, as going to church—to "purge her out," to "cleanse" her bowels. It was given, in cold medical ritual, in a silver soup spoon, flavoured with brown sugar and the juice of half a luscious green lime. And to make certain that this "medicine" performed its function, she was given a tablespoon of thick cane syrup from the Plantation House, and then a shot of cognac, and relegated to the house, in close proximity to the WC.

She turns the lights on. In the blaze of new light, she looks around the room in which she had lain so long, at the debris on her bed, the two crumpled, thick blankets balled up into the shape of valleys and hills; and at the Bible with half of its black back almost torn off; and at her silk dress with the blue and white polka dots, that she had packed, weeks ago, in her valise, when the trip to Saskatchewan, with Josephine, was still on.

This silk dress still on her body is like an extra skin. She can smell the pungency of her body.

She walks into the bathroom, and sits on the toilet, and she opens the hot water tap at full blast, and watches the water pour down in torrents on the porcelain white bottom of the shower stall, held in by the twelve-inch ridge, which she can also use as a bathtub. Her landlord had measured wrong, and made the bottom of the shower into a crude bathtub.

The steam rises and clears her head a little. And she pours about a gill of Limacol from Barbados into the water. From the medicine cabinet above the toilet bowl, she takes out a small brown paper parcel. The parcel contains bush. Medicine that her Mother, knowing the virtue of bushes, had grown in her kitchen garden along with the lettuce and the beets, for supplementing their diet, and for selling some through the kitchen window, back in the Island. Her Mother's taking and relying upon bush, for ailments, for working obeah—witchcraft—and for terminating undesirable pregnancies, was handed down, she told Idora, from Africa. African bush. *Lignum vitae* was the principal one. Then Sersey, and Miraculous Bush, and bamboo leaves. And more.

This bush was old now. This bush had been sent to her years ago, so long ago that she had used some of it on BJ when he had contracted a chest cold that doctors could find no cure for (two large bottles of drugstore cough medicine could not do the trick), when he was a baby . . .

The bush has retained its strength and its curative power, miraculously. She empties half of the envelope that held the bush into the water. The heat from the steam seems to swallow the leaves, and devour them, and then bring them back again, to life; soft and almost fresh; and to break up the small branches still attached to the leaves. The smell is not pleasant. Not like the smell of Barbados Limacol. It is a smell of lime, strong and nauseating, the smell of curative power. And of strength. Power in the bush. The smell of cleanliness. The smell of disinfecting power to wipe out all infirmities.

She touches the surface of the water, and flinches. She turns the hot water tap off. And runs the other tap while she undresses. She lets her clothes fall at her feet. And when she has unclipped her corset, and unclips the fasteners on her brassieres and stepped out of her panties, she bundles them up neatly; wraps them, along with the silk polka-dotted dress, and places them in a green plastic bag, as garbage.

She admires herself in the looking glass, covered halfway from the floor with steam, and sees that her hips blossom at the waist, and that her shape is like an hourglass . . . a large hour-glass . . . "But what the hell?" . . . and she smiles at her reflection; and at her beauty. "I look damn good! And younger! Sweet!"

From her cluttered bureau drawer, she chooses lipstick of a reddish colour; and face powder which makes the complexion of her face lighter. It makes her appear as if she is wearing a mask. The skin outside the oval of the mask is her natural colour: darker. She rubs a Kleenex tissue, wet with her saliva, over the face powder, and reduces the sharp contrast in the outline of the mask, until the skin round her ears and neck and forehead is the same colour as the rest of her face. She softens the mask of her makeup with complexion cream.

She had always wanted to wear white. There was no other colour suitable; or symbolic enough. She takes out her only white sweater from the bureau drawer, and a white skirt and white pantyhose, barely heavy enough for the cold weather; and lays them out on the bed. A strand of off-white imitation pearls round her neck completes her white attire.

She knew all along that she had to wear white on a day like today. For white is the colour of coming out. Coming out, like a new mother, from the days and nights of labour, in severe pain, fighting with her conscience and her body; a pain that refuses to be appeased.

It is Sunday.

When she stands on the top step, she braces herself for the cold journey she has to undertake.

The houses on her left are shut up still; and on her right there is only the Park, and the Armouries to the west of the Park, that have life in them. Everything else is dead. The road is empty except for the three tottering men coming towards her.

And so, to keep her own company, she starts to hum; sing without the words: loud and melodious in her contralto, not caring how she appears to the three drunken men, now upon her, and how they appear to her, on this Sunday morning; she is singing out loud, as if she is already standing at the altar in the Apostolical Holiness Church of Spiritualism in Christ.

The three men smile, just as she draws abreast of them.

It is a cold Sunday.

She is already at the altar call, taking part in the altar call. She puts more swing and rhythm into her singing:

"I'm ah-running for my life!
I'm ah-running for my life!
If-ah anybody asks-ah you, what's the matter!
With-ah you, tell them . . ."

The Sherbourne bus is slow and cold. And from the front, beside the driver, where she puts her ticket into the slot, to the back, where she walks like a queen, in the slush of melting snow, and water from the thawing boots, oblivious to the smells in the bus; and the pieces of paper, and chewing gum, and potato chips boxes, and pages from the weekend *Star* newspaper, strewn on the floor like confetti at a wedding; she walks like a woman with a new lover; and a new love. She feels like a bride who is about to walk up to the altar in the Apostolical Holiness Church of Spiritualism in Christ, to enter into holy matrimony, to be the bride of Jesus Christ, her God.

A white woman and a white man are nodding. She sees them. She is standing over them; and she prays for them.

"God bless the two o' you," she says, loud enough for the man to look up and wonder, "What the hell's going on!"

The woman beside him just smiles.

The driver of the bus, it seems to her, has no driver's licence—unless he had got it from Dominion supermarket, just around the corner, she joked, in her mind, as he jerks the bus so suddenly that she strikes her head against the metal pole; and he jerks it more severely when he comes to the next stop. The men and women, even those holding on to the overhead aluminum bars, and to the leather straps, stumble, and bounce into one another. No one protests. Most of the passengers are immigrants: she could spot them, conspicuous as if they were in a Caribana Parade! Immigrants. They are all well dressed, in suits and long white dresses under their short windbreakers, that did not keep the wind out on this cold Sunday morning. Some wear black. They all have their shoulders hunched and stiffened as protection against the driving cold wind. The women, mostly, hold their Bibles in their hands, displayed for all to see, and with a show of superiority, and religious disdain for the sinners on the bus with them. The few white people, mostly men, are not dressed for church. To Idora, they look as if they could be heading to the Greenwood racetrack. "That man" comes into her mind, with a shortness of breath; and she casts him, like Jesus renounced Lucifer, immediately from her thoughts. The Pentecostal song is a better source of happiness.

"I'm-ah running for my life . . ."

The bus passes clumps of men, sitting on the steps of a church at the corner of Sherbourne and Dundas, men who look sick; and sickly, as if they are on drugs; or prescriptive medicine. As if they are exhausted. They are mostly nodding, after the ravages of Saturday night; and there are women walking along the sidewalk flinging their arms about their bodies, this way and that, as if marching; and jerking their heads left and right, looking for "fares" behind the tinted glass of speeding SUVs. And if she was back in the Island, she would have said these women suffered from St. Vitus's dance. But, in spite of this cavalcade, this tableau of sadness, and being on this bus with men who are already drunk, or stoned on crack cocaine, this Sunday morning, she has in her heart a sudden, great love for them. A love she knows that only God could put into her heart. She is no longer penitent for her past attitude to their poverty, not like Saul on his way to Tarsus, smitten by a manifestation of old guilt. Her sentiments this Sunday morning are more like the manifestation, and her acceptance, of the reality of poverty amongst which she lives. Her understanding of all this poverty. All this neglect. All this hopelessness. She is, with her pride of superiority, and her insistence that she is better off than any of them, she is still their neighbour. They live together; and as her Mother would say, "They pee in the same po. In the same potty." She can escape down to the Kensington Market, and buy fancy food from back home; or walk down to the St. Lawrence Market, and pretend she is a tourist. But when it comes down to brass tacks, she shops more often at the No Frills. Yes, it is her neighbourhood; and their neighbourhood. Her world, and their world. Her No Frills, and their No Frills. Her city. Her Canada.

She has always ignored and refuted the lies the newspapers write about them; and her; and her neighbourhood. The newspapers are prejudiced. If not racist. She knows that.

What else would they write about me? And about these poor men and women in bad health, who live in "Lower Cabbagetown," and who are described as "the residents of the Hood"? Others call this neighbourhood of Dundas and Sherbourne "the Cocaine Centre of Toronto."

But she does not pity these men and women. She sees them more as poor bastards out of luck than as men and women with a tarnished morality, worthy of the "toleration" from city hall. Some of them, buying crack cocaine and sniffing some, choose this Dundas–Sherbourne corner as their drawing room, their rec room, their den, because it is safe—safety amongst the pitiable, "amongst the downtrodden."

Years ago, according to Josephine, this corner was the home of the best jazz club in the city. Castle George? She was not sure if that was the name.

And on this Sunday, Miss Idora Iris Isabelle Morrison—if you please!—Assistant Deaconess, grieves for the women in the crowd who walk in dramatic contortions of their bodies, caused by the same crack cocaine they touch on their tongues and then inhale with the snot from head colds, to give them courage to conduct their lives on these hard, mean, street-cornered streets. Yes, she loves these men and women.

It is a cold, damp Sunday.

She is happy and she is sad. And she prays for these men and women, as the bus travels north; and she prays even harder that the bus driver would stop jerking the "blasted bus," throwing her against the other passengers, some dressed in black, with large black purses, with hairnets that control their processed hair, with hats worn at the correct angle of conservative Christian-mindedness, who hold their Bibles in a bragging, threatening manner, as if they were weapons to be banged against the heads of sinners and the ungodly, giving her, as a Christian woman herself, like them, the impression that only they are upright, and clean, able to be passing through these dens, these streets of iniquity, and still remain pure.

She prays for the bus driver to reach Bloor Street safely.

There had been only women there. That Saturday afternoon last week. Twenty women in all. And one man. The man was the hairdresser. The women had been talking among themselves about a Jamaican man whom the police had killed, many— thirty?—years ago, to the day. It was like a sort of commemoration of his murder, a memorial day.

Their voices were high. The heating system of the hairdressing salon was noisy. The women were young and old; married and unmarried. But judging from the rings on their wedding fingers, gold and diamond, most were married. Idora had no ring on her wedding finger. She had stopped wearing it for many years now. But later that Saturday night, when she had got home from the hairdresser, she searched up and down, taking apart the basement apartment, looking for her wedding ring. She did not find it. She was disappointed. And she was glad.

She knew enough about these women that, even if some of them were not married, were not "decent married women," still they would wear a wedding ring, for protection. If only to save themselves from the man-sharks in Toronto, and in bars and in the subway; and when walking the streets alone. These twenty women looked rich and comfortable and confident. They all looked well fed. They were all West Indian.

She had stood at the entrance when she arrived, for a while longer than normal, watching them, appraising them, admiring them, and listening to the background rhythm and blues music, on a stereo system. She recognized the tune. She had heard it often, on her favourite radio station, WBLK, coming over Niagara Falls, from Buffalo.

"Come in, come on in, lady!" the hairdresser had said. "And take a seat, girl. Be right with you, dear."

She had sat beside a woman who said she had been waiting for two hours, so far; "But don't mind, girl! Kameel Azan is the best in Toronto! In Canada, if you ask me! Anything that worthwhile, you does have to wait for! Everything."

The woman passed her a copy of *Ebony* magazine. She had read it, two times, she told Idora, while waiting. The magazine was one year and five months old.

"Read the article 'bout American Negro women demanding too much from their Negro men," she said to Idora. "By the way, my name is May." She took the magazine out of Idora's hand, turned to the article in question, gave it back to Idora and said, "If I still was married to one of these Negro men, I would kill his arse!"

Idora shuddered. And then she said, "My name is Idora, as in 'eye' . . . your eyeball . . . short for I-dora."

"May, short for Maybelle," the woman said.

"But I prefer I-dora," Idora said.

Idora was turning the pages absent-mindedly, right to the back pages, where she examined the hairstyles of American Negro women. She recognized Maybelle's own hairstyle in the magazine.

Idora had been going to an Italian hairdresser, on special occasions. Otherwise, she fixed her hair herself, with an ironing comb, heated on a ring of her stove. At the end of each treatment she gave herself, there remained small singes where the skin on her hairline was burned off by accident, where the hot ironing comb had touched the skin on her ear or her forehead.

"Well, I will tell you something," a woman was saying. Her voice was so high-pitched, it brought about great merriment. "I could tell you about a girl I know who would rob a bank and give it all to the blasted man she living with!"

Laughter broke out in the beauty salon. When it stopped, a woman was saying, ". . . bosey, he must be damn good!"

And another woman completed the thought, and said, "In bed, you mean!"

And the roof of the salon collapsed under the screams and the hollers and the fun. Kameel Azan was bending over, laughing too.

Idora loved this beauty salon. And after talking about good men and men good in bed, the conversation turned and settled on their remembering the Jamaican man shot dead by the police.

"And child! All that blood! What a thing, eh?"

"And did you see the pictures in the *Star*?"

"In all the papers, too!"

"Yes, they show you how that police went in with guns blazing . . ."

"Toronto is the new Wild Wess!"

"And the two thrildren hiding behind she! Scared as hell! . . . Two girls, I think I read in the *Star* . . ."

"And his wife, poor soul, down behind the table, hiding. From the bullets . . . her two hands covering her head and her two ears!"

"One picture show how the street was empty. And it was a morning. It must have been seven or eight. And the garden in the back was so nice, with such lovely red—"

"Roses!"

"Yes! The papers said they were roses!"

". . . flowers that he was growing . . ."

"Roses, as I said! They was roses!" a woman said, demonstratively.

". . . and vegetables, too. And other . . ."

"My God, his roses, I hear, were so pretty! Just like back home in Jamaica . . ."

". . . vegetables, yes! Vegetables, and flowers too!"

"Trinidad, too! What the hell? It have culture in Trinidad too!"

"Don't leave-out Barbados! Don't leave-out Lil-Barbados!"

This was Idora, interjecting in her broad, flat, superior accent, which made all the other women laugh. "Don't omit Little We! Lil-Barbados!"

"You mean Little-England?"

And they laughed again, even louder. Kameel Azan was bending over, holding on to the top of the double sink, shaking it and shaking his body in rhythm, in hiccups of his merriment.

"We does win international prizes in international competitions, for gardens and horticulture! Eh-eh!"

"Things grow so nice, back home," a woman said, with sadness in her voice, "and how they does blossom so nice and pretty, eh? You know? And all of a sudden two police appear, called by Mr. Johnson's malicious neighbours! And you're charged for breaking the peace! They complain your music too loud. Or the SUV in the driveway is not yours! You can't own nothing in this country so nice as a SUV, unless you thief it! . . . And you working your arse off, holding down two jobs. Sometimes three!"

"Sometimes I does wonder, 'Why worry?'"

"Yeah! Why break my ass?"

"Were they two police, or t'ree?"

"There was t'ree! Not two!"

"I hear they were two."

"No, man! Three! I counted t'ree, myself. There was t'ree police, who shoot the blasted man!"

"Two! They sent two. Two police went to shoot him, man!"

"Mr. Johnson?"

"No-no-no! The fellow they say that thief the SUV! And after he dead, with a bullet in his head, they find the ownership papers! The blasted car was in his name!"

"Legal possession! My God! But he was dead already!"

"Oh! I thought you meant the number of bullets that—"

"No, I mean three. The police!"

It was the hairdresser, being emphatic. He had been holding a woman's head over a square, black porcelain double sink. "There's usually three cops on assignments like that. Backup, they call it. I saw it in the *Star*, too," he said. "And on television, the night."

"What did I tell you!"

"Whether there be two or three . . . those bastards . . . Did you see the blood? Did you see the blood? Police violence in Toronto, boy!"

"So much blood! But I did-still like watching the pictures, though."

Idora didn't think so many others knew, and cared, and remembered poor Mr. Johnson, even though none of them seemed to know him personally. For the first time, she learned that his wife, Mrs. Johnson, had to hide behind the dinner table! Or was it the chairs?

". . . and the man's eyes turned colour, and changed shape? The whites of his eyes . . . right in the man's home! And on a Sunday?"

"Here in Toronto, they say your home is your castle . . ."

"What kind o' bullshit is that?"

". . . no home is no castle, if it own by a Negro . . ."

"Free passageway!"

"Free passage."

"Yeah. Free passage. Thanks."

"A nigger, you mean! If your home is owned by one-o'-them!"

"If you were a decent person, a decent Negro person, your home would be, in true, your castle. But otherwise, you are nothing but the N-word . . ."

"This Toronto is the new American South. And the Wild Wess—Calgary and Alberta, and all out there in the wilderness of the West! This is like Birmingham, Alabama."

"Birmingham-Alabama? Or Birmingham-Atlanta? To me, is like Haiti!"

"And Birmingham-England, Notting Hill, Paris-France, South Africa, Holland, Montreal . . . I leff-out anything? Racism gone international, now. We, in this country, watching the outsourcing—is that the word for it, now—of racism . . ."

"I thought the right word for it was *multiculturalism*."

"Multiculturalism, my ass! Who they fooling? They think Wessindians is fools? Because we don't carry-on, and shed tears, and demonstrate when a piece o' racism lash our ass, they think we is fools?"

"I *like* Toronto, though."

"I like multiculturalism, still."

"Multiculturalism? Is multiculturalism, you say? What is so multiculturalistic about Toronto? Toronto is a collection of ghettos. Ethnic ghettos. Cultural ghettos. In other words, racial ghettoes, and—"

"Oh Christ, I never looked at it this way! That's right!"

"You got Rosedale: Anglo-Saxon people. Jane–Finch: black people and visible minorities. High Park: the Poles. Sin-Clair, all up there by Dufferin and Eglinton: the Eye-talians . . ."

"Don't leave-out the place up north, where the cheapest house cost a million. The rich Eye-talians . . ."

"And all 'long the Danforth . . . Danforth Avenue . . . is the Greeks . . ."

"This Toronto-Canada? Six o' one, and half-dozen of the other!"

"But what you know about Haitians? You's a West Indian!"

The waiting was patient and loud, and long; and argumentative. Idora hadn't been in this environment for years. She watched the hairdresser as he held a woman's head over the square black sink.

"You scalding me, man!" the woman cried out.

The hairdresser had walked slowly towards her. Idora thought his pants were a bit tight.

"Now, what can I do for you, pretty woman?" he said to Idora.

"I want my hair fix, and I was thinking . . ."

And together, they went through various hairstyles, while he called her "a lioness" because of the strength and thickness of her hair; and then "a beauty queen"; and she told him she wasn't a lioness, because she was not born "in no zoo," nor in July under the sign of Leo. And he complimented her on her "ratid sense o' humour"; and he suggested the "Banana Split"; and they both laughed at the name; and he said that the "Page Boy" could be worn by women of all ages; and he even asked her how old she was; and she stiffened in her chair, and refused to tell him.

"You are damn fresh!"

"Sorry, ma'am."

"You're welcome."

"No offence meant . . ."

"But in future, watch your mouth, boy!" And then she asked him, "You know this Jamaican man we were talking about?"

"Which Jamaican?"

"The Jamaican."

"I know a lotta Jamaicans. I barn in Jamaica!"

And both of them almost killed themselves, with laughter . . .

And when it had finished, when Idora left, she was a new woman. She felt years had been taken off her body and her spirit, and her face, by her new appearance; years taken away from her gait; years taken away from her attitude to herself. Her hair was a deep mauve; and shining, and smelling of lotions, and the smell of the hairdressing salon. It was seven o'clock when she had stepped down from the chair; when she left the beauty salon, that night. The Saturday night before the Thursday when she first took to her bed. "Sweet" was the word for how she looked!

The subway is crowded. There are many more black men and black women in the coach with her, this Sunday morning, than there had been on the slow-travelling, jerking Sherbourne Street bus. She does not know the population of black people who live in Toronto. And the newspapers never gave her a number she could trust. Seeing all these black people, this Sunday morning, so close to her, she thinks there must be millions of them living here; or that the Caribana Parade must be taking place this Sunday. "But it too damn cold to be summer!"

She tries to see, in her reflection in the windowpane, how her hairdo looks. Did she allow Kameel Azan to put too much colour in her hair? Was she looking more—or less—like a woman of easy virtue? She liked the term. "A woman of easy virtue!" She says it aloud. She wishes she was a woman of easy virtue. And she repeats it to herself many times; as a matter of fact, each time that she steals a glance, and sees her reflection crammed with other reflected faces, in the glass of the window of the subway coach. Now, travelling underground, she can see only cement walls, until the train slows into the approaching station. She is no longer sure she wants to be "a woman of easy virtue." And she smiles, once or twice, at the thought; and at the man sitting close beside her, whom her knees are touching; but she knows that the man made their knees touch, not because of the small space of the seat, but because he can see a few inches of her skin above her knees. Her knees are full and shining in her white pantyhose. Yes, she had smiled at this man, who was not "dressed for church"; was not in his "Sunday-go-to-meetings"; but is wearing a jeans jacket, blue jeans trousers, white and blue sneakers, and a T-shirt which has UNIVERSITY OF TORONTO, 5T9 written on it.

She goes back, in that flash of touch, his knee rubbing against hers, to years before, when she dated a university student; and more recently, to last week, on that Saturday afternoon in the hairdresser's salon, when, with more casualness than accidental determination, she had allowed her eyes to rest on the hairdresser's tight-fitting pants.

It is all right, she thinks, even on a Sunday morning, on the way to church, to think about sex. Sex is such a natural thing. Sex is life. Is blood. And the body needs life. And the Bible is full of sex! This person begetting that person; and that person begetting somebody else. And this woman lying with that man . . . Even kings were doing it in the Bible, with more frequency and, consequently, with more offspring than in Toronto, now starved and crippled by a limping birth rate. And she

remembers the words of Louis Armstrong, singing "Let's Fall
in Love" . . . because "bees do it, snakes do, even educated
fleas do it, let's do it, let's fall in love . . ."

"If there were more West Indians and more black people living here, the way they breed, this country would really see big
populations! Lord, there would be people like peas, in Canada!
Like India! Or China! It is all right, on a Sunday, to think of the
flesh. So long as the flesh you are thinking about is not the piece
that belongs to thy neighbour!"

And so, on this cold Sunday, dressed in white because she
had come to the end of the "forty days and forty nights" of
monastic meditation and fasting, she thinks perhaps it is sinful,
after all, on a Sunday morning, to be thinking of carnal knowledge on her way to the Apostolical Holiness Church of Spiritualism in Christ. And sinful to be painting these thoughts of
depravity and of the flesh, on the way to church, when it was
agreed between her and the Pastor that she would present the
message today, to the congregation, on the text of Jonah in
the Belly of the Whale.

So, this Sunday morning, punctually at nine-fifteen, Miss Idora
Iris Isabelle Morrison (as she now calls herself) is armed with
her songbook, marked in three places with pieces of Kleenex
she had torn off to make bookmarks, for the songs she had
chosen for the altar call, and will lead the congregation in. She
had got off the subway, and had taken another bus to get to
the Apostolical Holiness Church of Spiritualism in Christ.

She sits on the very first seat, which she alone occupies. Her
perfume sweeps the entire bus, strong as a pleasant wind in
Barbados. Her back is straight. Her "bubbies" are pushed out,
and her flesh can be seen just a little bit, through her leotards,

under her rich white dress, the colour of pearl; and through
her formed brassieres. She ought to button up all the buttons
on her white winter coat. But her mind is on Jonah. Poor Jonah,
and Mr. Albert Johnson, the Jamaican man, in the midst of
happiness and sleep; one, with his red roses; the other, in his
bunk in a big ship; happy as a lark. And then, Fate or Satan!
Satan or Fate stepped in, and altered their lives, just like that!
She wondered if she could give the Word of God such a liberal
interpretation. Why not? The members of this congregation,
her congregation, mostly women, will understand this kind of
liberty with words and meanings; if this licence were used to
portray their known misery and troubles; if they could see their
lives measured, almost word for word, in these new words, to
God. In the Bible. They would know. Yes! She could give the
Word of God this common interpretation, this everyday appli-
cation, and this vulgar interpretation.

When she had crossed the road to take the second bus, she was
standing at the regular weekday bus stop. The ugly, large bus
came, and did not stop. She knew that the driver saw her. She
could not make out the face of the driver of the bus, because
of the dried snow and dust on its windows. But she accused him,
and swore that his behaviour was un-Godly. When she realized
that she was not standing at the right stop, the special Sunday
stop, she made the Sign of the Cross, asked pardon for her
thoughts, and walked the short distance farther up to where the
bus had now stopped. Her high-heeled red patent leather shoes
were difficult to walk in; were already making her carriage
unladylike; and now to be attempting to run in them, on a Sunday morning, dressed so beautifully in white, with red shoes,
made her appear, in this haste, as if she was going to a dance;

and not to the house of God. But she got to the bus before it
pulled away from the Sunday stop. The bus driver was killing
himself with laughter. The bus driver knew her. Even with her
hair coloured red. He had spotted her at the wrong stop for
Sundays, and deliberately, and playfully, had given her this little scare. And she knew the bus driver.

"I was playing with you, dear," he said. He was smiling. He
was always smiling whenever he saw her.

"I break my arse the whole week rushing to catch a bus for
work. I break my arse rushing to take a bus to take me back to
my apartment. I do this five times a week, multiplied by two.
And on a day of rest, you want me to bust my arse . . . Looka,
niggerman . . . you want to make me run and sweat-up myself,
to catch this bus, this blessed Sunday morning too? Boy, you
need God. A bright Sunday morning! And you purposely driving this bus like you want to scare decent people? A Christian-
minded woman like me? On her way to serve God? Why you're
such a blasted sinner?"

And they both burst out laughing.

"Pray for me, then!" he said, still laughing. He took his holidays in Barbados, twice a year; and came back tanned almost
to the colour of a Negro; with two bottles of Mount Gay rum,
and one dozen fried sea eggs, for her. "Pray for me, dear. No?"
he said, chuckling. The other passengers were laughing too.

"I intend to. I intend to do just that, you damn sinner!"

And he laughed; and the bus laughed; and she laughed, and
said to him, "Boy, you see me here? I am running for my life."

"I thought you was running for the bus!"

"You are a real sinner. And a comedian, to-boot! I see I going
have to pray real hard for your soul, this Sunday morning!"

"Are you going to church? Or are you going to see your boyfriend? You dress' like you going on a date!"

And he laughed some more. And she laughed too.

"Well, you have a good service, darling." And they said little naughty things to each other, and he drove the bus right up to the entrance of the Apostolical Holiness Church of Spiritualism in Christ. "Don't forget to say a prayer for me, darling!"

"God don't forget, boy! God don't forget! You take care, you hear? See you next Sunday."

She rose from beside him; and he said to her, as if they were joined in a conspiracy, "How's your other boyfriend, the Jamaican fellow with the red flowers? Roses, ain't it? Heard anything, lately?"; and she stepped slowly on the step of the door, covered in slush, and said, "Not a word, boy! Not a word. But God isn't sleeping. Thanks."

"My heart is filled with joy, and with the excitement that the church holds out to me this Sunday morning; and my heart is filled with love: brotherly love; and Christian love. And also for the men and women gathered round the entrance of the church, which I sometimes call 'the tabernacle,' like those gathered round the entrance of that Anglican church that I pass, the one on Sherbourne Street, near Dundas, with the homeless men waiting for a free cup of Starbucks coffee, and a doughnut, or a bran muffin, or whatever else falls from the table of the halfway house and the social and community centres distributed by the workers; and talking about what happened to them on Saturday night, last night; talking about their children, wherever they are—some lost, some in prison, some in mental institutions; some living on the street; all badly off; and about the bad weather we're having; and the latest news about friends not so fortunate. And sons, little black boys out on bail, waiting to hear their sentence. The Don Jail? Or Kingston Penitentiary, doing hard time?

"But it is the men and women round the entrance to the Apostolical Holiness Church of Spiritualism in Christ, who talk mostly about the cold weather, and about the latest news of their friends, and what fools they are to be still living in Toronto, in Canada, in all this cold, that interest me this Sunday morning.

"'Wha' feh do, eh?' a man says.

"'We living,' a woman says.

"'And the money good,' a man says. 'More better than back home, whether home be Jamaica, Sin-Lucia, Barbados, Antigua, or even Trinidad with all the oil that they got . . .'

"'And the highest murder rate in the West Indies!' a man says.

"'As I was saying, or even Trinidad with all the oil they have . . .' a man says.

"'Had,' the other man says. 'Not have. Trinidad broke as any African country you read about, these days.'

"And I mingle amongst them for a while, and shake each hand extended; patting each child on the head; and leave behind with them a strong whiff of my expensive perfume, for them to wag their mouths about, as I know they will, the moment I turn my back and mount the two steps to the entrance of the church. 'These bitches!' I say in my mind, as I climb the steps made out of cinder blocks, resting my hand on the railing, getting back my regular breathing; careful because the railing is wobbly.

"'Oh, Sister Morrison! Just the person I want to have a word with!'

"It is the Pastor. My Pastor. Black and large, always sweating, always smelling sweet from the aftershave lotion he pours on his face, just as he pours the sweet words of damnation and of sinning over his congregation; and big in the thighs. I noticed this the first time I entered his church, one night in the week, during a revival meeting, 'A Call for New Souls to Be Saved.' And well dressed, in the wrong colour of suits for his black complexion. He is partial to deep, rich brown. Double-breasted suits, even in the summer; dark brown leather shoes which look red; light brown shirts whose colour has a sheen to them; and rich, thick, dark brown ties, with no design in them, and broad, 'my-God-in-heaven, so broad that it covers his whole shirt front!' He used to live in England; and claims that this is the way Englishmen dress in London-England, 'the best sartorical place in the whirl!' he says; and 'You know, all the Englishman is about, is all style!' And his voice, deep and as rich as the clothes he wears. And like a foghorn.

"This Sunday morning, he is wearing his long black robe over his brown suit. Immediately, I think of Mike in the Park. The Pastor's robe, embroidered and cut to suit the clerical rank he has ordained for himself (the equivalent of Lord Bishop), has red and green working round the neck; and a sash with two long crosses on it, made of gold thread; and a hood that university professors wear at Convocation. The Pastor had given himself the title Doctor. But he never told his congregation Doctor of what. He carries a large white handkerchief, which he is always waving in greeting to the women in his congregation, and moving over his face and his forehead to swat his brow and his neck; and when he removes it, his face and his forehead have the same oily sheen as before. 'It must be the kind of skin he has,' I think. 'Or his makeup.'

"'Just the person I want to see!' he tells me.

"'I want to have a word with you, too,' I tell him.

"'Praise His name, Sister!'

"He and me move to his 'sanctuary,' which is what he calls his office. But before he can open the door, he has to unlock two bolts; and then he says, 'This flu that going-round, child. This H'Asian flu that going-round. I'm not myself today. But I still 'ave to 'tend to my flocks.'

"'God's work, boy!'

"'Bless His name! So, what I want to h'axe you, if you don't mind, and seeing as how this H'Asian flu—' he began to say.

"'I prepared, Pastor. I come prepared.'

"'Praise His name!' he says. He is happy.

"It is as if, all week, and 'specially Friday night, God was telling me, 'Sister I-dora, prepare thyself! Sister I-dora, prepare thyself to do your Lord's bidding!'

"'Bless His name, Sister!'

"'His name!'

"'Bless His name, Sister Dora! And make it a message that going-'plenish the collection box . . . Bills, you know, my dear? Hydro, the gas-people, and the roof . . .'

"'As if, Pastor, you know when somebody is following you, but you don't see nobody following you, but you have the uncanny sense you're being followed? On the bus coming here, that feeling that somebody following me came over me, right up to these very church steps . . .'

"'Bless His name, Sister Morrison. But if you don't mind me saying so, you do look real pretty this blessed morning. Real pretty. Bless His name! You must have heard from Bertram! He find anything permanent yet, down in Amurca?' he said.

"'From Thursday night, right into Friday morning, all day Friday, and it only end fore-day, Sunday, this very morning . . . it was like the forty days and forty nights in the Bible, that God was talking to me, Pastor. Forty days and forty nights! It seem so. And it is Him who has me prepared, this morning.'

"'You sure look pretty in white, this blessed Sunday morning, Sister Morrison! Like a virgin, if I may call it that! You don't mind your Pastor using these term to describe your pulchritude, do you, Sister Morrison? As if you're going to a baptism, praise the Lord! Like an angel! Bless His name, bless His . . . or to a wedding!'"

Idora is nervous. Nervous in front of this large congregation. The congregation is the largest she has seen in the Apostolical Holiness Church of Spiritualism in Christ, on an ordinary Sunday. Perhaps, when she was going to St. James's Cathedral Church, this Apostolical Holiness was having a revival, was having crowds like this every Sunday morning that she was absent.

She mounts the pulpit. And places her hands on the shaky lectern. The pulpit is in the centre of a raised platform which serves as the chancel. In the Cathedral Church she attended in Barbados, where she sometimes took Holy Communion, the chancel was like the size of a temple of white marble, sparkling and enriching in its power, to make her think of heaven. And of hell.

She places her hands on the lectern. And the lectern shakes a little. She loses her balance, for a moment. She thinks this is an omen. But she dismisses it out of her mind. She regains her balance. What she knows now, and understands, is the reason

why the Pastor stumbled once, and almost fell over, during one
of his two-hour sermons. She had thought, like the congregation, that it was the "spirits" in him, descending upon him.

She places her Bible in the middle of the unpainted lectern,
and pulls the long cord of herringbone twine to turn on the
reading lamp. No light comes. There is no bulb in the brass
cylindrical shade. She is nervous. Perspiration forms on her
upper lip. This is another omen. The power of the words in
her head tells her, however, that it is not. But the nervousness
grips her, and turns to desperation, and then to determination.
"Give me strength, Father-God," she whispers. And, as she has
seen the Pastor do so many times at so many Sunday morning
services, she clears her throat.

"Praise the Lord!" the Pastor shouts. He is sitting immediately behind her, in the only chair there.

And then the congregation. Their shouted exhortations
frighten her. She is not accustomed to hearing their voices, from
this angle; from the front of the church. Their chorus sounds
strange and threatening, as she stands before them, apart from
them, now their leader, and their messenger of the Word they
have come to hear.

"Praise Jesus!" they shout. But it is more than a shout. It is
like an invective. An accusation. It is definitely more than a
shout. It is their urging, their encouragement. She is still frightened by their chorus.

But she is ready now. To begin. To give them all the passion,
all the hate, all the love, all the misery she has lived through for
the past four days and four nights, turned in her imagination
into the sackcloth of forty days and forty nights, like a miracle in
the Bible, like the Feeding of the Five Thousand; and it is this
kind of gathering, frightening in its number, that she is standing

up before, now; and it makes her put pressure on her teeth, to steel her courage and herself. A carnal flavour comes into her body, and she accepts it as a religious commitment to God.

"Praise the Lord!"

"There was a great tempest," she begins. The church falls quiet as a vault. "And the old ship began to really rock. And an old captain, by the name of Gennofeel Cappuah . . . I say, an old captain by the name of Gennofeel Cappuah!" she says, putting this narrative, this Gospel, in the ethnic dialect language of Barbados mixed with the more formal Canadian language. But there is more dialect than Canadian, for her entire congregation is West Indian.

Her choice of language is greeted by a loud exhortation that runs through the congregation, from the first row of chairs right through to the heart of the assembly, down to the last row of men and women standing at the back . . .

". . . by the name of Gennofeel Cappuah. And he say, 'I have been sailing these seas in this voyage, all my life. And never. Nev-verrr. Never have I seen. The old wind. And the ocean behave like this.'"

"Never!" a woman screams.

"'There must be something peculiar going on. Peculiar, I say. There must be something peculiar on board.' And the captain call the crew together. And questioned the crew. To see what they had done when he was in port. 'Something must have happen.' Sisters, something must have happened. And you know what that means! Something, brothers, must have happen; something, sisters, that never happen before. And the crew cast lots. And the lot fell on Jonah. The lot fell on Jonah . . ."

"Oh Jesus!" the same woman cries out. Her voice is high, and searing. And it frightens Idora.

"And ole Jonah was laying-down. In his bunk. In the ship. Fast asleep. And he thought. He had got away. From God."

"No, no, no!" the same woman screams. "He can't get-'way from God! He can't run-'way from God!"

"Then they came. And woke Jonah up. And tell him about the great tempess . . ."

The church is quiet now. Some women are clearing their throats. There is a little coughing. And then the quiet is broken by the crying of a child . . .

". . . Jonah confess. I say, Jonah confessed, saying, 'The fault lies in me' . . . Amen! 'The fault lies in me,' Glory-be-to-God! He said, 'Cast me overboard!'"

"Ooh, noooo!"

It is the same well-dressed, thin woman with the thin, dry voice. Idora had picked this woman out of the congregation as her point of focus. The woman is now moving from side to side, as if Idora's words are jabs delivered to her body, one in her left ribs, one in her right ribs; words addressed to her, personally; and she is trying to absorb them.

"The captain began to question Jonah. And the captain ask Jonah where he come from? Saying, 'Whence have you come? From where, Jonah?' Yeah! And what was his occupation? . . . Glory be to God, hallelulia! . . . Because he wanted to know . . . hallelulia! . . . he wanted to know about this man . . . amen!"

It was at this point in her sermon that the door at the back of the church, facing her, opened slowly. She continued preaching, even taking her eyes off the interruption; but inwardly, she was waiting to see who the intruder could be. Who would come in at this point, and interrupt her train of thought? For she was not quite in stride. The cold wind preceded the intruder. She saw the hand in a brown glove, first. And then the black hood, which covered most of the face. And in the same flash of recognition, she saw his clothes and the way the trousers fell off his waist, down to a bulge over his Reeboks, and she cried out, "Rashanan!"

"Hallelulia!" the woman with the high voice shouted. "Hallelulia! Thank you, Jesus!"

"Speak to us, Sister! Tell it, Sister Idora!" the Pastor said in a loud voice.

And the entire congregation was shouting and jumping up and getting into the spirit; and dancing.

"We're hearing voices!" the Pastor said. "We are hearing tongues from heaven, as in the upper chamber! Sister Morrison's speaking to us in tongues!"

Idora saw the person. And recognized the person. And when the congregation shouted again, it had disappeared. Like an apparition. But she had seen it.

She had seen Rashan Rashanan . . .

Only she knew. Only she would know. Such is the signature of God's presence.

A blow of concern mixed with a feeling of affection, something like passion, coursed through her body. She now had to fight the words and fight the congregation. She was regaining her focus. She had to have the power to whip them into shape, and she drew strength from her own torment over the forty days and forty nights, when she lay immobilized on her bed, and which took on the heat and the delirium of a fever, during her excruciating retreat from life.

"Why would God cause all this to happen? Why would God? Cause all this to happen? And why would God bring temptation to me, his messenger this Sunday morning, even as I am standing up here, in front of you, preaching his word? . . ."

"He's tessing you, Sister. God is tessing you!" It was the Pastor. So close behind her. She could feel his whispered words, as if they were his hands on her body. "He's tessing you, Sister!"

". . . why would God? Cause all this to happen? Just on account of one man? . . . Amen!" The thought of his hot hands on her white silk dress was taking away her concentration. "But what the ole captain didn't know . . . amen! Was that Jonah was running for his life . . . amen!" She is feeling hot, and she unbuttons the first button on her dress. She can see the lace at the top of her brassieres, like splashes of blood, matching the red three-leaf flower that is the decoration in the middle of her brassieres. "But my Bible tells me," she says, ignoring the small exposure, "my Bible tells me. After they cast ole Jonah overboard, God prepared . . . amen! . . . a whale . . . amen! It came along . . . amen! and swallowed ole Jonah up . . . amen! . . . Hallelulia-to-God!"

"Good Jesus!" the Pastor shouts. "Good Jesus!" She has heard exclamations like this, in a church, and not all of them are shouts of praise to God.

"And after the whale. Swallowed Jonah up. After the whale swallowed-up Jonah. God prepared the whale . . . amen! And it had vines wrap-round its neck . . . amen! Vines wrapped-round his neck . . . amen! So that he would not drown! No! Nor choke to death . . . amen!"

"No-no-no!" the thin woman with the thin voice screams. "Don't let him drown, Lord! Good-Jesus-Christ, don't let Jonah go down to the depths of the seas! Don't let him drown!"

"And not only that . . . amen! But God let him to be . . . amen! In his right mind . . . amen! Yesss! 'I going-take you outta your right mind, Jonah! And I going-let you know what I going-do to yuh' . . . amen! And out of the fish's belly, Jonah was crying out to God, 'I am the reason for my own affliction . . . amen!'"

The church goes wild. Women are jumping up, and stomping the floor in their high-heeled shoes, and are clapping; and the men in the congregation are stomping heavily on the floorboards. There are smiles on their faces; and tears in their eyes.

"'I am the reason for my own affliction!'"

The women are screaming.

"Jesus! I say, Jeee-sus! I am leaning on yuh!" Idora screams.

"Lean on me!" the women scream, in reply.

"Jeeees-sus!" Idora screams. "I'm running for my life!"

"We're all running for our lives, Sister!"

"Ole Jonah cried out . . . amen! . . . out of the fish's belly . . . amen! . . . and said . . . amen! . . . 'The Lord hath given unto me, another chance! I am going to pray! And maybe' . . . amen! . . . 'maybe, the Lord will hear my prayer . . .'"

The church is shaking. Everybody is standing and clapping.

The Pastor rises. And the noise dies down, slowly, like a wave travelling back out to the depths, crawling over the sand the colour of pearl.

Idora begins to lead the congregation in the altar call, in song. She begins with the song she has been singing in her basement apartment for the past four days and four nights. "I'm Running for My Life."

Five men, in black suits, stand; and then they go through the congregation, like five well-oiled and silent lawn mowers, holding the deep-red collection bags made of cloth. The men have many rings with gold and diamonds on many fingers. The bags they hold in their jewelled hands have a large cross embroidered in gold, on each soft velvet pouch.

She is sweating now, from giving the message. Jonah has fatigued her. She is happy and joyful. Jonah has enlivened her. And the congregation is singing.

> "I'm ah-running for my life-ah!
> I'm ah-running for my life-ah!
> If anybody-ah asks you what's the matter . . ."

The Pastor is standing beside her, on her left side. She can smell his aftershave lotion. And she can feel his hand on her waist, in a respectful touch, going straight through her white silk dress with the almost invisible floral pattern, also in white, right through her thighs. She can feel her clothes sticking to her skin. But the Pastor's hand is just a soft pat, on her waist. It is a pat, nothing more than a touch of congratulation. The congregation is singing.

The Pastor whispers something into her ear, and she leans closer to him, to hear. She cannot hear what he is saying. He moves away from her, and goes to the lectern. "I'll take over this part of the service, Sister Morrison," is what he was trying to tell her. The five men in black suits are walking towards him, with the heavy collection bags in their gleaming hands; and they approach him like security guards.

Idora takes out her embroidered cotton handkerchief, from the sleeve of her dress, and passes it over her forehead. When she removes it, it is soaking wet.

"Praise the Lord!" she says.

The Pastor takes up her exhortation.

"Praise the Lord!" he screams. "Praise Him for today! And praise Him for giving us Sister Morrison's message, this blessed Sunday morning!"

Before this building, the Apostolical Holiness Church of Spiritualism in Christ, was a church, a place of worship, it was a butcher shop. And she can still smell, or she tells herself she can still smell, the odour from slaughtered animals: pig and cow and calf and sheep; and now, with so many West Indians living in Toronto, goat; she can smell the smell of animals; and sees marks on the floorboards and on the walls where their carcasses used to hang, for a time, before they were then placed on the iron hooks. A few hooks still remain in the ceiling. There is one left on one wall of the building, erected by stonemasons who came over from Scotland; and from London, to the province of Ontario. But these hooks are painted white, to match the colour scheme of the interior of the church, and to try to wipe out any trace of that butchering history.

The congregation is singing. The Pastor's deep voice is carrying the bass line. And it tells her that he knows that the collection, on this Sunday morning, will pay for the hydro, the gas bill, and he will have enough money left over to pay down a deposit on the telephone bill, which is overdue; enough to subtract his cut for "sussinance."

The singing of the congregation comes full and beautiful into her heart. The Pastor's voice giving the Benediction sweeps over her like a warm wave. It is deep, and heavy, and emotional, and loving. ". . . and we have to thank Sister Morrison, for bringing such a stirring message this blessed Sunday morning . . ."

"Praise His name!"

It is the woman with the thin voice.

"I'm ah-running for muh life!" the Pastor screams. And the congregation responds. "I am like Jonah. I'm-ah gonna pray-ah, and maybe, maybe-ah, God will hear my cry!"

Idora is beside the Pastor again. And he places his hand on her hands on the lectern; and the two of them join in the singing.

"I'm-ah running for muh life!" the Pastor screams.

"He's ah-coming home, thank Jesus!" Idora screams.

"Jonah is coming home!" the Pastor screams.

"He's coming home where he belong!" Idora screams. And then "that man" comes into her mind, and she says, "He's coming home where he belong." She says this in a deep, hoarse voice, with her eyes closed.

"Jesus! Jeees-sus!" the Pastor screams. "I'm coming! I'm coming home!"

"Come-on home, Pastor James! Come-on home! . . . Amen!"

"And then, when Pastor James, minutes later, with the congregation thinned out, and leaving in their cars, closed the door of his sanctuary behind me; and then locked it, turning the two bolts that made a solid, final clunk; my blood moved in a rush to my head, and registered caution. But I could still hear the conversations of a few worshippers, outside the sanctuary, which had now become stifling and uncomfortable as a holding cell.

"I will scream. I will have to scream. Can I scream out loud, in a church? Would my Sisters, those members of the church committees, and the members of the Mothers' Union, the Deaconesses and the Assistant Deaconesses like myself, and those ordinary members of the congregation, would they believe I have good reason to scream?

"'Drunk, or sober,' Pastor James told me; and he does not, at first, complete the adage immediately, but he decides to complete it, nevertheless. 'Mind your business.'

"'The gospel-truth,' I tell him.

"'Don't let the left hand know what the right hand's doeth,' Pastor James says—smiling after he says this, at his wisdom.

"'The gospel-truth, Pastor James, the gospel,' I tell him.

"The sanctuary smells like incense. And old clothes. Or the lingering smell of dead animals. There is also a smell, a smell that a woman would call sensual. It is a smell I would say is a 'living smell,' a smell of living people.

"Pastor James goes to a metal filing cabinet, painted green, and, with a key on a bunch he takes from his waistcoat, opens the top drawer. He takes out two short, fat-skinned snap glasses from the drawer. On the table with his Bible and some papers is the bottle from which he had poured the Communion wine, earlier. He holds one glass towards me, nods gently, like a gentleman would, and without waiting for me to accept, he pours me a drink, up to a half-inch from the rim. And he bows. I expect him to click his heels, he is such a gentleman, exaggerating his good manners. He pours himself an equal amount.

"Suddenly, outside the sanctuary, there is no noise, no shuffling of feet, no clearing of the throat, no voice in conversation. The silence outside in the church comes right into the sanctuary with the two of us, and makes me feel real lonely. But being alone with the Pastor makes me feel also, in a strange way, the privilege of his favouritism.

"Pastor James, I know, is no longer married. His wife went back to Jamaica 'because of these damn Canadian winters! How you stand them?' his wife asked him. They are not divorced in the legal sense. Only 'to all intents and appearances and purposes,' in 'a practical manner of divorce,' he told me once. But his wife ignored his argument, and went back home, to Jamaica. There are no children born from their fifteen years of marriage.

"He gets up from his swivel chair and stands in front of me. I steel my body, and close my two eyes, not physically; but morally I shut them, in preparation of what he will do, next. I remain sitting. In the other swivel chair. Mine is noisy. Pastor James comes right up to me. I could feel his trousers touch my flesh, just above my ankle. I stop breathing. I stiffen my body, and stiffen my senses, and stiffen my resistance to what I am sure he is about to do. But I remind myself that the two of us are still in his sanctuary.

"He stands in front of me. Touching my flesh, accidentally, with the legs of his trousers. I do not open my eyes. I do not see how brightly shined his shoes are. How keen the creases in his trousers are. Did not have the chance to examine the rich material of his dark brown suit.

"He holds his body down to my level. He holds his glass of wine aside, slightly to the right, and he kisses me. On my forehead.

"'Thank you. Thank you, Eye-Dora, for this morning.'

"I open my eyes. They are filled with tears.

"'If I wasn't still a married man, in the eyes of the Church. And in the eyes o' God, and if . . . and this is more important . . . if I was a much more younger man, I would ask you, in all decency, to make a' honest man outta me, Miss Eye-Dora. I mean that. Marriage. God is my witness.'

"I am in tears now, crying now.

"'And if Bertram wasn't still in your life, I sure-would . . .'

"He does not finish the thought; or, to be honest, the wish. 'You are welcome,' I said to him.

"I take my kerchief, an embroidered lady's hanky, from the sleeve of my brocaded white silk dress, and dab it so delicately, so much in an act of what women call *civilized manner*, so beautiful and cultured, that he himself must be feeling the power of my delicateness. And then, as he says, he has regrets that he has brought up the subject, under the circumstances that my husband, though absent from Canada, is still down in America, still alive. God have His mercy!

"'Forgive me,' he says. 'Not meaning to upset you, Eye-Dora.'

"'You are welcome,' I tell him.

"'Look!' he says, as if he has passed an examination, as if he has reached the solution of a serious personal problem. 'Look!'

"He did not need words to conclude what is in his mind. He goes back to the green-painted metal two-drawer filing cabinet, and this time opens the bottom drawer, and from it takes a forty-ounce bottle that contains a liquid that is dark brown, something like the colour of honey. But not so thick. The bottle has no label on it, as if he is deliberately concealing its contents. But the moment he pulls the cork, after turning it around with his strong fingers, the strength hit me, bram! And the scent of the drink comes like a sudden rush of fragrance from red roses, to my two nostrils.

"'We's two adults,' he says. There is no smile, or relaxed expression, to register the state of mind he is now in. He is still serious, as if the suggestion he makes is so upsetting that he cannot yet erase it from his character, from his behaviour as my

Pastor. 'Two adults like we. Let's have a sip of the real thing.' With the water from a glass decanter that he mixes with the Communion wine to weaken it, he rinses out the two shot glasses we have just used. Into each glass he pours a half-inch of cognac. I can smell its richness; and its richness takes me right back to the mansion down in the Ravine, to the cognac, more expensive than this, which I drink to my heart's content, when I was a more younger woman, when an employer of mine was not at home.

"'But Pastor James,' I begin to say. There are tears in my voice. My voice is soft. Tender. Fragile. And very vulnerable. But most of all it is soft, and endearing, like an embrace to seal a friendship. 'But Pastor James,' I say, 'you and me are practically the same age! Your birthday is written all over the place. It was in the papers, once.'

"'I know that, Sister,' he says. 'I know that.'

"'If only Bertram would hurry-up, and find a permanent job down in America! Or do something!'

"'Nothing before God's will, Sister,' he says. He takes the last sip from his glass, and says 'Emmm!' in appreciation of the bite in the cognac; and to clear his throat. 'Thank you for this morning's message. That Jonah is something-else, ain't he? He isn't much more different from some o' the men in my congregation that I have to deal with . . .'

"'You're welcome,' I say.

He looks at his watch. And the concern with time is registered in the crease of his forehead.

"'If I didn't have to visit one o' these West Indian Jonahs in the Detention Centre, I could drive you . . .' he says. 'But I can drop you off at the Dufferin subway.'

"'You don't have to go out of your way, Pastor,' I say.

"'If I offer you a lift, I know I have to go out of my way!' He is teasing me. 'You becoming too Canadian!'

"'I am a Canadian,' I tell him.

"I watch him as he tidies the sanctuary, replacing the glasses and the bottles into the filing cabinet, and locking it; touching the edges of the hymn books, and his Bible, and making them form a symmetrical design on the white altar cloth that has a large cross knitted into it, in red, yellow and green thread; brushing a speck which I cannot see, which is invisible to my eyes, which is probably not there at all—only his fastidiousness makes him see one—off his jacket.

"He holds my hand, my left hand, and guides me into the position of kneeling down.

"'Let us pray,' he says. His voice is soft, and soothing.

"'Yes, Pastor,' I say.

"He holds my hand, and is kneeling beside me; and his other hand is on the arm of his swivel chair, while I hold the hand that is not touching his to my side, fumbling to pull down the hem of my white dress, and feeling my thighs, and the way the dress flows over my thighs, as the blood surges through them.

"I have no ear for the words of thanksgiving he is muttering; and can distinguish just a few. '. . . and Father-God, we are before you, penitent, confessing on our knees, all our . . . sins . . .'; and his words don't have to have meaning now, for the two of us, him and me, are now joined in a love which, as the Bible itself says, 'passeth all understanding.'

"'. . . take this woman, Father-God, and guide her in her loneliness . . . guide her along the paths of righteousness . . . continue to fill her heart with the tongues which she spoke in her

sermon this morning . . . help her to discover the whereabouts
of her son, BJ . . . turn him away from evil behaviour . . . protect him from the gangs ranging throughout Toronto . . . the
shootings and the killings . . . and bring Brother Bertram
home to this woman's side, to her bed, to her life, safe; and . . .
rewarded by landing a job . . . in Amurca . . . we ask all this in
Your precious name.'"

"When he turned the stereo in his black Mercedes-Benz on,
when I saw how pretty he was, shifting gears, I smiled to myself; and when I heard the voice of Roberta Flack, coming
through the speakers, when I recognized the song Roberta was
singing, 'Sunday and Sister Jones,' I smiled in my heart. Pastor
James, I am sure, didn't have a clue what was going through my
mind . . . and didn't understand the meaning of my smile. He
had probably played this song so many times that what it first
meant to him was now, with irony, erased by the repeating of it.

"'I sorry I can't drop you more closer to your home,' he said,
'but I have to be at the Detention Centre by two.'

"'Thanks,' I told him.

"'Thank you for the message,' he said. 'I going here to see
this modern-day Jonah . . . in the Belly of the Whale!' He
pressed my hand firmly. 'You were speaking in tongues, Sister
Morrison. I hope you know that! It was wonderful, Sister Morrison, just wonderful!' He winked his eye at me. It made me
happy. I was happy. And it was me who persisted in holding his
hand longer than the greeting of goodbye warranted. 'You like
Roberta too, I see . . .'"

"I felt light . . . light-headed. I felt buoyant. The words of the
song were with me, stirring up emotions and fantasies roused

first in the sanctuary. Now they were rawer, and more explicit, and I accepted them. I felt I was a new woman.

"The sun was shining. And I knew, from living in Toronto all these years, that the sun could look just like the sun in Barbados, but when I opened my basement door and climbed those five cement steps, and stand on the sidewalk, the entire North, the Pole up there, in the everlasting cold and Tundra, could strike me raw and frigid. Full, in my face. The sun in this place is no sun at all. But I got accustomed to this cold sun. And this afternoon. . .

"'Where the day gone?' I wanted to know.

". . . this Sunday afternoon, standing for the few minutes outside the Dufferin subway station, waving to the Pastor, and smiling at the playful seduction he and me had both indulged in, I was born again. I was in a new frame of love. Confident. Loving the fact that today, Sunday, I was living in Toronto. I opened my purse, and fumbled through it, to find my passport, my Canadian passport, which I do not need to show to anybody, police or bill collector, to vouchsafe my presence in this land. Nobody. Neither police nor immigration officer. Not one o' them would dare . . . nor demand to see my passport, unless the request is legal. I have legality in Toronto.

"I took the dark blue book out, and studied the Coat of Arms on it, and decided that the Coat of Arms of the passport of Barbados, where I was born, is prettier.

"It is prettier. But this is a Canadian passport in my hand! I said this to my Canadian passport. 'And this makes me a Canadian. I am not any damn visible minority; or immigrant!'

"When I clipped the purse shut, and started down the steep, shiny stairs to the subway platform, I was like on wings, I was buoyant, as if the climb which I am now taking backwards had given me a giddiness in my head. And the moment I reached the platform, and was standing in the unnatural light from the fluorescent bulbs, and was aware that I was below the ground, all the things that had contributed to my withdrawal, as if from life itself, lying on my bed for the four days and four nights— four days and three and a half nights, really; for it is only one-thirty in the afternoon, on this Sunday—calculated, symbolically, into forty days and forty nights, by the force of my imagination and my sense of things, caused my mind to go back over the history, in a narrative, of my life in this city.

"And now, in this gloom in a subway car, in this new environment of the underground, I am seeing things more clearly. And that is ironical. 'If I think so,' I said to myself, as I could have said had Josephine been beside me in this gloomy subway coach, 'if I can think of it, and make it so, then it is nothing but my wanting it to be so. And imagining it is so . . .

"'I just realize,' I said, as my mind turned to the next matter that had been troubling me, for weeks, months now; years . . . But my mind erased him, and settled on my son, BJ . . . 'I just realize that I have to find time to sit down and talk to that boy. If I ever find him! Could it be a vision? Something that isn't real . . . that you imagine to be real . . . my seeing him during my sermon? My heart is still connected to that boy. And suppose I was to lose that mother's love? I have to face facts, and confess my stupidity, and how close I came . . . and more than once . . . to evicting him. And now he has disappeared! Should I really have evicted him? Yes? Or no?'"

"I really hate that girl Josephine, sometimes! She made me go to the lengths of packing a valise, and the trouble of picking-out my best dresses, the three silk ones, even down to my panties, to wear to meet her mother, and see the farm she grew up on . . . and all of a sudden, because of—Brandon?—for that bastard Brandon, Josephine left me in the lurch! That's what she let Brandon do to me? Her friend? But, I don't really mind. Not Josephine! Josephine won't betray me. I surprise myself, and wonder how people see me and she . . . see me and her . . . whichever is correct . . . walking, and holding hands, as if we are . . . and laughing together . . . sometimes even skipping, like two teenaged girls. And my God! One of us white. The other black. In Toronto. In Canada. Only in Canada! As they say . . .

"Still, though, concerning the disappointment surrounding the visit, I imagined myself driving in from the Regina airport, in Regina, and seeing the expanse of highways that she tell me they have out West, stretching to the ends of the earth, as far as the eye can see. And what's those things called, now? What're those tall things that keep the wheat when it is reaped? Yes! Those *silos*. I would have liked to see those silos. And the three Prairie Provinces. A-S-M, the initials my geography master used to use, to remind us of their names. You can't even make a word out of these three letters! A-S-M . . . for Alberta, Saskatchewan and Manitoba . . . that I learned in Geography, in Barbados. Barbados is so close to Canada!

"But. That time when we were watching the Canadiens play the Maple Leafs, and we were eating Pringles and popcorn, and drinking Heinekens, and one thing led to another . . . this is something which, if I could put out of my mind, put it to one-side, in time, with the passing o' time, I may forget that it ever happened. I don't think anybody in their right mind, man or woman, who was to know about that night watching hockey,

at her condominium down in the suburbs . . . Jesus! . . . It is
no wonder she liked the Bluffs, so much! She lives next door to
the Bluffs. Why didn't I think of this?

"'That man' came close to accusing me of foolishness with
another woman. Only if he knew! Only if he was to know, how
close I came. How close, because of him, I came to committing
that fornication. Or is it carnal knowledge, when a woman do it
with another woman? . . . with a person of the same sex? . . .
and temperriment? What am I saying? When, as a woman, you
do it with a woman! When, as a woman, you do it with a person
of the same sex! That's better!

"I was so deep in these thoughts that I did not hear the train
conductor announce the name of the station I was coming into,
and now, oh Lord, I passed the stop. I paid more attention, now.
I could see the route map of the subway, and even with my distance sitting from it, and with the glare of the fluorescent light
on the map, I made out my station, and how many more stops
I had to travel, before I got to the corner of Yonge and Bloor;
and then would have to transfer south onto Yonge, and get off at
Dundas—and home!

"I suddenly started to feel closed in, incarcerated, locked
up in this silent, half-empty subway coach. Two young women
were chatting, and laughing. I did not hear the cause of their
merriment. A man was sleeping, with his mouth open. Another
man, dressed as if he had come from church, was reading a
paperback book. I could not see the title. I held my purse in
my hands, in my lap. I was becoming so sensitive about my
body, especially during my short time with Pastor James, in his
sanctuary. And now, some time after that meeting, I am still
conscious of my body, when I brushed my legs or my thighs

with my hand; even though my hand is not the same as the hand of a man, is not a hand investigating for consent and satisfaction, the touch still makes my body tingle."

She is going over the narrative of her life. "What, dear God, would you advise me to do? Father-God, I need your counsel." She went through, word for word, from memory, the last letter she had considered writing to Bertram, and had then destroyed, also in her mind; had it wiped from her memory. "Father-God, I have had my eyes wide open, and yet I seeth not! I am blind to the wiles of man and mankind—even including the man I married."

"When I was in the sanctuary with Pastor James, I was at first uncomfortable, for a time; but later, I allowed myself to relax, in that moment of playful seduction, which did not last. And I imagined, because I wanted to pretend I was not an accomplice in the seduction, nor consenting to it; I wanted to pretend that I was about to be seduced, not by Pastor James, but was being hit upon by Bertram. Similar to the changing of actors in my dream from which I had been awakened by the ringing of the church bells; and also, for decency sake, imagining that Pastor James was Bertram.

"But Pastor James bears not the slightest resemblance—not in height; not in colour; not in build; not in handsomeness—to . . . Bertram? Bertram was uglier; and more crude . . . to Bertram . . . Then I am only 'mama-guiling' myself, lying with a bold-face self-deception. But I am really glad I endured those twenty minutes I had in the sanctuary with a man who I know wanted to take me to bed, but . . .

"Not many women who do not have this experience of close-ness, religious and congregational closeness, to their Pastor can understand the heavy smell of sensuality that turns into sexual-ity, that is in the air, in the breath breathed out, in the words spoken and in the smell of breath when those words are spo-ken, in the glance of an eye, the touch of a hand on a leg, on a shoulder, the greeting kiss . . . Only those women who know, know.

"Only a few more subway stops!"

On the silent subway journey underground, in the quiet, dark sections when the lights go out for a moment, and then come back on brighter, she had felt disoriented as the subway was passing through dungeons and channels below the ground. The squeaking noise and the rattling of iron wheels as the train went round corners got on her nerves; and had made her skin crawl. All her past, all those ugly thoughts and memories; and her litany about the Jamaican man whom the police shot one after-noon, so many years ago, on a Sunday like today; when the sun was not out, and it was dark, Mr. Johnson was gunned down. All this past had fit into the scream of wheels as the subway rounded a bend beneath the surface of the earth. She wondered why the noise below the surface of the street was more foreboding and cruel, and was everlasting, like sea water in the ear; this noise, so eerie underground, so understandable on the street; and she wondered why there was a different shrill to the noise. All her past rode with her.

But then deliverance had come suddenly, as she realized, without the benefit of an announcement by the conductor, when the subway train had reached the Bay station. It was here, when she had climbed the twenty-one steps to reach the street, and had stood at the bus stop, coming out into the sun, still a cold sun, that she felt the cheerfulness of the afternoon, that she compared this feeling with the kiss of deliverance; and had walked in the weakened rays of the cold sun, restrained by the wind that entered the bone.

The joy returned to her. She could taste once again the Communion wine Pastor James had offered her; and when he offered her the cognac, it was not only that she had tasted cognac before, and a better kind, she was still joyful and expansive.

She had mentioned Brandon to Pastor James. Had told him about what Brandon had told her girlfriend, Josephine, about beating up young black men; boys, really. And that had caused Pastor James to mention his own community work with black youths. And she had asked him, what should she do, having a friend she loved who loved a man who beat up black teenaged boys? What should she do? Stop talking to Josephine? Have Josephine drop Brandon before she continued her friendship with her?

She discussed her worry with herself, and told herself, again, all the details, all the incidents: walking in public, she and Josephine, hand in hand; and not having the slightest sensual feeling for each other; walking like two sisters; and when she is at Josephine's condominium, she would unclip her brassieres when it got too tight, and hurt her skin; and discuss the history of her sexual life with Bertram; and this made Josephine tell her more details about Brandon and her; and when she discussed these things with herself, talking with herself; pretending that she was talking about someone else, not herself; imagining that she was not Idora, but was Josephine, so much did she want to fantasize that she was not herself, was not Idora; and that Josephine was not Josephine—it's all very confusing!—that Josephine was different, and was becoming so West Indian that she even, behind Idora's back, went back to the Kensington Market, and shopped for the "ingrease-ments" for making breadfruit cou-cou . . . "When did that damn girl remember that I showed her breadfruits in the West Indian store . . . and how we cook it? . . . and with pig tails, to-boot; and stirred the right way . . . be-Christ, with a real cou-cou stick that she bought!" . . . And on Saturdays, if she was on the night shift in the College kitchen, she would take a change of clothes, a jogging suit sometimes, a loose dress other times . . . and sleep over.

"You know what a sleepover is?" Josephine said to her once.

"A what?" Idora had raised her voice because she was in the shower.

"Sleep! . . . one word," Josephine said. "Over! . . . second word."

"You mean like 'turn over'?"

"Forget it!"

But she told her what it meant, when she turned the hot water off; and stood in the open door, with the steam and the mist behind her, drying herself with a very large red towel.

The closer the subway train came to the Yonge Street sta-tion, the more light-hearted she became, anticipating walking in the streets bathed in the cold sunshine. She had thought of walking a little to enjoy the sun, and extend its exhilarating effect upon her. She could taste its freshness. She could feel its touch on her body. She could imagine, back in Barbados, walking in a brighter, stronger sun.

She changed her mind, and got off the subway at Bay, one stop before Yonge; and stood in the freshened air at the bus stop.

It is a beautiful day, and her spirits are high. And she enjoys the rocking and the rollicking, and the jerks in the bus. This is a different driver. But he drives in the same reckless manner as her friend who took her earlier this same morning, right to her church door. This is exhilarating.

Idora is at the corner of Yonge and Dundas now, across from the large, empty, ugly space, Dundas Square. "Can't the Mayor do something about this?" She decides to cross the street, and walk on the east side, the side of the Square. One man, sitting with his head in his hands, has this vast cement cemetery all to himself. He does not look up as she passes near him. She is across from the Eaton Centre, walking in the vast, empty mausoleum called a Square, touching-distance from the homeless man. She wonders how it feels to be homeless on a Sunday. Or on Christmas Day. Or Easter. She walks on the sidewalk going south, and can, from the distance of the width of the street, across in the Eaton Centre, see her full reflection in the display windows of the store that sells jeans. Her white dress fits her more tightly than she had thought. In the cold sunshine, she has opened her winter coat, and the light and the glass, and the car that has just passed, break up the image of her white dress, and her face, in a playful, fleeting disjointing of her body. She remembers looking into the long full-length mirrors and looking glasses in the mansion of her previous employers, years ago, and seeing herself, and posing, and making faces and using her balled-up yellow tissue of Kleenex to wipe the perspiration from her face, and dip the same tissue into cold water and bathe her forehead. And afterwards, she would go into the first-floor restroom, and use her employer's cosmetics, applying face powder and creams until she changed her own complexion. In her own basement apartment, no light from her light bulbs was as sharp as those in the mansion, where they flashed off the huge glass panels which themselves served as mirrors and looking glasses. But when she stood in that light making faces, it was as cold as this. She had never, before this Sunday afternoon, seen herself in such a fractured reflection. And the light in her basement apartment had never really shown her figure and her face to best advantage.

She crosses the street, and stands before the glass with her reflection in it. And a car passing cuts her reflection into pieces, but only for a moment. She goes closer up to the glass, almost touching it, examining herself in it, and goes over her entire body. She talks to herself, in this showroom glass, as she would talk to herself in the restroom of the mansion, or in the bathroom of her basement apartment.

"It is near here," she says to the glass, "near this very store, where I saw the policeman that morning, with the workmen putting up the advertisement, and I thought—not thought, I took out his revolver—in my imagination. I nearly killed him . . . in my imagination."

She stands in front of the glass in the show window and looks at herself; and realizes that the white face powder she uses at home, and at work, is not in her purse, and she twists her mouth, closes her eyes, opens them, puts her head on her shoulder as models do, and walks off a little and then approaches the glass, as if the glass is an audience watching her parade on the catwalk.

And she stops posing. Stops modelling. And is serious. And

stands still. And is now the same size as her reflection in the glass.

"My God! My complexion is blacker than I thought. I am more blacker than all those other mirrors and looking glasses ever showed me! My God! What a thing! What a thing to find out, and on a Sunday to-boot! I love this country! The Maple Leaf. . ." she says aloud. ". . . forever!"

There is no one passing. She breaks into song. The National Anthem.

"O, Canada! . . . my home and native land!
O, Canada! . . . da-da-da-dahhh . . . daah . . . dah!"

She does not remember any more. She has never learned the words of the Anthem.

She is laughing out loud now.

Her reflection, like a magic lantern, comes to an end at the corner of the store, by the door leading to the subway. She is now walking towards Shuter Street.

She must turn left when she reaches the corner, and passes by Eaton's department store, so "Goodbye, Mr. Eaton!", where on Thursdays, her day off from being a domestic servant, years ago, she had spent her "off-duty" excursions, touching dresses and underwear and fur coats, and imagining they were on her body, and wishing that the small brown envelopes that contained her fortnightly wages held more cash in them; and were bigger; and her closeness to this store was like a magic lantern cutting to another scene: putting on three dresses to try them out for size and fit, and imagining not taking them off, and imagining walking out from the changing room, from the store. "Goodbye, Mr. Eaton!" she says to the store. The store is closed. "Bye-bye!"

. . . And now she passes Massey Hall, and she thinks about all those concerts advertised on its billboard, and in the *Star* newspaper, which she never went to, because of the price of admission, during those same domestic servant days; but she could hear some of the songs and tunes played by the artists, Harry Belafonte, Sammy Davis Jr., Miles Davis and others, on WBLK radio; and not have to go to the concerts themselves. Not in those days.

She passes by beggars, the homeless men who make a living with the small change accumulated in their hats, in their outstretched hands: "Spare any change?" Their voices, like the delivery of famous actors, change to suit the person petitioned, or the dress of the woman imprecated. "Spare any spare-change?" There are intensive hospital wards on either side of this street, now. There are beggars in their "stations," in their "offices," as one of them described his position, his station, one morning, to Idora—on one side of the street only. Each time she passes these two men in their "offices," she gives them each one toonie, equal to two dollars.

"God bless you, ma'am," each man says.

"Take care of yourself, now!" she says.

"Blang! blang! buh-lang! blang! . . ."

She can hear the bells of the church where the men with no homes, with no jobs, with no bedrooms, with no breakfasts, sit in the cold sun and wait for the distribution of homemade coffee and Starbucks doughnuts. Across from the church, as if to fill the soul with the symbol of God and Catholics, is the

St. Michael's Cathedral. "Blang! blang! buh-lang! blang! . . ."

"Bells calling worshippers to prayers!" she says. "Could be to Sunday School . . ."

She cannot get the tune the bells are playing. Perhaps these bells are not like the ones that ring from the steeple of St. James's Cathedral Church. Perhaps bells do not play tunes, or hymns, or psalms. This is not rock-and-roll. This is not rhythm and blues. But they make her soul light. And they bring back the joy of deliverance. And they seem to justify her affection for this city of Toronto, and for this country of Canada; and for this community of Moss Park.

She crosses Church Street, with its churches and pawnshops, and James McTamney & Co. And new apartments and condominiums going up into the sky. Then with its whores, whom she forgives, as Christ forgave the most famous of all whores in the whole world, in the whole Bible. She forgives all the whores on this street.

And then, the bells of St. James's.

Joy comes with the ringing of the bells of St. James's. She will go to church there, next Sunday, and sit at the back, and let the bells do things to her emotions and to her sensuality and to her love of God and of church music; and to her love, her Christian love, for the Dean. "The bells of Saint . . . Saint Something!" is the name of a tune played by bells. She cannot remember the name of that church, up in England. The Dean would know. She will go to church, next Sunday, never mind she cannot remember the name of the song. And perhaps, if she can get in earshot distance to her Dean, ask him, for he is bound to know, the name of the church whose bells are so internationally famous.

She has crossed the street, on the other side from the Armouries, walking on the north side of Shuter, beside the building that has a sign advertising GEORGIAN TOWN HOUSES, that has been boarded up against the invasion of homeless men, and rats, and intruders, for six years, keeping the homeless men and the rats from its bedrooms. Coffee cups, and plastic bags, and cigarette butts in the clumps of dying grass that look like a discarded garden bed are now the landscaping of this decrepit building. She is close enough now to see down the street, almost down to the wrought iron fence that guards her basement apartment from the intrusions of the street; and she can barely make out the collection of vehicles, not knowing yet in front of whose house, exactly, they are parked; and blinking; and she sees flashing lights, and she thinks she sees ambulances and two fire engines and police cruisers, and . . .

The closer she comes to the wrought iron fence that protects her apartment from the thoroughfare of the street, the easier she can count the ambulances and the white vans of the Emergency Medical Service. She can count four police cars. She can count two fire engines. The whirring lights on the ambulances and the police cars and the fire engines seem as if they are giving off noises, the wailing of sirens. Men in black uniforms, and some in white uniforms and in heavy suits, like divers, like whalers, in coats made out of tarpaulin, or oilskin, move round a stretcher, like surgeons round an operating table, busy trying to save a life . . .

She is close enough, now, to see where she is, to see blood, to see that there is a body.

She does not see, in her growing confusion, that her friend,

Josephine, is standing beside the gate of the wrought iron fence. She does not, for the time being, understand why there are so many men, in uniforms, and some neighbours; and so many lights spinning around her; too overcome to know what is happening at her gate. Perhaps somebody has been arrested for attempting to break into her basement apartment. Perhaps it is Bertram who has come back, on the impulse for sex, sooner than he had planned. Perhaps her landlord, just back from a long-distance trip to Timmins, has lost the key to his backyard garden. Perhaps it is . . . oh, no! . . . not him! . . . oh God, no! . . . not him!

A woman standing over the body, on the white sheet and the white canvas, is like a replica, a lifelike model, of a weeping matron, from the classical pages of mothers mourning at funerals long ago in history, in old leather-bound, crumbling books about processions in Victorian times, of state funerals of generals and of statesmen, and the wives of generals and statesmen . . .

Idora is too confused and shocked to know who this woman is. Idora pulls away the white sheet, and the sheet of white canvas away from covering the head. She must look full in the eyes of this dead boy, with her own eyes wide open, to see the truth, and to tell the truth after she has seen it laid out like this, in order that she might identify the relationship to her; and to touch the dead flesh, to tell how she is related to this unmoving body. She sees, as if she is identifying these items, his long black T-shirt over another long white one; and she examines the white do-rag, and his white baseball cap . . . and his blue jeans; and she sees there is no belt through the tabs of the jeans. She sees the black elastic band in the waist of his underwear. His underwear has the name of its manufacturer, the one she had bought for him, stamped into the elastic waistband. *Jockey.* And yes, she identifies his Reebok sneakers. She bought those, too. Going over these items, she does not utter a word. The sneakers look ugly on his lifeless, rigid feet. His feet look like a model's feet, lifeless as prostheses. In the middle of the body, as it lies on the stretcher, is his Raptors basketball white cap, with the number 27 on it. She does not know whose name belongs to the number 27. He had never told her. Seeing it there, on his body, reminds her of a fallen soldier's military funeral, when a helmet or a folded flag is laid on his uniform. Sometimes the army places a ceremonial sword where the white basketball cap is now placed. She still has not uttered a word. Nor shed a tear. Over this body. This body. There must be some reason why this body is lying here on a piece of canvas, on a stretcher inside her gate, beside the two red plastic flower-pots with the dead geraniums in them, no longer in bloom, all life dead, now that it is winter.

"Was he dead already?" she thinks. "Those three boys on the subway . . ."

She pulls the white cloth, or the canvas blanket, from the head; and she sees the face. And identifies it.

"First thing," she says to herself, as she rests her hand on the stretcher bearing his body, "first thing is to call Pastor James. Pastor James will give him a good turnout . . . and it will be next Sunday, and it will be a large funeral, leaving from the basement and coming up these front steps and leading up to Yonge Street, along Shuter, down Dundas, past Dundas Square, past Sherbourne Street, going through the neighbourhood where he lived, like a funeral procession back home . . . But I want this one to look like a demonstration . . . that we used to have in Allan Gardens, the park just north of here . . . against racial discrimination . . . And I want them to play music. The music will be 'Sometimes, I Feel Like a Motherless Child.' And then 'Poverty Is Hell' . . . and Pastor James will be at the head of the procession, and I will beat my tambourine . . . and I want saxophone music and slow drumbeat, and all the sex-workers, the man with the walker, and I want the crack users to join in, and like this, the parade of sadness, the procession of his death, will go along Shuter, north up Yonge Street, swing east along Dundas Street, the parade of death will flow like a broad, slow river, east down Dundas Street . . . with me holding the doll I made of BJ, dressed like a student of Trinity College in the University . . . close to my heart . . . close-close, carrying it in my two hands . . . this is a day of rejoicing and of death . . . the Lord giveth and the Lord taketh away . . . and I will dress his body myself, give it its preparation bath, things I learned from my Mother . . . the chain I gave him for his thirteenth birthday I will take off his neck, after I bathe him, and put scents and mothballs in the proper places . . . as my Mother taught me . . . and I will present the silver chain and cross to Josephine . . . and keep the Star and Crescent. I will wear it round my neck . . . to remember him by . . . and I will ask Missis Proposki and Cilla to walk in front of the coffin, behind Pastor James . . . and I will invite the ladies of the night and the sex-workers and all the homeless men to join in this remembering of him . . . making his final journey longer and bigger, because we will be walking from here, from my basement apartment, all the way to the Apostolicals . . . as if it is a Civil Rights demonstration . . . And all my 'babies,' my other children, will be on the coffin as it is pulled along the road on wheels. I will hold Mr. Rashan Rashanan—if you please—firmly to my breast . . . formerly known as BJ . . . in my two hands, close to my chest . . . All I have to do now is call Pastor James . . . and make the arrangements . . . And the third hymn I want for him is 'The Day Thou Gavest, Lord, Is Ended' . . . Yes!"